THE CRIMSON HUNTERS: A DELLERIN TALE

THE CRIMSON COLLECTION VOL I

ROBERT J POWER

DEPAOR PRESS

THE CRIMSON HUNTERS
First published in Ireland by DePaor Press in 2021.
ISBN 978-1-8382765-1-5

Available in eBook, Audiobook and Paperback.

www.RobertJPower.com

For Rights and Permissions contact:
Hello@DePaorPress.com

CONTENTS

For Jan.
I write these fuken books just to make you smile.
It's the best feeling in the world.
You are my muse, my love, my best friend.

1

AT THE FAR END OF NOWHERE GOOD AT ALL

Derian hated many things. Hating things was one of his more interesting pastimes and today it was the rain. The droplets of Luistra were bigger and heavier here than anywhere else in the world. Was that even possible, he wondered, hating them even more. Perhaps the source's energy affected them? That seemed like a perfectly reasonable explanation, so he went with it. Derian believed in ignorance. He considered it a powerful tool whenever he didn't understand why things occurred as they did. Like the source. *Ah, the fuken source.* Blaming the source was the finest use of ignorance because the source was invariably responsible for unexplainable things. Some opinionated peasants claimed the source was another realm of this world. Dark, eerie, and full of monsters. All trying to break out into the world. Derian really hated the idea of it. Even though he'd never been there.

A low-hanging tree branch caught him off guard and scraped his cheek, drawing blood. *Wonderful.* He hated nasty branches. To the fires with them all. Except the ones that stayed out of his way. He had no problem with them unless they wanted to start something.

As well as the weather, jutting branches, and his life, Derian also hated running through depthless forests pursuing feral demons. Much to his annoyance, this was exactly what he was doing this miserable morning.

The lecherous demon broke away from the path, uprooting a tree as if it were nothing more than a stalk of wheatcorn. Derian charged after it, leaping through the splintered wreckage as it fell around him, and received another painful slap from a branch as he did. *Stupid branch. Stupid lecherous demon from the source. Stupid rain and all!*

It was a hard life being a mercenary these days. Probably because he wasn't a very good mercenary. Derian was about as imposing as a drunk munket defending a jar of honey— and just as accomplished. It wasn't his fault he was unimpressive; it was the source's. He was smaller than a tall man and a lot thinner; some might say he hadn't fully grown into himself, while others might suggest he was a skut of a thing. His greasy hair was brown, cut to his shoulders. It matched the goatee he was growing, apart from the strands of red, which made little sense to him. His gentle eyes were a dark hazel and just as bland. His nose, however, was as attractive as most attractive noses. That was something.

He had earned no title to his name, nor had he any decent scars to display. Worse than that, he had done nothing extraordinary in this miserable world to merit either. Perhaps were he to march these lands a little longer he might become more impressive. *But who really has the time to master a craft these days?*

He thought himself young—only twenty years old, if he believed his father. Three years had been ill-spent as an apprentice in the worst mercenary outfit to march in the

Seven Kingdoms of Dellerin. They weren't the worst simply because they were brutal, vile, or dishonourable curs. *Oh, no. That would have been something.* Instead, the Crimson Hunters were just useless at any form of heroism, ability, or accomplishment.

"Get the cur! Get the spitting cur and… I don't know… Hit him in the—" a voice cried from far behind him. The sentence's ending may have included imaginative profanity, but it was lost in the wind, the turn of the leaves, and the howling of the hunted monster beating up another tree. Perhaps the beast also hates branches, Derian thought. That would be one thing in its favour. He pursued the demon alone, and he wondered if this had ever been part of the plan.

"Keep up, idiot! I can't do this alone… idiot!"

There came no reply from his cutting jest.

Come on, Natteo, you wonderful idiot.

It was a two-man job. *No.* It was a ten-man job, but there weren't ten members to call upon, so the Crimson Hunters had given Natteo and Derian the honour of performing their grunt work for them. Derian couldn't help but think it involved nothing more than a generous measure of running.

He cleared another fallen tree but tripped slightly on a branch with ideas above its station, twisting his ankle awkwardly. He stumbled, and a shard of pain shot up through his leg. He almost gave up there and then. *No, no, spit on that*, a little voice inside his head whispered. It made a good point. Enduring this misery was the best opportunity they'd had these last few days hunting their prey. Killing the beast would keep them polished for the rest of the year. *Worth a little pain.* He felt a crack, and then a pop—though it might have been a cracking pop—in his ankle, and he bit down the pain and continued running.

Derian thought it unusual that Natteo could not keep up

with him. Life had gifted Natteo many skills—like cursing, running, and avoiding unpleasant tasks. He was Derian's best friend and absolutely nothing else. He knew this because Natteo ensured that he knew this. Natteo also ensured that he would never need to fight off his legendary charms. Because of their friendship. Because Derian was not his type. Because he was ugly. Derian would have liked a say in the matter, but it was easier to just agree with him.

A good friend.

They were similar in age, but you wouldn't think it. Natteo had a young face with aged old eyes and a devilish grin. He claimed to be a poet first, a lover second, and when he had the time, a mercenary third. Derian wasn't jealous of his brazen confidence, wonderful charm, and good heart at all. *Not one bit.*

Natteo had likely slowed to a leisurely jog by now, taking in the grey flowers, counting the unsettled birds, or watching hissects buzz around as they avoided the bulbous raindrops amidst the ruin of felled trees. Natteo was inclined to notice things like this, or, worse, talk about noticing things like this. Having spent most of his life in the grey structures of Castra, depthless forests were a thing of splendour to him. Even if they shared the same sickly grey colour.

Crash!

It flung aside another tree, and Derian wondered why the beast would prefer to knock a tree from its path instead of running around it. *That's how demons behave, though, isn't it?* No consideration for the world they'd broken into. *Tree in way, stupid tree, knock tree away. No more tree in way.*

Another crash followed.

Demons behaved anyway they felt, and all Derian could do was learn as he went and improve with every mission.

4

That's how any inept mercenary became great, earned a few scars, and earned a proper title. Like Lorgan. *Technically.*

For every step the lecherous demon took, Derian needed to take two painful ones, yet still, he kept up. The beast was as wide as a cart and as tall as its driver, and it looked like it had been thrown together by a demented god who favoured leathery skin containing bulbous muscles and an overabundance of thick blue veins. Its stumpy legs were the same length as Derian's, yet somehow the monster stayed upright; it charged forward as though in a perpetual flow of tripping, like a certain drunken munket after it had consumed an entire jar of honey. Somehow, though, it never fell over. Instead, it used its massive long arms to keep its balance.

Like all monsters, its face was a gruesome description of unrivalled evil. Thin slit eyes, dark and grey, and sharp, pointed ears upon a bald grey head, but with ill-fitting incisors in an unsuitably small mouth. Derian wondered if the pain of teeth continuously breaking through its own lips was the reason behind the current rampage it found itself on. Perhaps the flaming arrow in its right shoulder might also have been a contributing factor, but a plan was a plan. Even a bad one. Even a good one, come to that.

"DO IT NOW?" Derian roared to those hiding in wait, somewhere ahead down the valley. Only now, in this desperate rush, did Derian realise he should have listened more to the plan. All he'd cared about was their just rewards. Killing this vile beast would earn him and his comrades some badly needed renown. Killing a few hundred more might earn them some grace in the Guild. Might even earn him his own title, and wasn't that the most important thing for any half-named mercenary?

Lorgan had made him read up about their quarry. Derian hated studying even more than the rain, and, according to the irritating written word, a lecherous demon was merely a servant to the greater evils of the source realm—fortunate enough to slip from the unnatural dominion into the living world to cause shit mindlessly. He also knew that a lecherous demon answered to a master. All demonic beasts did. Greater, more masterful demons with intelligence and will. *Grand demons.* That was it. That was all he'd studied, and it had been mind-numbingly boring. Well, that and something about there being at least seven grand demons, all with terrifying unnatural powers, horns, claws, and all that spit. He hadn't seen one, and he wasn't alone. In fact, no living mercenaries had ever seen a grand demon. Some said they were dead, torn apart by each other in a wild act of demonic madness. Others believed them slain by an ancient warrior a millennium before the source first revealed itself, and that that old warrior now lived as a god—eternal and restless, living off the souls of the fallen. Wise and wary, they said. Bored as bark, Derian imagined. Others, though, believed them to be biding their time, scratching at the doorway, desperate to come in and play. They said Anguis, the Dark One, had seen all seven, but that was peasant talk. No, it was peasant drivel, and nothing was worse than peasant drivel, peasant talk, and peasant understandings in the mercenary world. Unless it was the rebels of Karkur. They fell somewhere in between. Though their penchant for blaming the world's leader Anguis, the Dark One, for all things nasty got in the way of their credibility. They should have just blamed the source.

Derian believed the Dark One was only human. Terrifying as he was.

Don't forget the seven gods of Dellerin. Can't forget the seven gods.

It was easier to forget what he didn't believe in. He'd seen the actions of demons, yet never the actions of gods. Gods were supposed to be on the side of humankind, right? Derian wondered if the seven demons and the seven gods were the same seven entities lost in the retelling of stories. He wondered if the demons had killed the seven gods or if there had never actually been seven gods. He wondered if there were more than seven demons. Perhaps the strapping male demons had mated with pretty-looking lady demons and made loads more little baby demons. *Demon younglings? Youngemons? Demonlings?*

Concentrate, idiot.

Whatever the truth turned out to be, he doubted the world would ever know how many demons walked between worlds. However, every fool and scholar with thoughts on the matter agreed that a grand demon could tear an army of soldiers to a million shreds in one swift attack. No tale spoke of any mercenary group killing one, not even any of the fictional tales of those groups like Erroh's Outcasts or Heygar's Hounds. Maybe he'd be the first, and everything would be far easier after that. Or a thousand times worse. He'd long since learned that good things were swiftly followed by tenfold the fuken disasters. The night before, he'd had a pleasant, relaxing dream about a real pretty girl. She'd been reading a book. It wasn't a spectacular dream but it had been nice, and he'd forgotten how spitting awful his life was. He'd considered that a nice thing and now he was running through a dreary forest. Perhaps Kesta was correct in suggesting that his mind wandered at the worst of times.

"Where are you?" Derian shouted again, slipping through the roots and branches of yet another upturned tree. His ankle had stopped hurting, but the rain still poured down upon him through the growing number of openings in the forest's canopy. As he sprinted, the world blurred into one vision of grey and exhaustion, and he looked for familiar landmarks in this desperate chase.

He knew he should have paid more attention on the walk up the valley, but Natteo's stupid ramblings about the perfect arrow leaf had distracted him. *Was it possible to become stupider when speaking on stupid matters?* The scenery all looked the same at this pace. Forest was forest at the best of times, and this forest was just another stupid thing about this wretched island.

The unnatural grey was spreading. It had not taken this forest fully, but who knew a year or two from now. He'd seen it in different parts of Dellerin. Rich, natural green fading away to miles of ashen grey—as though all hope and life had been stripped from each tree's surface, like a painter's scribbles before producing timeless beauty. Even if these trees still bore fruit and grew larger with every season, he thought it an omen of bad things.

He knew why this deathly grey happened. He was certain that someone had told him. He had it on the edge of his mind. The land was grey in some parts because... because...?

Ah, spit on this. Stupid rain, stupid demon, stupid life. Stupid source making things grey.

Chasing an ugly demon through a rainstorm in the middle of a miserable grey forest of dreariness was a new low in the young life of Derian the Unspectacular. And he'd thought being a member of the Crimson Hunters was the lowest anyone could ever truly go.

He slammed his sword's pommel against his bronze chest plate and cursed aloud, creating the perfect suggestion of a pursuing mob. The beast didn't look back, but it did roar a painful retort before upping its pace and smashing an extra few unlucky trunks out of its way as it charged on. So far, so good for Lorgan's plan. Then again, many of Lorgan's plans had at first appeared solid. That's why most people agreed to them. Problem was, all plans could turn on their heads in a moment's notice. Derian had little understanding of the complexities of probabilities—he couldn't even spell the word or most other long words—but he understood that Lorgan's plans turned on their heads far more than probability demanded. Perhaps that was another reason why they were such a wretched outfit.

"Grrrr! Arrrrrgh!" Derian shouted, adding to the illusion that there was a big group of monster hunters pursuing. *Keep running*, he willed it, and the lecherous demon continued its fateful charge for a dozen more breaths before breaking free of the grey forest and heading out into an open dell that Derian didn't recognise at all. *Fuk.* He feared another change of plans was in his near future.

At least it's out in daylight. For as brutal and terrifying as most demons were, they suffered under the burning heat of the sun. It was the only defence this world had against the monsters who stole through. Daylight stripped a demon of its fight, so any day was a good time for hunting them. Though the rain didn't help. He could see now that the demon was suffering some fine burning, and he thought that was polished and all, but it was far from causing it any real harm. There would be some fight to come. There was always a fight to come. He thought again of the dream. He wished it had been nicer.

The monster slowed at the edge of the dell and leant forward to draw air into its monstrous lungs beneath the shade of a weeping oak. The burning arrow in its back was long since extinguished, and it appeared less a volatile projectile intent on scaring the beast into a charge and more an irritating splinter of wood.

"Oh, spit on me. Don't turn around. Keep running,"

Derian hissed under his breath, coming to a swift stop among the waist-high grass of the dell. This wasn't the plan, at all. The plan involved the demon running in hoodwinked fear, until the rest of the Crimson sprang the trap and tore it to pieces. That was the plan.

That was the plan.

Far behind, he heard the low thumping of Natteo following in the wake of destruction. The demon must have heard the solitary plodding steps as well, and it turned its head. Derian couldn't read body language on a beast so basic, but he would swear he read the expression on its confused face as it realised their ruse, and he felt the turning of the tide. Or to be more precise, the turning of another of Lorgan's well-thought-out, ill-fated plans.

THE GANG FIGHT A MONSTER

"Set the fire at the entrance and smoke the bugger out of the cave. They're stupid beasts—a little noise and a couple of arrows as it passes, and it'll charge brainlessly right down the valley. Me and Kesta will wait all cosy like," Lorgan had said, and he'd seemed so reassuring.

"What if it smells the smoke and ventures deeper into the cave?" Natteo had asked. His tone had suggested deference, but there'd been a spark in his eye. Derian had known this, Lorgan too, but he'd still feigned a smile and answered.

"Then we'll try something else, but I'd bet my life the cur takes flight towards fresh air, and once we get it running a while, it'll tire nicely in the daylight, and that's when we'll have our chance."

"I don't think I want any involvement in this part of the plan. Unlike yourself, Lorgan, I've never been much of a runner," Natteo had said, in that same tone.

Natteo had a wonderful ability to say the wrong thing. He also had the wonderful ability of finding out exactly what that wrong thing was. He also had the ability to find the exact wrong moment to say that exact wrong thing. Admittedly,

Derian was equally gifted in this practice, but that was more by accident. Natteo had willingly mastered the art.

"Listen, you little—"

Kesta had placed her soothing hand across Lorgan's chest and calmed him in one easy manoeuvre. For all the incompetence in the Crimson Hunters, Kesta was the worst mercenary of them all. She had an unambitious spirit and an uneasy disposition; her fighting skills were dreadful, her tracking was incompetent, and her privilege as second was unjustified. She had no feel for the work.

Still, though, Derian liked her. She had great hair. Derian knew this because Natteo always said it when he braided it for her. It was a service he provided any time she desired— so, most of the time. Her brown braided hair matched her skin. She was twice as old as Derian, though carried it well. She rarely smiled, and her dark eyes suggested that somewhere along the way, life had struck her a blow or two. That said, life had a nasty way of hurting everyone in Dellerin; Kesta merely kept her scars deep within. From the three years he'd known her, he knew little more than her love for the sky, books, and ensuring the rest of them were being the best little mercenaries they could be, like a clucking fowl. She had moments when she'd fall silent listening to the wind or watching the dawn. Whenever they came upon a steep ridge on a march, she would stand at its edge and take in what sights she could. Frequently, she would stare at birds in flight while standing there whispering delicate prayers to herself. Thinking of it now, he wondered if she wasn't just contemplating leaping to silence.

Well, she hasn't jumped yet, and she shows little desire to leave Lorgan's side either. She had a cold stare that would settle a Venandi night hunter, and when needed, she had a certain tone of voice so cutting that the Dark One himself might offer an apology and return the honey cake he'd stolen. Lorgan valued her more than Derian and Natteo put together. Probably because she was the first mercenary that hadn't left him or died under his leadership. To her credit, she kept the group together as a watching mother kept eyes over her young cubs. Derian suspected, though, that the Crimson was the level of her ability. She'd started the mercenary life later than most.

"Shut your mouth, Natteo. You and Derian will do what he asks, or I'll knock you both out," she had said, and Derian had heard a flock of birds above them fall deathly silent. Lorgan had walked away muttering under his breath, annoyed that she had settled the argument without a little battering to get the blood pumping.

"Knock me out? I could take you, no problem," Natteo had countered.

"Would you really take me, little one?"

"Probably not, Mother."

"Don't call me that, you little shit," she'd countered in a dangerous tone that Natteo knew well not to push.

When Lorgan had returned with the netting, his pale face had been serious, and Natteo chose not to mock him any further. There was only so much abuse you could give the warrior before he retorted with significant violence.

"Chase the little beastie down the forest," he'd told them. "It's like drawing out a flock of pheasants. We'll be watching. We'll line the net across whichever path it chooses."

"Yes, sir," they had both replied.

Derian slid the bow from his back slowly, and the monster watched him from the dell's far side—thirty or forty feet across. It tilted its head and looked beyond the diminutive mercenary. Like before, Derian could almost understand what confused thoughts ran through its apple-sized brain.

It looked left of Derian. *Nope, no hunting pack on that side.* It looked to the right. *Nope, no hunting pack on that side either.* It looked straight at Derian. *Little human, make noise.*

Perhaps had the beast moved with urgency, it might have been less unnerving, but as it was, it reached behind its muscular back and slowly, almost leisurely, plucked the limp arrow free. It eyed the bow in Derian's hands accusingly.

"Whoa—he looks bigger when he's got you in his sights," Natteo said, appearing beside Derian. "Where's the net?"

Derian had the perfect reply—a thorough and expletive-laden outburst, all about why Lorgan's plan had fallen to waste—but he never uttered a word because the monster charged them.

Natteo was quick. He'd always been quick. Such quickness was hardly born from practice or from running around. His was a quickness of the mind with reflexes to boot. He fired two small bolts from each wristbow before the lecherous beast could take a second step. By the time the bolts struck and their quarry had taken a further step, the mercenary was reloading for the next shots.

Derian's mind flashed to the pictures in *The Successful Mercenary's Compendium*. He hated that compendium as much as he hated having to read it. He did like the few pictures displaying techniques required for precarious moments, though. Tragically, there weren't any illustrations to teach him what to do in this precarious moment—beyond dropping the offending bow and unsheathing his sword in leathery silence.

What to do?
Panic?
Fuken panic?

14

Will that help?

"No," a voice in his mind whispered.

Lorgan would fume that his mind went blank. Another argument in favour of him learning to study more, he imagined. This was turning into a fantastic day altogether, he thought miserably as the features of the girl from his dream faded away. A moment or two from now, the dream would be gone altogether.

"Keep moving!" cried Natteo, and Derian roused himself from his stupor. He ducked as the monster fell upon him with wild lunging strikes. He met the attack with shaking hands upon the tightly-wrapped grip of his faithful sword, Rusty. It wasn't the name he'd have given it. He'd have preferred Lightbringer or Deathwalker or something splendid like that. Instead, his comrades had called it Rusty because its previous owner, a lowlife bandit with thin leather armour, had left it to fall into ruin. Even now, in the hazy light of a rainstorm, the echoes of its disrepair were clearly visible on its guard and pommel, but the blade itself was oiled and sharp.

"For the love of fuk, keep shooting it, Natteo."

"I'm doing my best, Derian. Why don't you stab it better?"

The beast swung its claws like weapons, and Derian met each razor-sharp strike with Rusty in a loud *clink*. Without the monster able to put its full momentum behind the attack, Derian could parry each strike without being felled like an unfortunate tree. To any incompetent swordsman, this appeared impressive; however, any mercenary worth his weight in silver would suggest his guard was a little high, his feet were spread too far apart, and his counterattack was non-existent. They would be critical; they would be right.

He wished Lorgan and Kesta were here with him now, bringing the fight to the beast, but at least for all his mutterings, Natteo was a fine comrade of war. Despite his reluctance to sprint through forests in the rain, the mercenary ran around the dell firing bolt after bolt from his spring-loaded wristbows, shouting loudly every time. Uncommon and favoured by grander men of leisure, the wristbow was a slick weapon, easily folded upon itself in more peaceful times and spring-loaded for swift violence in a pulse of time when it was needed for smooth murder at close range. They were expensive, though, and favoured by the sneakier mercenaries. Naturally, Natteo sported one on each wrist. The smaller bolts were less effective than any traditional arrow or crossbow bolt, but he looked polished firing them— and looking polished was as important as efficiency. That he broke skin less than half the time wasn't too important either.

"We have this!" he kept shouting, as though they did.

Derian slipped back and readjusted his footing as the pictures in the compendium suggested, and despite his better judgement, he brought his arms closer to his chest. The book suggested this gave the beast less chance to strike him, but still, it felt unnatural. The demon swung, and he blocked much more easily than before, but with his arms tucked in, there was nothing to cushion what power the beast had. He took the winding blow and fell to his knees. *Stupid book.*

The other claw connected cleanly across his chest. There was pain. Dreadful pain. All the pain in the world. There was also a strange sensation of floating, as the world spun his vision asunder. He heard a triumphant, monstrous roar, a best friend's cry of profanity, and the whistling of wind and rain as the demon flung him through the air.

Flying.

He landed painfully in a heap on the far side of the dell. For a few breaths he lay on his back in the dampened wild grass as his vision settled, and he reached down to his torn chest armour.

Far away he heard the trampling of undergrowth, and farther from that, the aggressive roars of battling opponents. His chest plate was wet—but only from the rain and mud. His father had assured him it was reinforced bronze, despite his misgivings that such a delicate piece would be effective.

"It is my only heirloom, son. Battered by a rodenerack smith for ten long years. Thin, sturdy, and worthy of you." His useless bastard father had placed the chest piece in his hands on the morning Lorgan had claimed him as a young apprentice, and a life of disagreements was lost in one moment of kindness.

There were three long gashes down its centre that hadn't been there this morning. Bronze shouldn't break that easily, he thought, and then thought how much of a dodgy cur his father had been. Why should a farewell gift in front of their small watching village have been any different? He'd probably had a dozen similar pieces in his trader's lockaway, ready to sell to those moved by his gesture.

Thanks, Dad.

Derian stripped the tin piece free and left it in the grass. It might stop an arrow from a hundred feet against the wind, but in its current state, it was little more than a hindrance and a gentle reminder of where he'd come from. Most little villages were drenched in peasant superstition, and his shitty clan had been no different. They believed in Seevas, of all things, the ancient hounds of the gods. They even had a shrine where they worshipped them. It was so embarrassing. He never mentioned that to ladies when trying and failing to charm them.

His chest stung as though he'd taken a dull lance to it, but he took a breath, and without a wet heave suggesting trauma, he wondered if today might be a good day, despite his bad feeling.

"Get up, idiot! It only knocked you thirty feet!" Lorgan shouted from behind him. The tall mercenary emerged from the grey, carrying half the heavy steel net with him. He offered a cursory glance at his fallen companion but didn't break stride. Kesta followed, carrying the other half of the net, and they dropped it beside him. So much for the net plan.

"Up you get," Kesta said, as though he were a little pup with a dislocated ankle and running it off was the only way to pop it back in. When she used that motherly tone, it was impossible not to agree. She held him for a moment in a sturdy grip until he steadied himself. "Come on, little one. Let's go earn our crust."

3

THE VECTOR

The three mercenaries fanned out around the dell, one at each corner, and drew the monster's attention. They shouted and hissed, and Natteo slipped away from the creature's sight through the grass and took his place in the mercenaries' formation.

"That's not a lecherous demon," hissed Lorgan, holding his sword in one hand and his shield in the other. If he ever looked the force of nature his experience suggested, it was when his plans turned on their head and he resorted to straight-out battle. He glided towards the bolt-ridden monster. "It's something far fiercer."

"What is it?" muttered Derian, gripping Rusty.

"At least thrice the price that they promised us," the old mercenary suggested.

"Wonderful news, boss. You go attack him, and I'll wait right here," Natteo suggested, disarming his wristbows in a flash before pulling out two short swords. He'd tired of stinging the beast; now came the cutting.

They formed up around the demon, as was typical in the slaying of any monster, according to that annoying book.

Though he had not shared this with his comrades, Derian had had a bad feeling all morning. Maybe it was knowing today was to be the day he died.

He hated being right.

He also hated being forced to stare at demons. Something deep within him always recoiled. He imagined that was what most people felt. The monster stood like a statue in an archaic cathedral of Venistra. Only its wide, hairless chest gave any suggestion it was a living thing at all. It took slow, methodical breaths, and for a strange moment, Derian wondered if it wasn't reconsidering its inevitable attack. Something in the eyes. Something in the way the shoulders sagged. As though in its weary state it had lost the will to fight, ruin, and devour. Did demonic creatures like this have feelings? Did it experience fear? Regret? Did it feel that today was the day *it* would die?

Did *it* hate being right?

The collapse of his best-laid plan hadn't disheartened Lorgan. He remained poised and controlled. Most mercenaries wore no headdress, and he was no different—for good vision was more essential than avoiding a good headshot. He also moved more smoothly than the rest of his comrades because he carried less armour than they did: a few leather pieces with sparse shards of light steel plating. Not to mention easy-release strapping. Derian had always wondered how he'd lasted so long without heavier armour covering the rest of him; he'd asked him once, and Lorgan had merely smiled sadly and he'd never asked again.

The monster snarled and bloody spittle dripped down its chin, and for no reason at all, Derian lost his will to fight— until he caught sight of something hanging along its neck, standing out from the grey of its skin.

It was a golden necklace with a sapphire amulet. He

thought it a strange thing that the demon could carry such a piece through from the other realm, but he didn't fret on the matter, thinking how much more value such a journey added to the piece. The contract would earn them a fine little pouch of gold as it was, but a jewel like that would fill their pockets for the year. They might even get to travel back home in the lap of luxury upon an airbarge this time. Might even be treated to a week in the pleasure houses of Castra, while they were at it.

Oh, yes, greed was a wonderful thing, and Derian's fear ebbed away in the glimmer of that shiny, polished jewel, along with his mercy and wariness.

A whimper echoed out across the dale. It had come from the monster, and Natteo eyed Derian curiously. *Since when do monsters show emotion?*

Kesta was unmoved, however. Without warning, she leapt forward, drawing first blood from their prey. Instinctively, Lorgan followed her attack, and both mercenaries met the beast with blade, hate, and violence. The air was alive with the clanging of claw on steel, healthy amounts of growling, and a Natteo's amount of cursing.

"Die at my wrath!" roared Lorgan, as though he were a hero of the old tales, and his pompousness was heartening.

Derian gripped his sword, awaiting the moment for heroism, or, failing that, a little stabbing. Preferably in its back.

Even Natteo roared eagerly and leapt into battle. He spun his blades impressively in both hands and looked as much a hero as Lorgan. Perhaps he'd noticed the jewel?

They came at it, not as one collective attack, but rather in four lesser, swift sequences. Each warrior was allowed a moment to strike, and as they cleared the swinging claws, another would follow and take the beast's attention with it. It was an archetypal tactic when bringing down any monster of great size and strength. One little mercenary running around firing bolts while another stood toe-to-toe with the enemy was not a tactic Derian was keen to attempt again—and one that Lorgan wouldn't even consider.

If Lorgan was fierce and loud with magnificent bravado, Kesta was disturbingly quiet. Her face was a grim veneer of hate as she attacked with all the skill her body would allow. She tore a blade across the monster's side and slid beneath its hulking, laboured counter-strike. She dared a second stab before it could take hold of her, but the demon swung its talons a little too swiftly and she stumbled as she leapt away. The beast could have had her, but Lorgan appeared, cracking his shield fiercely against its nose before rolling away from its distracted grasp.

As Natteo glided behind the monster's back and dug both his small swords into its spine, Derian was imagining what shiny new armour he could purchase with his share of gold.

However, both Natteo's swords held tight, trapped within muscle, bone, and organ. "Ah no," he groaned, as the demon spun towards him, striking him with its unforgiving fist. Derian watched in horror as Natteo was sent sprawling through the air, far back into the deep grass. The sight of deep claret stains on the monster's claws shook Derian to the core.

This is bad.

"Help Natteo!" shouted Lorgan, stepping between fallen comrade and demon. Anyone who knew the Crimson Hunters knew that Lorgan never left companions behind, and he never sacrificed innocents for a mission's success. These were honourable traits to peasants and even soldiers, but to mercenaries, they were flaws.

It required a certain nastiness to succeed. Lorgan was a good man, and as the demon fell on him with a flurry of swift combinations, Derian wondered how successful his leader might have become if he hadn't spent thirty years looking after his mercenaries instead of wielding them as the weapons they were. Aye, he would have lost many more friends than he had, but a rich man could buy all the friends he'd ever need. The Crimson Hunters were unspectacular in their undertakings, and the blame fell upon their leader.

Derian was still young, but he had no intention of staying a pauper in this outfit for the rest of his career. Or his life. He had big plans beyond the little town of Treystone's contract for a lecherous demon. Natteo felt the same. They had already been whispering about the prospect of forming their own little outfit in a couple of years.

"We should have brought a net," moaned Natteo weakly, and Derian raced through the grass to reach him. When he did, he found a ruined man with a bitter grin on his face. His chest was punctured wide open, and both his legs were splayed unnaturally to either side. An ocean of red accompanied the many shards of bone protruding bloodily through his clothing. The fallen log he'd landed on was jagged and painted an unnatural crimson colour. It matched the tainted grass around his friend.

"I like sunny days," Natteo said dreamily, trying to rise, but the task bested him with the breaths he had left. A terrible river of red flowed from his mouth, and Derian's heart dropped as Natteo's heart slowed. He could have stayed with his friend as he slipped into darkness, but he clasped his weak hand once and left him to die. His companions were still fighting for their lives, and they needed him. It was what Natteo would have wanted, but he'd never have said it aloud.

Having withstood the onslaught from the demon long enough, Lorgan took the fight to it with flurries of his own. Sword and shield hammered loudly from each side—striking, cutting, and hurting—and despite the demon towering over him, he forced it to retreat a few steps. Perhaps he knew Natteo's fate and had become enraged, for the bearded warrior roared with every strike and appeared as mighty as any legendary warrior could.

"Let me strike!" screamed Kesta, eager to relieve him and continue the assault, but Lorgan was deaf to anything but the battle; he charged upon the beast.

"To the fires with you, thurken cur," he growled, using old-man swear words, and he stabbed the demon in the heart and it fell away, taking the sword with it. Lorgan didn't stop. With two hands he swung his shield like a farmer scything wheatcorn. Each dull, teeth-shattering blow echoing loudly in the air matched each curse the grizzled warrior spat out. But a shield was only half a weapon, and suddenly, the monster grabbed the half-weapon in its mighty grip and held fast. So Lorgan kicked it in the groin, for all men will fight desperately for their life in the last moments. It was a fine kick that did little damage.

The monster sent the old mercenary flying like his comrades before him. He landed upon his head beside Derian with a horrific crack, and Derian knew Lorgan would never get up again. He lay motionless, but his eyes blinked rapidly as though he were struggling to understand this impossible angle his neck found itself at. A little trickle of blood came out of his mouth, and he began to slip from life.

"NO!" screamed Kesta, and fell upon the monster in maddened grief. She struck it through skin and muscle several times, and it spun towards her. The world became still, and for a moment it didn't fight back. Instead, it looked upon the warrior as though she were something to study rather than fear. Kesta wailed as she swung with her sword, plunging it deep inside the creature and drawing much blood, yet it did not fall to her wrath.

"Leap away!" Derian cried, preparing his attack, but as with Lorgan before, Kesta was deafened to typical tactics by a haze of anguish.

Then, to Derian's horror, he saw a dull blue sheen cover the monster. The wounds it had suffered began healing in front of his eyes. He felt the burning touch of fire in the air, and as though he were standing before a charging carriage with no route to escape, he knew this was the end.

"You fuken piece of—"

The monster took hold and lifted Kesta in the air above its head. She was fierce, she was brave, and she wasn't a very good mercenary at all. She continued to stab with all the hatred she could muster, but it twisted her like a small bundle of kindling. Derian heard the ripping snap as it broke her in two. She didn't scream—the pain took her consciousness—as it flung both parts of her aside like a child's toy before spinning around and charging the last standing Crimson Hunter.

The ground shook, and he thought he'd try to escape, but a terrible surge of hate engulfed him and kept him in his place. His limbs felt impossibly light, as though controlled by thought alone. He desired to raise his sword, and he did so without feeling the action. In that moment, he knew his mind was abandoning him when he needed it most.

He thought he'd be terrified at the end of his life, but he was only angry. Not for dying; that didn't matter. He was angry that he couldn't kill the demon and raise its decapitated head above his own in triumph. That he couldn't gorge himself upon its blood, for that was the greater insult. The demon took him, and he thrust his sword towards his vanquisher.

It wasn't an impressive strike, but his wrist was stiff and straight, his blade's pointy tip reassuring. He plunged the tip through the demon's neck, and as he did, he shattered the dazzlingly beautiful amulet for good measure.

The world exploded in a pulse of black and magenta fire. Blue lightning too. He felt his body rip and separate, and as his vision burned away, his last sight was his limbs tearing free and taking flight—and with them went the glorious anger. He spun in fire, blood, and pain, and the world went dark as Derian died in a wretched dell, in a wretched country, in the wretched rain.

4

AFTER THE DARK

B *irth.*
   Birth was painful, terrifying, and terminally inescapable. She knew this because she'd been through it all before and thought it a nasty affliction. At least with traditional birth, there was a watchful midwife and a caring mother waiting with open arms and warmer hands, but as this familiar moment enveloped her, Seren felt no comforting call.

As bad as birth was, a second birth was worse—though she didn't know how she knew this. She knew she must learn to think like humans again.

Humans have many thoughts, don't they? Flying through her mind like flutterbyes. Close yet elusive. *Also pretty.* She hadn't thought like a human in so very long. *How long?* Well, she didn't know. She also didn't know how she knew what a flutterbye was either, but knowing was delightful.

One of her first thoughts was *This world is bright*. Her eyes burned like the sun, and though she tried to cover them and hide again in the eternal darkness, she did not cower, for she knew her eyes would overcome this horror. Also, she had no hands yet, only molten eyes. The world spun, and she felt

7

its embrace. From her stinging eyes flowed tears of agony, release. Oh, she had old thoughts, but they forsook her and flittered away to whence they came. Like a particular hissect. Would they return? *He said they would.*

"He said I would forget," she whispered, and her voice was unnatural and croaky as though she hadn't wet her throat in a thousand years. No, that wasn't true. It was more like twenty in this realm. *What was a year anyway?* She felt the world's winds upon her skin as it formed around her bones, and the pain was deliciously maddening.

She felt her tongue and it was strange. *Slithering.* Her burning eyes floated in the air and then they became surrounded by muscle, ligament, blood, and bone. A head, hair, a face grimacing in torment. A body clenched in a demon's wrath, broken and torn. She felt herself as she would be, and she felt the blissful cold all around her as though emerging from her mother's belly into a freezing life of struggle, pain, hunger, and death—and she loved it.

"Thank you," she whispered to her master, and it hurt more, and it was wonderful, and she tried to thank him again but he was gone; gone longer than she could understand. Just like he'd said he'd be.

I'll see you on the other side.

Her knees became whole and they buckled beneath her as though she were a witch of a thousand years. Further thoughts slipped from her mind, replaced by the wonderful new.

Imprisoned. Mother. Demon. Dark One.

"Hunting."

She fell to the ground, blind to the dreadful burning of day. She wept majestically and manically, like babies when tasting the world for the first time. *For the second time and still without a mother and father.*

The ground was wet; she remembered wet, and other

things, and she wept in joy a little more. There had been no wet where she had been. Her thoughts and understandings from the darkness slipped away as thoughts of this new world replaced them. How did she remember what wet was?

She couldn't sense him anymore now. She couldn't even remember who he was, apart from his fierceness, his love, his kindness, and his eternal hope.

Grandfather.

She felt cold, her hands were wet and muddy, and she felt happier than she'd ever felt in her life. *Her first life.* Her eyes blinked and focussed, and this too brought a fresh wonder. She was on her hands and knees; they were attached to the rest of a woman's glorious body, and she was free. *Free to bring doom to them all.* She drew in air and realised the delirium of a deep breath, and the world around Seren focussed completely. *Seren, Seren, Serenity.* Everything was sharper—as sharp as a tormentor's wicked knife—and her eyes tried to focus upon the grassy strands interspersed between the muddy patches in her vision.

"Where am I?"

She was alone, and it was beautiful. The world focussed, and a half-life of blurred darkness gave way to the delicious brightness of day. She was Seren, and she was alive after years of imprisonment, and she knew little else. It would return, her mind, when the moment had passed. When she'd become born fully. *Any wonderful moment now.*

She stood up, and this time it was her cold, muddy feet that betrayed her, and she fell again with a wonderful *plop* all over the wet, muddy ground. To be alive was a precious gift, and she cherished it in these first few moments, for though she couldn't quite understand why, she knew her fleeting life would be entrenched in blood, horror, and misery. She knew this because he'd shown her what was coming. For now, she was happy because it was raining. *Yes.* Raining started the wet. *Brilliant.*

It was raining, and she was naked, and she was free.

She rose once again as the last memories of her tainted imprisonment slipped away completely, and she cried aloud in an ecstatic, wailing bray of liberty. Her eyes became her own, and though they hurt with such dreary bright light all around her, she soaked up what vision she could. She felt the world come alive in honour of her birth, for he had enchanted this moment. Made her heal to life. Made everything heal to life. At least, for a while.

Maybe not the vector demon, though?

A self-healing vector demon would be a terrible thing. *Or a wondrous thing.* She couldn't remember at all. She smelled the richness in the bitter-cold air, and she knew that fragrance. Around her stood a forest of grey, and she thought it beautiful. She stretched her arms out wide and spun around in a circle, giggling. *Yes:* to dance was a human thing of such merriment, and she remembered that vividly. She wondered what else she would remember as the moments passed. She'd need to remember the art of killing. What a strange thought, and how strange that it reassured her.

She could hear the raindrops all around her, and they felt larger than she'd remembered. It didn't matter, for she was awestruck by the simple wonder of it. She opened her eyes against the wind, sting, light, and rain, and she looked upon the glorious dell.

At her feet were countless tufts of green long grass, wilted and scorched by her birth. *Resurrected too.* The scarring on the ground spread out fifty feet in a great arc, and she thought this another reason to dance in appreciation, though she couldn't be certain why. Just in case, she spun around in a delicate pirouette and caught her foot on a jagged rock. She remembered pain. Sharp, unavoidable, and a reminder that a breath was a gift. She felt a gash in her foot, and then she felt it disappear as the last of his enchantment fizzled out and disappeared into the dark eternity. And then she saw the bodies.

No longer alone at all. They were human creatures like her own body of flesh, and all of them were spread out around her. All of them ambling as though being born like herself.

She saw the woman, lying in the grass, and she watched her rise, just as she herself had only a few moments before. This beautiful dark-skinned woman had unsettling hair. Long and thick and decorated in beads. Her eyes were tragic, like the eyes of a beast from the dark. She would be no threat. Nor would the young man lying in the grass be. He said something, but she lost his words in her hearing. In her understanding. She was not fully born at all, it would appear.

He spoke again, swiftly, and she wondered would they be friends?

It was the tall figure with shield and sword that shook her entirely, and she sensed his destiny of sadness. He also spoke, and slowly the words formed in her mind, and she began to remember the act of coherent speech. She tried to listen, but her body carried her around the glade as she took enjoyment from everything she happened upon. Until she came to the last human.

She liked him most of all. Him and his bow and arrow. She felt her new heart already skip a beat, for she sensed something in him. Something near yet far away.

She could sense his essence, she could feel his vitality, she could see his terrified eyes, and she thought them pleasing. Did she like to instil fear? She knew fear was a potent source of vigour. Oh, she had an overwhelming desire to leap upon him too. After so many years denied, such primal thoughts flooded through her frantically happy mind.

Mating is what humans do?

She tried to smile. She walked to him, and with every step, the world grew loud and vibrant, and Seren gorged herself upon it—as a drunkard did after a barrel of ale and no evening supper. How did she know this? It didn't matter. What mattered was walking to the boy and ripping his clothing free so he could be naked like her, and then they could be close.

She wanted to spin around and give a cry of joy for her birth. She very well might have, but suddenly, an ache stirred in her stomach and thrust itself outwards—like a creature with jagged teeth, long claws, and too many legs. She imagined it tearing and ripping from deep below, out through her newly-formed muscles and skin. She screamed like a beast in its trap.

She could feel the mark upon her skin. A demonic tattoo of knowing, and she tried to remember what he'd said of it. Painted in goldstone, knitted into her new skin by a monster of a purest divine wrath: she carried the mark, and she carried it openly. It ruined her and elevated her all at the same time. So, she did what newborns did once delivered. She screamed deafeningly so the world would know her pain better.

And the beautiful young man shot her in the head with an arrow.

5

KILLING THE GIRL

Derian woke from the explosion and found himself surprised he was capable of an achievement like waking from an explosion. The world around him was hazy. His body felt a ruin, but not as bad as his soul. He felt a misery, shared only by those who'd survived the desperation of battle, and in the dreaded hush of its aftermath he recalled that all his comrades were slain.

Torn, snapped, ripped.

The Crimson Hunters were disbanded in blood, pain, and violence. All of them dead, and he was alone.

How?

His mind was a blur of darkness. He crawled through the grass with limbs he'd believed thrown asunder by a fireball. He didn't know where he crawled, only that he kept moving lest death return and discover him nearby. His legs would not move beneath his will, and he almost cried out. Had the monster crippled him? Was he torn apart like Kesta but just too stupid to die?

A lesser man might have just lain in the wet mud, crying out in anguish. He looked behind at his legs and thought them impossibly heavy and long. They stretched out uselessly, and there was a deep crimson trail gushing out from behind him. A terrible thing to see; a worse thing to overcome. He dropped his head and wailed pitifully for his fate. Giving up was acceptable too.

He tasted the bitterness of mud, and he hated everything. He remembered the fireball and wondered if these were just a few lost moments before the end. Was he already dead? His face felt numb, as though his mind hadn't recognised the agony he found himself in—or else the pain was so potent, his mind had blocked it out. His skin had burned away like a swine's deliciousness upon a spit, and he tried to remember anything beyond fire and burning shards of muscle, but there was nothing.

He had his scars now, he thought miserably. Nobody would ever get the chance to ask him how he'd earned them.

"This is how I die," he whispered to the rain, as its cool droplets fell upon him for the last time. He would have preferred a blue sky with the sun warming his face at the end, but mercenaries rarely died well. At least he wasn't moaning like a rodenerack after you'd stolen its cheese. Dying alone with dignity was better than nothing, he supposed, and he felt his bladder release.

He turned over onto his back and stretched out as though felled spectacularly. His bones would look rather impressive, he pledged, and then he noticed his left leg had a terrible itch. Then he noticed the seeping blood had slowed its escape, and after that, he felt a tingling in many parts of his body.

Was this all in his mind? A last, distracting gift before the end?

Then the feeling began to return to his broken legs. Each breath he took brought him a step closer, so to speak. A few breaths later, he began to feel the gentle urge to move, like a little spark throughout his body, and he thought this amazing.

And then a naked girl walked by him and he thought this even more amazing.

She was faded as though stuck between two worlds, like the spirits of Brimlor Fields, and she stumbled and fell, and he thought her nakedness wonderful from this angle.

He felt a sudden strength course through him, and far away he heard the mutterings of Lorgan as he recovered from his own impossible injury. Derian saw the old mercenary kneeling in the mud looking thoroughly bewildered, but something drew him back to the naked girl. Perhaps it was her nakedness.

"What in the seven dead gods just happened?"

He knew that voice. Deep, feminine, and motherly. Derian pulled his eyes from the wonderfully naked girl burgeoning into the world and saw an equally bewildered Kesta resting her hands on her hips, exactly where the beast had snapped her irreversibly.

What enchantment of weaving was this? The naked girl began spinning and laughing, and he wondered was he in fact dead? Blown to bits by a lecherous demon—which wasn't actually a lecherous demon, but rather something far more volatile. Perhaps this was the world beyond the source, where all dead friends took unlikely breath and pretty girls with wonderful breasts danced around giggling?

"Who made it?" Kesta called out. She looked around the glade, unable to focus on object or comrade, blinking as though her eyes worked for the first time. Derian felt the same with his limbs.

It felt like a strange dream had befallen him—befallen

them all, really. Everything around them appeared ethereal, unnatural, and a breath of time seemed both an eternity and immediate.

Strangely enough (as if there hadn't been enough strange things already), Derian's body felt better than he could remember. A life on the march usually left any mercenary's body covered in bruises, from crown to toe, but he felt no pain at all. In fact, he felt like running a dozen miles at full pace without rest.

Dead.

Yes, he was dead; he had to be. He'd joined the last ranks of the fallen mercenaries. The Crimson Hunters were done. Chapter done. No more tales to tell.

"Well, we're not dead, that's for sure," Lorgan said, staring at his hands as though they were new appendages to him. "Vector demon. Nastier than I'd heard."

Derian hadn't heard of such a thing himself, and if Lorgan had more to say, he fell silent because the beautiful naked girl with flowing long raven hair walked past him whispering little sweet nothings to herself.

"Who are you?" he asked, stepping after her with feet less stable than usual, but the stunning naked girl had no intention of paying him any attention. Her bleary eyes resembled those of a patron at a lustre house in the wicked quarter of Castra. Derian had never been to that isle, but he'd meant to—as soon as he'd led his first mission. Lustre houses weren't as popular these last few years, according to Natteo, but it was a rite of passage any successful mercenary went through, and one he held a great interest in "enduring." The naked girl would fit in nicely with her dancing, he thought.

He tried again. "Excuse me, miss. Why are you naked in the forest?" The girl flitted closer into existence, and she glided across the dell back towards his leering eyes. He could have been a gentleman, but Derian had never seen a girl in such blatant undress before. Well, he had, but that was a different story altogether. He hoped this story ended in a more rewarding way, and with far less bruising.

It was Lorgan who snapped from her glamour first. "She's an alleerier servant."

A pulse of fear ran down Derian's spine like an ice-tipped blade. He recognised that monster, all right. There had been no picture, but the word just rolled off his tongue. They were wilier than most. They could transform their bodies into almost anything, but they favoured the appearance of a human to better hunt a human, for human meat was tastiest above anything else. To get this difficult delicacy, they deceived prey with desire and allurement and other such salacious things. Derian couldn't keep his eyes from the naked woman's body, and now he realised exactly why.

He recovered his bow and then looked at her a little more.

"Brought into this world by a vector demon, and now she is free," Lorgan hissed, and Derian still didn't know what a vector demon was, though he had an idea.

"I've heard of stranger things happening."

Because of the source.

"She's no alleerier," cried Kesta, stepping in front of Lorgan, doing what all would-be mothers did by protecting defenceless prey. Derian wanted to agree with her, for all passionate young men would happily be friends with a girl who was naked, but he knew the truth, and the nasty witch had to die.

"What's an alle... allllereeer... erier?" Natteo roused himself and did so with the misery of a man whose cherished trousers were forever stained in blood. "Whoa," he added, when he got to his feet and set eyes upon the beautiful girl with no clothes on. "Hey, Derian, there's a naked girl attacking us. Or saving us. Or, you know, whatever."

"Kill her!" screamed Lorgan.

"Who are you?" Derian demanded as the girl without clothes spun around and faced him, eyeing him with sharp, clear eyes. Blue like the ocean. Immediately, like a crack of lightning, he felt a connection to her. He also felt like connecting to her, and strangely enough, he believed she reciprocated his passion. She looked lovingly upon him as he notched an arrow, and she smiled, and she was naked, and a vector demon had blown him up, and none of this made any sense.

"Don't kill her!" Kesta cried.

"Strike that lewd witch down this instant," Lorgan ordered.

"How about we all just calm down and find out if she has any male friends?" Natteo argued.

Derian tried again. "Are you from the source?"

She looked right through him as though he weren't there until, without warning, she reached for her stomach and moaned loudly and the moment became lost. She *was* an alleerier. She had to be. Such an attractive girl would never look at him twice. He wasn't a troll to look upon; more she was a goddess. Or more accurately, she was a demoness.

"She stepped across worlds. Carried by a vile beast powerful enough to break through," Lorgan cried, and he recovered his sword. "Kill her, Derian. Kill her."

The air was volatile, like a hidden sine distillery beneath the ground. Any moment, someone would ignite a torch and blow them all up. Derian held the bow and arrow, wondering would it be him.

"I shouldn't."

"Leave the girl alone," hissed Kesta. She pulled at Lorgan and held him in place.

"It is no girl. She'll kill us all."

"We should take a moment to breathe. She might be worth something."

Derian drew back his bow. What a waste of a perfectly naked young lady, he thought, and the girl roared aloud like a demon of mercenary tales. Her stomach glowed like fire, and only then did Derian notice the tattoo upon it.

"Kill her. Kill her now. DO IT!"

"Don't."

He didn't want to—deep down he knew she was no threat. He knew it like a child instinctively knows its mother's touch from birth. Lorgan charged from Kesta's grip, barking orders to kill "before she regains her powers," and calling forth the last scraps of his ability as a mercenary, Derian obeyed orders; he would attend to repercussions after. Lorgan knew monsters better than most. The moment became eternal, and Derian felt his heart skip. He felt surging anger deep down open its eyes and desire murder. Murder most likely for the witch claiming to be this pure vision of a girl.

She looked at him once more with beautiful deep-blue eyes that he could sail upon. He released the arrow and sent the projectile through her head, killing the beautiful naked girl immediately and saving them all, like the hero he was.

6

LASTING IMPRESSIONS

Murderer.

Derian didn't have a great deal of skill with a bow; but he had enough to hit a demon and flush it from its cave, sending it on a rampage down a valley. He also had enough to send an arrow through a naked girl's hand as it attempted a block, through her forehead and into her brain, killing her instantly. Almost instantly.

She managed one solitary noise before she died. Nothing spectacular, just a whimpered squeak of such sorrow and surprise that even Lorgan grimaced. He'd have thought alleerier witches would have gone out with more grandeur and probably more fight.

Instead of thrashing and calling upon ancient monsters of the dark, she remained motionless at first as her final-ever cry echoed and disappeared beyond the glade of deep green. The arrow pinned her hand to her head in an undignified pose, and for a breath there was no blood. Then it began to flow as her heart beat its last few efforts.

She stood as though betrayed by the world; gone, yet too surprised to collapse. He could see her stunning eyes locked evermore in a look of heartbreak, but there was no glimmer behind them, and he no longer desired to sail upon them as a lover would.

Eventually, she fell backwards in a dreadful wet splash, and Derian dropped the bow in knowing horror. He'd killed before; it was never easy. To his pathetic name he had a few bandits, a dozen source beasties, but never a monster pretending to be a naked girl. He doubted a kill like that would earn him a title. As she collapsed, the glade seemed to silence itself. Perhaps it was just his imagination that the world recognised he had just committed a terrible crime.

It was an order, he told himself.

Kesta fell down beside the dead girl as though she might help, but death was forever. He'd seen his mother slaughtered as swiftly. They never came back. "What have you done, you little idiot?" She dropped her head, and he dropped his own, for something at the back of his thoughts began to sting. Some veiled truth he wasn't ready to accept.

Kesta pulled the arrow free from the girl's head with a dull thud and let her still-punctured hand fall onto the grass, arrow and all, staked like a demonic witch's would have been. "Oh, what a waste," she cried, and Derian stared upon the dead girl's face and felt disgusted with himself. She was stunning, even in death.

The terrible hole had spilled blood all over her face and ruined it, and Derian wanted to throw up. So he did. He'd had eggs and rye bread for breakfast. He wouldn't be eating either again for a while.

"She was certainly pretty," said Natteo, stepping to Derian and leaning over to hold his brown hair away from the mess erupting from his mouth. He tied Derian's hair with a little strip of cord, performing the task with the delicate skill of a man who might have had another career in Castra under different circumstances. Sometimes, Natteo did the exact right thing at the exact right moment. "Are you okay?"

Derian sniffed away the bitter, warm tears coming down his face. "She was a demon. It had to be done." He spat some strange pieces of carrot from his mouth. After a moment, he realised that they weren't carrots at all. His stomach stung as though a beastly creature had reached a jagged claw down his throat and wrenched it out.

Kesta was far from finished. "We could have captured her alive, you idiot, but oh no, the boys have to shoot a treasure, right in the face, before we can do anything."

Even Lorgan appeared contrite. He shrugged. It was the best defence he could summon.

"Is she definitely dead?" Natteo asked, patting Derian's back. Kesta checked the girl's neck pulse a second time.

"It's a strange thing that there was no reaction to the arrow in the head," Lorgan said, and knelt over the body, examining her as though she were a hunted beast slain for devouring during the Festival of the Boar. "They're supposed to be a little louder at the end." He dug his finger into the little hole and felt around, nodding approvingly at the damage the arrow had done. Derian threw up a few more carrots and allowed the beast to wreak havoc with his insides once more. "She didn't even soil herself either," he added, as though he'd just chosen cucumber soup as first course in an evening meal.

Natteo stared at him in horror. "Why would you notice something like that?"

Lorgan knelt in close to the girl. He pressed hard on the strange golden pattern at her navel and muttered under his breath. He checked her teeth, sniffed her skin, and grimaced before shaking his head.

"What is it?" Derian asked.

"It's nothing. Best we bury her and leave it."

"Tell me!"

"It won't take long," he added.

"TELL ME."

He took a breath. May have been a sigh. "I think she might have been partly human, maybe all human. If you hadn't killed her, we might well have known," he said, as though the cucumber soup was a little salty.

"Oh, please no."

Murderer.

"Please tell me this isn't true."

"Murderer."

"Please, Lorgan." Derian gasped, backing away from the murdered girl. "By the gods of the source. What have I done?"

"You killed a girl," Kesta snapped.

"It was an order." Derian fell away from his handiwork. His mind was a turmoil of sorrow and remorse. His thoughts flashed like lightning beneath a storm. She was beautiful. She was defenceless, and he had killed her. "I didn't mean to," he wailed, but he *had* meant to. He had meant to shoot that fuken witch down, for that was his job. He would hang for it. He should hang for it. But perhaps not, he thought. Who would know? Who might tell on him? No one would tell, would they?

No one needs to know.

He would know. Could he live with that? Such beautiful eyes, and he'd extinguished the light behind them. He was a murderer, and he deserved punishment.

"Murderer. Murderer. Murderer."

Derian suddenly gasped for air. Something took hold of his chest and squeezed furiously. He knew what it was, for it was an ailment he'd successfully concealed the three years he'd marched with this outfit. It came at the worst of times. Usually, anger followed and pulled him from the precipice.

You deserve this.

Who wanted to hire a mercenary who struggled with bouts of panic, anyway? He fell to his knees, and the world began to darken. And Natteo was beside him to comfort him. He was a murderer, and she didn't deserve this, and he started to cry. Would they bury her here and say a few words? Should he give the eulogy? He only knew the mercenary's prayer to the night. The grip tightened.

Slap!

The loud crack woke him from his fit.

Slap! again.

His friend eyed him warily and held his hand up to slap him a third time. He didn't need to, and instead, he accepted Derian's counterpunch and rolled with it as he did. They spoke no words, but Derian nodded what gratitude he could. He felt a little better. He caught his breath; it cowered beneath his panic and misery.

And then the dead girl opened her eyes and started screaming.

7

EVERLASTING REPERCUSSIONS

"I'm not shooting her again!" screamed Derian, backing away from the wailing girl in the grass. He stumbled and tripped on the offending bow. Stupid weapon causing all this mess.

"Whoa!" cried Natteo, joining Derian in his retreat. His feet squelched in a carrot-like substance, and if he noticed it ruin his boots, he said nothing. Instead, he turned his backwards retreat into a full stumble. His wristbows were already reloaded.

Lorgan's voice cut through the panic as it always did. "Form up." He raised his sword. His shield hung out in front of him, waiting to protect, and Derian pulled his own sword free.

None of this made sense at all. His mind recalled pictures and a few jotted notes in terrible handwriting from his mercenary guide, but all explanations eluded him. Dead meant dead in all realms, right?

Kesta remained calm despite the resurrection. She remained at the girl's side as she howled like a trapped lurcher in a spring cage. She spun and contorted, and Derian felt the suppressing grip of fear upon his chest, but he fought it off this time. One fit per day was enough. Even if a dead girl he'd murdered was not dead at all.

Was he still technically a murderer?

"Shush, little one," Kesta said, gently enough to soothe, but forceful enough to rise above the cries. The girl didn't respond. She rolled in the grass and caught sight of the arrow still protruding from her hand. This brought fresh mania, and Derian's stomach clenched. Was she a demoness after all?

"Aaaaaagh."

"It's okay, little one."

"Aaaaaaaaaagh."

"Shush, shush, you are safe. No one will hurt you." Kesta took hold of the girl in her strong arms. For a moment this seemed to help, until she caught her breath, sobbed a little, and resumed her braying. In the demoness's defence, dying and coming back could be a jarring experience.

Kesta released her and did what any kind mother would do—and perhaps this was where Natteo had picked up his healing hands. She struck the girl fiercely across the chin. A strange enough strike that left no wound but scored a clean point, if it was a contest of pugilism.

There was a dull satisfying *thunk* as jawbone met rock-hard mercenary fist, and it dazed the girl. In a flash, Kesta pinned her down and slid across to sit upon her arms and chest. In the same movement, the old mercenary snapped the arrow and wrenched the piece from the girl's hand.

"I'm sorry," she offered, as the girl's temporary stupor shattered.

"AAAAAAGH!"

"See… look… Better now," she said, displaying the broken arrow to the girl, who, despite the frenzy, focussed upon the arrow. The screaming died away to sobs. A flood of tears followed, and Derian hated this melancholic outburst more than anything else.

Actually, he'd hated the death yelp more.

"What in Silencio's spitting name is she?" Natteo demanded from somewhere behind the tree he'd used for cover. Kesta smiled, stroking the terrified girl's cheek; she spoke the language of the comforting mother over a little one's scuffed knee, and she spoke it just right. The girl's frantic (wonderful) chest resumed a more regular wave of breathing, and were it not for the sobbing, Derian might have smiled. *Not a murderer.* Her forehead's wound was already sealing up as though knitted together by unnatural things, just like his own body before. Was there something about this place?

"She is human." Kesta hushed the girl a little more.

Lorgan knelt down beside her, and Kesta glared a warning. He shrugged in self-defence, and she sighed. He grunted, and after a moment, she nodded. After a few breaths, Lorgan nodded. It wasn't the first time such a silent argument had occurred between them, and even if Lorgan had won out, Kesta seemed satisfied with the outcome. He passed the iron bind across to her and stepped away.

"It's okay, little one. This is for your own good," Kesta whispered, and she slipped the iron bind around the girl's neck and locked it with a click. Lorgan took hold of the thin chain at the other end and completed the capture in less than a breath.

"Human, but she came from within the source," Lorgan said, and he wrapped the chain to his waist. "Such a thing is rare. Worth her weight, no doubt."

Natteo dared a few steps closer. "I'm glad she's not dead and all, but humans don't heal like that."

"You seem to have," Kesta whispered. Her eyes never left

the stunning girl lying in the grass all covered in mud and nakedness.

"It's because I'm special."

"We all healed quick enough," she said, and the girl became transfixed by the larger woman with brown skin and great hair.

Natteo grew braver and removed his tattered cloak, draping it over the naked girl's stunning, shivering, naked body, and she became less naked. Derian supposed it was an honourable gesture, and it disappointed him he hadn't thought of it first.

The girl gripped the clothing as if the freezing breeze of the day had suddenly struck her like a friend might, during a panicked moment, and she looked at Natteo in careful gratitude and then her eyes caught sight of Derian.

Derian offered his warmest smile. He didn't know where he had learned such a thing, but people thought his smile was one of his finest features. Perhaps it was his teeth. He chewed enough eucal-twigs to keep them unspoiled. So, when he smiled with his wonderful teeth, he'd expected a better reaction. "Hello, my name is—"

She began to scream again, a melody of primal terror and terrible panic, and he instinctively took a step forward, eager to ease her distress. This brought about further shrieking, and Lorgan sent him away with one glare.

So much for being a hero.

8

POLISHED

Derian sat in the grass on the far side of the clearing as they tended to her. He replayed the battle and its explosive outcome, over and over, until Lorgan sat down beside him. The chain binding him to the naked girl clinked gently in the grass.

"How do you feel?"

He looked at his hands again as though they'd grown a different colour this past hour. "I feel wretched for what I did. If she is to die again, it won't be by my hand. I will not strike her down a second time," Derian argued. Never again would he obey an order unquestioningly. It was no way to behave, he told himself.

"If I order you to kill her, you will kill her," Lorgan replied. "However, I don't believe I'll have you kill her a second time. At least, not today." His voice was quiet but fierce, his eyes cold and resolute.

"That's good to know… sir." Anger flowed through Derian unexpectedly. He took a deep breath and pledged to hold his tongue.

"I need no master," the voice inside his head growled. Its anger matched his own.

After a moment, Lorgan's features softened, and he patted Derian on the back. "You did well keeping your nerve, young mercenary. You might be some use to the Crimson Hunters after all." He looked back to his hands and clenched and opened them a few times. He smiled every time.

"What is she?" Derian asked.

"Our responsibility. Our valuable responsibility. She is worth a fine price."

"So we traffic humans now?"

"We will find quite a few suitors for a girl who appeared from beyond the source. Better we find a price rather than delivering her into the hands of the Dark One," Lorgan said, and he left his hands to their own devices. He looked better than usual. Healthier. There was a glimmer in his eyes. Perhaps the prospect of a fortune had refreshed the older man something fierce.

"Slavery is a shameful practice, sir."

"Well, it's better than killing her and leaving her in the grass, like you were happy to," Lorgan countered.

"I was follo—"

"You were following my orders?" Lorgan interrupted. "What's done is done. Until we know more, she is in our care."

"You mean to say she's our captive."

Lorgan shrugged, but he was thoughtful. "She is our responsibility, Derian. When we know a little more, perhaps we won't require the chains. As it is, keep your weapons ready, for strange things are afoot."

They watched Kesta tend to the girl as she calmed her to normality—whatever that was. Her skin was deathly pale, though that might have been the fright. She had stopped screaming, which was something.

Lorgan lowered his voice. "Do you remember what happened? I remember falling and not much else."

Derian recited the battle, as he had been last to fall.

Last to die.

Lorgan raised an eyebrow at the mention of the necklace and the final strike, which had brought an end to the demon and the explosion thereafter. It was a strange tale, and Derian wasn't certain he did it any justice in his retelling. Still, Lorgan appeared satisfied with what he learned.

"What do you know of vector demons, apprentice?"

Vector demons?

Wonderful. His ignorance would show again. "I'm not sure, sir," he offered and found a stone to look at. He heard the disappointed sigh, but at least he was saved the disapproving glare.

"You need to learn to read fluidly, Derian. Education is the mark of a polished man. How else will you understand all tricky matters of a bounty? How can you learn what beast you hunt without the true gift of knowledge?"

"Seems to me it didn't really matter what they wrote on this bounty, sir. We almost met our end chasing the wrong monster."

Lorgan didn't like that. No master liked to be questioned mid-tirade. A smarter move might have been allowing the older man to correct him. They'd had a rough day; they'd died. Lorgan was entitled to say whatever he wanted.

Still, though. "If it weren't for me, we'd all be dead in the mud, sir." Derian understood the word *petulance*, though he could not spell it. *Ungratefulness* was another word he struggled with, but he couldn't help himself. Derian had unwittingly saved them all. His first time, in fact. It had hurt more than he expected.

Truthfully, this wasn't the first time they'd nearly died in a haze of failure. Usually, it was Lorgan who saved them all, and he did so without rubbing it in their faces. Derian knew he should have behaved similarly, but he had done what all fire-blooded young mercenaries did. He'd attacked again to strike home the point.

"The plan with the netting was stupid, anyway," Derian muttered. Lorgan's face tightened as he clenched his teeth, and Derian focussed on the stone in the mud. It was quartz. There may have been some sandstone thrown in there. Valueless. "It wasn't my idea to shoot the girl either." Derian reached for the stone and cast it far into the green forest and regretted the act immediately. If he'd just held it, he could have studied it for a few moments longer and avoided the deathly stare from the grizzled old mercenary.

"Listen, hero. I appreciate you doing your job for us, but know your place in the world. We keep score. You might find yourself far below the value of Natteo." He spat his best friend's name, and Derian understood the extent of his misstep. "I gave an order, but you were the man with the bow. If you were certain it was the wrong decision, what type of man kills without questioning? What type of man fears the wrath of an ancient mercenary like me?"

He laced every word with such disappointment that Derian dropped his head in shame. "What would you have done if I'd refused?"

"Shot her myself and then you," he said, and Derian believed it true. "But you would have had a few pulses to convince me otherwise, little one," he added, and Derian believed this also true. He felt he should apologise. The moment was right to apologise, but a hot-blooded youth was disinclined to show sense. Sometimes it was easier to find another rock to gaze upon and wait for the world to settle. "If this is how you feel, perhaps you would be better leaving this outfit altogether." Hearing this, Derian's stomach churned. Getting kicked out of the Crimson Hunters was certain to become a tale for the ages. His leader had made his point.

"Sorry, Lorgan."

"Study your damned book. Am I clear?"

"Yes, sir." Derian met the eyes of the older man. He wasn't angry. It was a strange thing to see Lorgan not looking angry out on the march. Even on the warmest sunny days, he would frown and mutter unhappily about how the day had too much glare. He clenched his hands again, and Derian nodded sheepishly. "I don't want to leave the Crimson Hunters. I like this outfit," he said, and he realised that he really liked the outfit, and he didn't want to leave. At least, not yet.

Neither spoke for a time. Across the dell, Kesta and a wary Natteo helped the girl to her feet. As they did, her cloak fell free, revealing her wonderful nakedness once again. Lorgan looked away, but Derian didn't. He couldn't help himself.

Kesta slung the cloak back over her swiftly, tragically returning her dignity. The girl held out her hand where the arrow had punctured right through, and she appeared perplexed at how the hole had knotted itself over, leaving only a faint mark as though she'd hidden it from the sun. She brought her recovered hand to her forehead and its similar mark. Then, suddenly, she looked across the glade in both anger and horror, and he looked away in shame. *How could any person apologise for that?* Natteo would probably charm a smile out of her and make her believe it her own fault, but Derian would stagger over mumbled words.

The chain at Lorgan's waist clinked gently, and he freed it

from a snag in the ground. He held it for a moment, and Derian wondered whether he was considering releasing her.

"Perhaps this necklace entrapped our little naked prisoner within," Lorgan said, dropping the chain and clenching his hands into fists once more. "Tell me this, Derian. Your mind feels wretched for what you did, but how does your entire body feel in this moment?"

"I feel polished." He did, in fact. His sore ankle wasn't even bothering him anymore.

"For twenty years, my fingers have suffered dreadful arthritis. I am not unique. You find me a weathered mercenary without pains from riding saddle or holding a sword, and I will show you a thurken liar. Then I'll strike him down for being a liar, and then I'll hit you for being so gullible." He spat on the ground and appeared to annoy himself, and Derian smiled despite his shame. Lorgan held out his hands, and they were free from lumps and misshapen things. He clenched and released them, grinning as he did. The grin showed how much younger he appeared as well. For a moment Derian imagined Lorgan as a young mercenary, and he imagined him impressive.

"They look healed," Derian gasped.

"Perhaps the pain will return as the enchantment fades, but for now, I feel marvellous. You call yourself a quick-witted merc, but why haven't you noticed the colour of the surrounding trees?" he said, and as though emerging from a river of waterlilies, Derian saw the world properly. It was stunning and green in a great arc from where she had appeared. Many surrounding trees had returned to their lustrous green and bore the bright fruits that had long been a dour grey, and despite the rain and mud, Derian thought this a wonderful place.

"That is impossible," Derian whispered, tearing a leaf from a tree above his head.

"I'm an old man of fifty. There's no worse thing than an old man declaring older times were greater. I remember a world before they slaughtered all the weavers in Dellerin. I remember when things like this occurred and we gave thanks to the source." He was wistful, and a sense of sadness fell upon him again. "I remember when the source was a thing that served us, healed us, and made us better. Before the Dark One." He shook his head and reached for a leaf with remarkably nimble fingers. "I suspect it won't last too long, but fresh life has been born into all of us. We were lucky, but luck is a fine ally to all mercenaries, be it good or bad."

"So what do we do now, sir?"

"It's time to get paid for a job well done. We have an extra mouth to feed."

9

AFTER THE DRAMA

D erian loved horses. As a child, he'd believed them to be elegant, proud, and precious. As an adult he really thought highly of them. Any mercenary worth his weight in gold could ride like the wind, and Derian was better than most. He would kick his beast forward and will it to great speed effortlessly, for he had a kinship to them, and all mounts he sat upon would trust him as he trusted them. Derian was happier upon a horse than anywhere else.

Though he'd never say it aloud, when he was a scrap of a thing he'd considered earning a life in the Mounted Legion. They filled their ranks with the finest riders atop the greatest warhorses in all of Dellerin. That they'd had a rein-gripping hand in killing his mother was probably the reason he'd never enlisted. Who knew what awkward questions he'd have asked? But despite their barbarism, cruelty, and affinity to murder, they had really pretty horses, and in this rain-drenched moment, he wished he had one of them to call upon.

He wished he had any horse to call upon, really, but the Crimson Hunters had suffered another bad season with derisory contracts, and they had needed to cut expenses.

Who needed two proper meals a day? A mouldy apple was a perfectly reasonable dinner—especially with a few fruitworms inside as additional protein.

Who replaced marching boots that had only three or four holes worn through? Feet didn't smell nearly as bad with fresh air at them.

Who needed to repair armour missing a few panels of metal here and there? Had anyone ever died from a stray arrow in the shoulder?

Who needed horses to carry you through harsh regions in a fraction of the time, anyway?

Who needed…? He had more to complain about, but feared for his bad mood returning. Truth was, the Crimson Hunters didn't have the money for anything as luxurious as mounts, so they slung their bags upon their backs and began the long march back towards payment.

And maybe a trip home in an airbarge.

It was at least two days uphill through dense forest, and Derian knew he would curse every step taken. They marched in line to disguise their numbers. Kesta took her place at the back, with Natteo just a step in front, and it suited the group, for their clashing conversations were a distraction from the miserable muddy slog—Natteo with his stupid opinions of himself, the world, and everything in between, countering Kesta's disdainful, monosyllabic retorts. It was a well-played battle of wits, spanning years, and frequently ended when Natteo struck a golden jest, rich enough to break Kesta's stern gaze, resulting in the gift of a grin or the treasure of a snort.

Lorgan travelled lightly, but today the chain at his waist weighed him down. He had allowed the girl a few feet of freedom and little more. She walked ahead of Derian with her head bowed, her shoulders slumped, and her body quivering ever so. She was a wretched sight despite her beauty, and she looked upon the world around her with the same naivety as a child upon seeing the Open Lands for the first time during the harvest season. She glanced from tree to flower to mud to grass as though these natural things were new to her, and perhaps they were. When he'd first seen her busy eyes, they'd burned with unrivalled joy and excitement, but since then, she'd lost a spark. Perhaps she'd lost it in the gentle pull of the thin metal leash around her shapely neck, bruising her slightly every time she fell behind. Perhaps it was something else. He wanted to apologise. Oh, how he wished to form the words to make her forgive him.

The cloak wasn't the only garment she wore. Her keepers had gifted her a few scraps to stave off the cold and rain. A thin pair of breeches here, a bland cotton vest there, and she had accepted them with a cautious smile, but as she marched, her feet splashed miserably in every puddle, and finally he went against mercenary instinct and pulled out his spare pair of boots. Her feet were tiny, delicate, pretty, and his boots would be awkward, uncomfortable, and unstylish. However, she would be dry. It was all he could do, for he had little skill in offering apologies. He chose his moment; he formed the words and glided up behind her.

"I'm sorry for shooting you in the head. I hope you feel better," he said in his warmest sorry-for-killing-you voice. Startled, she leapt away from him, screaming loudly, and tripped on a branch and would have fallen were it not for the iron collar around her neck. This wasn't a good thing, however.

He remembered once watching a performing show in Dellerin City. It was nothing more than a curtain opening up to a dimly-coloured jester standing upon a little makeshift wooden stage. He remembered the juggling was unimpressive, but the fool's impressions of various animals were remarkably funny. Derian had been alone in his enjoyment, however, for the audience remained mute. Perhaps had he laughed loudly, others might have joined in, but he had been too embarrassed to stand out. Perhaps not as embarrassed as the jester, who tried and failed miserably to pull a reaction from the crowd by including crude jests in his performance, which admittedly weren't as entertaining.

It was the long holding hook swiftly emerging from the edge of the curtain that had quelled the stirrings of booing before they could catch fire. He remembered the holding hook sliding around the oblivious jester's neck like a choke chain upon a cornered hound. Only then had the crowd begun to laugh in cruel expectation. He remembered the jester's naïve smile, believing that he'd breached the audience's defences. Mostly he remembered his sudden look of fright as the hook looped and tightened and the jester realised his performance's fate. *Mostly.* With a slight tug and a shocked gasp, they had dragged him from the stage, and the delighted crowd had offered a standing ovation. Perhaps the jester was used to such practices and had prepared himself for the violent yank; Derian told himself this each time the guilt stung at him.

The girl, however, wasn't ready for such a thing, and for a horrible moment, Derian wondered if her neck had broken in half from the force. Lorgan attempted to move with her as she stumbled, but failed. Her cries were cut short in a desperate gasp, and Derian tried to help her as she fell to her knees, panting.

"She doesn't want your help, Derian!" Lorgan bellowed, and he released his hold, allowing her to crawl forward through a deep puddle as she tried to catch her breath. She'd lost whatever warmth she'd had from her new clothing thanks to his blundering, and it was in that exact moment that Derian understood the vast amount of grovelling he would need to perform while attempting to charm her.

"I just wanted to give her these," Derian muttered, and Kesta snapped the boots from him before tending to the delirious girl. Natteo patted him on the back, the knowing pat of an ill-fated man who knew the pain of unrequited love.

"Wish I'd behaved like that when you tried to befriend me, Derian. Maybe I'd be well rid of you now."

"Shut up, Natteo."

Kesta helped the girl to her feet, and the tearful smile she offered in gratitude for receiving the gift of boots annoyed Derian.

"They're not from her," he cried, and Natteo hushed him to silence. "Fine—it's better that she has them, I suppose." Derian continued walking with Natteo behind him.

"I know you are terrible with women, but killing them isn't a good way to meet them."

"Shut up, Natteo."

"I'm not sure that's how they tell great love stories."

"Shut up, Natteo."

"Maybe don't do that again, perhaps?"

"Shut up, Natteo."

"Unless she's into those types of things. Do you think she's into those types of things? What a strange girl."

"Shut up, Natteo."

Silence. Derian knew that silence well. His friend was creating further jests.

"What would you bet that I could bed her by the day's end? How about your sword for my hairbrush?"

"Shut up, Natteo."

"Perhaps I wouldn't even need to bet. She's attractive enough to stir something in my trousers. Not a lot, but enough."

"Seriously, shut up, Natteo."

"Or what if—"

Slap!

Kesta, meanwhile, kept the girl company; she spoke quietly, searching for understanding behind those stunning eyes, but the girl never replied with a word. At most, she gestured, and Kesta continued on regardless, for she was persistent if nothing else. Kesta had taken a shine to the younger girl, as though enchanted in some strange way.

With Natteo nursing his cheek and waiting for the right time to retrieve the conversation, Derian amused himself by wondering about worrying things. He wondered how long they would keep the girl chained as she was. What would happen if she tried to escape? Did she have a future among them? Did Lorgan believe her price would be worth the dishonour of slavery? He wondered if he could go along with such a thing. Would Kesta? Would she have to?

Perhaps when the girl spoke, there would be proper answers.

Hours of marching passed until Lorgan's voice silenced the group entirely.

"Ah, spit on me," he cursed, and fell to a stop between two leaning seeping oaks; he raised his hands in the air, and Derian looked out into the endless grey to see the clustered nothingness of the deathly forest surrounding them. Kesta reached for her sword, but Lorgan shook his head and she held.

"You have us. We offer no fight!" he shouted.

10

AMBUSH

"I don't believe this fuken shit," Lorgan hissed, as the forest came to life around them. No, not alive: something else more unsettling. Kesta drew her sword regardless, and he heard the gentle click of bolt upon wristbow as Natteo stood poised and ready. Nobody could see Derian's fingers quivering as he reached for Rusty. They felt numb and awkward. Twice he tried to pull the weapon free, but fear denied him a grip. The sight of walking shrubs as tall as men was the most unsettling thing he'd seen since a vector demon had blown him up.

There were only three of the unnerving monsters, but they scared the spit from his mouth. It was as though all of the fallen leaves from the surrounding trees had gathered together on the mossy ground and, through some evilness, had knotted themselves into unnatural grey abominations. Rustling gently in the wind, they stood watching like guards of the forest, and Derian's heart hammered in terror. Terror mixed with the will to grab his sword and go out swinging—or else take hold of a rake and deliver the terror right back onto them. However, he had no rake. That was just another thing the Crimson Hunters couldn't afford.

Nothing happened for a moment, and Derian dared to dream that they were harmless. Or perhaps they were intending a little barter and nothing more sinister. Perhaps all they desired was a tax for walking these parts? Then he remembered their usual luck and imagined the embarrassment of falling to a few bushes. *Stabbed in the heart by a twig* would be a terrible engraving on the Guild's tunnel of remembrance, he thought.

"Lower your weapons, mercenaries," a deep voice cried, and the largest monster stepped forward. His outline was that of a human who had submitted to a forest's will. He pulled at his head for a moment, and Derian watched uneasily as it pulled its head free from its body, revealing a human face beneath. Only then did he understand the illusion of the forest suit. It was no trick of weaving or a monster made of bushes: it was, in fact, an intricate design of camouflage, and though there were three strangely dressed men standing before them, the forest became an altogether scarier place, for if one couldn't trust one's own eyes, who or what could one trust?

On second glance, though, there were obvious differences between each man. All wore the same deep grey colour, but each had chosen different patches of leaves to cover them. Someone had gone to great trouble to make these outfits, and if they were bandits, they were bandits of wealth. If they were mercenaries, Derian and his companions were in real trouble.

"You heard the man," Lorgan hissed when none of the Crimson lowered their weapons. Though his decision making and leadership could use improvement, his ability to smell any ambush was unmatched. Usually. Derian wondered if perhaps, in dying, he had lost some of his wilier skills.

The girl didn't appear fussed by events at all. As they all

fell to a ready position, she continued walking; her eyes were transfixed by the three figures. She squeaked in joy when the first man revealed himself, and she walked closer until the chain tightened and held her in place. She reached out to touch his beard, and for a moment, Derian saw a small smile appear across her lips.

"Is this a mugging?" Lorgan asked, tugging on the chain. The girl hissed as though denied the taste of a sweet cake by a fatter little child and fell back behind the older mercenary. If looks could kill, hers would, at least, have scarred. She gripped the chain at her neck, muttered some incomprehensible mumbles, and spat on the muddy ground.

"This is no mugging at all, my friend. Might you be the Crimson Hunters, perchance?" the man intoned.

Though Lorgan didn't draw his sword, he gripped its handle more firmly. "Might be. Why would a few leaves be enquiring?"

Bad thing getting stopped by walking bushes in a forest. Worse for them to know your name. Derian finally took hold of his sword's grip, but he did not draw it.

"We are the Army of the Dead. You might have heard of us."

Natteo cursed under his breath. He drew his fingers through his hair nervously before running his hands down his grubby cheeks. *The Army of the Dead.* Derian knew that name too. Most mercenary groups did. There was one thing worse than a mercenary outfit knowing your name, and that was a mercenary outfit you knew the name of, knowing your name.

The Army of the Dead were renowned through the Seven Isles of Dellerin. They got their tasks done through necessity, through heroism, and through blood. Derian had always thought their name stupid. *Mightn't be the best time to say it, though*, he mused.

Lorgan bowed, and the other two mercenaries removed their headdresses of grey so they might get an unobstructed view of those they planned to mug.

"I am Mowg, the tall one is Blood Red, and the sturdy one at the back is… the Assassin of Death," Mowg said, and he held them in a steely glare, as though he hadn't said the three stupidest names ever.

"So, does the Assassin work for death, or does he actually kill death?" Natteo whispered.

"I am Lorgan of the Crimson, and yes, we are the Crimson Hunters. What business do you have with us this fine evening?"

Mowg was their leader, it appeared. While the other two mercenaries snickered with delight at Lorgan's admission, Mowg stepped forward and offered his hand. For a swift, delirious moment, Derian believed these dangerous curs might not have bad intentions at all. They might just be out walking. They might not even know of the bounty on their collective heads in Dellerin. Still, though, they weren't in Dellerin, were they? Did a bounty in Luistra even count? It would also be a big job getting four dead bodies all the way across the world for a measly few bags of gold.

Derian watched both men shake hands and realised Mowg was far too confident. Lorgan was twice the size of him, yet he never flinched in his grasp. Four against three was a fair fight, and if the Crimson Hunters took out the Army of the Dead, it could serve them well in future employment. Still, Derian wondered if they were all in attendance. What kind of pathetic outfit had only three members, anyway?

Blood Red stepped forward now. His movements were awkward and restrained, as though he was concentrating all his efforts on not striking someone in anger. "It appears the town of Treystone didn't believe you capable of your task."

"Is that so?" Lorgan replied.

"How long are you hunting the monster? A week? More? It appears their needs were so pressing, they desired a second outfit to complete the task." His gritted teeth hid behind a thick bushy beard of black with tinges of grey. His hair was similar in colour. There wasn't any red to him at all.

"Now, now, Red. We are all friends here. Less of the mockery." Mowg laughed and shot a glare at his companion. A "let's-kill-them-later" glare, which Derian didn't like at all, but if Lorgan caught it or took any offence, he showed nothing. In fact, their fearless leader was remarkably calm despite the rising threat.

"Typical peasants, wasting your time. We did the deed," Lorgan muttered, and upon hearing this, Mowg suddenly found interest in the girl, and Derian's face flushed. He wanted to tell him to find other interesting things to gaze upon. *Maybe that tasty shrub over there with the deathly berries?* He wanted to be brave and step forward as the mercenary gazed upon her with murderous eyes. However, Derian said nothing and did less, and Lorgan allowed Mowg to slip past him.

"What's this?" He took hold of the girl's chain and tugged her to him, and she looked at him warily. He opened her cloak and caught sight of the bottom half of her navel tattoo. The top half was obscured by a ludicrously cut short shirt that Natteo had pledged had served him "during the promiscuous parts of his youth." Mowg lifted the cotton shirt of faded white to reveal the rest of the tattoo, and again Derian fumed but said nothing. The girl must have sensed the threat, for she allowed Mowg to look upon her, but her eyes were cold and unforgiving. Derian recognised that look.

Mowg appeared to think about touching the mark. His finger almost reached out, but as if wary of scalding himself upon a hot plate, he drew away from her. "A terrible shame. Easy contracts are a rare thing, and a lecherous contract would have been a fine bounty to fill our time."

"That's true." Lorgan sighed as though conversing was beneath him.

"Tell me, Lorgan. Do you have the beast's pelt as proof?"

"No pelt. It went up in smoke and fire. It's my word and nothing else."

Click. Natteo loaded a second bolt and one of the opposing mercenaries eyed him. Derian felt a clawing fearfulness rise and threaten to take over in the volatile air.

Practices like assassinating an entire outfit were rarer now than a few decades ago, but still, there were many instances every year wherein groups took out other groups. These were usually attributed to a botched bounty or an egregious grievance, but sometimes they were just plain old envious exterminations, more often than not in quiet forests with no one around. There might be a Guild's inquest after, but all was fair in money and blood. Especially if the victorious outfit discovered there was a bounty on those already slain.

"Now that is a shame, for we might have offered a satchel of silver for the piece," the Assassin of Death muttered from behind, and stretched his arms as though preparing for sudden violent actions. He rested his fingers on his sword's grip, which was peering out from beneath stitchings of twigs and leaves and a few wilted flowers.

Lorgan nodded in agreement. "That would have been a fair offer." It wasn't a fair offer at all. The contract was for fifteen gold, and a satchel of silver was worth a satchel of silver. A satchel of silver wouldn't even feed them and get them a barge off this miserable, wet island. Well, maybe it would get a small barge with a drunken captain, but it wouldn't get them a lift back home in an airbarge like Lorgan had promised. Even Kesta had shown interest in such extravagance. Perhaps she'd never had the pleasure of journeying in an airbarge. Derian had only seen them up among the clouds. Little specks of black against eternal blue.

"The girl has nice eyes," Blood Red said, and Mowg nodded in agreement as Lorgan allowed him to inspect the girl's teeth and nails. Kesta stared at them, and Lorgan was careful to keep himself between her and the girl. Her sword had silently returned to its scabbard, but she was clearly itching to retrieve it.

"She'll cost a little more than a satchel of silver." Lorgan spoke as though he were dealing with cattle at a fair, looking to get the best deal. Derian wanted to hiss loudly that she was no deal to be struck. Instead, he said nothing and felt wretched. This was a mugging. Blood was in the air.

"Who is she?"

"She's just a bandit we caught rummaging through our packs, and we weren't sure what to do with her. I'm not keen on bartering a human life, but if you offer the right amount, I'm sure a deal could happen," Lorgan offered, and Mowg seemed happy.

"You speak my language, Lorgan of the Crimson," Mowg said, taking their leader's hand again and shaking it, though this time in genuine respect. "Come, sit with us at our camp," he said, and with that, four more mercenaries in similar attire emerged from the grey cover. Each of them sheathed their crossbows and longbows.

Natteo cursed again, looking uneasily from each man to the next. He unloaded his wristbows as he did.

"There were far more of us than you realised," Mowg said, pleased with the great reveal.

Lorgan laughed with him, as though he'd had no idea there were more curs watching them. "It's a fine thing we spoke as friends, so," he jested, signalling the rest to follow their potential captors away from the path and into the deathly grey forest.

11

THE ARMY OF THE DEAD

I t was an unsettling thing to walk in silence through a
forest at the best of times, but walking with this quiet
outfit was so much worse. Even Natteo was unusually frugal
with his words. There was tension in the air, and Derian
considered slipping into a cluster of trees and fleeing his
comrades. He doubted he'd make it more than a dozen steps
before they caught him. They were surrounded, and it was
unlikely their positioning was accidental. If he was a captive,
it was very polite captivity, though. They never asked for his
weapon, and he never produced it; there were no chains, no
shoving or mocking, just a forced march through the
undergrowth.

Along the way, Lorgan and Mowg loudly discussed the
girl's price, and each counter-offer sickened Derian to the
core. Still, he said nothing, convincing himself that it was
Lorgan's prerogative to deal with her any way he desired. If
Kesta was angry, she showed nothing in her face and marched
beside the girl, watching the men out of the corner of her eye.

Derian wondered about their intentions for the girl.
Murder, a little thievery, and even slave trading with bandits

were acceptable mercenary practices; however, rape was never tolerated in the Guild, and whispers of rape could lead to a unit's removal from it altogether. To lose the Mercenary Guild's perks was something no group could afford. Nor could they pay the thousand-gold bounty immediately placed upon each offender's head. Disqualified mercenary outfits were usually snuffed out quicker than an assassin's wick.

Derian should have felt reassured. However, who knew the depths of depravity of despicable men in forests? His stomach turned, his eyes filled, and his disappointment in Lorgan grew. Still, he said nothing and gripped that shame tightly, knowing that if he were in Lorgan's large boots, he would do the same thing.

Eventually, they came upon a wall of shrub and branch, as tall as a man on a mount and spreading thirty feet across. Mowg grinned and pulled at a concealed rope. As if enchanted, it fell away like canvas upon a drying line, revealing a large camp within. It was an expensive and entirely impressive camouflage.

It was a fine camp, indeed. Derian noticed the hobbled warhorses in the far corner first. Fayenar war mounts—expensive, rare, and fiercely aggressive in battle. Skins of freshly-slain beasts were stretched out upon tanning racks, and countless weapons were set upon stands for swift use at a moment's notice. A large, deep cart filled with supplies stood in the centre, and Derian's face flushed with jealousy. It would take his own outfit a year of hard successes to earn such riches, and these men left them unattended in an abandoned camp. What treasures did they keep in their stronghold?

As accomplished as they were at ambushing travellers and displaying their riches, it was their hosting which was most remarkable. Moving like well-oiled cogs in a machine of demons, they set a large slab of boar meat to cook across a long metal grill over their campfire. From somewhere within the riches of the cart, they rolled a barrel of ale out and let it sit at the centre of the gathering for all to use. As though rubbing the wealth in their guests' grubby, resurrected faces, they distributed silk cushions to all, and despite himself, Derian took one and found it a divine resting place for his rear.

They wrapped the girl's chain around a nearby tree and offered her a blanket and cushion to improve her imprisonment ever so. But as much as Mowg and his men were hospitable, they never cracked the barrel nor sliced the meat to offer food and drink to their guests. There weren't even jests thrown into the wind. Instead, they sat in a circle and got down to the business of negotiating.

Conversation between both leaders intensified as they came closer to striking a bargain. As easy as it would have been for the hosts to slay the Crimson, if they struck a deal, there'd be no bloodshed, no awkward discussions with the Guild.

"Don't be talking any more about silver, my friend. She's worth more than that," Lorgan said for the third time. This time with steel in his voice.

"Twenty gold and a hundred pieces of silver," Mowg countered, and it was a weak bet. Precarious position or not, Lorgan wasn't selling the girl for anything less than a decent price.

"Fifty gold."

"That's no price. She is a beauty, but that's hardly a reason for exorbitant requests," Mowg snapped, but his eyes were willing. Derian wondered what else was willing, and he shook that thought away. Better to believe the deal would benefit the girl.

Truthfully, he'd had foolish thoughts of her beyond simple desire. He wondered whether she might have talked her way into earning her freedom in the Crimson. If she couldn't fight, she might have learned like Kesta. If she couldn't learn, perhaps she might have a flair for cooking. A chef was just as welcome as a master bowman. Unfortunately, it was a foolish thought from a foolish love-struck boy; he knew her fate, and it was not with them.

"Forty gold and a bag of silver, so," Lorgan said, playing the defeated merchant perfectly. The food, the ale, and the cheer all waited; the moment had not yet arrived. Derian could see a clear drop of fat from the meat drip into the fire, and he licked his lips as it caused a delicious spark in the flames. The fine feast was so close he could feel it, they all could, but there was no deal struck yet, and all of it could end in tears. Derian caught sight of Blood Red staring intently at the girl, and his appetite waned. They couldn't do this. Could they? He wanted to throw up. And straight after, he wanted to leap upon Blood Red and kick his fuken head in. That mightn't help negotiations, though.

"Strike the deal, Mowg, so we may eat," Blood Red said, and every mercenary licked their lips in reply. Reward was in the air, and it smelled like sizzling meat.

"You strike a fine deal, friend," Mowg declared at last, producing a large bag of gold and a larger bag of silver. With the swiftness of a rodenerack, the mercenary tipped forty gold pieces into a little pouch and another thirty silver into a second, and Derian cursed at how paltry the girl's price appeared when compared to their fortune. Lorgan could have pushed for more, he thought in disgust.

He wasn't alone in his disappointment. Kesta stabbed the earth with a small dagger and dropped her head, unable to face the group of men around her, and Natteo's pale face became hard, for he knew well her future, did he not? If they didn't rape her, her life might still take a terrible turn. Men would pay quite a price for her attentions in the pleasure houses of Castra. Oh, she might leave the employment after she cleared her price, but not before her keepers had drenched her in the wonders of the dream medicine called snow. She'd lose her mind and will. What a fuken waste.

"What a waste," Derian said aloud, and one mercenary turned to him.

"What's that, young hero?"

"Nothing. I said nothing," he said, and he felt the coldness of fear and melancholy wrap him up tightly. He willed himself to steely bitterness, for this was the way of a mercenary's life. The nameless mercenary clapped him fiercely on the back, and Derian also wanted to kick his head in.

"Let's drink," Mowg declared, and the uneasiness in the air dissipated immediately. They uncorked the barrel, filled tankards, and raised them high.

Lorgan addressed the gathering now, tankard in hand. "Shall we test our wills? To the traditions of the march." He downed his beverage in one massive assault, and their new comrades cheered him on and followed. With the toasts done, games were afoot now, and challenges offered between friends—who would be the last man standing? Or woman, for even Kesta cheered and eyed her challengers with a rare smile. She attacked her lightly-bubbled ale with relish and was impressive. Natteo, who had grown up on the finer sines of the entitled and believed peasant ale beneath him, still joined the drinking, though he did so cautiously. A gentle shove and a quiet word of insistence from the young Army of the Dead mercenary sitting beside him, however, convinced him to drink heartily.

Within no time, Derian's tankard was refilled, and he joined the gathering with jests and wit. He sat farthest from Lorgan, in a futile attempt at protesting their leader's actions. Truthfully, though, Lorgan had done the right thing, cruel as it appeared. Lorgan attempted to catch his eye and share a few words with him as he did the rest of the Crimson, but Derian pretended he didn't notice. Let Lorgan know his disappointment with no words. When Lorgan finally gave up, Derian took the victory.

Their hosts threw the rest of their names around, but Derian caught none. He thought one was called 'Bob,' but he wasn't certain. He had blond hair and shiny armour, and Derian wondered whether he was the unwilling recipient of the Natteo charm for this evening.

After a time, knowing their names didn't matter. He referred to each as 'friend,' and they were happy enough with that. Moreover, he earned the same title for the rest of the night, and if truth be told, he came to enjoy their company. They were fierce on the outside but unusually open and warm once they had a bit of ale in them. He realised they might not commit immoral acts with the girl as he'd believed. He held that thought and locked it away, allowing himself to relax a little more.

As the evening wore on, they spoke of nasty incidents throughout Dellerin. Another uprising failed and fractured. Weavers whispering in the island of Fayenar. They told of warring clans wiping each other out over trivial matters, and they spoke of many more things beyond. Even Blood Red lost his intimidating glare to easy grinning, and around him, the cheer was so healthy that inevitably, the ugly truth reared its enticing head.

"I'm glad we could strike up a deal," Mowg slurred, and drank from his unusually frothy tankard. The task was beyond him, and he spilled half its contents down his vest. He seemed very puzzled and spat the gathering of froth from his upper lip. Ever the gentleman, Lorgan, who had taken leadership at the edge of the barrel from the first pouring, spotted Mowg's catastrophe and swiftly poured the frothiest of drinks Derian had ever seen. Within an instant, he returned the tankard to Mowg, who downed it before Lorgan even offered a retort.

"I feel it might have ended badly for me and my comrades had we not struck a deal," suggested Lorgan, and eyed his new best friend.

"Don't take it personally, Lorgan. Money is money, slaves are slaves, and… well…"

Lorgan cut him off and took his shoulder in his powerful grip. "Blood is blood, Mowg. Have no fears, my friend, for I know the tale. You must look after your flock, and I must look after mine," he said, and both warriors exchanged a nod of respect.

The world is tough; we do what we must.

"Tell me, Lorgan. Did you suspect her true value, or do you think I paid well over the odds for her?" Mowg asked, and Derian listened with interest.

"Is it the tattoo of gold upon her belly you allude to?" Lorgan said. "I know its significance. I know its danger."

Danger?

"She's worth tenfold what I offered. Is that something you can accept come dawn?" Mowg asked.

"I know you will get fifty times what you paid. I know a demon's mark when it spits in my face." Lorgan tapped the gold pouch at his belt absently, as though the small bag was worthy compensation. Derian was distraught. Terrible to lose a goddess; worse to lose her for a paltry fee. And what was a demon's mark?

"Well, for what it's worth, had we to kill you over the matter, it would have been swift, and with a heavy heart. I am sorry, friend," Mowg said, and a few of the mercenaries listening shrugged guiltily and shuffled their feet. It was strange for a mercenary to admit such a thing, yet Mowg did it openly. Was it overconfidence? Was it his conscience? Was it bravado?

Only Natteo appeared to take offence; he immediately stepped away from the mercenary named something like Bob and glared at the tall warrior the way a husband would upon discovering his wife down in a tavern with a new 'friend.' A glare like that could have sliced tin armour with one strike. The blond mercenary dropped his head in shame and offered his brimming tankard of ale as an apology. Natteo shook his head swiftly, but after a moment, he slid back beside the good-looking young man and drank deeply from his own, less impressive tankard. This heartened the good-looking mercenary, but Natteo's eyes were colder than usual, and Derian wondered if Bob hadn't blown his chances at going for one of Natteo's midnight walks. At least none of them would have to listen to the salacious details of his adventures come the morning, Derian thought. Entertaining as they were.

Perhaps Lorgan had tried to save face in the delicate threat, he thought. Perhaps it was the truth. Perhaps it was something to say after worrying revelations.

"I'm glad we'll rid ourselves of her," Lorgan told Mowg. "There is no guarantee that Treystone will pay for us killing the monster without proof. We can't afford to get her all the way to Dellerin. We don't even have horses, and at some point, swiftness might be the key to her survival. She would be safer from the hunt in your hands," he said.

The words hung in the air, and Mowg nodded his agreement. Derian was furious. Lorgan had known more than he'd let on. More than that, he'd known her value and kept it from them. He knew she brought a great risk to them and had said nothing of this either. Who hunted her? Yet again, Lorgan had fled from risk. It was typical of things in this outfit.

One mercenary stumbled a little, and much to the merriment of his comrades, he fell against a tree away from the fire's glow and threw up his last beverage all over the grass.

"This evens the odds in our contest. Come, Mowg, your cup is already dry," Lorgan bellowed, and he took Mowg's tankard again and began to refill it. The last grievances had been raised and aired successfully.

"The barrel isn't even halfway drained, and already the Army of the Dead have one man fallen!" Kesta roared with such unusual mockery that Derian couldn't help raise his drink in victory. Her eyes were wild, her face taut. Perhaps competition brought out another emotion in her.

"I'm fine. I'm not out," muttered the sick man, who caught his breath and then began retching loudly. "Get me another drink." More retching. "After someone finds me a bucket…"

The group laughed at the man's misfortune as he slipped away into the darkness. Derian saw the girl laughing along with them, and he felt compelled to try once again to seek forgiveness. He ventured towards her, elbowing his way through the boisterous group, and with a boldness in his heart and nerves of tin armour, he sat down in front of her.

"I'm sorry," he said, doing his best not to envision her nakedness again.

She shrank beneath the cloak around her and his heart dropped. She had the form and splendour of a young woman, but her eyes sparkled with the naïve beauty of a god. She blinked those eyes and offered no reply. Instead, she clutched her knees and held them tightly against her chest as though seeking comfort.

Derian cursed himself once again for not studying more; he wished dearly to understand the mark tattooed upon her glorious stomach. "I'm sorry for shooting you. I'm sorry…." But how could he apologise for Lorgan selling her? "I'm sorry Lorgan wants to sell you," he said, and she eyed him with a disdainful wonder; as though she did not understand his words, but still despised him for them.

He wanted to try the apology again, but Lorgan distracted him. It was a strange choice of words he used, for they referred to a terrible time a season before when food poisoning had struck him and Natteo down. Both had spent a miserable weekend losing half their body weight.

"Hey, Derian, remember that time we went fishing in Malell?" he said, and he smacked his leg as though it were the funniest wit ever spoken aloud. Derian's stomach churned at the nightmare memory, and suddenly he realised. He looked out into the darkness for the sick man and spun around to the girl, and her soulful eyes were alive with delight once more. They were looking away from him.

"Don't worry, girl. Everything is all right," he whispered, and the air became laden with the sounds and stenches of violent heaving.

12

AFTER PARTY

Seren hated Derian.

Hate, hate, hate.

Is that the word?

Yes, it is a wonderful word. It is an emotion.

Yes, hate.

She liked hate.

She enjoyed remembering what words were, and where they went, and how some of them had more than one meaning, and how others could be different words altogether yet still have the same meaning. She also liked… *Wait… no, there is a better word for* like? *… Adore. Yes, adore.* She really adored that word. What was her point, she thought? She couldn't remember, or else she had forgotten.

Hmmm… forget is a fine word. It's nothing spectacular but perfectly fine… anyway….

She thought further on words and decided the word *like* was the correct word. What a waste of thoughts she thought, and started over.

Seren liked her captors, but she reviled Derian.

Reviled. Ooh yes, reviled. Reviled, reviled, reviled the spitting thurk.

"Spitting thurk," she whispered, and she enjoyed how curses rolled off her tongue. She said the words again just as silently and enjoyed how they made her feel, but she couldn't put words to it.

Is this what irony is?

No, she decided, it was just a girl's mind rebuilding itself after a birth, and an arrow's catastrophic consequence after that.

And the world does not want me walking this plain. She thought on this cold thought and it flittered away.

So, she watched them argue over her, as though any of it really mattered. She knew her path, and it was not likely with the forest men. But then again, how could she be sure? That thurken arrow had ruined her mind, hadn't it? She knew little, but she knew that she should have grasped more comprehension by now. The fuken idiot's arrow had split her in half at the worst moment, and now sanity was a feather floating above her. Tantalizingly close, but effort took it further.

Fuken idiot Derian. Fuken. Fuken. That was a fine word too, she supposed. It felt less familiar. Her master had never spoken it.

Anyway, fuk Derian, the thurken cur. Smiling, she wondered if she should turn around and stab him a few times and be done with it. It would make her feel better. It might even make her feel wonderful.

Wonderful.

She wasn't afraid of him, but whenever she met his eyes, she felt the arrow plunge into her forehead. Was that trauma?

Trauma.

Perhaps when she found all the words and recovered all

her thoughts, she could summon the strength to kill him. Maybe not kill him in its finality; maybe just gouge his eyes out, or set him on fire a little bit, or just throw him into a frozen river. Good things would return eventually, but for now, she was limp. She was gelded. She was without a path.

I want to tear myself free of this broken form and taint everything.

Her broken mind gifted blurred visions of the old eternal man who had released her from the demon's hold.

Not old.

As her knowledge of pain, cold, and hunger, and a filling bladder returned, she seemed to remember less and less of the man. Who may have been old, but then again…

Grandfather.

"Grandfather," she whispered aloud. She wondered if she would ever grasp these thoughts, remember his teachings, do his bidding, and be waiting for him when he returned.

When he returns.

Those three words had not faded. Burned into her mind like a swine's branding. He would return, and with it, there would be a terrible vengeance to last an age. *No, to end this age.*

She slumped in her seat by the tree and massaged the bruising around her neck. Kesta had whispered to her that the holding was fleeting. *Ooh, fleeting. Nice word.* It also meant temporary. Like her gelding.

"Perhaps I am not a good person?" she whispered. No one was listening to her, though.

Perhaps it would be better if the Army of the Dead took hold of her, she decided. They were fierce, and she would need fierceness. Being good men or bad was irrelevant. She didn't know how she knew this, and she fought a pang of frustration and fought it off swiftly.

The idiot's arrow happened for a reason. Trust in reason.

"I must walk to Dellerin in the last days," she whispered to herself and sighed, thinking of the vast distance from here to there. She needed to fly, though she had no means. She felt other things impossible to name, to understand, to fear. But mostly, across the world, she felt the girl's energy and she felt the stones. And oh, Seren was built to stray from any set path. A spark spat out of the fire and caught her gaze, and her thoughts left her again.

Girl and stones? What path? What?

"Stupid thurken cur," she hissed, searching for sanity and losing it again.

Stupid Derian.

She heard the two fine warriors strike the deal and questioned her certainty that the Crimson were her keepers. *No, that's not right. They are my companions.*

She wondered if predestined things could not be altered. Perhaps the Army of the Dead would walk with her. What if they fought the Dark One, she wondered? What if they were in league with the Dark One?

"The Dark One," she whispered and found words spoken aloud to be less tasteful. She was drawn to the Dark One, whoever he was.

Love, maybe?

Hatred?

Family?

She tugged at her stomach and waited for the pain. In the moments before it struck, she usually felt it coming, like a morning wave leading the high tide. It would surge. She was a breaker, and the pain was excruciating. When the pain reached its crescendo, the world would become a darker place. This she knew for certain.

Like a prospective mother, she massaged the tattoo more

and more. Sometimes it made her feel better, and sometimes it drew her attention away from the demonic scraping. She rubbed her stomach a little more, watching the men shake hands and bond as friends, and she was quite pleased with her value. She found it strange that she understood the finer economics of the world and the art of bartering, yet the importance of eating for sustenance had eluded her until watching such actions in practice had sparked her mind.

Stupid Derian with the pretty smile.

"Bite and chew," she whispered to herself, and she thought her favourite words were those with plenty of watery-sounding letters in them. "Thurrrrrken currrrrrr," she whispered, but no one was listening. "Fuken. Shit." Enjoyable, yet not as smooth and imaginable.

She watched Lorgan slip the strange juice into each of the tankards he poured. He was boisterous, and no one saw the little bottle concealed beneath the shadow of his palm. *A fine trick.* She saw that the clear fluid made the beverages a little frothier, and she licked her lips and remembered her guardians never allowing her to drain tankards. She felt the emotion of sorrow and a need for comforting sweet nothings whispered in her ear. Perhaps these emotions were not her own, for she felt Lorgan's terrible desolation even from across the campsite. She didn't begrudge him his desire to rid himself of her. He had lived a life not destined to him, and she wondered how she knew this. How she knew that he fled from greatness like a young weaver from the two paths of the source world and its terrifying inhabitants.

Kesta's sadness was unfathomable, born of a life of ruin. A wise mind wasted by hollowness. She was a shell, left in the wake of horror. She cared only for those who needed her care. It was all that kept her afloat. It wouldn't keep her afloat forever. Eventually, she would stop fighting the current.

Natteo said something outlandish, and it drew Seren from her agony. She liked the good-looking young man because he never stopped talking; his sharp tongue was a gift to the world, and she relearned most from his mutterings. He hid his horrors better than most, and she liked that too. He chose love over pity. She wondered if it would be the right choice.

Derian sat down beside her, and she felt an arrow break through her head, and she almost screamed. She nearly reached for the phantom projectile to stab him in his manhood, but stopped and caught her breath sharply. He didn't notice her discomfort as he kept talking and apologising, and she wanted to reach out and take his stupid sword and put it through his eye. *Would that kill him?*

She believed it might. However, it was no arrow through the mind, was it?

There's no healing enchantment bonded to you anymore, is there?

Is there?

She rubbed her stomach and looked around at the collection of warriors, and she could sense their goodness behind the growls. It made her smile, and she doubted all at this gathering would survive the coming war. The thought of war and death made her smile, and she didn't understand why.

Destinies are torn asunder in wartime.

A cold feeling ran down her spine. Why did that ring so deeply?

Stupid Derian looked into her eyes as she reached for his sword to cut him. *Just a little.* Before she could attack him, though, many of the group began throwing up the contents of their stomachs and distracted her. She thought this was an unusual occurrence, and she also thought it delightful. Derian said something that was both annoying and reassuring, and she hated him.

"Spit on you," she countered, but he was already away, out of earshot and out of reach. She watched him and his rear and remembered her first thoughts of attraction for him and despised herself for it.

The Army of the Dead fell about the camp, retching violently, and her guardians took advantage. Lorgan led the assault, and he was inspiring. With fists like chunks of raw ore, he waded into the melee of nastiness, hammering two hobbled mercenaries senseless as he went. Each concussive blow was more deadly than the last; he worked himself into a frenzy and roared mightily as though he were fierce in battle, and despite herself, she too formed a fist. Lorgan was broken, never to be restored, but he was a leader.

Kesta never left his side, and Seren clapped each time the older woman ducked a weak strike and countered with a brutal head butt or a kick to the groin. Seren didn't recognise every sound of this world yet, but the retching squeals caused by Kesta's strikes were fascinating.

Natteo was the smallest at the gathering, but that didn't stop him throwing around what weight he could. He settled upon battering his blond companion to the edge of the camp, where he left his quarry to his semi-conscious, vomiting misery.

Even stupid Derian was nearly impressive. She could see how inept he was in his attacks, but he was relentless. He made straight for the one they called Blood Red and swung at him, delivering feeble strike after feeble strike. On an even day, and refusing to call upon his more violent abilities, Derian would have fallen, but focussing upon the larger man's unsettled stomach, each punch was a winding blow. Within a half-dozen strikes, he'd felled the mighty man completely, and because he was Derian and he was an idiot, he raised his hands in triumph as though he'd single-handedly saved an entire town from a swarm of monsters.

It was a wonderful spectacle of violent things, but tragically, it was all too fleeting. *Fleeting.* Within a few breaths of foul-smelling air, the battle was waged, fought, and won. It was a hollow victory, bound to breed long-lasting repercussions, but for the day, the Crimson had won out, leaving seven of the most elite mercenaries unconscious.

"Lay them out on their sides," Lorgan said, and they placed each beaten warrior so, and Seren thought it humorous to watch unconscious men throwing up through split, bloody mouths as they slept. It was Lorgan who released her from the tree while the others began raiding what treasures they needed. She caught sight of blood trickling down Lorgan's nose from where Mowg had struck a blow between dry heaves. She placed her finger into his nostril and he flinched. After a moment, she took it out and a quick gush of blood streamed down his thoroughly amused face. Her fingertip was crimson, and she wondered what blood tasted like, but he caught her wrist and shook his head.

"Thurken idiot," he said, and she smiled happily at his choice of words. He led her to the waiting cart, and Kesta helped her aboard. She sat down as the rest of the Crimson Hunters formed up on mounts of their own, and she thought this far better than traipsing over muddy ground. She watched Derian whisper sweet nothings to his horse, and she thought his conversing with such a wild creature to be a natural thing.

"Let's ride!" roared Lorgan, and Seren sat back in the cart, rubbing her tattoo. She was exactly where she needed to be. Her stomach burned, and she felt the call of the dark closer now. She felt the clawing upon the door.

Not too long now.

13

THE ROCKY ROAD TO TREYSTONE

"Just do it, Lorgan,"
"I will not."
"You are a better man than this."
"Stop asking and know your place."
"My place is at your side, making sure you don't make stupid decisions."
"I will not repeat myself."
"Just… do… it… Lorgan."
"I… will… NOT!"
"…"
"…"
"You are a better man than this."

Between the roar of the wind, the thunder of hooves, and the hissing of the rain, Derian could barely hear the argument growing among the group. Instead of taking joy in an unlikely victory, the wealth of supplies, and the swift open road, Kesta had decided Lorgan had taken long enough to do the right thing and that it was time for her to intervene. They were not slavers; they were not jailers. The girl was no demon or witch. They would release her from her chains. More than that, Kesta implied that this would somehow induce the girl to stay as a comrade to them. Considering they'd likely signed their own death warrants with the Army of the Dead, perhaps keeping her as one of their own was a better gamble than trying to sell her for a little fortune. Still, though, allowing her to join them after just a day seemed peculiar. Even if he secretly thought it was a great idea.

He considered entering the argument, but landing on Lorgan's wrong side for a second time that day seemed like a bad idea. Besides, Kesta had this.

Perhaps she saw something in the girl similar to what he saw (without desire muddying everything up). Perhaps she thought another girl would add a little grandness to their troop. Or maybe she just needed someone else to care for, but he doubted it. The Crimson Hunters were enough for any mother's care. Regardless, whatever her well-intentioned reasons, Kesta countered Lorgan's every argument on the matter. It was a rare thing to see them bicker so openly, but after the events with the Army of the Dead, having a girl in chains was probably only asking for further trouble, if not precarious questions. Who knew how the peasants of Treystone would react if they discovered her origin?

They would act like spitting peasants.

Natteo assisted Kesta, even though she didn't ask, arguing only for her freedom. Perhaps he was afraid of the girl who'd arrived in the middle of a fiery explosion. Perhaps he didn't trust her piercing eyes. Perhaps he just found her silence unsettling. *Perhaps he has a point.* Regardless, he offered his own informed and well-constructed thoughts on slavery. This was no surprise, as Castra was rife with the slave trade. Derian had long suspected that his best friend came from a wealthy family, whose sins were many. Slave running was likely to be one of them. Perhaps that was why he hated his family so much. Perhaps walking as a mercenary was Natteo's way of forsaking his lineage completely. He could have asked him about it, but Natteo had his reasons for not speaking of such painful things. Derian would have been just as happy to talk about himself, but there really wasn't much to him, admittedly. Also, nobody ever really asked.

Lorgan, for his part, argued as to her value, her mystery, and her potential threat, but as much as he fought his side, Kesta met his arguments with short, cutting retorts. Eventually, he began to give ground. Perhaps he wanted to agree with her, Derian thought, for he'd offered sterner responses in arguments past.

The girl sat behind Kesta in near delight, swaying with each thundering roll of the wagon's wheels through the deep forest as though it were a game. She didn't speak, but she broke her silence every now and again by humming a few irritating notes of music under her breath. He hummed the same tune and cursed its annoyance.

They raced the rain across the sky, resting sparingly for no longer than needed to let the horses recover their breath. The vile potion of rotted swine juice would take a few hours to run its course through the Army of the Dead, and though the Crimson had taken all their horses, they knew the mercenaries would track them. Once the bouts of explosive diarrhoea dried up, there wasn't a rock big enough nor a cave dark enough to conceal them. Best to get ahead, get to Treystone, and get out of there all nicely polished, he thought.

They made good time, and as night drew in, Lorgan brought them to a stop. Without saying a word, he unlocked the metal hold around the girl's neck and left it sitting in a clinking bundle at the back of the cart. She immediately took the chain and tossed it to the muddy ground below. Lorgan laughed and bowed; she had offered her own thoughts on the matter. She would not be chained again.

"You want to march with the Crimson Hunters until you find your way?" he asked, and she smiled.

For a few hours more they travelled, the Crimson and their new companion, and though he didn't have any confidence in his gut feelings, Derian felt happy with this new arrangement. With the low light of the moon above their heads and the clear glimmer of a thousand stars setting their course, Lorgan brought his horse alongside Derian's.

"You've taken the lead for long enough. Let me take the catalight," he said.

Glad to be free of the burning flame and the frequent sparks, Derian unhooked the six-foot-long pole of light from his horse's saddle and passed it across. The forest's shadows danced menacingly around them as Lorgan attached the marching light to his own horse and patted the beast forward.

"I'm glad you freed her, sir."

"I'm certain enough that she won't burn us as we sleep," Lorgan replied, adjusting the catalight to shine as much light ahead as possible. A spark fell down into his grey and black beard, and he wiped it away absently.

"What'll we do with her?"

"I imagine if word got out about a girl from the source, the Dark One would soon hunt us down. We'll likely put her on an airbarge and get her to the Guild in Dellerin. She'll be safe enough under their protection. Let them decide." He smiled in the light, and Derian could see the worry. The Crimson Hunters had condemned themselves to a life of waiting for a vengeful pack of rabid mercenaries to come knocking at the door. The smarter move would have been killing all seven and taking everything they had, but that just wasn't the Crimson way, was it?

"What is the tattoo?"

"If you studied your book, you'd have all the answers you'd need, Derian," Lorgan retorted.

"Idiot," Natteo muttered, from somewhere behind.

"Do you even know what the tattoo is, Natteo?" Derian countered.

"Course I do."

"Then what is it?"

Natteo took a breath. A cynical man might believe he was forming a lie. "It's a piece of golden art that defines her as a person. She need not speak to let us know who she is. And why should she? That tattoo tells us everything we need to know of her soul, her heart, her life. If you can't see that, Derian, there's no point in me ever trying to explain it. The body is a canvas, Derian, and tattoos are the masterpiece scrawled upon—"

"Shut up."

"Oh, will both of you shut up and I'll tell you!" Lorgan snapped. "It is no tattoo. It is a grand demon's mark. It wasn't until it started to glow that I knew for certain."

"What's a demon's mark?"

Lorgan sighed in defeat. "Most fools know that a grand demon can only breach our world through a shattered monolith. However, that is only half the task. The way through is a difficult path. That mark is a shining beacon to light a demon's way."

"So, we should keep her away from any monoliths, then?" Natteo asked.

"Well, yes, that would be a fine start."

"And if we accidentally come upon one?" Derian asked.

"There are none in Luistra. How do neither of you know this?"

"It wasn't in the book."

Natteo asked what Derian was thinking. "What if she is a servant to the grand demon? What if she knows the whereabouts of a hidden monolith?"

"A big jutting unnatural rock of onyx is hard to miss. There's no hidden monolith," Lorgan said, ensuring both young mercenaries knew what a monolith was. He needn't have bothered. Derian knew as much about monoliths as most. Which was, in fact, very little—except it was believed they were the locks that held the two realms apart from each other. Some people believed the seven gods had given up their lives in their creation. And weavers, before they were wiped out, had been known to flock to monoliths as if they gave power. Perhaps they did. Five stood throughout the Seven Isles of Dellerin, all of them shattered and cracked. Some people believed there were more.

"Maybe it's hidden somewhere clever," Derian suggested.

"Like in a cave?" Natteo added, and appeared rather worried at such a thought.

"It's not in a cave. If you two just studied, I wouldn't have to deal with idiocy," Lorgan muttered, and he kicked his horse forward, away from irritating questions and ignorant apprentices.

"Do you really think she's bad?" Derian asked Natteo.

"I think there is more to her. Anyone that pretty usually has something to hide."

"She is beautiful," Derian said in agreement.

"You have no chance, brother."

"Course I do."

Natteo mimicked Lorgan's sigh. "You will end up with a nice swamp troll. Although for your sake, I hope it's one of those Addakkas trolls. The ones with the lowest standards," he mocked.

"Love is blind," countered Derian.

"Like I said, troll."

"Naked girl or troll, at least I'll be in love," muttered Derian.

"I could fall in love too, if I wanted to."

"You'll never find someone stupid enough to fall in love with you. And even if you do, you'll swiftly find a way to ruin it," Derian mocked.

"That might be true," Natteo said, falling quiet.

Near midnight, they set down a few hours' ride from the town. Derian suspected Lorgan didn't want to spend a few silver pieces on a night in the tavern, and he didn't begrudge the old mercenary a little miserliness. Despite the huge treasure on offer, they had stolen only the girl's price, but it was still more money than they usually had. Lorgan wasn't too eager to spend it on civilised luxuries, so instead of fresh straw, clean sheeting, and the mutterings of a tavern, there were worn blankets, damp ground, and the whistle of hissects, and it was good enough for Derian.

They nestled in by the fire beneath the clustered grey trees, and Derian did what he'd never once done in his life: he took out his book, his parchment of lettering, and began to study with no prompting.

The girl watched him as he struggled with the trickier words, and he dared an embarrassed smile. She hissed at him. Kesta lay on her back, staring at the open night's sky above, while Lorgan was quieter than normal at the edge of the light, allowing Derian's mutterings to fill the air.

Natteo leaned over and whispered mockingly to him that he was 'the goodest little studious munket,' but when Derian turned to retort, he spotted Natteo's own notes in his hands. As usual, his best friend was thinking similar thoughts. The Crimson Hunters were a doomed outfit. Going to war with the Army of the Dead had guaranteed that. Best they learn what they could now before slipping away from a terrible fate. Maybe when Mowg and the boys caught up with them in a few seasons, they would have their own skilled unit. Or else have perfected their apologies.

Maybe they'd be hiring if Lorgan and Kesta hadn't gone out quietly?

"Turn to page twenty-seven," Natteo said after a time. The chosen page had several images similar to the five-pronged tattoo covering the girl's wonderful navel region. There were other pictures involving mirrors between two worlds and demonic horned beasts stepping through and other nasty foreshadowings. It was wonderfully unsettling.

He tried to understand and memorise, but his feeble mind was slow. He could never comprehend how some scholars could read so naturally that it appeared as easy as breathing. Each line took him an eternity to master, and its meaning even longer. He didn't like to think himself stupid, but when reading, it was impossible not to. He preferred ignorance.

Lorgan stood up from the fire to tend to things, and as he walked past, he patted Derian gently on the shoulder. There was no finer compliment than 'the pat' after a deed accomplished. Natteo called it 'Lorgan's love stroke,' and they had a competition to see how many each had received. This pat put him three ahead. He smiled triumphantly toward the irritated Natteo, but as Lorgan walked by him, he also received a gentle pat. Grinning, Natteo held up his fingers to indicate the difference between their scores. Derian gestured in silent reply, but his friend was already back studying.

After the tough marching, Derian felt himself relax. The fire was warm, his stomach was full, and he suspected Lorgan might let them sleep until after dawn.

And why wouldn't he?

It had been a busy day. They had slain a demon, fallen, died, been resurrected, met a naked girl, survived an ambush from a renowned (if a little too trusting) group of mercenaries, 'earned' a small fortune, and now stood to increase their wealth with a bounty fulfilled. For a pulse of blood, Derian felt good. He looked up into the trees and wondered when exactly it had stopped raining. It didn't matter; he took it as a fine omen.

With a start, he realised the girl was standing up, facing them. "My name is Seren," she said to them without preamble. "I think I am important." She looked bemused by her own voice. "I believe I am good girl, but I think I need… kill," she added, and her tone was terrifying. It sounded like she was hanging from a cliff, and the person cutting the rope had argued that she would reach the ground faster this way.

Before Derian could speak, the moment was lost as a hundred demonic monsters emerged from deep within the forest. Screeching, howling, and snapping wildly, they came straight towards their campsite with a sound like thunder.

14

THE CRIMSON HUNTERS

D erian had seen them before. Not in the real world but in the scribblings in his book, and he really, really wished he'd learned more about them. He tried to remember their given title, but most rational thought beyond a hundred demonic beasts charging straight towards them eluded him completely.

Their fierce howling pierced the serenity of the night, and Derian fell back, away from the light of the fire, tripping on a tree root as the first four-footed beast reached the camp.

Someone screamed, "Canis demon!" and a flicker of a memory touched his mind. Canis, the doglike creature, though far larger. Closer to a furless lion, but without a tail. *What happened to their tails?* Also, their backs were covered in jagged horns all the way down.

The canis beast leapt over the cooking fire and veered away from the light as though burned by its brightness. The ground rumbled under its massive charge, for though it was far smaller than a horse, its weight of muscle was remarkable. Why did all demonic beasts have to be robust doom bringers? Just once, couldn't the monsters be slow-moving fat blobs of

killable evilness? he thought miserably. The world of the
source did not allow monsters of weakness, though, and the
thing snapped hand-sized teeth at Derian, who stood directly
in their route. Without thinking, he did what all legendary
warriors did when faced with mean, nasty monsters. He leapt
for the nearest tree.

To an athlete of the Drydern Games, reaching a tree and
its life-saving branches only a horse's length away in less
than a pulse of blood was no great accomplishment, but to
Derian, it was a near-impossible feat.

With a gracefulness he'd never called upon, and an
impressive spring to his step, Derian leapt clear, and
somehow, he took hold of a nasty branch a few feet above his
head and swung away.

Don't break. Don't break. Don't break.

"Get off the ground!" roared Lorgan, leaping over the
fire with shield raised out in front, as Kesta, Natteo, and the
girl, whose name he'd already forgotten, scrambled up onto
the parked cart. Within a breath, and possibly against
Lorgan's will, three sets of human hands took hold and
pulled Lorgan up to higher ground. It wasn't very high
ground, but it was higher than the level of the monsters.
They drew what weapons they could to meet the attack, but
the monsters kept charging by. Not even the herd of hobbled
horses at the edge of the treeline drew the monsters'
attention.

What makes them run like this?

Derian's feet still hung over the edge of the cart, dangling
like fishing lures above the first invading beast. He'd always
ignored Lorgan's insistence that he should build his strength
by hanging from nasty branches and pulling himself up a
dozen times every morning. He wished he'd listened, and he
truly wished he'd attempted at least two or three pulls a week,

for his arms were thin and unimpressive, and as he struggled, their burning was agonising.

Snap!

A set of teeth almost took his ankle as the first monster leapt and missed and continued charging onwards down the path. Right behind it, another beast attempted the same attack.

"HELP ME!" Derian cried, swinging back and forth above the charging beasts. He tried to pull himself up again, but could do nothing more than tuck his legs closer to his chest and swing like a honey-drunk munket at a fairground. With his life precariously close to ending, his mind wandered to thoughts of a recurring dream he'd suffered frequently throughout his life.

It usually started with him being thrown overboard, swimming in a stormy ocean and watching the rise and fall of surf while everyone he'd ever cared for was sailing away into the darkness on a barge. They always begged him to swim after them, promising 'nice honey cakes with cream, that needed eating,' but as hard as he swam towards the barge, the farther it would slip away. Eventually, he would become swamped beneath larger waves. It was usually then that his feet would become entangled in sea vines, monsters' tentacles, or something slithery like that. He hated that dream more than any other dream he'd ever had; the loneliness, the desolation. The uneaten cakes.

Until that moment, he'd never felt as tragically left behind as he did in the dream, but now, with a plethora of snapping monsters below him and his comrades near, yet still so very far away, he found it curiously familiar. So familiar, in fact, that he wondered if this was a dream.

You can fly in dreams.

"DERIAN!" Natteo screamed from across the camp,

standing on the top of the cart in relative safety. From Derian's swinging view, it looked like that barge full of deliciousness.

"No cakes," Derian whimpered, and his body shook uncontrollably. The tree shook as well. The air was sticky and warm with panted breaths, and each monster came near enough that if Derian wanted a fight, he'd need only drop and take hold of one as it passed. For a strange moment, his heart began to beat out of time and a terrible fury overcame him. Maybe he should drop below and kill them.

"Kill them all."

Rusty was swinging from his waist, whispering for release. It was that or the pulsing blood in his body making him delirious. Then his cowardice took hold and calmed his cascading mind.

Who was he to attack a perfectly reasonable stampede of demonic beasts charging through the forest in the middle of the night, anyway? They made no genuine effort to attack, so why show prejudice? They might be good little doggy demons out for a midnight run, he argued.

He caught sight of Seren's tattoo glowing against her open cloak. She stood beside his comrades watching the monsters pass beneath them, and rubbed at her belly with her hand like a woman carrying a child, and a strange sense of doom engulfed him.

"Who are you?" he whispered, and shivers ran down his spine. Did the beasts sense and fear her? Were they fleeing what hunted her?

Ooh, I don't like that thought.

The beasts thinned out, and then, as swiftly as they had appeared to ruin their night, the last monster passed by and the Crimson were alone again. The only hint of their charge was the stench of rancid meat and raw faeces in the evening air and deep clefts in the soft ground.

"I will not complain about nasty branches out to get me anymore," Derian said, dropping to the ground. To his dismay, he discovered a patch of dampness at the front of his pants, and he gave thanks to the gods of the source that he'd favoured black this morning.

"They could have torn us all apart," Kesta said, watching the route they'd taken. Her eyes were heavy and filling with hate.

"They must have caught the smell of Treystone in the wind," Lorgan said, sheathing his sword and clipping his shield to his back. He followed the demons' dust cloud into the dark for a few steps but stopped before leaving the security of the campfire. The ground at their feet began to fall silent as the sound of hooves faded into the eternal darkness, and Derian took a breath.

"So what do we do?" he asked, recovering his book from the mud. Its crumpled pages were wet, but he wiped them clean and held them to dry over the fire. To the others, he looked like a scholar finding love in study, but really, he was disguising how close he wanted his trousers to be to the fire's warmth.

"They have no right to flesh," Seren said, and caught Derian looking at her. She hissed at him as though she were part demon herself.

Natteo must have thought the same; he edged away from her like she'd sprouted a horn upon her shapely head. "They are running down upon Treystone," he said. "Their walls won't hold that horde for very long."

"There are children there," Kesta called out to Lorgan, who stood watching the darkness.

"Children are not defenceless. They can fight horrors too," Lorgan muttered.

"What could we do, anyway?" Derian asked, shuddering at the thought of those monsters turning tail and coming back at them. "Maybe we should get our horses and run away?" It sounded far more pathetic than it had in his mind. Still, though, what could they do?

Kesta tended to the shaken horses. She whispered calming sounds and began strapping four of the beasts back on to the cart. The horses were wild and raring to run. She did the task with the skill of a woman used to controlling precarious things, and then she ordered Natteo and Derian to follow suit. Derian complied with a heavy heart.

"Is this not Lorgan's decision?" he muttered, holding the catalight lantern out over the fire until the phosphorous dust ignited brightly in a spitting buzz.

"Lorgan will get there in a moment," she whispered, and Natteo cursed before slipping away to don his armour.

"We need kill them," Seren whispered, but her voice was fierce. She had a general's tone. A legend's tone.

"Kill them all? Okay, pretty girl."

Lorgan continued to stare into the darkness, and Derian could almost hear the swinging pendulum in his head easing him towards wretched nobility. "If they tear that town apart, I'm not sure they'll be willing to pay what they owe us."

Derian shook his head in despair. Stupid Kesta, knowing him better.

"Might be that we can earn a bonus to the bounty outstanding," Lorgan added, and Derian climbed atop his mount. "We are the Crimson Hunters. It's time to do what we must." He spun around to see his mercenaries already a couple of steps ahead.

"Oh, this is just polished," Natteo cried, and he kicked his horse forward.

"Spit 'n' polished," Derian added, and he took the lead, lighting the path ahead. He felt a chill akin to the one he'd felt before the vector demon tore them apart, and he willed his nerve to hold. It wasn't fear chipping away at his courage; it was just knowing that this was the end. A thousand foolish warriors might argue differently, but the truth was definite. When these monsters stopped running, whoever was around them would not see the dawn.

To ride towards doom was foolish, destined to end in tears. It wasn't gold or renown for Lorgan or Kesta that drove this group of mercenaries. It probably never had been. The crux of the Crimson's misfortune was always doing the right thing. And that was bad business in Derian's eyes.

"I need out of this fuken outfit already," Derian spat.

"I'm with you on that, brother," Natteo called.

15

END OF THE LINE

What are you doing, Derian?
        Saving peasants, that's what I'm doing.
This is not your fight.
It isn't theirs either.
"Let's kill them all savagely."

He was not sure how parts of his mind were split with opinions, but now was not the time to worry on this. The catalight rocked wildly to the beat of Derian's mount as he led the chase, though he didn't have a great desire to catch his quarry. Riding alongside, Natteo cursed and complained, and Derian could see the fear in his friend's face—and it matched his own. No matter how fast the wind rushed or the booming thunder roared from hooves on the ground, they could hear the sound of death in the cool night air, and it came from the distant chorus of evil things racing along the path ahead.

Death never comes in silence.

He had regrets. He had so many unsaid words. Where could he even start? He might start by telling Natteo that he was the best damned friend a mercenary could ever have, but what type of fool said meaningful things like that, anyway? Besides, Natteo knew he loved him, and he loved him right back. He regretted following Kesta's orders without proper argument—and Lorgan's after that. He also regretted that he agreed with them.

So, I'm an honourable man now, am I?

"You are a glorious killer."

The loud rattle of the cart kept pace behind them, and Derian imagined most of their ill-gotten supplies lost in the desperate charge. What use were bags of apples or loaves of bread to the departed, anyway? Kesta drove the horses fiercely, and he could see Seren clinging to its sides, a hand on each edge, squealing in neither delight nor terror, but somewhere in between.

This will end in tears.

"And rivers of glorious blood."

He was no skilled watcher of the sky. He couldn't tell how long after midnight it was. It was a skill he really should have learned by now. As it was, by the time they reached Treystone, dawn would still be far out.

As inadequate a mercenary outfit as they were, a town of peasants would need their help in fighting off the demonic beasts. A hundred of the things was a terrifying prospect, but with the Crimson Hunters assisting, a town of peasants might have a chance.

It didn't take Lorgan too long to catch up. His powerful mount came alongside Derian's, and though he was just one more person, Derian felt fiercer with him present. Lorgan's hands gripped the reins tightly as though untouched by years of wear, and he roared all of them onwards. It would likely be his second doomed mission in as many days, but who was counting?

As the miles passed beneath him, Derian's mind wandered to a terrible place. He thought of himself and realised he wasn't kind in spirit or heart; he wasn't caring in soul or mind; he had no faith in anything or anyone. He was a waste of a man and not even brave enough to stop silent tears streaming down his cheeks. He began to despair, and he began to cower. And then something strange happened. Though his rational self whispered the inevitable truth in his mind, and his better senses suggested doom was upon them, something else began to influence him. Something that had kept his fingers firm upon the reins without him knowing. Something that now stirred him towards belief. Belief in his companions and in himself. They chased a hundred demons through the darkness, yet somehow, now, he knew they could survive this.

Idiot.

He could not enjoy this feeling of hope for long. With no warning, the forest whittled away; the path opened up wider, and the claustrophobic hold of the night disappeared altogether. They charged from a grey forest out into the openness of a valley he recognised immediately.

The valley of Treystone was quite an impressive valley as far as valleys went. A half-mile-wide expanse of fertile openness with a gathering of structures nestled deep within its centre. Derian shouldn't have been able to make out the town, but it was alive with fire and the sounds of shouts and screams and snarling.

They stopped as one at the lip of the valley to steel themselves for what was to come, to take in what horrors they saw below, and to concoct worthless plans, hoping to convince themselves they were not about to endure a suicidal last charge. Derian patted his horse's mane, and the exhausted beast took the respite gladly and chewed upon a clump of grass at its feet.

Brave, nameless horse, you've no idea what's about to happen, he thought, looking out over the town.

"Doomed," Natteo said.

"There will be much bloodshed tonight," Lorgan said, and something within Derian moved with fierce anger. This anger was rousing itself more and more these days. He thought of a child taken in the night, and the anger fuelled a desire to kill the beasts.

All of them.

"All of them."

"The town has spread itself out too much," muttered Lorgan, and he was right. It was a perfectly adequate settlement nestled around the valley's slow, bubbling river. There were many wooden and brick structures peeking over one wall of long timber spikes. *One spitting wall. Not even a killing ground to focus upon.* They must have believed the walls would be high enough to hold fast a wandering pack of threats, and they might have been had the townspeople manned them adequately.

Treystone was a growing town, fuelled by the wealth of a healthy mine and overlooked by the richer city of Gold Haven a few days' ride away. It was no surprise it was larger than most settlements in this region, but while the structures and wealth within grew impressively in such fortuitous times, a wiser mayor might have recognised the need for recruiting more able-bodied soldiers to keep the town safe.

This wasn't the first time Derian had seen peasants behave with narrow vision. Why feed and pay for a battalion of soldiers a season at a time, when they could send out word as needed to any hapless passing mercenary outfit wanting to earn a small fortune eradicating a pesky monster seen in the area?

"Peasants," Lorgan muttered.

"They don't have a clue how to defend a town," Natteo added.

"They should have a general at arms," Kesta hissed.

"The monsters need die," Seren said, and nothing in the world sounded sweeter in Derian's ears.

They stood side by side, watching the growing melee below, unsure of what to do. The monsters had reached the town far more swiftly than they had. Given the sheer numbers of them, and the dreadful noise, they hadn't been the only pack of charging monsters, either.

"Can you name the beasts which attack this town?" Lorgan said aloud. Strange time for a lesson, thought Derian.

"Canis demons and anculus demons," Natteo replied.

"How many are attacking?"

"Too many."

At least a dozen tall monsters stood in the thin grass outside the small gates of Treystone. They were over seven feet in height and stood upright as though human. Their spiky bodies were covered in tufts of fur, and long, sweeping blades of sharp bone jutted out from each arm. Some said anculus demons were born in the likeness of the first grand demon, Silencio himself.

"They are masters to the little ones," Lorgan said, and Derian's stomach dropped. They stood watching the monsters fan out tactically, each with a ferocious pack of canis demons under its command. They hissed, and the smaller brutes howled in return—it reminded Derian of a herder whistling his swine in for the night.

"So that's why they didn't attack us on their charge," Lorgan said, as though reciting a line from his book.

Why couldn't it just be simple? Why couldn't it be primal monsters attacking mindlessly? Derian thought miserably. No, it had to be mindless monsters under instruction.

"They're still coming," Kesta said, and Derian's eyes were drawn to the edges of the valley on the other side, where more of the beasts were emerging from the treeline. Three hundred? Four hundred? Probably more.

"What evil is this?" Natteo asked, and beside him, Derian heard Seren gasp. Was this somehow her doing? Had she broken a wall between the two worlds? No one answered, and no one dared to move, for it occurred to them as one that they watched an army. An army of demons upon the battlefield of Treystone.

"The peasants are brave," Derian said, and his comrades nodded in agreement. It wasn't much, but it was something. Along the top of the wall stood dozens of villagers, each with bows and torches, and they combined the two as best they could. They could hear the panicked roar of the defenders as they fired volley after volley down at the demons, but it was a strange thing to see humans outmanoeuvred by monsters. A smarter general might have sent a dozen archers after one or two targets, striking them down and moving to the next, but as it was, each man upon the wall chose his own target and they filled the valley with hopeless fireflies dying in the wet grass.

The beasts must have understood this, as they fanned out along the outskirts of the wall, screeching, hissing, and barking. Treystone's defenders answered this taunting with wasted ammunition, while smaller groups of monsters slipped between the fiery projectiles and took ground beneath the bottom of the wall. With massive paws, they tore at the wood, eager to make a hole before arrows did finally strike them down, but by then, another would have taken its place and another after that.

It was Kesta who pulled them from their stupor. She stood atop her cart and stared down upon the melee. When she spoke, her voice was a cold whisper, fragile like a waif's. Her hands shook, but after a moment, Derian realised that it was her entire body that shook.

"This town will not fall tonight," she intoned. "These beasts don't want to waste the warm-blooded meat." Silent tears streamed down her face, and she let them flow. "They want to eat while the heart pumps it fresh. They will take what they want—husbands, wives, children—but not all of them tonight. They will take their time and then, come dawn, with squirming prey in their jaws, they will disappear." She wiped her eyes and spat onto the ground. The world was motionless, and even Natteo was silent.

"They come at night," Kesta went on, "because they like to sleep with full bellies through the day. And as they sleep, the youngest and fiercest human warriors, those who are left, will track them with shiny, puny swords and thurken fire." She spat again. "Those brave warriors will find the monsters and quickly find themselves overcome and devoured, for they will never return," she said, and her voice broke, and Derian reached out and placed his hand upon her shoulder. He didn't know why some pain was contagious when passed by words.

"And it might be that yet other young warriors will flee in terror and leave their kin altogether," she added. "They might just up and abandon those waiting behind the walls and spend a coward's life earning regretful breath." She spat again.

"But every night, the monsters will come, and those few left behind the wall will get better at holding them back, get better at stabbing their black hearts, get better at killing, but it'll be futile because everything's lost, anyway.

"Everyone they'll ever love will be dead."

"After a few nights, there will be few villagers left.

"There will only be a few monsters left.

"Then it'll just be one person on the last day.

"They'll never know why or how they survive." Her voice was cold. It was like steel.

"All they'll know is they'll never rest until every thurken demon in these lost lands is dead," she said, before wiping the last tear and flicking it away in disgust.

"Won't happen tonight," Seren said, and Kesta nodded in agreement before dropping the reins into the goddess's lap and taking her place at the back of the cart. She wrapped some rope around her waist and attached it to each side tightly and strapped herself in. She emptied a set of quivers out in front of her and knelt down against the edge with notched bow. Natteo notched two bolts and gripped his mount's reins. His face was pale, and he offered Derian a 'fine life while it lasted' nod.

"Kesta and the new girl lead us through the pack," Lorgan said now. "We charge at them and break through to the town's gates. We stay alive, and once we're back in behind the walls, we make a new plan," he said, and Derian thought it so stupid that it might just work.

"Let's go earn some gold!" he roared, striking his sword loudly against his shield.

"Let's kill every one of them!" shouted Kesta, and she fired one arrow into the valley below, signalling her murderous intentions.

"Let's go be heroes!" cried Derian, feigning bravery and trying to ignore his bladder suddenly filling.

"Let's go die like idiots!" shouted Natteo, and he wiped a tear from his eyes and gave a demented sneer.

"All die together," Seren said, and she brought the cart down towards the battle.

16

THE BATTLE OF TREYSTONE

Any talented bard or drunken storyteller will tell a middling story and embellish just enough to make it impressive. With no respect for practicality, they'll suggest a thousand fiends felled by one victorious hero, they'll pledge that a bond between lovers overcame all odds—including death itself—or they'll insist that goodness always won out.

Derian could accept most embellishments with a smile. All but one, that was. Time. He didn't know why time irked him. Only that it did. Storytellers would have you believe battles stretched for hours, days, or longer, when really, they were fought in moments. Horrible, ugly, violent, and bloody moments. It took only a single pulse for blood to begin to spill, and it took only a breath for any heroic warrior to take their last.

It didn't take hours to charge down a valley of fire, blood, misery, and monsters, and it didn't take hours to become a hero in battle. However, it took only a moment to be forgotten, and as Derian followed his comrades towards doom, he wondered whether there would be any great tale told of their foolish heroism.

It all went wrong from the start.

The first anculus demon to spot the attack was the first demon to die. From its place at the edge of the battlefield, it turned to the sound of its vanquishers and managed a scream as it fell under the crush of Seren's charging horses and the massive wooden wheels they led. Unfortunately, the cart bounced awkwardly on the creature's exploding head, veered wide, and nearly flipped. Were it not for the ropes holding her, Kesta would have been flung swiftly into the night. As it was, Seren recovered control, but the charge pulled her away from the rest of her companions. Wary of stopping to get back into formation, she followed her momentum and disappeared from Derian's view into the mass of demon bodies.

With no cart barging their way through, Lorgan led his horse forward to break through the rear guard, swinging indiscriminately at any grey flesh he could see. He drove his horse down along the valley, aiming for the gate, and he was impressive. However, like a fist clearing the way in an ocean's lazy wave, what space he made swiftly closed behind him, and Derian and Natteo could not follow. Watching helplessly as he raced towards the gates, falling under some protection of the line of defending archers, Derian and Natteo pulled away, searching for a route of their own through the hostile grounds.

Derian, ever calm atop his magnificent beast, chose agility over speed. He guided Natteo among oblivious monster after monster, both men dodging the monsters' delayed instinctive blows as they passed.

It worked wonderfully for at least three moments, before a flailing claw struck Natteo's horse and caused it to rear in fright. Instead of correcting the horse's reaction and continuing with Derian, Natteo fired two bolts into the offending monster and swiftly reloaded as a dozen canis demons attempted to surround him. Derian screamed out for his friend, but his survival instincts and his route took his best friend from his sight.

"Honourable man?"

It didn't take long for Derian's route to become crammed with the enemy, who were slowly realising they faced an invasion of their own. All around him they snapped and growled, and still, he pressed onwards towards the gate, knowing that at any moment he could be torn from the saddle. He held his breath and waited for the end, and his limbs became numb as though not his own, and then, without warning, Seren and Kesta rumbled by him and earned him a reprieve. And in so doing, they also earned renown worthy of legends all by themselves. Weighed down by what supplies remained, the cart and horses had now become a thundering weapon, trampling all beneath thunderous hooves and unforgiving wooden wheels. They raced through the battlefield in a great arc, sowing confusion and devastation as they went.

"I want to kill them all."

All canis fell beneath their charge, leaving a trail of smeared demonic mulch in their wake. Atop the cart, Kesta fired at any anculus unfortunate enough to come into her sights, and she was unusually accurate. With limbs no longer reacting to his will, Derian charged recklessly away from his route, towards the biggest brute he could find.

"I'll start with this fiend."

"Come on, you piece of shit!" he roared, and did what all reckless heroes did in tales, and he didn't really know why he did it: he leapt from the saddle with Rusty already drawn.

"For honour and glory!" he shouted, because all heroes hid their terror behind war-cries as they felled great monsters.

He wasn't sure he'd struck gold with that outburst, but by the time he thought of something else to say, he'd already fallen upon the monster and knocked it to the ground. So he struck down upon it with all his might.

Unfortunately, he hit one of its horns and the sword rebounded backwards. The tarnished grip snapped in half, leaving him defenceless and looking a little foolish. Only then did he notice the demon was already dead, killed by one arrow—either a crack shot from Kesta or a rogue shot from the town.

"Ah, Rusty," he moaned, and picked up the blade, holding it to the grip as though the source would weave them back together. The source made no attempt, and his horse, sensing the opportunity for escape, ran off through the mass of monsters, leaving him rightly fuked.

The hold upon some canis demons around him diminished with their master's death, and they scattered like a shoal of fish. Unfortunately, there were plenty to take their place, and Derian found himself surrounded again.

Suddenly, a shrill whistling sound filled his ears, and a volley of arrows landed all around him. They only struck two of the monsters down (in a pathetic show of ineptitude), and he heard a cheer from the ramparts. Though he didn't know why, he waved back in appreciation. Less for the kills but more for the flaming arrows, which had caused a nice burning distraction.

He held Rusty in his grip and lamented the loss. It looked less like an average sword and more like a larger-than-advisable dagger.

Dagger.

He reached beneath his armour, tore some strips away from his vest, and began wrapping the old threads around the

end of the blade where it had snapped free, because that's
what unskilled mercenaries did instead of giving up.

"This will do," he said aloud, as a body came tumbling
from a passing horse and rolled to a painful stop at his feet.

"You idiot. You lost your horse and broke your sword in
the same breath!" cried Natteo, eyes wide with terror. He
scrambled back to his feet and fired at a rushing demon
who'd stepped over a burning arrow, hitting it twice in the
head before it collapsed on the ground.

"I thought I lost you," Derian said.

"You owe me money."

"Why did you come for me, brother?" Derian demanded,
and Natteo grinned manically.

"So we can walk into the darkness together."

The demons formed up around them. Snarling cries filled
the air; their vile features were doubly revolting in the
glowing embers of the arrows burning up around them. And
so, as though their deeds were being sung by the mouth of a
drunken bard or talented storyteller, Derian and Natteo went
to war. Back to back, they shed what blood they could,
knowing it could never be enough. The monsters kept
coming, and the pair kept killing. Natteo fired bolt after bolt
into the swarming masses, and Derian stabbed swiftly with
his long-dagger any who neared. As though they were blessed
by a god from the source, somehow not a single jagged set of
teeth fell upon them, and no flailing claw tore them open.
They moved and turned with the sway of battle, screaming
and cursing and massacring all beasts who stood near them.

"We can do this. We can survive!" Derian roared.

"We really can't," Natteo replied, and he was right.

17

EVERYONE DIES... AGAIN

As swift as battles were, massacres were even shorter, and the massacre of the Crimson Hunters was shorter than most. If it had been a tale to tell the masses, it would have been underwhelming and symbolic of their ineffectiveness as a mercenary outfit.

Derian never saw the first of his comrades fall; he heard only a defiant roar, louder than any demonic wail, and through a break in the bodies, he caught sight of Lorgan, striking out at anything near him as he bravely attempted to regroup with his comrades. He'd lost his horse along the way, and he swung shield and sword with such force that monsters fell to the ground all around him. As he drew nearer, however, Derian could see the unnatural strain in his movements and hear the heavy panting of a man taking his last few breaths. Finally, Lorgan broke clear and fell at their feet in a wet heap.

"Fight with me, boys, so the girls might reach the gate." He sounded as though he spoke from beneath a lake, and Derian caught sight of the deep gash along his side. Lorgan rolled in the grass and tried to rise, and Natteo fell to his knees beside him. Derian froze, seeing so many white ribs protruding through broken flesh into the night air, and he held back a wail of melancholy. He'd felt this pain before, at the side of his mother's trodden body as she gasped her last.

"I don't know what to do, sir," Natteo cried, and he took Lorgan's hand as he convulsed. Still, Lorgan tried to rise again before cursing his own blood as it streamed out, soaking the ground where Derian and Natteo knelt.

From a few feet away, a monster had the audacity to disturb them from their horror and charged. Derian stepped to the beast and drew its attention, sending his dagger through the monster's brain effortlessly before knocking it away as though it were no threat at all. Other monsters circled them, but they made no move to strike, as though silent orders were being whispered in their ears.

"Help me up," Lorgan said, even as his lungs filled with blood, and then he stretched back in the grass as the last of his strength left him. Natteo patted his shoulder but did not help him rise again, for the old man was already slipping towards the darkness.

"There is no need, sir. We have won this battle," Natteo said, and Lorgan gasped lightly.

"I feel I am drowning," Lorgan croaked, and he spat crimson blood from his mouth. "A terrible thing to drown, not worthy of any hero's legacy," he whimpered, and he looked past Natteo to something in the darkness beyond.

"We are lost," Derian cried, and fell away from Natteo and the dead man.

"No mercy."

He tasted metal in his mouth, and he wanted to kill them all. He wanted to rip them as they ripped others. He wanted to kill as many of those curs as he could before they struck him down. Without thinking, he charged into the waiting horde recklessly. In his blood-covered left hand was old Rusty, and in his pristine right hand was Lorgan's sword. It was heavy, reassuring, and he waded into them with it, covering himself in their blood, and the world became a blur of snarling, claws, hatred, and death.

He was no great warrior, but a furnace of rage moved him. He struck harder than before and suffered fierce blows, all the while pledging to himself that he'd treat his injuries after the battle, even though he knew these to be grand lies. He gave himself to the fight, and for moments, he was a true mercenary—violent, cruel, fierce, and victorious. And to any of the watching eyes from the wall, he was a hero with spinning dual blades.

At least, for a time.

A slip of the hand undid everything. A small beast on four hooves charged past him, snarling, only to receive a strike from a plunging blade that went deep through skin and muscle but held fast. The dying monster howled and broke clear, taking the sword with it, leaving Derian with only his untrusty long-dagger.

A moment after, he didn't even have that.

In his defence, his last actions seemed like a good idea and not just another attempt at attaining Seren's forgiveness before he died. For the second time.

The cart had delivered wonderful mayhem, charging through the horde, knocking the larger demons asunder and killing the smaller ones outright. However, there were only so many collisions in the terrified horses' resolve before their power dwindled, before the cart slowed to a trot. After a few laps around the battlefield and with nearly all of Kesta's arrows drawn and fired, the wagon became less an undefeatable war machine and more a target. But now, instead of pulling the fatigued mounts from the melee,

Seren had dared one more deathly charge and doomed them all.

As the cart struggled to regain its crushing momentum, a large anculus demon leapt aboard and fell upon Kesta with slashing claws. It plunged a jagged talon into her stomach, and Derian sprinted towards the cart even as he knew full well there was no hope.

The demon tore chunks of meat from her neck, but she was defiant. With her last arrow in an iron grip, she stabbed repeatedly until the shaft split, and she had only a twig in shaking, bloody hands. Kesta cursed loudly as the beast impaled her with its massive claws one last time and lifted her high into the sky before tossing her into a group of chasing monsters.

"Derian!" Natteo screamed, but Derian could do nothing but charge for the cart.

"Deria—"

From somewhere behind, he heard a sudden silence take his best friend, and he refused to look back, for seeing Natteo torn limb from limb would be too much to take.

He watched the demon turn on Seren as she tried to free herself from the rider's seat, and still he had not neared the cart.

"Save her."

Something deep down within him whispered in his mind. Something from a different realm. Something that guided his thoughts, guided his ability.

"Save her."

Rusty really was a terrible weapon. He flung it away. He thought it a strange throw, too. It arced high in the air, above the horned heads of those who would kill him, before coming down at a swift, deadly angle and embedding itself in the head of the demon standing over Seren.

Derian roared in triumph as the beast fell soundlessly from the cart, but in avoiding another invading brute, Seren turned the cart suddenly and with the turn, she brought it charging down upon Derian.

"Be carefu—" he screamed, and caught sight of the girl, and he thought her beautiful, even as the horse struck him and he fell beneath the cart's dreadfully swift spinning wheels.

Seren screamed as Kesta stepped from the world. She felt her passing and wailed aloud like a daughter upon losing a mother, for Kesta's will and heart were incredible, and she had been kinder than all others. Even as she died, the woman fought, and Seren thought this the finest part of being human.

Human.

She was becoming a fine human; she was very sad it would end. There had been moments where she'd believed she'd get out of this one. Had seen it like a murky dream. But her path ended here. She screamed in fear and panic, and she pulled the horses to the side, hoping to knock the beast clear. Her horses obeyed and, incredibly, the beast lost its footing and fell away, and she kicked the horses forward again, but she pulled too severely and they veered wider than she expected.

They hit a large rock, and she felt the world teeter unsteadily. For a moment she thought the entire cart would flip, but it didn't. She roared in triumph, and there was a flash of white skin as she saw stupid Derian in front of her, but it was too late.

Spittle formed in her mouth. She hated him, but still, she tried to pull the horses wide of the idiot, but he fell beneath her and a stream of blood splattered up and splashed her in the face. His body broke into a million pieces, and the wheels flattened his face to nothing, and she felt some sorrow. Not much, but a little.

Then she felt something far fiercer than pity or regret. Her stomach erupted in fire, and she screamed aloud. It was no mere wail of agony; it was a howl, fiercer than any demon's cry, and it erupted from her body like a molten ocean, deep beneath the ground.

Not yet. I'm not ready.

She fell from the cart as if thrown and crumpled in the dirt and screamed as though her tormentor was trying to tear right through her body—and perhaps her tormentor was. Her tattoo of gold was glowing and burning as if on fire, and it became solid.

Not here; not this close to the town.

She grabbed her stomach and cried as she felt darkness engulf her. Unconsciousness claimed her, and her life drained away.

Darkness.

A little less darkness.

She opened her eyes to the settled night. The demons were still around her, but now they were still as they sensed their master coming. They tried to retreat from the light, and, buoyed by this, she struggled to her unsteady feet, but the pain in her stomach caused her to cry out in fresh agony.

Childbirth?

Demonbirth?

Unsteadily, she stumbled through the darkness and tripped over the dead body of Lorgan, and she wailed aloud again. His eyes were open, his face frozen in a grimace of pain, but beneath the dim, deathly stare, she saw the glimmer of triumph, for his shield still dripped warm blood.

She stumbled farther, lost beneath the haze of darkness, and came upon a beast feeding on Natteo. Stretched out in the grass, he'd embedded the last of his bolts in each shoulder of his massive killer. His daggers protruded from its stomach. It wasn't fair, she thought bitterly. Each should have been a killing blow, but steel and grit couldn't slay some monsters.

Some take fire and fire alone.

"Where are you, master?" she whimpered as the tears fell from her eyes. She called out to the weaver who had saved her. Delivered her from the source. The great weaver, lost for decades within the source. Lost from her mind.

No, not fully lost.

She thought of the book, and the stones, and the girl, and through the pain, she tried to put them all together into one coherent thought.

What does it mean?

She touched the tattoo upon her stomach and it burned anew. The demon would be along. *No, not demon.*

Fiore, the demoness of the source, vile and cruel and waiting.

"I chose my guardians well," she whispered, and the tattoo tore at her again. She could feel the beast close now, cracking the door between worlds. She tried to hold on, but the pain grew too much. She stumbled through the darkness

"Leave me!" she roared, and the demonic beasts understood as though she was their master, and she was, for they answered to the one surging through her. Speaking across the darkness.

They fled from Seren, but only towards the town. Within a breath, the town started crumbling under their assault as they attacked once more in a frenzy from all sides. She heard a moan from her mouth and it was not her own. Fiore was trying to get through, and Seren was the light to guide her way.

She stumbled through the battlefield and willed the source

to obey her wish, and as the last pulsing throb of pain took her, she knew the hour was here. The last trapped grand demon was to walk.

She gripped the symbol and hated it. The mark was only the guiding light. She knew this because her master had whispered it in his teachings, and she had been a good student. *A good student.*

"A good student," she moaned, and the night was alive with the screaming of the dying and she didn't care, for she remembered his last few words, and she clawed at the tattooed symbol and hated it with everything she had. It was the symbol that had enchanted the glade and returned her body to birth. It was the symbol that would lead Fiore back through once it broke.

But not through my broken body.

"To the fires with you, demoness!" Seren wailed, and she felt flame erupt around her fingers. She tore at the tattoo on her skin as though it were a rock embedded in the ground. Her hands became fire in themselves; beautiful magenta burned and bubbled her fingers and charred her arms, her face, her breath. She felt her clothing burn to nothing, and she realised she would be in death as she had been born, and this consoled her.

She felt the tattoo harden into something like stone. No, not stone, but gold, for that is how they scribed all demon marks.

With burning fingers, she pulled that five-pronged, spitting piece from her body like a leech from a sickened old wretch. She tore it free and burned herself away to death, and the demon mocked her fiercely for the pain.

There was no stopping Fiore walking the world; but a legend of a different era might conceive a way to release a fierce fighter free from imprisonment at the same time. Seren held the piece above her head and knew it had one gift left to give beyond delivering life.

"Please," she begged the dead gods of the source, and she glanced to her fallen comrades, even fuken Derian.

"A last gift," she cried, and she snapped the mark in two and succumbed to the fire completely. As her eyes burned and melted, she felt a greater pulse emerge from the shattered gold, and it tore her body to pieces. The pain was horrific, until everything went eternally black.

The young mercenary opened his eyes and felt his head and was happy to discover everything was exactly where it should be, though he couldn't recall exactly why. He sat up in the grass and realised dawn had struck, and he was very much alive—though he had gained a strange phobia of wagon wheels. He tried to remember what had happened.

He stood up and fought a dizzy spell and discovered a beautiful girl sitting naked in the grass beside him. Well, mostly naked, as there were shards of burned clothing stuck here and there to her perfect porcelain skin, and he tried not to leer, but she was naked and she held a flower in her hand, as though it were the prettiest thing she'd ever seen. She placed the flower back in the ground near its kin, and when she let go it stood upright as though never plucked.

Only the foul language of Natteo pulled him from his gaze. His best friend was staring in disgust at Lorgan, who busied himself hacking a fallen demon to pieces. Derian tried to walk, but he stumbled in the sunshine, and the reassuring grip of Kesta caught him as she appeared from behind.

"It seems lightning struck us a second time," she said, and she held Derian in a motherly embrace a moment longer than needed. Beside them, Seren stretched and sighed wonderfully, and Kesta bade him look away. Instead, he removed his cloak and held it out to her.

Many demons lay strewn in the surrounding grass, either dead or having a wonderfully deep sleep in the glimmering daybreak. Their skins burned in the light regardless, and this was as beautiful as a naked girl with a flower.

He looked to the town's wall and saw many of the defenders rousing themselves as though they had fallen asleep mid-battle, and he thought all of this peculiar. So did they, judging by their astonished expressions.

"Can't birth again," Seren whispered, and she took his cloak with a grimace of distaste before wrapping it around her body. "Broken now." She flung a piece of gold far into the healthiest-looking grass he'd ever seen.

"What happened?" Derian demanded.

"Nothing. Stop Fiore birth," she said. "When she comes, we die," she added, as though it were nothing, as though any of this made sense.

"Who is Fiore? When will she come?"

Seren spun around and eyed him coldly. He didn't like that look. He didn't like it at all.

"Today? Next day? A century? Don't know. But she come, tear Seren's soul apart," she said, as though her impending doom were nothing at all.

"I pledge myself to protect you, Seren," Derian proclaimed, and he offered his warmest smile. The smile that could launch a thousand apologies and have each one gladly accepted. He placed a grubby, blood-covered hand upon her shoulder and squeezed it gently. It was not a touch of lust nor desire, but merely a gesture reassuring the girl that all would be well.

"You are one of us, Seren," he whispered, and wondered, was it too much or just enough?

Just right.

She sighed, deep in thought, and he sighed in agreement. They were in this together. Friendship first; perhaps in time, a little more. Her voice was strong and delightful to the ear. She looked into his eyes right down into his soul. His heart skipped a beat.

"I hate you," she said, and walked away, tightening her new cloak.

18

AFTER THE STORM

D erian stumbled towards his friends. His limbs felt unused and weak—as though freshly grown. Grisly images of demons and decapitations flashed through his mind, but he couldn't recall everything that had happened. He felt as though he'd just woken up after a debauched night's leisure and was only now remembering the evils committed. They should have been dead, torn apart into shards of raw meat for carrion, or moving through the belly of a monster, but they weren't. They were alive, and it was polished. Again.

"What did you do, Seren?" Natteo demanded.

Seren shrugged and held her cloak tightly around her, fending off the dawn's biting chill and denying the world any further sight of her nakedness. *Oh well. Living is enough.*

Natteo hid his fear well. "I remember pain, I remember teeth... and darkness... and something strange beyond. Something menacing. Did anyone else feel it?"

Beyond the darkness?

Somewhere beyond he'd sensed someone... something. A deity of great curiosity and greater power.

A grand demon?

It hadn't felt menacing. Though he had little memory of the ordeal beyond, it hadn't seemed too bad dying. Maybe he was getting better at it. "I felt something."

Derian's head hurt just thinking on the matter—much the same way it hurt when he looked into a night sky and wondered where it began and where it all ended. Sometimes, ignorance was a gift. Ignoring the pain and anger of death was also a gift.

"Reborn in fire. Boom, demon boom," Seren muttered, and she held her stomach where the peculiar tattooed mark of shining gold had once been.

"Demon boom?"

"Boom. People unboom." She made her hands into a vague circle and brought them out as though the circle grew. "Whoosh."

"Whoosh?"

"What else can you do?" Natteo asked distantly. He looked across the devastated battlefield as though remembering where the Crimson Hunters had charged into death, found it, and somehow crept away from it. It was hard not to be in fearful awe.

"Seren not make rebirth boom," Seren said, reaching down and taking another flower. After a moment, she returned it, but unlike before, it did not immediately recover. It wavered as though caught in the wind and fell in the mud. "Fading," she muttered to herself, and Derian left her to her savage murdering of flowers.

Even in the warmth and beauty of the first sunny morning since they'd landed on this cursed island, the field outside the town was a miserable sight. Scorched and sizzling demonic bodies of both canis and anculus lay strewn upon the ground, all the way from forest's edge to the gates of Treystone.

Steam rose into the sky where skin, not built for the harshness of this world's sun, burned where they lay. All the brutes lay flat where they'd fallen, as though a great explosion of cleansing wrath had killed them in one fell swoop. *Boom.* It was glorious and it was terrible, and Derian was scrambling through the bodies, searching for his dagger, when without warning something began to stir in his thoughts, in his gut, and something primal stirred his instincts.

"Oh, this cannot be?" Lorgan hissed.

"Oh, please, no," cried Kesta, for something unsettling began to happen around them.

Like a river's serenity lost to a skimmed stone, the valley began to ripple and churn. The bodies upon the land began to move. Scarred flesh, demonic spikes, and fur began to tremble and writhe, and the ripple became an ocean.

They were slow, as though they were moving through thick honey. The field became a rising cacophony of hissing and snarling as the sun's unforgiving rays continued their assault upon the creatures' bodies. Few of the lesser monsters of the source could stand the sun, and what charring had begun as they lay in near-death continued as they attempted to rouse themselves.

For a strange moment, Derian wondered what awfulness the beasts must have felt, to wake so feebly, in such pain. A part of him almost felt sympathy. Not a lot, though.

Thankfully, not all had survived the boom. Those nearest Seren's scorch mark were eviscerated. However, there were still hundreds remaining.

"They are too slow to be a threat," Natteo declared. He hovered over the still body of an enormous beast, and as though recalling some terrible event from another life, he shook his head and began digging around the creature. Within a breath, he recovered his blades and stabbed the motionless beast through its eye sockets until there remained only two open holes. "To the fires with you," he cursed, and then he stabbed it three more times where the heart might have been. The anculus still made no movement, and Natteo appeared dreadfully disappointed he couldn't kill it for its crimes. "This is too easy!" he shouted, falling upon another anculus demon crawling through the blood-soaked grass. He drove his dagger through the beast's head and held it until it fell still. "Good little beastie. Silencio is calling you."

"Kill them all."

Derian's mouth watered, and he found himself eager to join Natteo's murderous wrath. Instead of fear, he found himself exhilarated among the ruins of horn, flesh, and teeth, searching for his weapon.

"Slow, yes, but they are many," hissed Kesta, wading further into the river of bodies with blade in hand, stabbing and cutting. "Help us!" she cried to the figures watching in anxious silence at the wall of the sieged town.

Derian looked up and saw rows of faces, dazed like his own, looking back. Many had not fully awakened, and they lay strewn against the top of the wall with arms drooping lazily over the edge. The more alert struggled just to stand upright.

"Peasants," Kesta cursed, and spun back to task.

Lorgan recovered his own blade from the body of a canis beast. "This is on us, my comrades." He seemed perplexed as to how his weapon had gotten so far away from where he'd fallen, but soon enough he went to task again like a farmer tilling at the turn of season: a few steps forward, a quick thrust down through flesh, a swift recovery of blooded blade, on to the next. It was oddly rhythmical, and Derian, now with his own blade firmly in hand once more, found himself in similar poetic movements.

Even Seren joined the massacre. She recovered two arrows from vanquished monsters and fell upon any foe in her path. Her movements were graceful and assured, her speed was incredible, and her technique was flawless. Most of all, her knowledge of killing points was worryingly efficient. She struck flurries of combinations at every monster she passed, striking a weak point every time without breaking her stride. She appeared to stroll through the battlefield, killing effortlessly, and Derian wondered how a girl like that was so accomplished at such a young age.

Fighting an army of burning demons in the middle of the day was easy, he found, although he knew that some peasants with ideas above their stations might have an issue with killing supposedly defenceless monsters.

"Let's try to broker peace with these creatures, for they have braved the darkness to live in this world with us," he imagined them saying to each other in the safer back alleys of Dellerin, believing their own spitting rot, having never once faced something they couldn't tame with a few harsh words. Derian hated demonic beasts, but he truly loathed pompous, outspoken peasants and their entitled values.

The world isn't fair. Monsters are real. Bad things happen. Sticks and stones may break my bones, but demons are far worse than a few harsh words.

No amount of peaceful talking would stop these beasts from smothering the life out of the innocent villagers behind the wall, he knew. To the fires with the ill-informed, thought Derian. He would kill as many beasts as he could before they escaped.

He didn't know how long he waded among the monsters, slashing and stabbing, only that he killed a lifetime's worth in his first charge. By the time some of the creatures had recovered their senses and begun fleeing towards the treeline, most of the villagers had roused themselves enough to cheer. Derian didn't think any less of them for their appreciation of the brutality on show. He knew full well what terrors they had endured. Perhaps the path to recovery from anguish began with seeing the monsters vanquished this way?

The crowd howled triumphantly when Lorgan slipped behind a larger anculus beast as it attempted to stand, snapping its neck with a satisfyingly loud crack.

They roared lustily when Kesta, with gore-covered arrows, struck down a retreating canis who was but a couple of steps short of salvation beneath the shade of the treeline.

They applauded when Natteo giddily plunged both his blades into any demon searching for shade beneath the wall, and they took delight in the colourful curses he delivered as they died.

They cheered Seren loudest of all every time she sent an arrow into a creature's ear and out the other in a swift plunge, leaving her victim convulsing in the dirt.

It was easy; it became pageantry, and Derian appreciated the growing whoops and cheers the longer the slaughter continued. This felt like success. This felt like heroism. They were not some failed mercenary group with barely a recognised win to their name. They were elite warriors; they were champions; they were becoming legends. They might even get paid.

"Perhaps they've very little entertainment out here in the muck lands," Natteo suggested, sliding his dagger across the throat of a canis. He held the beast's spurting throat at an angle, allowing just the right amount of spray to fill the air, and a few members of the crowd clapped in appreciation. It was a smooth move, despite the goriness.

"You like this spitting mess?" he cried, offering them his most demented grin. If any other person wore that grin, it might have been unsettling, but blessed be that charmer. He was charismatic in his mania. "Yeah, you love it." He laughed wildly as he caught sight of another canis demon slithering away, desperate to escape but unable to summon its swiftness in daylight. "I bet you wished you'd stayed in your nightmare realm, you little fuker! Let's play!" he cried, falling upon the beast, and the crowd loved him for it.

"Show some decorum!" barked Lorgan from behind his mound of freshly reaped corpses.

"I just want to show them my swords," muttered Natteo, taking offence at Lorgan's reprimand. He had a point. They were some fine swords.

Efficient as the Crimson were, many nasties still needed killing. Many demons escaped their wrath and disappeared into cover. Perhaps had the peasants left the safety of their wall, they might have helped to wipe them out altogether. But peasants were peasants, and peasants didn't understand the way of things. The mercenaries knew the tables would be turned come nightfall. Come returning monsters.

Perhaps there are more things to worry about than a few hundred beasts, Derian thought.

Perhaps there really was a damaged monolith, hidden somewhere in these lands, and Seren had unwittingly breached it?

Perhaps her grand demon was already marching through the forest, drawn to this place like her demonlings.

Perhaps there were darker things afoot.

Perhaps this was an invading army sent by the Dark One in his attempt to control Luistra.

Perhaps these attacks were occurring throughout every isle of Dellerin.

Oh, spit on this.

Whatever the reasons, Kesta was right about the demons' predilection towards ruination—even at the expense of their own lives. Come nightfall, hunger would stir their simple minds into a frenzy. Those scarred and sun-scalded brutes who had escaped the battlefield would slither back with gnashing teeth and prey upon whomever stood behind the wall. Once again, Treystone would face the same horrors Kesta had endured. The Crimson Hunters had done fine, honourable things, but perhaps all they'd really given the town was false hope.

Derian thought on these miserable things for longer than he should have, and only the unexpected emergence of a massive anculus demon, rising from beneath the bodies of its brethren, drew him from his dreariness.

With skin sizzling like swine upon a spit, it stumbled awkwardly through the shards of bone and shredded entrails, and Derian spun towards it theatrically with dagger in hand before leaping gracefully.

He soared, the crowd cheered, and he cried out magnificently. It was epic—until the beast reached out and caught him in one powerful claw.

Not like this.

It lifted him up high, and Derian could see the burning steam emanating from the creature's bulbous arm. He thought this the funniest thing he'd ever seen, though he couldn't understand why.

"Should have worn a cloak," he gasped. His feet dangled in the air, scrambling for a foothold. The crowd gasped. A few cried out as though he were a favoured knight, felled in a tournament of gold. The beast roared demonically, for it knew no other way, and Derian felt the crunching pressure as his killer sacrificed the safety of retreat in favour of a final kill. His heart hammered and adrenalin pumped through his limbs as the call of darkness engulfed him. Yet he was not scared. He was furious with himself for allowing this doom to fall upon him.

Darkness.

Brightness.

Derian blinked a few times and wasn't sure what had happened. The darkness in his vision dissipated, and strangely enough, he stood unvanquished in front of an ocean of blood, a desert of intestines, and a tundra of bones and viscera. He vaguely remembered a large anculus demon having stood in that exact place only a few moments before.

"Whoa, that was brutal," Natteo offered, creeping cautiously up to him. Lorgan and Kesta kept their distance, savouring the moment and the respite it offered. Seren stood motionless, staring into the forest; she'd snapped both her arrows, but she still held them as though they were pristine killing tools. Perhaps they still were, given her ability. The battlefield had settled to a reassuring stillness. The monsters were either dead or retreating. At least for now.

"I did this?" Derian muttered, staring at a mess on the ground before him.

"Oh yeah, you did."

Derian couldn't look at the ruin he'd made of the creature. He felt foul, his head thumped, and a vast emptiness took him. He felt as though his very essence had been stripped away and thrown asunder. He lost the last few moments to a blur of horror and shimmering darkness, like waking from a dream so revolting that grasping it was like catching a burning ray of flame.

He felt as though another had taken his mind and body and swayed him to actions he thought horrendous. Through the daze, however, he knew what he had done, and he knew that he'd enjoyed it. Perhaps such cruelty was too shameful to remember.

Am I possessed?

Am I evil?

He had taken the demon apart with brutal savagery, and he had done so slowly, deliberately. He could have stopped sooner, should have stopped sooner, but killing the creature hadn't been enough. If Natteo's performance had been distasteful, his own had been abhorrent. He'd never thought panic could gift such ferocity and viciousness, but it had given these things generously. He'd broken away from the beast's grip by cutting its hand from its wrist. A clean cut, bone and all.

"You are a sick, sick boy," Natteo added, lifting the creature's frozen, eyeless head in the air. The stump of its neck bore marks where Derian had removed it with his teeth. *Wait, what?* Had it been his teeth? He remembered it had involved teeth.

"It needed doing," Derian offered, and that felt like the truth, but he knew better. He'd drenched his body in crimson, and his stomach sloshed with the warm fullness of demonic blood. He wondered should he speak to a healer about it? Or perhaps he should find a nice dark corner somewhere and throw up a pint of acidic hell juice? He didn't look forward to relieving himself any time soon.

"I think you scared the last of them off with that thing you did to its tail." Natteo picked up the chewed strip of flesh and sniffed it disapprovingly. Derian remembered a loud crunch and the astonished wail accompanying the act.

"That was the teeth part."

"I don't want to think about it."

"This thing must have tasted like—"

"Shut up, Natteo."

"In a good way, I mean," he said, as though his friend's sudden aptitude for torturous violence didn't upset him at all. Perhaps that was what best friends were good at—telling you it was okay to be a psychopathic demon slayer. "Gory things happen in battle. Better that than collapse in panic, I suppose." He tossed the tail back into the mess of demonic waste. "Or worse, collapse with a crushed windpipe—" He stopped mid-sentence and looked at Derian seriously. "I will never grab you by the throat ever again... Although if you could do what you did with my... tail... though a little more softly, then we can talk," he said, and Derian felt better.

"We survived this, brother," Derian said, and Natteo nodded in agreement. They had better get paid for this.

"Fine work, hunters!" Lorgan called from across the field. He trudged over, dragging his sword along the grass to remove what demonic blood and discarded intestine he could. He looked both exhausted and exhilarated. It was the same look any mercenary wore whenever payment was in the air. The terrible deed was done, and money was on all their minds.

He beckoned them over to stand with him at the front gate. "Try to look the part," he muttered through clenched teeth, as a gore-covered Kesta and a pristine-looking Seren joined them.

"Now that we've dealt with this, I have a genuine worry," Natteo whispered, as the town's gates swung open and daylight appeared between them. "Do you think the Army of the Dead will hold a grudge for what we did? It was better than killing them, right?" he added, convincing himself that using a bout of food poisoning was fair game.

Derian smiled and welcomed his friend's levity. "I'd say they've already placed a hefty death bounty on our heads from their chamber pots in the woods." He could see that Natteo was distraught. He got upset about the strangest things.

"Shut up, you idiots," Lorgan hissed.

"Sorry, sir."

"Sorry, sir."

The figure standing between the gates was unmistakably feminine—shapely despite the heavy garments. In the morning light, her hair shone a radiant blonde, and if she had been ten years younger, Derian might have formed charming courting words to offer. She was attractive, and she looked upon them with kind, striking eyes. Her smile was welcoming, and she swept gracefully from the entrance down through the debris of war as though walking upon a glade of marigolds and spring flowers.

"Thank you, brave heroes," she called out in an endearingly pleasant voice. Her boots were awkward in the terrain, her dress dragged out behind her and became stained in the blood, and her leather chest armour bounced loudly with every step. She looked like a peasant before battle. Prepared, but not well enough. She allowed excitement to get the better of her, and she greeted them as kin she had not seen in an age.

She reached Natteo first, took his hand, and fell to one knee, holding his grimy palm to her forehead. "Thank you, sir," she whispered, and Natteo was delighted. She then slipped away from him and took Derian's hand, repeated the greeting. He caught sight of the impressive gold and jewelled wedding band on her finger. Whoever she was, she was of money.

"You are welcome… madam?" he replied, searching for the right term.

She nodded in delight before turning to Kesta, who received the same greeting. However, instead of dropping to a knee, the woman stroked Kesta's thick, curly hair closely and muttered something like, "Brave, brave warrior goddess."

Kesta merely nodded and tugged her hair away as politely as she could.

The woman then offered Seren a careful smile and took both her hands in her own. "You are one of them, aren't you?" she whispered, and Seren raised a curious eyebrow. The woman's tone was wistful, like that of a zealot of faith. He'd heard that same tone from a few lunatics in his home town. Ooh, they were the worst. Judgemental, erratic, and easily manipulated. All it took was someone mentioning seeing a vision of a dog in the clouds and they would take to the hills worshipping. Derian had always ensured he chose the rainiest of days to send them on their dreary pilgrimages. There wasn't much too do in his village for entertainment.

"I am Seren."

"I am Keralynn, the Watcher of Treystone. It is good to meet you, Seren," she offered, and then she slid away from her to greet Lorgan, whereupon her smile become magnificent. Lorgan stood as straight as he could, though, as usual, he betrayed himself as a man worried. He had business to conduct.

"Where is Olmin?" he began.

"Olmin died the first night," Keralynn replied. Olmin had been the man who set the bounty for the lecherous demon.

"He was one of the first taken back over the wall by a clawed monster," she said, placing her hand upon Lorgan's chest. "There were two dozen fiends the first night; they tore us apart."

"Well, I had business with him," Lorgan countered, unmoved by news of the man's death. Money was money, and death complicated matters. Out here in the mud lands, the Guild's interference into broken contracts would take months to rectify. Nothing was ever easy.

"Any business you had with him is now with me," she said carefully. She kept her hands upon his chest. Without warning, she took a breath, gazed into his eyes, and kissed him upon one cheek and then the other. She finished by kissing him lightly upon the lips. She did not break the kiss immediately. It lingered a fraction of a breath longer than was usual for a traditional greeting kiss.

"She's using her tongue," whispered Natteo.

"So is he," Derian countered.

"I think Lorgan will like the new leadership," whispered Natteo, as the woman withdrew, blushing, and began leading them into to the town. Lorgan's face was stern with worry, but there was a crack of a smile trying desperately to free itself.

"Shut up, you idiots," Kesta hissed, though she too was biting back a smile.

19

WIPE YOUR BOOTS

K eralynn hid her awkwardness beneath a hasty retreat towards the gate and the growing procession within. She bade them follow, and the Crimson Hunters obeyed her wishes as a pack. The sound of the crowd, which had fallen silent in her wake, began to grow once more.

"I think you might have a potential suitress there," Kesta said, shoving her commander lightly as they walked side by side.

"I'm not sure we can trust her," he replied, allowing the shove to unsettle his march, and Kesta's sigh was loud enough for the rest to hear. Even a spectacular victory in view of an appreciating audience wasn't enough to lessen his apprehension about what awaited them. "Besides, she might look to undercut our deal or offer further employment," he added, and suddenly Natteo and Derian's smiles faltered.

The town wouldn't survive the next attack—the walk up towards its entrance had told them that much. The walls were cheap timber, and they were neither sturdy nor tall enough to keep out a horde of either humans or monsters. They had not even treated the front gates with the craftsmanship deserving of a town as big as Treystone. No reinforced timber beams to hold against an unruly mob's crush, no ironed spikes atop its crown, not even a proper guard post to stare suspiciously at them as they marched through.

Forget additional work. Let's get the money and get out of this town before noon.

A few feet above the gate was a long platform, and Derian saw heads peeking over. Some were children, but others were nervous adults. All were keen to see the heroes who'd appeared at their lowest ebb and saved them all from certain death.

"We're not staying long, are we, boss?" Natteo asked.

"Don't you worry, little one. We'll stay as needed," Kesta interrupted, before Lorgan could commit himself to anything, and Derian felt a sinking feeling.

Please, let there be no madness again.

The night before, a wave of insanity had fallen upon them. They had waged war on an undefeatable enemy, and though nobody spoke it aloud, they had died, and they had died brutally. Seren suggested the tattoo had been the link to their resurrection, and as appealing as her navel was without the gold design marring it, he'd prefer her with the rebirth boom enchantment any season of the year.

There would be no third resurrection, he decided. In the light of day, with no rash thoughts of heroism to a failing town, things changed, and they would make better decisions. A job was a job. Only a fool took payment for suicide. Unless the money was life changing.

"They have come two nights now, and it has taken its toll. They took many and left as many dead behind," Keralynn called as she led them through the waiting crowd. The wretched inhabitants gazed gratefully upon him, and Derian avoided their eyes lest they see how desperate he was to flee as soon as possible. He felt pats upon his back, whispered thank-yous, and source blessings, and he tried to ignore them all.

Derian could see scattered signs of invasion throughout. The first clue was the splotches of blood along the inner wall, where monsters had scaled it and slipped over. The next clue was the vast numbers of dead. He counted at least two dozen broken bodies laid out, all neat and formal, at the corner of the entrance. Carrion birds watched in stony silence from the wall, now and then dropping silently, hoping to peck at bloodied, staring faces, but they were quickly scattered by those sitting vigil.

Some towns had their own traditions for sending the dead into the darkness; some used fire, and others opted for burial. This town had a river running right through it. It wouldn't have surprised him to see the townspeople float the bodies on down the valley, each one with a garland of flowers resting upon their chest. As it was, however, he could see the beginnings of a pyre, and so he offered a delicate, respectful bow to those gathering the layers of kindling. He had no time for these types of rituals, himself— dead was dead.

As for his own kin, well, he'd placed the ruined body of his mother upon the passing cart and watched it trundle away slowly with the rest of the murdered, and that was that. His father had allowed him to get drunk for the first time that night. He'd then started a fight with an older girl he'd always had a fancy for, and she'd knocked out one of his teeth. She'd still kissed him later that night—and delivered other naughty things the hour after that—so overall, he'd decided it was a good day. He'd really liked that girl until she'd knocked out two of his oldest friend's teeth a week later, and, well, things had occurred as they did. He ran his tongue through the gap in the back of his mouth and decided he didn't really miss his youth at all.

They continued through the town's small square, and his feet squelched in the mud that was typical of all small towns lacking stone pathways. He hated towns, always had. Nothing good ever came from collecting humans together and forcing civility upon each other.

He looked to the sky and the rising sun and began counting the hours until it set again. When he wasn't having nightmares about monsters dragging him down to the darkness below, he'd frequently suffered uncomfortable dreams of being dreadfully late. Walking this town reminded him of that feeling.

"Thank the gods of the source you came to us," Keralynn said, finding her voice and distracting him from his worry.

"There are no gods in the source," countered Lorgan. "If there ever were, they're absent now. All that're left are demons."

"Oh, find some faith. All things happen for a reason, Lorgan of the Crimson Hunters," she countered, before delivering a smile that could have felled trees. A cynical man might think she was playing a part, a believer might believe she was quite taken with the older man seeking love, but a wise mercenary might suspect she was one of those allured by the work of mercenaries. A life spent without adventure bred desires for excitement. It caused strange attractions for those who walked close to death. Derian wouldn't have minded one of those reserved ladies—he'd heard that desperate ones even had an eye for apprentices. Raw and wriggling and all that. He'd happily play, as long as there was time before sunset.

As they walked farther in, more and more of the crowd gathered around them, marched with them, and called out to them until Keralynn, keen to keep Lorgan and his mercenaries all to herself, took charge.

"Leave them be," she called. "There is no rush to meet and wish good things upon the heroes." Derian didn't like those words. *No rush.* Neither did Natteo, who raised the most suspicious eyebrow he could muster. The crowd parted but continued their cheering. To be more accurate, they filled the morning air with grateful, desperate, pleading cries of gratitude.

Derian tried to offer no smile, for fear that they take it as confirmation that salvation marched in red-tinted battle gear, but it was a difficult task as his every step received a round of applause. Natteo received the same treatment and took it all in his stride. He accepted each pat on the back as though he were a war general observing a pleasing parade of arms. Even Lorgan allowed some grubby hands to take hold of his own. He grunted a few appreciative words and eased past the gathering crowd, who, despite their enthusiasm, parted in the tall man's wake.

Only Kesta appeared uncomfortable with the praise. She hung back and muttered blessings for the fallen under her breath, and the crowd must have appreciated her gesture, for they allowed her a moment's quiet before she caught up, whereupon she accepted healthy and hearty embraces that she had little intention of enjoying. Stray hands grasped at her impressive braided hair, and she hissed them away easily enough.

Seren trailed a few steps behind, her eyes alive with apparent delight at seeing the calamity that had befallen the town—the signs of claw and hoof on the wall, the mud, and the shattered doorways of the small buildings they passed. "Hello, friends," she said with wonderment as a portion of the crowd fell upon her with unrestrained reverence. But they did not embrace her as a friend, hero, or anything in between. Instead, they fell to their knees in the mud and whispered in prayer, and she, their deity, came alive. There were a couple dozen worshippers, and Seren stared as their whispers grew to muttering, then to humming. Whatever the melody was, it was unsettling. They were demented in their adoration, and Derian had seen how swiftly adoration turned to muggings among the zealous. *Especially if we piss them off by leaving this town.*

Seren must have sensed it too, for she smiled warily before bidding them rise, but her followers would not be silenced nor moved. They liked it in the mud, apparently. They continued their humming, and Derian wondered what they had seen of the battle from the safety of the walls. He had a sinking feeling they had seen … everything … and now believed Seren was capable of resurrecting the dead. She'd suggested it was not of her doing, but Derian had an uneasy feeling that this crowd might argue differently. Maybe he could spot a few false omens in the clouds to distract them should things take a turn.

"Strange, pretty," Seren whispered, as though hearing the worshippers' melody for the first time. It had turned to nonsensical singing now. After a moment, Kesta tugged her gently to follow.

Treystone's reaction differed from the usual suspicious glares the Crimson Hunters suffered when entering settlements. All mercenaries faced derision when entering a town, no matter its size—for the blood on their hands, and for the tasks they were hired for. It wasn't always heroic demon-slaying. Sometimes it was a little dirty assassination that brought them over a town's threshold, and any group appearing at a town's gates was watched with unease, especially by folk with things to hide.

It didn't matter that Lorgan would never accept a murder contract. He'd always said 'Those contracts could change the world dreadfully,' and insisted that he 'wanted none of that.' Derian thought it was foolishness; some people just needed killing. As long as they were bad and the pay was good, what was the problem? He'd argued as much to Lorgan, who'd sighed and walked away without offering his own thoughts on the matter, and Derian had taken the win.

"We've never needed a night watch along the walls, so when it happened, we weren't ready," Keralynn said, pointing to a few buildings where the splattering was thicker. She led them towards the far end of the town, following a path between two lines of small hovels, all made from light brick with yellow pinewood walls supporting thinly-thatched roofs. Derian counted twenty on either side, all the way along. Some had little fires burning outside, and others looked abandoned. Some had life and others did not. Derian wondered how many former occupants were lying cold in the mud at the gates.

"Different land, yet same spitting life," he muttered to himself, peering through one gaping doorway and seeing the small familiar beds, side by side, where a young couple might have cared for a child. No space for more than a few cupboards and shelves for food and a few bottles of sine to drink the frustrating life away. Give him a bed beneath the stars with the trees as his privacy over such luxuries any day. Give him a sword over a shovel for the land, or a shield over a pick-axe in a mine.

"What did you say?" Natteo asked, and Derian shook his

head. No point discussing his miserable childhood in a little hovel with unloving parents in a town that worshipped Seeva beasts. He wondered if this town had any such beliefs. Probably, considering how swiftly they'd fallen to their knees before Seren.

He watched the sun again and reassured himself they would be free of this place soon enough. Keralynn led them onwards, past the smaller hovels to the larger structures reserved for those of a wealthier disposition. Those who'd benefited greatly from Gold Haven's interests. There were far fewer of these, but they were four times larger than the hovels and stood two floors up. All of them were closer to the outer walls and had been hit much harder than the hovels.

"They ravaged the elders' quarters most severely," their blonde host whispered. "It's why I greet you now and not Olmin."

They passed a long building with a few delicately-painted letters above its front door, and Derian surmised it was a tavern from what he could see within. Beyond that were a few wooden stalls that counted for a fledgling unattended market, and at last they crossed a bridge over a swift-flowing river at the town's far corner. Unlike their carelessness with the gate, the townspeople had had the good sense to ensure that the hole in the wall where the river entered was secured with iron bars.

"What's in there?" Lorgan asked, pointing. On the other side of the dark, muddy water stood a massive warehouse, likely filled with a cold season's storage of food and such. One of Gold Haven's bonuses, no doubt. Derian's mouth watered at the prospect of raiding the stores during a quieter moment. Maybe not him, but Natteo could slip in through one of the upper windows with no problem at all. He felt a little ashamed at his wandering mind. These people were going through bad times as it was. Why add to their misery by stealing some honey cakes? However, when the town was overrun, it would go to waste anyway. Better someone enjoyed the rewards within.

"Um… eh… nothing at all," Keralynn lied, and Derian licked his lips thoughtfully. *More than honey cakes, so.*

"This town is an open gate to those beasts," Kesta said suddenly.

"We tried to man the walls, but were it not for your appearance last night, we would have suffered even greater losses." Keralynn looked at Seren. "That healing, life-returning light you brought shone brighter than the day… and it took the night from them completely."

Really don't like that tone.

"It was a godly thing," Seren whispered.

Rebirth boom.

"A divine miracle from the source," Keralynn said, and Seren shrugged—for her interest was drawn to a gathering of children who emerged from the warehouse. They were bolder than the adults. Word travelled quickly in a town as small as this, and they came to gaze upon the heroes who had brought daylight to night. They were dressed in muddy clothes, like most children in dirty little towns, and many of them bore dark reddish splatter-marks on their dreary garments. They watched and whispered, and their daring encouraged some of the adults to creep forward, Seren's admirers most of all. From a safe distance, they began chanting, lauding her apparent greatness—as though she were a dog-shaped shrine, Derian thought unkindly.

The group walked onward in Keralynn's wake.

"We have some business that you must honour," Lorgan said, when they reached an official-looking office in the shade of a mill's sails at the far end of the town. Derian remembered it from their first visit. Happier times, accepting a generous contract.

"We will give you whatever you need," Keralynn said to Lorgan, and Lorgan alone, as she opened her office door and bade him enter the dark room within. Keralynn had the lure for their fearless leader something terrible, and Natteo sniggered loudly.

"Enjoy yourself," he said, his eyes alight with mocking, and Derian could see that holding his tongue was near killing him. Keralynn ignored him and, with practised, waving hips, she glided through the doorway, leaving the mercenaries behind.

"You, with me," Lorgan muttered to Derian. "Everyone else, keep a watch," he added, keeping his eyes away from Kesta's murderous glare. She was always his second when conducting and concluding business. When a deal was struck, the most precarious moment of the mission was collecting payment. As was ensuring no payment was placed upon a long finger. All for the promise of further riches for future exploits.

"If you speak, then speak wisely, Derian. Best you learn this part of our art," Lorgan said, patting the younger man's shoulder. Derian suspected that Lorgan would choose payment now over Kesta's honourable ways.

No problem. Also, leading by three pats again.

"Keep your dagger handy. Nothing more precarious than a little bartering," he said.

"Don't sell us a weak bidding," Natteo warned, taking hold of Derian's shirt. He pointed to the sky and the growing sun, his meaning clear. The sands of time were slipping.

"Trust me. I'm no idiot," Derian promised.

20

DEALS BETWEEN DOOMED MEN

"We have the gold. Oh, don't worry about your payment. We keep our word just fine," Blair said. No, that wasn't accurate at all. He didn't just say it: he sneered it.

It was painful doing business with a man like Blair, thought Derian. Thin face, clean-shaven—despite the two-day death watch—and black greasy hair, slicked back with cooking fat, no doubt. Cold, politically-minded eyes and all. Derian did not trust this man. Not one bit.

Lorgan, however, didn't seem to mind doing business with the recently promoted town's leadership in the form of a slithering snake of a mayor ruling from behind a desk and an attractive blonde in arms caring for the town's defences. It was more or less like most other governances.

"A word is a fine thing," the old merc offered. He sat in a leather chair facing the greasy mayor and Keralynn. With welcomes secured, business got underway. Worryingly, new deals were in the air.

Derian stood behind Lorgan, keeping an eye on the window of the little official office and the rising sun shining through. Plenty of hours left, he told himself. However, the sun seemed brighter through the glass now, and after brighter light the day would speed by. Soon after, evening would sneak right up.

A man could go mad sitting in an office counting the hours, Derian thought absently.

"In fact, how about a little honey for the... miracle at the front gate?" Blair said, and he slid a second pouch across the desk that separated them. He let it rest by the first pouch, and Derian smiled. There was nothing prettier than those golden coins with the demonic flying dragons upon their shimmering surfaces.

Lovely.

"What did it feel to know death? And to rise above it like an angel of the source?" Keralynn asked quietly.

Lorgan took the pouch. "Can't really remember what happened after I fell, except that I got back up." He began counting their fortune.

Derian remembered some of it. His mind flickered back to the vast emptiness and the strange presence.

After a swift shudder of the soul, Derian looked around the office, searching for a distraction. It was a fine office, he supposed. There were a few shelves of files and ledgers running the length of one wall, and he surmised that every mining town needed books to keep itself in order. He shuddered a second time, thinking of living a life with nothing but words. Writing and reading and spelling. Not to mention the suffocating evils of grammar. He thought it a wasted life, and he counted his ignorance towards scholarly things as a blessing in a place like this.

The only real object of interest was a picture hanging high above the window, away from the sun's glimmering rays. It was old and sloppily finished, but it was a striking image of

Heygar, the last real hero in Dellerin, the lost leader of the Hounds. The legend who would return when the world had fallen to ruin.

How much worse can the world get?

The figure stood magnificently in shiny silver armour, radiant despite the artist's weak strokes, surrounded by his comrades, epic and undefeated. Stories of the Seven were a nice tale for children, but Derian thought it strange to hang such a piece in the place traditionally reserved for a town's coat of arms.

"The girl is no deity. She is a weaver," Blair muttered to Keralynn, as though he were a bitter wretch of an instructor speaking to a dunce. To Lorgan he spoke coldly. "We do not welcome weavers in this town, and sieged ruin or not, we wish to have Treystone remain as it is. We will do anything to ensure this," he warned.

"So best we conclude our business swiftly," Lorgan said, and Derian liked this talk.

"Hush, Blair. The girl is welcome. I pledged for her," Keralynn said, and Blair turned to argue, but after a moment's pause, he fell silent. Perhaps threatening the mercenary they were attempting to coerce into employment wasn't the right move.

She continued, leaning back in her chair, allowing her impressive breastplate to look its best. "We are nothing but a humble town of farmers and miners. A fine company like yours could earn enough gold to swim in, should you come to our aid," she said. Lorgan shrugged in indifference, and she was crestfallen.

Not the hero you were hoping for, is he?

She touched her lips with quivering fingers. Her bright demeanour hung by a thread. Derian was learning the art of deals first-hand from his master, and he thought it an interesting thing. Saying nothing of value, Lorgan had easily pulled the rug from under their boots and swiftly doubled the cost of whatever they dared offer. Not that they'd take the offer.

"What do you offer?" Derian asked, and Lorgan gave him a quick glance of approval. He wasn't there to listen. Better they know two men needed impressing.

Blair leaned forward in his chair. "We need you to fight for us. We need you to set up defences that can withstand a horde. We are no fools; the demon's stone caused this. We are no strangers to a few nasties making their way to our gates, but this swarm is too much, and—"

Lorgan cut him off. "Whoa, there, my friend. What demon stone?"

"The one in the cave in the forest."

Oh, spit on this. A hidden monolith.

"Are you telling me there is a source monolith stone standing somewhere near this town?"

"I assumed you knew. I assumed Olmin told you before you took the contract."

Oh, no. Oh, no. Oh, no.

"I think Olmin forgot."

The air in the room thinned.

Blair went pale. "As a rule, in this town we don't speak of the vile, jagged rock. The last thing we desire are *his* acolytes of the dark making their pilgrimages to this place, searching for enchantments that no longer exist."

Lorgan was furious. "You are near a monolith and you think you can keep it a secret?" Derian could see his knuckles turn white.

Blair appeared to have had this conversation before. "We stay silent, and the world remains undisturbed. Anguis, the

Dark One, has no need to cast his sight near us. Tell me, does it really matter?"

"Where is it?" Derian demanded.

"A day's ride or so south, where the forest is greyest," Blair replied quietly, as though revealing the location would make matters worse.

"I think I know the place," Lorgan muttered, and he eyed Derian. Sounded like a fine place for a hidden monolith to stand. Also sounded like a fine place to find a vector demon and a naked girl.

Derian shook his head.

Idiot peasants.

"You brought a weaver to our gates, so let us call our misstep as making it even, my friend," Blair hissed, and this time Derian's knuckles whitened.

"We could have located the lecherous demon far quicker had we known of this rock sooner," Lorgan said, and his voice was deadly calm again. He'd concealed what anger he'd had. Derian was incensed, however.

"Typical peasants," he growled, and Lorgan hissed him to silence. Being called a peasant meant little to any land labourer, but to a mercenary, it was the gravest of insults, implying that rather than fighting to survive, they merely cowered behind walls, hoping for miracles. There was no greater criticism. Derian had more to say. "Maybe that's why—"

"You could have told us," said Lorgan, cutting him off mid-sentence.

"Olmin could have. So, take up the matter with him," Blair countered, hiding his irritation behind a false apologetic smile. He was nearly as skilled as Lorgan.

Derian almost blurted out that the monsters were attacking because a certain event had shaken the stone's ability to keep both worlds locked away from each other. He almost suggested the severity of this event happening so close to the stone.

Oh, right.

Derian suddenly realised why Lorgan gave nothing away. If Blair learned of Seren's 'birth,' there might be a few more questions. There might be resentment from the peasants if they added up all the factors and counted their dead. Perhaps they might truly despair to learn a grand demon was close by, just itching to get through. Perhaps it was wise to stay silent and give nothing away. They thought her a simple weaver, and that was fine for now.

Maintaining his hard-won calm, Lorgan said, "We will not speak of the stone beyond these walls, my friends." He passed both pouches to Derian, who gladly received their healthy, clinking weight. "You have my condolences, and you have my hopes for fortunes, but the Crimson Hunters are not interested in earning anything more."

Fantastic, thought Derian. It was a fine plan to get Seren far from the stone. Things might settle down with her gone. Or get far worse. Who knew?

"Help us," Keralynn cried. She took Lorgan's hands and squeezed them warmly. A few days earlier and Lorgan might have grimaced. As it was, he allowed her touch. She had a nice smile and a nice touch of desperation to her.

"You suggest we will swim in gold? I think we'll all drown in blood," he whispered, but he did not pull his hands away.

"Take a moment, Lorgan," Blair said, his previous arrogance giving way to despair. Lorgan was no gold-blinded mercenary, and the man had now discovered it.

"I don't have many moments to spare."

Blair shook his head in desperation. "We have walls and

willing defenders, we have weapons, and yes, we have wealth —more than anything you've ever dreamt upon. But for everything we have, we are not wise in the ways of warfare. We are the body; we will respond to your will. Please—we have sent willing riders out for reinforcements. Our town is too important to be ignored. A few days is all we need before a battalion from Gold Haven reaches us."

"You know this for certain?" Derian asked, and Blair squirmed. *So a week, more likely.*

Keralynn shook her head. "They will come within two days."

"That's a fine offer," Lorgan said, "but we will not stay behind these walls to die. If any of you want to ride out with us this day, you are welcome," he offered, and Derian knew that tone. Nothing would change his mind. Not even Kesta.

"We have old, infirm, and injured. We are not mercenaries! We would never leave others willingly to their doom!" Blair shouted, and Keralynn hissed him to silence. A spitting argument full of venom would hardly turn the deal.

"Do not beg us to die with you," Derian said, and once more Lorgan nodded in agreement. Derian wondered if he had a natural gift for this game.

"I trust you will allow us safe passage to leave?" Lorgan asked, and Blair nodded in defeat. He gestured offhandedly to the freedom of the doorway and the doomed world outside, and despite his earlier disdain, Derian felt sorry for the man, whose face had turned ashen.

However, if Blair had admitted defeat, Keralynn was resolute.

"Mercenaries have no gods but the weight of their pouches," she whispered. "Surely in honour of the greatest of your kind, your brave Crimson Hunters might lead us to survival."

She pointed to the picture of Heygar and his Hounds, and Derian almost laughed at the attempted con. As though a legend was likely to sway any of them. As if things like lost heroes returning at the darkest hour to save them all could really happen.

Oh, hush yourself, pretty lady. At least double the bounty before playing upon sentimentality.

"He was our chosen son," she whispered with unrestrained awe, and Derian sighed loudly in reply. "And he was my kin," she also whispered in that same tone, and Derian admired her commitment.

"Is that so?" he said mockingly.

"This is my mother's painting. A gift she created from the memory of her only brother so that all who do business in this town would know its legacy. His legacy," she said, trailing off as she touched the painting, and Lorgan laughed bitterly.

"I'm sure every man, woman, or child would claim as much to get their way. Or else they might just as swiftly claim to know his fate, should they have need of it." Lorgan stood up to look at the painting more closely. He was overcome with sadness, as most mercenaries were when talking of heroic legends. All mercenaries wanted to be Heygar of the Hounds or Erroh of the Outcasts. Who didn't want to be a legend? Who didn't want to walk their path?

"It is an unusually accurate representation compared to most other pieces I've seen," he noted, and Derian could now see the glimmer of resemblance between painting and woman.

Hey, maybe it is true. Heroes had to be born someplace.

Even Blair softened as he gazed upon the picture. "What Keralynn says is true enough, and though you might forsake us in our darkest time, a better man might resist mocking our history in the same breath as the one condemning us to doom."

"All apologies," Derian offered, and got to his feet. It was time for him and Lorgan to leave with their fine pouches of wealth. A few hours in the saddle were calling, and with them a nice taste of escape from death.

Lorgan, however, touched the painting as Keralynn had. He did it like a man who believed in prophecies. He looked like a man wanting to honour a legend. He looked broken, and Derian thought this worrying.

"So, you suggest we might swim in gold?" Lorgan asked, sitting back down again.

21

IT'S WHAT WE DO

Outside the office, the crowd were positively delirious upon hearing Keralynn's address. She must have been born for public speaking, as she controlled them with ease, and they loved her for it.

And why wouldn't they? She was delivering them from death.

Natteo leaned toward Derian and spoke in hushed tones, but there was no disguising his dismay at hearing the news— nor avoiding whose blame he believed it fell upon.

Still, though, Derian tried to stand his ground. "I don't know what happened. We were out the door with gold upon our waists, and he just turned his thoughts with no warning," he whispered, meeting Natteo's killing stare. He could see it in his friend's face: Natteo would get him back when he least expected it, and Derian wouldn't begrudge him a little vengeance either. Derian felt just as aggrieved.

"We'd already be out the gates with bellies full of wine and the wind at our backs, if I'd been in the room," Natteo hissed.

"I know."

"I can't stay in this town." He dropped his head in despair and pulled a small dagger free, eyeing it in the sun before spinning it a few times until it was nothing but a blur. It was something to do while panicking.

"I'm sorry."

"You can smell the looming death!" he snapped, and then caught himself before saying anything more, lest one of the townspeople eavesdrop on him. He leant back against the stone wall and shaded his eyes from the sun, all the while concentrating on spinning his dagger. He'd once told Derian that he only felt alive when he held a weapon. They were his only treasured possession. Derian had asked, but he'd never given the reason. "Maybe if I cut you a few times that would make me feel better," he muttered, like a child denied his first glass of sine.

"Not the face."

"Then what's the point? No one will notice 'I love Natteo' branded on your rear."

Derian smiled weakly and turned back to watch Keralynn address the crowd. He could feel a hundred sets of eyes upon him, on all of them, and a trickle of sweat ran down his forehead. He hadn't stopped revisiting the conversation back in the office. Even now, he didn't think he could have done anything differently. "I'm as angry as you," he whispered out of the corner of his mouth, "but if it'll make you feel better, my skin is your canvas," he joked, and Natteo smiled hopelessly.

"I'm scared, Derian. I'm really scared."

"I am too."

"Actually, I'm always scared, but this is worse. This is something I feel deep in my bones. I've died more times than most people I know. I really don't understand why martyrs are into it so passionately. Death is spitting awful. And… and… there's something beyond the dark."

"We might not die," Derian argued, and the false positivity tasted like ash on his tongue.

"I've far too much love to give this world. Also, I think I'm in love," he said grinning, as though humour could carry him away from dread. He spun the blade once more before returning it to its scabbard at his waist, but not before swiping it at Derian's forearm, drawing a thin line of blood. Subtle enough that no one saw. "You had it coming, and I aim to get my revenge before I die," he hissed.

"I didn't think you'd cut me. I expected a slap. At most, a punch in the face," Derian muttered.

"It's so you remember me when I'm dead."

Derian suddenly felt compelled to embrace his friend. *Perhaps not in front of the crowd.* "If you die, I won't be far behind, brother." Derian examined the cut. It wasn't too bad, but it would sting something awful.

"No, you will survive this. I feel that in my bones, too," Natteo said, and he spun away from Derian to return his charming gaze back to the crowd—to play the part of heroic mercenary like the rest of them.

Kesta took the news of their employment as though she were a rodenerack gifted a delicious wheel of cheese curd on a sea barge. She offered nothing as extravagant as a smile, but her eyes burned with more vigour than usual. Upon hearing Lorgan's quiet affirmation that death, destruction, and disastrous defending were in their near future, she'd swiftly fallen into duty. As Keralynn addressed the crowd, she stared at the town's banner hanging out over the wall and mumbled a prayer for the dead under her breath. Derian wondered if she would have stayed in this town, regardless.

What does she have to live for?

Peasants said all mercenaries hid desires of their death in warefare, and perhaps Kesta was no different. He thought about her painful words the previous night, and he wondered if she hadn't always been waiting for something like this. Perhaps she was satisfied to die with her Crimson family.

Seren was indifferent on the matter, and she had fine reason to be, for the peasants distracted her with their worshipping. Somewhere along the way, they had learned her name and now sang chants of her greatness. The tunes were unnervingly catchy, and she appeared oddly unhappy with the matter. At least she was no longer casting venomous glances at Derian every few breaths. That was something, he thought.

Keralynn finished her words, and beside her, Blair stayed silent. Lorgan began to speak now, and he did so as if he'd spent a lifetime in the realm of political strife.

"Cut that chanting crap," he barked, and the crowd of worshippers fell silent. "My name is Lorgan, and we are the Crimson Hunters. If you want to live these next few nights you will listen. You will obey every word I say, and every thurken word that any of my mercenaries say." He took a moment to wipe a little spit from the side of his mouth and eyed the watching faces. Derian thought he was impressive. "There will be no hesitation, no challenge, and no whining like cantuses, lest you meet my sword." He tapped the hilt of his weapon and continued on threatening the crowd for a while. Derian imagined that if Lorgan ran for office, he was the type of politician who would stand at the ballot with a weapon in hand and earn whatever votes he needed.

Who'd argue such a tactic?

As it was, Lorgan's first speech seemed to inspire the

confidence of the townspeople. Emboldened, he next led them to believe that his mercenaries were an elite outfit. Derian couldn't help standing with his chest puffed out, as though this praise was routine. It felt like a hundred pats on the back. When Lorgan finished, the crowd applauded wildly, their eyes bright, apparently filled now with a depthless faith in their new saviours. He ushered them away with orders to eat heartily and rest for a few hours, and to their credit, they filed obediently away to their homes, or what remained of them, and left the mercenaries to their peace.

"This is all going to end in blood and tears—and a mushed Natteo," Natteo muttered unhappily.

"We are mercenaries, young one. It won't be the first time you've faced unenviable odds," Lorgan replied.

"It'll be the last."

Lorgan slowly took in the town and its shabby barricades. Any fool could improve the obvious weaknesses in their defences, but to survive a focussed attack for any amount of time was likely to take some wilier skills. Skills learned only in great conflicts. However, none of them had ever tasted war, for as reviled as the Dark One was, no collection of lands had ever gone up against him. At least, not since the beginning of his reign. He had brought nightmares, misery, and segregation between races, but he'd also brought a delicate kind of peace. It was a bad time to be a soldier waiting patiently in a barracks for any word of conflict. The world had not known open warfare since the fall of the last king, Lemier the Wise.

And the slaughter of Karkur.

"We will probably die, but we will die well, Natteo. Isn't that a worthy cause?" Kesta asked quietly.

"No, that's just stupid. I'd prefer to live and get drunk, get married, get a better haircut, and maybe get a cat while I'm at it."

Lorgan countered, and his words sounded deluded as he did. "This town is sacred. We will defend it. We just need to rouse these people into a little warmongering. We have a wall, and we have warriors willing to fight atop it. What else do we need?"

Natteo knew the answer. "We have peasants with pitchforks. That's what we have. It's pathetic and pitiful."

Lorgan smacked the back of his head.

"Look beyond your terror. A few hard days and we'll earn enough money to live well. We'll earn great renown and make a name for ourselves, and we'll even get entitled status in the Guild." He placed his hand upon Natteo's shoulder and held it like a father would. "We'll do enough to look ourselves in the mirror."

"I already enjoy looking at myself in the mirror," muttered Natteo, but he didn't pull away from their leader's grasp. It was worth at least two pats on the back.

He's catching up.

Kesta continued to stare at the banner waving delicately in the wind. "I'm proud of what we are doing, Lorgan," she whispered with such warmth that Lorgan smiled.

"This is idiocy," Derian hissed.

"The idiot is right. We will die in this place," Natteo agreed, standing with his friend.

"No, this is an opportunity. You complain about wealth, about grandness, and you pledge to yourselves about what fantastic mercenaries you are both going to be when you've learned to grow hair on your chest," Lorgan growled.

"Wait, you can learn to grow chest hair?" Derian asked, and received a slap of his own.

"I feel something has destined us to do this," Lorgan said.

"Not everyone die," Seren said. "Only some."

"See? The strange girl from the demon realm agrees," Kesta said.

Natteo folded his arms as petulantly as he could. He saved this for precarious times only, when he'd lost the argument but hadn't yet had his fill. "Pledge to me I will definitely not die in this place, Lorgan, and I will offer no further argument," he said.

"On my honour, I promise that you won't die in this place," Lorgan said, and he spun away towards the nearest ladder reaching up to the small walkway along the wall. Seren strolled along after him, no doubt eager to see the world from a different perspective. Kesta followed, and Derian did a step after that. Discussion complete, it was time to move on.

"You know, I'm not sure he meant that," Natteo muttered, following them.

By the time the sun had moved another arm's length, disbelief and disappointment had turned to focus and fortitude. In fact, it was Natteo who first pointed out that there weren't enough ladders spread out along the wall for swift ascent, and Lorgan scribbled a few words into the little leather journal in which he planned most failing plans.

Derian pointed out that all beasts of the source feared the touch of fire, and Lorgan approved of the little knowledge he had, while Kesta suggested raising the townspeople's morale as a keen ally in battle. Lorgan scribbled this down, too, and drew a few lines beneath one of the chosen words. Seren pointed out that the blood spilled from the demons would 'make land fertile.' Lorgan didn't appear to know what to do with this knowledge, but nodded appreciatively anyway.

They walked the town wall twice in a few breaths short of

an hour, and Derian watched with curiosity as the villagers went to their regular tasks as though this were just an ordinary day. Some, but not all. For every man or woman who fished from the river or picked vegetables from small patches outside the walls, there were two others tasked with mending damage along the wall or replacing the blood-splattered doorways and windows of recently vacated homesteads.

A tragic few sat or stood at the tavern doorways, staring blankly into nothing as they recalled miseries and tragedies. Lorgan left them to their memories and took no note.

Eventually, when the sun had moved another arm's length across the sky, Lorgan took a hammer to the iron sheeting upon the gate and began to strike it. A terrible clanging sound rang across the town.

"Look impressive," he told them as the crowd gathered again. He continued to strike the gate for longer than seemed strictly necessary, and the crowd stared up at them uneasily. After a while, Derian felt naked beneath their gaze. So he did what Lorgan asked and tried to appear as impressive as he could. Standing erect, he placed his arms behind his back and kept his face stern. Beside him, he noticed even Natteo had forgone his usual disinterested pose in favour of a straight back and a brooding glare to those in attendance. A few of the younger peasants glancing his way seemed to find him impossibly attractive.

At last, Lorgan ceased the assault, and the crowd fell deathly still. There wasn't even chanting. Keralynn stood in front of the worshippers who had once been the loudest. She looked expressionlessly upon Seren, allowing only a trickle of a smile to appear upon her freshly painted lips. Lorgan offered her a bow, and Derian could see her face flush—so she was smitten with the man. Her wedding band was absent too, and

Derian wondered if Lorgan had chosen this deathly deal to
impress her. Perhaps that was his only way of courting her.
Perhaps, at his considerable age, he had such little faith in his
charms that he needed to kill himself—and his companions—
just to spend a night with her. Derian thought it tragic and
beautiful, and suddenly felt better about his own inadequacies
with women. He took a step closer to Seren, but she only had
eyes for Lorgan as he addressed the doomed townsfolk.

"Look around you, my friends. Fate has dealt you a cruel
blow. We stand here at the edge of the flame with no water
pail to call upon. Only the cups of our gathered hands." He
glanced back at Kesta, and she nodded subtly.

*A fine start, Lorgan. A very fine start. Maybe hold off on
the symbolism though*, she seemed to silently say with her
dark eyes, and, in turn, it seemed to reassure him.

"We have work to do. We chased them away, but they will
be back… and in greater numbers, too."

A strange feeling of calm had fallen upon Derian as he
listened to these words, and he wondered if he was moved by
the terror in the townspeople's faces or by a desire to show
them how skilled he was in killing. Deeper still, he felt the
stirrings of contained fury. There were insurmountable odds
cast against them, and though he couldn't be sure why, part of
him desired this challenge. The angry part. He gripped his
sheathed, makeshift dagger and wanted very much to stick
Rusty into something snarling and demonesque. *"Kill them
all."*

"From behind these walls, we can kill any nasties that
scale them," Lorgan continued, "and we can do it for long
enough that when reinforcements arrive, we will still have
some fight in us." As before, they hung on Lorgan's words.
They were terrified, but there was now a spark of hope in the

eyes of some as they watched the five figures standing before them.

Lorgan pulled out his ledger and ran his fingers along a few scribbled words. "I need the children first. They are in this fight too. Any five years or more, come forward." He did not ask; he demanded. There were immediate whispers of dissent.

What does the man want the children for?

Never in the world's history had the answer to such a question been in any way acceptable.

"I will not ask again," he called, and the whispers fell to an anxious silence until a young girl pushed through the crowd and stepped up before him. There was a strength to her, hidden behind her pale, quivering features. Her garments still carried the blood of loved ones. Her eyes betrayed her sorrow; there were clear streaks in the grime all the way down her cheeks. She couldn't have been more than eleven years old. A few more children followed behind her, and Lorgan tapped his notes absently. "Good girl. What is your name?"

"Eveklyn."

"A fine name. Are you alone in this world?"

"Yes, sir."

"Can this town count on you, Eveklyn?"

"Yes, sir."

Lorgan crouched down on his haunches and spoke softly so that only those closest could hear. "You are now a first general, Eveklyn, and you will command the rest of the young ones in this battle."

"Will we get to fight?"

Derian's heart broke at her tone. Only she knew what terrible things she'd seen—the same things that drew her to foolish questions. She was a child, and no, she would not fight.

She will not fight.

Right, Lorgan?

RIGHT, LORGAN?

"No, little one, you will not spill their monstrous blood, but there are tasks needed to be done—unsavoury and important."

"I will do it, sir," she said, and Lorgan was pleased.

He spoke louder this time so the crowd would understand his brutality. "Lead the rest to the field. Bring what axes you can carry. Fall upon each of the monsters and hack every limb free of the torso. Scatter their ruins all across the valley so the rest of them will smell their dead."

The crowd gasped as one, appalled. Eveklyn's face was expressionless. Perhaps hacking apart those who had taken everything from her was a welcome task.

Lorgan continued. "Take their heads and hang them from the top of each wall. Do these things merrily, little ones," he said, and the crowd again gasped aloud. A few mothers and fathers clutched their younglings closest. Others began to cry, and Derian tried to remain unemotional despite his revulsion. "I will leave the oldest parent out at the front gate this evening if they deny their child this task." Lorgan pulled his sword free as though, in that moment, the town might spit on his leadership.

As it was, they were simply terrified villagers. If the children hacking up a few body parts was all they would face, it was a task worth enduring. No man or woman argued as their children slipped from their grasp and raced home to find their tools for the grisly deeds. All but Eveklyn.

"I still want to fight, sir," she said, and Derian wondered

what strength the girl must have to accept leadership despite such grief. Lorgan patted her shoulder.

"Not tonight. Ask me tomorrow," he said, and sent her on her way.

"I need the best tree fellers this town can call upon," he said, addressing the townspeople once more, and then began barking out further orders. He read from his notes for a time, and the people set to task under his bidding. Eventually, the crowd petered away to nothing, until the Crimson Hunters were alone with only Blair and Keralynn.

"Using children for such tasteless tasks is rather savage," Blair said, and Lorgan turned to him.

"If you had a problem, you could have voiced your objections. We need all the hands we can get. Children are stronger than most people think. In fact, it is a child's duty to be stronger than their parents. And a parent's duty to allow them. Overly protecting them just makes them weaker in life. There's nothing wrong in pushing them that little bit further, because at some point they will see and endure things there can be no protection from. Better they see the monsters, better they learn to stomach brutality, and better their parents see them do it."

"And what scars will you give them for life?"

"Better they have scars to learn from. Better a scarred life than none at all."

"You are lucky you didn't lose the people with your first order," Blair countered. His compact body was tense, his face flushed a rich cherry, and he fought his anger. Derian wondered if Lorgan hadn't lost the man's confidence. Lorgan must have wondered the same thing, for he stood over the man and placed his hand upon his shoulder.

"These children know leadership, they understand nastiness, and they were the first to blink and turn away. They have accepted me and mine, just as you did, my friend. Things will become terrible soon. Better they know they have a vile fiend willing to do tasteless things to save them. Tell me, Blair, do I have your confidence?"

Blair took a moment—a full breath or two—and Lorgan did nothing but breathe. A moment more and the man nodded.

"With you to reassure them, how can we possibly fail?" Lorgan said, squeezing the man's shoulder before sending him away with a rough shove as only a comrade could in wartime.

"Will we survive tonight?" Blair asked.

"Course we will. With no great losses, either. It's whether we survive the night after. Or the one after that. These creatures are not mindless. They will pick, scratch, and find some way in that we haven't noticed," Lorgan replied cheerily.

"And when they do?"

"We'll have thought of something else by then," Natteo said, and Lorgan nodded in agreement.

"It's what we do," Kesta said, and deep down, that stirring, unnerving urge to kill began to gnaw at Derian once more.

22

THE QUIET BEFORE

Derian didn't like this room, not one bit. How could a man sleep in a place like this? How could he relax his beating heart for a solitary hour, before the true terrors of the world engulfed him?

"I hate this rotting place," he mumbled to no one.

Speaking aloud in this room was easier than thinking in complete silence. Darkness brought nothing more than desolate thinking, he'd always thought. Perhaps, had the room been blessed with any light, he might warm to it.

Yet, there were no candles at hand to counter this dreariness, no oil lantern hanging above his tired head, not even any tinder to set alight in the little stove in the corner. It was dark and musty, and he couldn't even brew a cup of tea to prepare himself for the cold night ahead.

His predecessors hadn't bothered to prepare the place for him, *the inconsiderate curs.* He suppressed a bitter snort at his tasteless humour, sat back in his chair, and placed his hands on its oaken armrests. It was a fine enough chair, with a plump cushion beneath his rear and a sturdy arch supporting his back.

What else could a tired mercenary need?

He reached over and removed his pack from where he'd discarded it on the bed. He hadn't noticed when he'd first come in, but there was a stain of blood soaking into the layers of blanket and sheeting. More blood had seeped right through onto the ground below, and despite the room's warmth, it still hadn't dried.

Just sleep on the floor and have words with management tomorrow.

"If they are still alive," he jested to the room. "If *I'm* still alive." He closed his eyes and silenced a forming whimper.

His mouth was dry, his body ached, and all he desired was a hard floor, dry pillows, and perhaps a few blankets against the growing chill. "I could find those things with light," he hissed, and hated this room a little more.

He imagined this shack might have some charm with the sun at its zenith, but the sun had moved on him; the demons were on the run, and he wasn't ready for the responsibilities placed upon him by his master.

"Hold the left, lead their strikes, and make each kill," he whispered, thinking of Lorgan's commands.

Hold, hold. If nothing else, hold.

He wanted to weep. Not only for fear but from exhaustion, too. His mind blurred like an image on a spinning coin, his bones ached as if he'd been dragged through a vice, and his soul was as empty as his stomach.

He remembered having a pleasant dream the last time he'd slept. Something about a girl painting a picture or some shit. Too many hours without sleep since then. He'd endured exhaustion as bitter as this, but only out on the march. Among the trees of green and the ground of mud, in rain and cold, he'd endured three days and kept walking, but somehow sitting around was worse.

He thought about locking himself away; the bolt was only an arm's reach behind him. The door was new and sturdy, unsullied by beast or human blood. He could still smell the freshly cut cedar wood, and there was no dab of varnish applied, but that was fine. It was still a fine door. The heavy bolt was attached at the centre, and though it wouldn't stop monsters charging through, it might halt them long enough that they'd decide to seek another prey.

"Maybe a child?" *No.* The children would be safe tonight, locked away in the warehouse with Eveklyn keeping watch, holding a battle axe far too big for her. Not for holding back the monsters. Lorgan had chosen her to care for the littler ones—those too young to chop a few demonic beasts apart, but old enough to know horrors in their last terrifying moments.

"It won't come to that. Not tonight, at least," Derian whispered, and he wondered could anyone hear his mutterings, or were they sleeping where they could before the great battle? He shook his head. There would be no battle tonight, just a slaughter, and the soldiers of this town would believe, and their faith would be misguided.

Tonight, Lorgan had resorted to what tactics he knew. Predictable tactics to anyone who had read a book before. Any greater or lesser siege was built upon the same few notions, and this town was no different.

A barricade here; some fire there; a shack-load of arrows along the way.

These reliable tactics would only work so long, though. The town of Gold Haven was too far away.

"We're so dead." He kicked at the unlit furnace as though it were Lorgan's shin. The metal clinked loudly, and the kettle atop bounced precariously towards a fall but then settled.

"Sorry," he said to the ghosts of this abandoned place. To

the poor unfortunate wretches who'd settled down to sleep that night and never arisen. Although they might well have made it to their feet at the dreadful thunder of their door shattering all over them. *Two beds. One large and one fit for a newly born. Both ruined now.* He allowed his anger to simmer in his stomach.

"I hate this place," he muttered, and wondered about Natteo. He, too, had accepted the offer of an empty shack, and was billeted in a similar structure across the path. Derian smiled, thinking of his friend convincing some foolish damsel or impressionable young man to join him and turn his hovel into a palace. They would scrub and clean, and he would sit and regale them with tales of magnificence and bad poetry involving trolls and roses. Natteo should have been a fine bard with the golden waste that spilled from his silver tongue, even when morbid terror was consuming him.

"Be safe, brother," he whispered, and realised it was a prayer to gods he had no belief in. He reached for his clothing and thought of Seren. She had also been given a shack of her own, and Derian thought this most disappointing of all. Perhaps if Lorgan had insisted she share with Derian, he might have wooed her, earned her favour, or maybe just lessened the hate she had for him. She was about five shacks down, give or take. He knew this because the chanting had started up again outside it, and he'd heard an irate young girl (who looked incredible without the burden of clothing upon her) shout colourful, broken abuse at her worshippers in an adorably strange accent before slamming the door. They had fallen silent then, until one brave acolyte in the "Church of Seren" had begun the chant again. Soon after, the singing had returned, quickly growing in intensity and urgency. They were seeking resurrection, it seemed. He understood their desperation. But still, enough of the singing.

"I love you," he whispered, and mocked his own childishness. He didn't love her at all. He just wanted to know her body better than anybody else. He closed his eyes and thought of her nakedness and how alone he was in this room and smiled. *Later.* Best he keep his strength for the battle if needed.

As for Kesta and their fearless leader—it was good to be the king, wasn't it? he thought. They had each taken one of the larger and finer houses farther up towards the wall. Perhaps to be closer to the action when it happened, or perhaps to send the right message to those they were to protect: they deserved the finest. He didn't begrudge Kesta or Lorgan their upscale lodgings, however; Derian was merely jealous that he and the other apprentices had been put in their place in plain view of the villagers.

DONG!

Without warning, his silence was shattered in the form of a bell ringing—this time, a proper bell, gifted to Lorgan by an accommodating blonde citizen. The clanging echoed, and Derian took a few breaths and remembered what little he knew, summoned what misty memories he had, and checked each of his clasps was tight before opening the door to the growing night.

"It's time to go to war, General," he heard Natteo mutter, emerging from his shack across the path.

"See you on the other side, brother." Derian clanked his new sword against his newer leather chest plate.

"Let's give these spitting fuks the warmest of welcomes."

23

GELDED

S eren listened to the manic clanging and thought it a pretty melody, for it brought excitement to the world. It was terrifying, daunting, and miserable excitement, but it was excitement nonetheless. She liked the room, despite the darkness. It was her first-ever room. And she liked darkness.

Easier to remain hidden in the night. Easier to strike.

"Burn." She looked at her fingers in the dim light and wondered what she needed to bring a little fire to her fingertips. She was a weaver.

Weaver.

Yes, I know that word.

She knew it like she knew her name, but little else. She knew of untapped abilities, but attempting to take hold of them felt like plunging her mind into a vat of black, charring oil and searching for gold.

Thurken Derian cur.

Spitting arrow.

Her words were forming in her mind more easily now. More slowly from her mouth, though. Perhaps in another day or two, she might be capable of holding an entire conversation.

"Unfinished."

She knew she was a warrior, but also nothing. *Lifeless, gelded.* She thought more about this and smiled. If nothing else, confusing things made her smile. She knew her master approved of conviction; a lesser person *like Derian* might crumble under a perfect lack of understanding. If nothing else, she would rise higher despite it.

"Idiot Derian." Her voice rose above the clanging darkness as footsteps thundered past her door, racing towards death.

"Death. Deeeeath." She did not enjoy pronouncing this word. There were no pretty letters to wrap her tongue around. "Tongue." She didn't like that word either.

People would die tonight; she didn't know how or why, only that they would. She felt sorrow at the innocent lives that would be lost, but this was the way of things, she supposed. When the monsters came, humans bled.

"May death find Derian."

She felt guilt condemning the foolish mercenary with careless wishing. She thought crushing his head to a mush would make her feel better, but no, she still hated him. At least they were even now. She tapped her forehead unconsciously and flinched at a bitter, swift memory. No, they were far from even. He'd stunted her recovery, and she would never apologise. Besides, it had been his stupid fault for standing in front of her.

Birth boom.

"Booooooom."

She hadn't meant to return his soul to his body. She hadn't meant to save all of them, but it had happened, and she was thankful. She wished she knew how to perform enchantments like that on demand; some things were impossible now, after the arrow. Some things were easier. She saw moments now. Not from these times, but of times to come. Just glimmers. Dipping into the source had tainted her, ever so. Had she been able to ask her master, he would have known. She wondered, as her mind recovered, would she understand these moments better? Would she see more? Less?

She knew in moments that those who chanted were those who could punish and murder. *Many steps to take before that.* They whispered chants, begging her to return life to those dead at the gate. Oh, if only such a thing were possible.

"No healer," she whispered, and a dreadful sorrow overcame her. It were as though the entire world's grief touched her mind for a pulse of blood, and she almost collapsed to the floor. It wasn't until a screaming child from somewhere out in the night pulled her from her thoughts. The manic screech faded as a panicked parent's cupped hand silenced the wailing.

Lorgan's plan was sound, she thought, even if some of it would go wrong tonight. As it did for them most of the time. She very much liked the Crimson Hunters. There was something about them she couldn't place her finger on. They were fiercer than either they themselves or the world realised. She had need of fierceness and their delicious… *Delicious? Was that the right word?*

She licked her lips. "Delicious." She allowed the last letter to ring out like a serpent's hiss.

Their *delicious* souls were strong, and their hearts were unshakeable. They would go to some dark places; she couldn't think of better companions to call upon. She would have a place among them if the world turned as she'd seen in her glimpsed moments.

It didn't really matter that they were terrible mercenaries, either, because she was a terrible servant of war. She could be so much better.

Delicious war. Ooh.

"Many will die." She reached for her blue dress. It was too tight a fit; it grabbed her in places she didn't expect, and it restricted her movement to dainty little manoeuvres. She despised this generous gift from Keralynn, but Kesta had assured her that fighting without clothing might only earn her further followers. Her chanting entourage was irritating enough, so she bit her lip and lifted the dress over her head, letting it fall upon her smoothly. She caught sight of herself in a small mirror hanging beside the bed. In the dimness, she looked like a wraith, lost and scared, not belonging in this world, without a path, destined to bring ruin to destinies.

She froze, thinking on this, and her newborn mind struggled and sought out a memory.

So close. So fuken close.

As swiftly as the thought appeared, it was lost. So she lifted the mirror and looked upon her face. Was she beautiful? Was her hair an appealing style? Did her smile fell suitors like trees? *Is that a saying?* She couldn't tell, but she thought her teeth shimmered a vibrant white. Maybe her teeth drew Derian to her like an immoral mongrel. If he continued to chase after her, she'd show him how strong her bite was.

"Better," she said, reaching for her armour, and upon tying the last of the clasps, she took the mirror again and approved of how warrior-like the wraith appeared. With Lorgan's call echoing through the cold night, she opened the door and had never felt happier.

All around her was a swarming mass of panic, but she could not be fearful with them. She believed herself destined to fear other things. Bloody and horrendous things. Fiore was nearing now, and she had her vindictive sights upon her.

Seren could no longer feel her presence, but she could sense the hunt. Closer now, slithering like a serpent. *Undelicious.* Was undelicious a word?

"Burn," she demanded, holding her hand out in front of her. A fine hand with no burns, and it displeased her. If she had fire, she could burn the beasts where they stood. Or lift them to the sky with invisible, godly hands. She might also be capable of saving herself when the time came. She felt herself shudder. *That is only something that could happen.*

She tried again and no flame erupted, and no pulsing force of invisible power left her soul.

"Burn." She willed a stunning blue flame to emerge— fierce, brutal, and uncontrolled—but nothing came.

"Burn." She willed a flame of most divine black, but her heart was not twisted by sadness and tragedy. At least, not yet.

"Burn," she hissed, louder than before, and willed the burning force of magenta fire to escape, for this flame was bright enough to give a grand demon concern.

"BURN!"

Nothing happened, and this time she lamented. People would die, and buried in her mind, deep beneath the memory of a jagged projectile, were the skills to save them. She couldn't release even a yellow spark to light the path ahead. Though she celebrated her mind's growing cohesion, incredible things still escaped her. She needed her master more than ever. Wherever he was.

Whenever you are? Is that right? Is that what I meant to say?

She marched towards the front gate, trying to distract herself from her inadequacies, and found distraction in something else entirely. She felt the warm glow of a fire and allowed herself a moment's hesitation. She stood just beyond the light of the blacksmith's shack, watching the owner and his two young apprentices sitting in a frantic circle, whittling timber into arrows. The blacksmith held little strips of thin wood over the flames and desperately moulded them straighter; one apprentice slit, cut, and shaped flights from hard leaves, while the other moulded them into place. They were careless and swift in their efforts; their hands had endured rough labour, she saw, for they were bloody, blistered, and bubbling from singeing, scalding, and scraping, and she thought them incredible. Not every arrow would fly true, but they only needed most of them to. At least a thousand lay in neat piles outside the workspace already, and villagers grabbed pouch after pouch of them as they passed, yet still they worked. Who knew how long these men had been busy? They didn't appear to notice their stocks swiftly depleting. They simply continued with their craft. Their heroism was not that of war, but equally impressive. *A good leader notices these things.* She bowed to them, but they were lost in their work, so silently she grabbed a few arrows of her own to hang loosely upon the quiver at her waist.

"Good… leader."

Lorgan did not trust her to lead, but he trusted her to fight, and she vowed to earn her place among the Crimson—and if not tonight, then the night after. The night after that was nothing at all. Again, she feared the unknowing and she looked at her fingers once more and felt no stirring of energy within, and she cursed loudly and felt better about it.

Archers stood along all four walls now. To be more precise, farmers, miners, and labourers stood along the walls. All had the freedom to fire upon any enemy they chose, while each of her Crimson comrades commanded a dozen archers of their own to focus upon the individual targets they selected.

"Death by numbers," Lorgan had suggested, and Derian had taken the left side of the wall. She watched him now, and the vision of the arrow in her mind was fading. *Trauma.* He walked along the battlements, looking nervous and idiotic. In another world without arrows, she could have lain with him. He would have grunted in her ear. Her stomach churned, and she tasted bile and she knew it would have been lovely.

Natteo's responsibility was the opposite side across, while Kesta and Lorgan stood atop the enticing front of the town, barking out orders to their respective units on either side of the gate.

No mercenary commanded the rear, as the wall was highest here: an additional four foot or more higher than the rest of the walls, with foundations secured in brick and a small river running alongside. It was a tragedy that the town rulers hadn't secured all the walls similarly. The back was the easiest position to hold, and so Lorgan had stationed the oldest, weariest, and most decrepit along its side, and Seren agreed. A risk if the enemy knew this, but all battles needed gambles. Backlit by torches and with bows in hands, they stood proudly, and Seren thought it a strange, wonderful sight. If the monsters attacked, they would fight hardest and few of them would run.

Seren would never run from a battle. In fact, tonight her responsibility was running *into* battle. She had no wall to stand guard upon. Instead, she was among the reinforcements. She stood in a reserve of twenty archers in the centre of the town, placed only a quick sprint towards any side. Lorgan had charged her with stemming the tide if the monsters spilled over the walls.

She wondered how well her surrounding comrades would fare, though. It was one thing to stand upon a wall, firing arrows down at nasties and slowly growing into battle; it was another to coldly rush into death. She wasn't capable of retreat. Perhaps that was why her master had found her.

Saved me from Fiore.

A terrified young man looked over at her, drawing her attention. His face was pale, his lips quivered, and he looked at her with desperation. 'Save us,' his eyes cried, and she had no words for him because she was gelded. *For now.* He held her gaze, and it was an uncomfortable thing to be a drowning man's driftwood; she could see him desperate to cry out, to release his bladder all over his ill-fitted armour, to beg the dead gods of fate to let him live his quiet farmer life.

"Don't," she countered with her own eyes. Panic was temporary, but it was also infectious, and when he could no longer help himself, he cried out and it was so much worse.

"Ave… emmmmm…. Seeeeerrreeeeen."

Oh, spit on me.

"Shut up!" she cried, and he dropped his bow and reached for her.

"Shut up, shut up, shut up!"

"Silen… ceeeeh eeeeooooom ava Seeeeerrreeeeen…" he wailed, and a few of his brethren joined him, and she hated this rotting mess as they chanted the song.

"Pick up bow, then chant," she said, spitting in the dirt in disgust. This town was a town of idiots. He nodded as though her words were gospel and recovered his bow.

"Long night," she warned.

24

BREAKING THE SEAL

"What is your name, friend?"

The nervous man's bow shook, and the crude arrow could barely rest in place. Derian took hold of the jagged projectile and pulled it carefully from his grip.

"My name is Keri." His eyes were wide and crazed, and they darted from growing flame to forest to wall and back again.

The walls they stood on were ten foot high, but Derian would have preferred to watch from double the height with a wider walkway. It was a peasant's wall in its purest definition. Adequate for discouraging human bandits, less so against snarling, scrambling demons.

The wall was a hand's length in width, but the builders had put fine work into the attached platform. That was something, at least. The foothold was a few feet wide, with supports every dozen steps: a satisfactory platform upon a flimsy barricade. Skill and attentiveness, mixed with a little ignorance of practicality. *Peasants.*

"That's a very good name: Keri," Derian said, feigning interest before returning the arrow to its owner. "No one needs to notch an arrow yet. Rest your hands. It could be quite a time before they need us. You'll find easier kills with a rested arm." Derian called loud enough that the rest of his dozen chosen fighters would hear. "This will be easy, like honey cake. She was a prostitute I used to know." He looked into the night and heard nervous chuckles around him.

The children had done well. They'd smeared the landscape in entrails and reserved the most grotesque of the slain demon's heads for the walls. He caught sight of one hanging below his feet. Whoever had slipped the thin rope through the holes in both ears had performed their task admirably. The beast grinned at Derian, reminding him of an old drunkard from his town.

"Your name is Charly," he told it, and tapped at the gruesome trophy with the end of his longbow. It bounced in its place, causing a few of the other demonic horrors along the line to join it in a demented, grinning dance. Derian sniggered, thinking of the dozen bouncing heads awaiting a charging mass of monsters. *As if that'll intimidate them.*

"That's a very good name," offered Keri, watching the bouncing heads. He wasn't alone either. All of his archers were watching. They smiled and chuckled again, and Derian made a note to congratulate Lorgan. Perhaps there really was something to morale during warfare.

"He looks like a Charly."

"Oh, yes. I see it now."

They fell silent, watching the night and the flames. "Will the spikes help?" Keri asked, and Derian almost lied. He almost said they would scatter the beasts and discourage them from clustering, but lying would only suggest Derian knew less than he did.

Truthfully, those charged with felling the forest trees had failed spectacularly. Perhaps they were lazy degenerates;

perhaps they were unskilled in their craft. More likely, it had been fear of a beastie sneaking up on them while they worked that had resulted in such disappointing numbers. Only sixty spikes had been cut, sharpened, and then dug into the ground.

"Those spikes will do nothing tonight." Derian knew Lorgan had hoped for at least thrice the number, but he would have settled for double. As it was, he'd secured the thinnest line of defensive spikes in a circle around the town, and it was a shameful spectacle. A careless demon might impale itself, but only if it were charging blindly. A better few days of labour might produce enough to fill the circle, but the spikes would be worthless tonight.

The second defensive line, however, looked more promising. It was a wondrous circle of fire, enclosing the town. Every table, chair, and barrel had been laid out, drenched in night oil, and kindled with dry leaves and sticks. The heavy smoke spread out across the valley in the wind before rising and disappearing forever. It had been visible for miles until full darkness fell upon them. Those who'd performed the task had pleased Lorgan. He'd even patted a few of their backs.

"Do you think someone in Gold Haven saw the smoke before the sun fully set?" Keri asked, squinting as he tried to make out the deathly black clouds soaring up into nothingness among the emerging stars.

This time, Derian did lie. "I do. There might already be a full battalion being assembled as we speak. This town's mines can't afford to be lost." Derian wondered had he said too much? Only Natteo had mastered the true art of deception. Not only in the telling, but in knowing when his telling was far-fetched. He always said just enough before his victims caught onto the ruse.

"That would be nice," Keri said.

Lorgan had timed the lighting perfectly. The fires wouldn't last the night, but they would burn for a few hours. Lorgan had attempted to entice the monsters to attack from the front by keeping the flames there only a foot in height. He'd stationed most of the defenders at this end and would roll the dice of fortune.

Derian watched him marching back and forth over the front gates, bellowing out a rousing speech to those under him. His words were lost in the flapping of flame and the brush of wind, but whatever words he chose were likely to be the ones he usually chose before a mission fell apart. Something about 'honour,' something about 'bravery,' and then there was usually 'eternal victory' thrown in at the end. Some men needed to say words and others needed to hear them. Derian wondered if the defenders under his own leadership might need inspiration. They could wait a time, he decided; he was no wordsmith, and speaking to any crowd was one of his many fears. He heard an approving roar and hands clapping, and he turned to see Lorgan punching the night air. Many of his listeners did the same. Turning back to his own anxious comrades, Derian sighed. He coughed loudly because he'd seen Lorgan get attention this way.

"When they come, fight for those you love. Do that and you will fight well." There were a few nods. Derian turned and saw Natteo also addressing his warriors. He'd have no problem, he thought.

Derian cleared his throat and turned to his own group. "If they breach, stick them with the pointy end," he said. There were a few laughs. "Not that we will get breached." His voice lost a little of its bravado.

Finish strongly and it will satisfy them, Derian thought, and a crude Natteo jest formed in his head.

Wonderful.

He ignored the opportunity for a perfectly placed jest and cleared his throat again. "They will not breach us tonight…. because… because a breach would be terrible," he mumbled. "And some of us would die." He couldn't stop himself. "And I don't want to die tonight."

A few people muttered in agreement, and in the distance, Natteo declared something and his archers began laughing. He'd said something about victory and eternal honour and maybe finishing strongly. It didn't help.

"That said, I'm probably the unlikeliest of us to die," Derian said, and hated himself.

Shut up, shut up, shut up.

"Because if they breach us, I'm better than most of you with a sword, so I'll last longer," he said, finishing weakly and leaving his listeners thoroughly unsatisfied.

Idiot.

Only an hour after sunset, with darkness engulfing the town's boundary, a lone, howling cry came from the treeline, and any subdued conversation upon the walls fell to silence.

Derian caught a gasp in his throat and stood straighter, peering out into the night, searching for the monsters come to hunt them all. The cloudless moon was bright, but the flickering flames beneath tricked his eyes towards blindness. Though he struggled to see, his ears worked just fine, and a second wail from across the valley joined the first. A breath later, another joined the monstrous melody, and another after that, until, like a pack of demonic wolves announcing their presence, soon the valley shook with the creatures' braying threat.

They speak to each other, he thought, and fear gripped Derian's chest.

"I see one in the break of the trees on the right!" a voice along his wall shouted, and Derian followed the instruction. Squinting and searching. As they all did. *There. And another.* Derian searched through the flickering yellow dance and as his eyes adjusted, he saw the pinpricks of glittering monster eyes gleaming back at him. Every beat of his heart felt concussive, and his chest constricted further. He felt a claw take hold of his lungs and squeeze the breath from him, and though he desired silence in the moments of serenity before the storm, he did not hush the panicked voices that grew around him.

"Another ugly one."

"There, up at the gap."

"At least a dozen."

"They're just staring down at us."

"They're everywhere."

"That one is laughing."

The cries of discovery became too many to count, and without warning, his heart's beat suddenly calmed, and the surging adrenalin that begged him to move, to attack, to kill, steadied to a strange tranquillity.

Am I that scared that I've gone beyond terror?

Is this acceptance?

He felt relaxed and hated it. He needed fear keeping him alert. He knew this because his book suggested fear was a mercenary's best friend. That and tight silken underwear.

"Hold your nerve," he told himself, but his mind spun, and his mouth had become parched. He reached for his water, and the canister did not shake in his grasp. He drank deep and wondered if this would be the last drop of water he'd ever take. He wished it were something stronger. Maybe a cup of tea. He really wished he'd been able to make one last cup of tea before the end. Maybe have a honey cake with it. That would have been nice. The howling reached a crescendo, and he found his stomach grumbling, and he realised dying with an empty belly was the true tragedy. He drank again and re-tightened the clasp for further use.

"They're coming. Oh, thurk me, they are coming," one of his younger soldiers cried before leaping from the platform to the ground below. He squealed in pain as his ankle gave way in a sharp crack, and Derian cursed his cowardice and braced himself for the inevitable following tide. The man limped away into the darkness, and Derian watched his scuttling. They all did, and truthfully, it was a pathetic sight.

"There's always one idiot who ruins it for the rest of us," he shouted. "Let them come. Let the nasty little beasts run down and attempt to breach these fine walls!" A few warriors stamped their feet on the platform in warring agreement.

"LET THEM COME."

They must have heard Derian's challenge, because they came.

The canis demons emerged from their hiding places in large groups, driven on by their anculus masters. The ground rumbled beneath their charge. Their snapping teeth tore at the air, and the night was alive with feverish wrath. Even in the bad light, he saw hundreds emerging from the trees; there were more than the night before.

You didn't even survive the first time, he reminded himself.

"There's no cart up here to crush me."

He shook doubting thoughts from his mind and looked to his terrified comrades. They weren't hardened mercenaries; standing in the way of charging demons was not their place.

"This will be easy!" he shouted, stamping his feet upon the platform.

"Well… that would be nice," Keri said doubtfully, looking back towards the horde of hunters, and Derian realised words would not settle his comrades. Death was in the air—and they knew it.

Ignoring the desecrated bodies of their brethren, the demons charged through the line of spikes with nothing more than a side-step, but the fire gave them pause when they reached the town's boundary.

Most of them halted. Denied the first kill of the day, they snapped and growled in disgust, while a few leapt instinctively into the flames. They howled in pain for a few breaths, then stumbled towards the wall before at least a dozen arrows set them to quiet. Derian patted Keri's back absently as he watched their first combined kill come rolling to a stop beneath the wooden wall. At least six arrows protruded from its body.

"Well done, heroes," Derian said, and there was victorious cheer.

The moment didn't last long, however, because now the beasts did something strange. He'd expected them to test the flame a second time, but as though some greater intelligence stirred and controlled their minds and actions, all of them began to behave as one impressive pack.

Without any discernible signal from one of their anculus masters, they took off in a charging line, three or four abreast, down along the burning ring of fire. Like an expanding shoal of fish, they raced as one, allowing those in front to lead while each monster waited patiently to join the stampede as they passed. The line gathered speed quickly and charged up along the edges of the wall Derian stood on.

"I've never seen such a thing," he muttered, cursing his

own amazement. Humans had learned a great deal while fighting demons these last thirty years, but Derian was certain this was something new.

Their numbers stretched out to half the wall's length, and they charged towards the rear of the town. Behind him, Derian heard the panicked roar of Lorgan barking out order after order as the last canis demon followed the first, leaving behind a few dozen anculus demons stalking through the ruined battlefield, staining their hooves with the blood and entrails of their kin. The anculus demons howled as one, a deep, guttural cry, and kept themselves far away from any archer's arrow.

What is going on?

"Why are they attacking us, anyway?" he heard one of his comrades cry out.

Then another, this time pleading. "Why didn't they just go after Gold Haven?"

"Why aren't they trying to clear the flames?" a curious voice asked, and it might have been Keri.

"This plan won't work!" another shouted in anger.

Anger is good; anger is a gift.

"Whisht, fools, and watch their actions," Derian commanded, and all around him became silent.

A few muttered, "Yes, sir," and it satisfied him that he'd countered a wave of revolt. The last beast passed them now, just as the leading pack leapt across the shallow river and out the other side before turning the far corner of the town and disappearing from sight.

Please don't attack that side.

Those at the back wall watched on in silent terror as the horde moved beneath them. Within a few anxious breaths, they reached the other corner and turned back up towards the last section, where Natteo and his archers stood.

"Weaknesses," he whispered, and gripped Rusty's freshly wrapped grip for comfort. He felt a growing thumping in his head, and it matched the vibrations from the charging pack. *Like a grand cantus searching for a fault in a night barge's hull.* Derian wondered how wily these monsters might be.

He followed their charge until they returned to the front gates once more. They showed no sign of stopping. Lorgan led his archers in an aerial bombardment as they passed, but they did not scatter nor deviate from their chosen path; they sprinted on with only a paltry number lost, like race riders beneath the gaze of a thousand fools who'd bet their livelihood on the contest's outcome.

"So much for planning," Derian whispered to himself. Any mercenary could hit a running demon from far beyond the flames, but most farmers or miners would struggle with the task. Lorgan and his mercenaries had discussed at length how far from the walls they should set the flames. Perhaps there was no definitive distance near enough to entice some canis to leap over, while still far enough away that archers could pick them off before they gathered beneath the wall. Until this moment, Derian had thought they'd done well enough with their choosing. Problem was, the beasts weren't behaving like themselves at all. The fire should have slowed them and allowed the defenders to strike them down from a comfortable position—taking the heart from their charge while giving the defenders some belief. It was typical, he thought bitterly, that Lorgan's tried-and-trusted tactic still found a way to fail miserably.

They'd expected a hundred would fall in the first few salvos, but Derian couldn't even count a dozen dead demons lying at the wall. They had argued that the fires would hold them for a handful of hours, but that didn't matter if they could not whittle down the number with each passing moment. There were no other tactics to follow. Something nasty was brewing. His head drummed louder, yet still, he was calm. He licked his lips and remembered the taste of demonic gore, and he took hold of Rusty's grip once again.

"Soon."

"Maybe they really fear the fire," Keri said, notching another arrow. This town would be defended easily if they feared the fire. Nothing was ever that simple, Derian thought, but said nothing lest his companions lose what little nerve remained. He also thought it better to keep quiet his worry that some higher intelligence had seen through the ruse and willed the creatures to find a weakness.

The demons thundered back around towards his section of the wall now, and to his own astonishment Derian did something he never usually did: he came up with an idea and acted on it.

"Prepare yourselves!" he roared, and pointed to a pathetic spike standing unimpressively out at the edge of the field. "As they pass that spike, take the second beast out. Not the first. Allow the wind to drag the arrow lower, and aim a foot above their heads." Derian ran along the wall, making sure his archers understood. Better they aim at one fixed point, he told himself as the terrifying line of monsters reached their section.

"Get ready!"

"..."

"Now!"

The arrows released with a reassuring whoosh and silently sailed into the night. Many missed, but they felled at least five in the first barrage.

"Again!" he roared, holding his hand high and signalling his team to reload. He was terrified, he was exhilarated, he was a general, and this was working. His Crimson comrades watched, and he felt stirrings of pride. He dropped his hand and a plethora of crudely made arrows, just sharp enough to pierce skin, and just straight enough to fly the distance, let loose and split the night again. Another five or six creatures died in that moment, but better than that, those in pursuit trampled a half-dozen more, before knocking another handful howling into the flames to meet a terrible end.

"I'm proud of you!" he shouted to his men, then watched wide-eyed as Natteo gave his own archers the same order as Derian had given. They, too, celebrated wildly at their own impressive assault on the hunting pack when the monsters came back around.

Keri pumped his fist in the air. "We can do this, sir." He wasn't alone in his belief; a sea of fists pumped around him.

Derian's heart swelled: in a few swift-thinking moments, he had turned the mood and caused heavy losses on their enemy. "Be ready for them to come back around," he warned, but his smile betrayed him. Perhaps he could be fine at this leadership thing.

After Natteo, Lorgan, and Kesta had all ordered their own similar blows to the circling pack, more victorious cheers rose into the night air: the great defence of Treystone had struck a mighty blow for humankind.

More of the attackers fell and died, and the leading monsters widened the arc they took as Derian stood out at the edge. Along the wall, he could see faces beaming with pride and the glorious spark of vengeance emerging. Nothing bred talent like a little experience getting some easy killing.

"Get ready, heroes!" he cried, raising his bow and appearing magnificent in the fire's light. 'Derian, the Legend of Treystone,' they would say. There were worse things to be known for, he supposed. It was better than 'The man who shot a goddess in the forehead.'

But then, as the canis demons came around again, the leading pack suddenly spun away from their charge. They veered far out into the battlefield, appearing as a strange, gigantic snake leading its lazy body away from killing things, and Derian wondered hopefully, were they retreating as one?

No.

As one they fled, and then, as one, they turned in a swift curve as if shying away from a depthless crevice. They turned back towards the fire and sped up towards the wall Derian stood upon.

Oh, no!

"Fire!" he shouted. "And keep firing!"

The first four beasts, leading hundreds behind them, charged directly into the fire. They did not leap nor avoid the burning collection of beds, barrels, and bales. They charged directly into the fire and died for their actions. As did the demons behind them, and perhaps the ones after that, but their sacrifice was impressive and unnervingly shrewd.

With a roar like thunder, the rear guard of the beasts trampled over the bodies of their fallen comrades, which had smothered the flames where they lay. Derian cursed. If they'd had more time to prepare, they could have foreseen this tactic and perhaps stretched the fire's width and depth. Or they could have dug a trench at the front so the beasts would have struggled to get a foothold in the unforgiving fire, but this had been a hastily created plan with inadequate hands to call upon.

This battle is already lost, he thought, as the first creature reached the wall a few feet below him.

25

SLAUGHTERED

The wall began to bulge inwards and Derian stood atop it, firing arrow after arrow down upon the beasts as they swarmed and formed themselves into an unnatural mound of horror. He knew it would take a thousand arrows and a thousand hours to cut through their terrible writhing mass, and still they would never strike those nearest the bottom, but still, he fired. Fed by the line of monsters flowing through the break in fire, the creatures' looming mass grew steadily in height and width. Closer and closer it came, every moment another foot nearer.

Archers on either side delivered death, but it was like swatting at a nest of hissects with nothing more than a needle. There were too many. Suddenly, the platform shuddered as though struck by a giant's fist, and Keri lost his footing. He grasped wildly at thin air and then, arms pinwheeling helplessly, fell down to the brutes below.

He screamed as he dropped—the shrill wail of a man realising his doom. He bounced off the mass, spinning like a helpless child's toy before rolling towards the flames. He never reached them, because a dozen set of snapping teeth fell upon him. He lived longer than expected. Derian knew this because of the screams. Perhaps, in that last moment, Keri might have struck one or more beasts with a flailing fist, but without his sword, it was a tragic last stand. Derian could have avoided watching the monsters tear and drag away what meat they'd earned from their victim, but his eyes were riveted to the horror. Keri had seemed a nice man. No man deserved that end. Derian felt a surge of raw hatred boil up inside him and fought back a suicidal urge.

"Leap down and take them all on. They'll never see it coming."

The wall shifted again, and Keri was lost from Derian's thoughts as he notched and released his next arrow. He hit a demon between the eyes, and it howled before falling back down and dying in the fire. A small victory after such a loss.

"This side, this side! They're only taking this side!" Derian screamed, praying his Crimson comrades understood the sudden turn. Praying the Crimson were swifter on their feet than usual.

The old wood of the platform, weakened by the blows from the monsters below, now began to creak and break beneath his feet. Its splintering snapping filled the night as the monsters tested and found a breach in the defences, and he spotted Natteo rousing his warriors and charging down towards the failing wall with a pack of confused archers in tow.

Too far.

The world was coming undone, and all of it was doing so under Derian's watch. The wall rocked again, and he thought of Seren. She would come, he told himself. He couldn't see her with so many buildings obstructing his view, and he despaired.

Will she come?

Surely, she would realise a thousand demons spilling over the wall wasn't part of the plan. He wondered would she race into death trying to save him? Or would she cry out as he died gallantly defending the town, defending her? Would she miss him? Would his bravery be enough to earn her love?

He saw Lorgan and Kesta charging down along the wall. Behind them followed several warriors, but they were still too far, and his anger raged inside. *This isn't fair.*

"Killing them all is fair."

"Kill them all!" Derian roared in a strange voice. "We hold or we die." Fate would decide the battle in the next dozen breaths. "Make them pay!" he cried again, hoping to rouse his fighters to an unlikely counterattack. They fired down, but just like before, as one snapping horror fell, three returned in their place. The beasts used their own fallen brethren as a foothold, and like ants frenzied by a midsummer feast, they swarmed upwards towards the top of the wall, while those at the bottom dug fiercely at the creaking foundations, hoping to make a breach of their own.

"Use your blades!" he cried, and pulled his sword free, plunging at the first monster who reached the edge. With a sickening squeal, the beast fell away, but another snapped towards Derian, who met the attack with equal violence.

Beside him, a young girl with sturdy forearms, long blonde hair, and rosy cheeks took Keri's place. He'd spoken a few words with her before the fighting began and wondered about sharing a drink with her come dawn. She had seemed unimpressive at the time, with a heavy Luistrian accent, but she had smiled warmly enough to pique his interest. In this moment, he thought her heroic. She wore the same armour as Derian, and she fought as fiercely as he. They matched each other's attacks—she would swing on his right; he would swing on her left. A wonderful dance of violence and energy. Bed mates bonded over lesser things.

She swung killing blows every time and held the wall magnificently, until a claw reached over and caught her unawares. With a lazy swipe, it tore her throat from her neck. She kept stabbing for a gushing few breaths before her body realised the devastation. The girl fell heavily against Derian, spilling her warm blood all over his hands, and the shock almost knocked him into the ocean of death below.

She held on, screaming silently as her body failed her. She held him fast in a vice-like grip, and her eyes pleaded for him to fix her. Her armour was so heavy. She spat blood from her mouth and tears streamed from her eyes and the world stopped, and they wobbled precariously along the edge like a balance upon a scale. He wanted to save her. He wanted to take her pain and soothe her into the night. He wanted to ask her for that drink.

Instead, he shoved her desperate, clutching arms from his shoulders and tragically sent her over the top. He told himself that she was already dead as she fell, but he knew better. She watched with terrified eyes as she went. Better her than me, he told himself. What good would come from accompanying her into death when he still had fight?

I'm sorry. So very sorry.

The beast that had attacked her pulled itself over the wall now and leapt upon Derian, knocking him back from the surging walkway. Somehow, amidst dodging, plunging claws and snapping bites (which would have torn tin armour apart like paper), he plunged Rusty deep into the monster's head and ruptured its brain. It died instantly, even if its teeth snapped three more times a finger's length from his throat before the creature wheezed gently and fell still.

He rolled away from the dead weight just as the monsters

fully breached their defences. He should have ordered the defenders to fall back—to drop away and find sturdier ground below—but he didn't, for Lorgan had ordered him to hold the left side, no matter what.

"Defend your ground!" Derian screamed, and his warriors obeyed. Each doomed soldier atop the wall stood bravely as a rising tide of monster flowed over them like a lake over a failing dam. In a pulse of blood, the wall was awash with fur, horns, teeth, and claw.

His comrades performed admirably; they were fierce, they were brave, they were heroes, and they were inexperienced. Perhaps an outfit of seasoned mercenaries might well have survived this wave; they might have pushed them back. Instead, they died in a breath of time.

From the side of the invading tide, Derian could only stab and plunge at the canis demons too distracted to attack him. They had set their sights upon dropping into the town below and tearing at the meat. "Keep fighting!" he demanded of the other defenders fortunate enough to be standing on the other side of the breach.

I can't do this.

"Yes, we can."

"Defend the town!" Derian's limbs became laboured as though he were swimming in a sea of thick soup, yet still, he swung both sword and dagger as though controlled by another entity. He felt like a drunkard, blindly returning home regardless of his ineptitude in the saddle. His body fought while his mind sought flight. Away from the wall, back into the town, and then disappearing into the darkness to take refuge in any house within retreating distance.

"Keep killing," Derian demanded, all the while searching for a means of escape. Then he caught sight of one lone defender in the middle of the wall. He was at least fifty, with a bushy beard. He wore old, unpolished armour that fitted, his sword was long and heavy, and he stood proudly despite monsters surging over on either side of him. He struck only what was in front of him, and not a single beast had breached his foot of wall.

"Kill with him."

Derian's eyes widened as the man turned to swing his weapon again: where the warrior's left arm had been was only a bloody stump. His mind reeled; he couldn't understand the will of any man who continued the fight after receiving a blow as debilitating as this. He thought the bearded man incredible. Perhaps it was stubbornness, perhaps he had Seeva blood coursing through him, or perhaps he had a family he would do anything to protect.

Perhaps he doesn't know the demons have severed his arm.

Perhaps he needs a hand, so to speak.

Derian waded into the struggling, slithering monsters as they climbed over, hacking with both weapons, and slowly moving towards the injured man. He did not know why he charged forward, only that he desired nothing more than standing with this falling man and dying with him.

"Help us!" he cried to any remaining warriors, and he pushed on as though navigating a rushing waterfall over a depthless drop.

"Help us!" he cried again, but really, he knew that all who'd stood with him were dead.

"Help us!" he cried to the gods of the darkness who were deaf to prayer.

"Help us!" he cried to anyone at all.

Soundlessly, beneath the shrieking, hissing, growling, and snapping of the beasts, dozens of arrows landed in front of him, behind him, and on the ground below him. Most of them found a home in monster flesh, but some embedded themselves in the wall he defended, and it slowed the swell for a moment.

Naked girl.

Seren stood below him with her group of archers and he had never thought her more incredible. She notched another arrow, and they followed her lead—albeit more slowly— letting loose and sending them sailing silently into the night all around him. Her arm became a blur of movement as she released an impossible number of arrows. In a couple of breaths, she'd fired a dozen arrows and felled as many beasts. *Naked girl has skills.*

Maybe Kesta should have driven the cart, he thought, but the strange sight of a dozen archers firing in his general direction distracted him from his epiphanies. The arrows landed all around him, yet somehow none hit him.

"Get away from the wall!" screamed Seren, but he did the opposite. With the rush held for a pulse, he raced along the top, kicking injured and dying monsters from his path as though it were no matter at all. However, the sight of the next wave of monsters on the outside scrambling up over their dead brethren crushed his spirit.

He reached the one-armed man just in time to face the invaders' retaliation. The dying man effortlessly decapitated the first over the edge, and Derian matched the broken man's power as he killed the next monster that was foolish enough to peek over. More followed, and more died as the warriors took the fight to them. With Seren and her archers clearing the way from below, and the fierce duo of Derian and his companion holding their section, the defenders held long enough for Natteo to reinforce them.

"For Treystone!" he roared, and his archers fired, delivering death to any beasts that Seren had missed, and for a glorious moment, the wall looked likely to hold. The defenders spread out, while others climbed atop the wall on either side of the breach to bring the fight to the monsters still racing through the break in the flames.

Though a great storyteller might suggest this battle took hours, it took only moments, and Derian enjoyed every slaughter-filled moment of it. Ravenous hate devoured any fear he had. As he put sword or dagger through flesh, he cursed the beast's soul, and soon the curses became nothing more than guttural snarls. Even his wounded companion became wary of his roaring and eyed him curiously when he wasn't busy defying his own death.

The man said nothing, never gave up, and neither did Derian. They met the curs along the top and sent the nightmarish beasts right back over. Derian called upon strength he'd never thought himself capable of. He'd heard stories of warriors summoning terrific power when losing, and so he roared and embraced his newfound fearlessness. He delivered great ruination upon every monster he faced until a beast knocked his sword from his grip. As the canis attempted to tear through Derian's broken defence, he swung a punch so fierce it snapped one of its long incisors in half and sent the unconscious beast flying back over the wall.

"Who needs a weapon!" he roared with a voice less his own and more a monster's. He punched another canis back over the wall, sending it flying into the crowd of its comrades below, and though this method of dispatching them was impressive, he realised he'd probably kill more with a weapon. Another demon came over and leapt towards him, only to fall beneath a hail of arrows. He spun around in disgust and howled "MINE!" The archers who had taken the shot seemed rather perplexed, but they aimed their next shot elsewhere.

"Mine. Kill. Mine."

His head spun and a rush of blood took his senses, and he embraced the fresh anger coursing through him. He snarled and a new fear took hold. What was happening to him? Was he enchanted? Was he infused with demonic blood? Had the savageness of war taken his insanity?

"It doesn't matter, Derian. Trust me."

It didn't matter, he told himself, charging back across the edge and ignoring a hail of arrows landing around him, for he was cutting, slicing, and killing, and it was glorious. He felt all-powerful, dominating, until, with no warning, the monsters stopped charging over. The demons slowed their invasion through the fire's breach. They stopped climbing up the writhing, demonic mound. The edge of the mob became still; they howled from down below and, farther out beyond the flames, those still in the darkness howled in reply. They vented their primal frustrations, they shrieked in delirium, they gorged upon human flesh they'd reached out and taken, and they fell away as though in retreat.

"We did it, my brave friends!" Derian cheered, raising his hand in the air, and Natteo raised his own in silent solidarity. He formed a fist and punched his chest three times, and Derian returned the gesture.

Seren, ever stunning in the flickering light of the wall's torches, offered a smug smile. She raised a perfectly attractive eyebrow and bowed her head a full three inches, and he'd never felt more alive.

Some of Seren's new archer companions climbed the ruined barricade now to reinforce the breach. There they stood as one, firing down at the large mound without fear of the demons crawling back over. Derian's heart swelled in his chest: the defenders of Treystone had held secure the line, and Derian had led them. A smile crept across his blood-covered face. He held it for an entire pulse before his one-armed comrade dropped to a knee beside him.

Done.

A great exhaustion came upon Derian, and even though the act of raising his arm took more energy than he thought himself capable of, he reached for the broken man, who felt impossibly heavy.

"You did well, brother," Derian whispered. The man's face was as pale as the day, and he knew the wound had almost bled him dry. "Without you, we would have been lost." The man nodded slowly and appeared to appreciate the words.

"We held the wall, you and I," the broken man whispered, as a few more archers pushed past them to finish off the swarm of beasts below. Derian wanted to cheer them on, to rile them up, to have them deliver such bloody vengeance that losing his comrades didn't hurt as it did. He wanted his dying companion to know the canis were being slain brutally, so his final sleep would be sweeter, but he kept silent. He didn't even know the man's name. He almost asked, but lost the will.

"We held the wall," Derian reassured him, and the dying man's sword clattered from his grip. It fell to the ground below, where many of his victims and friends lay dead or dying. Around them, the loud creaking of pulsing wood filled the battlements, and Derian cared only for the last of his warriors.

"I hear them coming through," the dying man whispered. "Help me back up and let me fight."

"There's no need. It is almost dawn," Derian lied, and he thought it fitting.

"Then I might rest." The man's voice was weaker now.

"Close your eyes, my friend." Derian waited for the man's

breath to catch and drop. Just a shudder after that, and his fight would be done.

"I'm not scared, for there is someone here with me now, in this darkness. He is fierce, he is powerful … and he watches you." The bearded man shuddered, and his breath caught, and then there was nothing but an empty, soulless husk dripping the last few drops of blood onto Derian's armour.

"Sleep, brother," Derian said, and released himself gently from the dead man's burdening weight.

Do not crumble under this, he told himself, and realised his ill choice of words, for, within a breath of time, the world beneath his feet began to crumble. Only a pulse of time after that, a piercing roar of breaking timber filled the air, and the platform beneath him shattered to a thousand pieces.

26

REMEMBER BREACH

Those sneaky monsters had been up to no good, Derian realised as the sky whirled overhead. While those who streamed over the wall met their end, the rest had busied themselves tearing at the wooden stakes below. In the melee, they had gone to task eagerly and without interruption as their brethren had climbed upon their backs and continued the distracting assault. They had hacked and slashed with their vicious claws and never let such a thing as suffocation or the incessant push of a bloodthirsty horde stop them. Eventually, they had breached the wall—and they had done it spectacularly.

The wall split now with a deafening roar and crumbled inwards from the swell; it gave way in countless shards of splintered wood, opening a gap wide enough that a marching army of canis demons could charge through. The warriors who had been standing above could do little more than collapse helplessly along with the tumbling debris, many becoming impaled upon the broken, jagged edges of shattered timber.

Derian fell among the ruin of canis and comrade. He

dropped into the abyss of churning darkness below, and with a terrible, crunching crash, he landed heavily on his back. The wind was knocked from him, and he fought back the urge to drift into soft, warm blackness. It called to him like the last whispers of a dying man, far beneath the rising tide's surface, and above him, as in a dream, the monsters poured through, battering him even further, though he felt nothing now.

"Don't sleep."

The mass of a thousand claws dragged him along and spun him as though he were a leaf in the wind. They caught him in their hate-filled wake, and he couldn't say how far they carried him or how many times he rolled—only that the world spun in a blur, coming to rest only when, as though waking from a dream, he shook himself, grabbed hold of a leathery neck and clung on tightly. The demon tried to shake him free—leaping and rearing like a prize mount unwilling to accept a rider. It fought, and among the ruin of the wall, Derian clung beneath its struggles and bested it, for were he to fall away, he knew death would follow.

"I have this."

He felt it again: the terror gave way to calm. He felt his limbs become a stranger's, yet they did not betray him. He savoured the fight; he savoured each breath; he savoured the story he was writing and the great telling he would deliver. His fatigue dissipated beneath the phantom power emanating from within. It was familiar, and he wondered, this close to death, had he weaved that strength from somewhere in his own soul? Had he gifted himself one last, titanic effort to survive? One last surge of courage that drove him to kill, tear, and destroy anything before him? *For* him?

The beast stumbled and leapt away from its charging comrades, and he felt a roar form in his lungs, upon his lips. Primal and ancient.

What is happening?

"Surviving."

He was brutal because he craved brutality. He locked his arms around the beast's fleshy throat and squeezed himself close, close enough to smell its vulgar stench, to feel its warm spittle upon his cheek, as it snapped at the unreachable parasite gripping on desperately for dear life. There was no desperation in his actions. He brought himself closer. So close that he could have opened his mouth wide and bit the demon —and this was exactly what he did.

Polished.

He gnawed deeply at the tough, sagging flesh below its neck, and it felt like biting into undercooked steak. He dug deep with teeth controlled by another monster, just below its jaw, and pulled vital entrails free, and this felt richer, like tearing delicious flesh from a chicken bone—and just as satisfying. The creature howled, and he tore again, swallowing warm blood as it sprayed into his face, and the beast stumbled and rolled itself and landed upon Derian, trapping him beneath.

"Not like this!" he roared in the voice unlike his own, as the terrible weight crushed his chest and stole his breath.

On both sides, canis demons surged past them, forward into the town, flanked by their following anculus masters, who roared them onwards like vile shepherds from a demon realm. Derian tried to roar again, but he lost his breath, and he felt the tempting embrace of unconsciousness beckoning him again.

Not like this, his mind begged, challenged, and wailed from deep within, and he fought the darkness as arrows struck the attacking monsters coming through. He caught sight of his Crimson comrades at war—Logan, Kesta, Natteo, and Seren—forming up in a line only twenty feet from where he'd fallen, while those they protected fled away into the town like the terrified peasants they were.

"Not like this." He felt a strange, familiar power and remembered his strength from outside the town, when a monster had taken him by the throat and squeezed. He'd bitten that brute as well.

"NOT LIKE THIS!"

Derian did not push the monster from his chest, for he felt incredible. *Unstoppable.* Instead of heaving the beast from him, he struck it with all his might, with a clenched fist of stone. A fine strike, fiercer than before, and it caught its jaw and snapped it cleanly in two, and Derian sent the carcass rolling away like a child tumbling down a hill.

He climbed to his feet beneath the ruin of the wall, with the enemy flooding in all around him, and instead of leaping towards better footing or retreating towards his comrades, he clenched Rusty in his grasp, roared in defiance, and struck the nearest monster to his right. The dagger blade went deep as he broke the monster's skin, and as it charged, he braced his blade against its weight and spilled its innards as it passed. He never knew if he killed it, for there were a hundred more charging in, but knowing he'd inflicted pain was something wonderful.

What is happening to me? he wondered again, and savoured how much killing he had to do. He spun to the next monster and plunged just as fiercely, roaring primitively—for he was magnificent.

Like spilling myself under a woman's touch.

He waded into the monsters, and his companions were beside him and it was glorious. Heroes all of them, and he a legend in waiting.

Natteo for his part offered himself as prey to the monsters, and he did so like a master. Allowing his armour to take most of the burden, he gladly accepted a few violent shakes from each set of clenched teeth before plunging both his swords into his attackers, one on each side. As they howled and died, he found a wonderfully profane description for every demonic spirit he sent back into the darkness, and Derian's savage self loved it.

Kesta drove her mighty long sword into every monster that moved, as if something ethereal possessed her, as well. She no longer resembled the awkward mercenary blessed with miserable motherly traits and little else. Now, she offered no mercy, plunging her sword down into each monster's body in turn, lest it rise for a second snap at her—or worse, escape with its life. Her face was cold and relaxed, except when it came to the killing blows. With these, she smiled, and Derian loved this too.

Lorgan matched Derian's viciousness, likely earning the right to Keralynn's bed with his performance. He was ferocious with both sword and shield. Using both as devastating weapons, he charged brazenly towards each anculus demon as though their breach were an affront to him personally, and perhaps it was. Such was his savagery, the beasts that broke through scattered beneath his wrath. He performed like a lost legend whispered to return at the turn of the dark.

Even Seren leapt into the fray fearlessly. In badly-fitting armour and a dress that had no place on the battlefield, she spun and cut like a grizzled mercenary of thirty years. She moved more swiftly than her usual laboured march, as though this were her calling. She looked less her usual goddess self, standing upon a pedestal displaying her divine beauty and gazing down on mortals with beautiful, knowing eyes—well, she still looked like all of those things—and more a Crimson Hunter. He'd never desired her as much as he did in this moment. He wanted to live long enough to win her heart. Or at least furrow her until dawn.

He shouldn't have seen any of this; he saw through the eyes of a nameless creature. As his body contorted, plunged, stabbed, and struck, his mind wandered from his actions, yet still, he knew to trust himself. Perhaps they'd spiked his drink? He could have thought more on this, but everything suddenly changed. As though commanded by one voice, squealing in a frequency no human could hear, the demons fell away from the defending wall. They retreated mid-bite, mid-claw, mid-kill, as though time had frozen itself as solid as ice, and Derian felt his frenzy release itself.

The exhaustion struck his limbs again, as though the sudden silence was a poison to his charge. He began to feel the injuries he'd incurred, and the urge to fall to his knees was overwhelming. He wanted to collapse among the frozen monsters, and he also wanted to attack them where they stood, but the enchantment of the moment held him in place, as it did them, and he was unwilling to shatter it.

The monsters set their hateful, deferential gaze upon Seren, and from her place among the three or four carcasses at her feet, she stared right back at them, returning their animosity tenfold. He looked to the gaping hole where they'd entered, and he could see dozens of beasts there, equally motionless, and he thought this a strange thing too.

"Shoo, little doggits," hissed Natteo, stepping beside Seren. He stood ready to counter their charge should the moment erupt into violence. Only then did Derian notice the badly taken blow he'd received; blood dripped heavily from a deep gash along his neck. It seeped out beneath his metal armour and down his favourite shirt. If the injury didn't kill him, Derian would endure a month's worth of complaining about his misfortune. A fine way to deal with horrors. Derian thought him a better man for it.

"Silencio is calling you," Natteo said.

Perhaps the attackers understood his meaning, for without looking from Seren, they scuttled away from the battle as one, like a burbling wave at low tide. They did not leave empty-clawed, however: they dragged away what riches they'd earned. Derian watched two of the creatures retreat through the breach clasping a one-armed body with them, leaving only its bronze helmet behind. Like raiders pillaging a market, the demons swept all the human carcasses from the ruin of the platform. Derian heard a few weak moans as the fallen were dragged away, and he moved instinctively toward them, but Lorgan took hold of his shoulder as the last monster disappeared through the break in the flames.

"No need to give chase, lad. There'll be plenty more fighting to do. Those they've taken are already dead—or will be soon enough. Best you calm that wild heart of yours, if you don't want it exploding before night's end," he said.

"It's no way to die," hissed Kesta, distraught that the fighting had ended without nearly enough monsters dead at her feet. From the darkness, a few of the villagers returned with weapons and torches in hand. They were frightened, shaken, and Derian imagined some were suspicious at the fiends' sudden retreat, but slowly and steadily they converged upon the last five defenders. Those who hadn't fallen along the wall, or fled outright from the horrors, looked back out into the night with hardened, newly-experienced eyes, as the retreating monsters fled from the valley.

"Well, that was a disaster," muttered Natteo, and finally he collapsed in a ruined heap, his face and hands soaked with his own blood.

27

LONG NIGHT

S ilence. Nothing but silence played in Derian's ears, and that was fine with him. The rushing wind brought silence, as did the crackling of the flames only a dozen feet from his place of watch. He liked how these natural things brought quiet, deafening his ears to everything else around him.

He ached, and each breath felt like he'd sprinted twenty miles in blazing heat without respite. Whatever had fuelled his rage and fierceness had now departed, leaving him weak and vulnerable. Lorgan was gone, his arms heavy with the broken body of his unconscious friend. So much blood had drained from Natteo. But he would rally, Derian told himself.

He'll be fine. Right?

Natteo was stronger than most others, despite his appearance. A few stitches with a careful hand, a few cups of ale, and his strong heart would pump some fresh blood right back into him. *Isn't that how it works?*

It probably said so in his book, but the section on human anatomy was heavy with complicated words and gruesome pictures. He thought of recovering his book to study the night away. Who knew how boredom would affect his thoughts as the night dragged on? Better, perhaps, to advantage of the silence.

No, best to keep an eye on the night, boredom or not, he told himself, and he made a good argument. Somewhere out there in the dark were demons, and he wondered if they watched him as he watched for them. He looked around at his comrades, at the crackling fire. There was probably no place he'd rather be in this town while waiting for dawn.

Standing upon each side of the breached wall stood archers. Twenty on each side or so. Enough to stem a sudden attack while they raised the alarm, he imagined. All of them behaving as statues would. Each lost in their own thoughts. There was no cheer, no whispered words; only uneasy eyes watching into the night.

Below them, anxious labourers went to work preparing for the day ahead. They were quiet in their tasks; they feared another sneaky assault by the clever demons, and rightly so. If Derian listened past the wind driving through the gap and over the sound of the dancing flames, he could hear their mutterings, their proposals, their manoeuvring of long timber poles, and their calm repairs. He didn't know why, but it calmed him. Perhaps it reminded him of the value of civilisation.

Certain the beasts had gone for the night, Kesta had slipped away to rest, her face grave from memories and the fear of losing another loved one to monsters. Natteo's blood had stained her worn fingers, and she'd spent a long enough time staring at them.

Derian turned to Seren, who stood beside him. She had been there for an hour now, and Derian was grateful for the silent comfort she offered. She hadn't spoken, but she was familiar, and familiarity was as reassuring as silence.

"Soon, will be light," she said at length.

He nodded, then turned away again and took a few steps through the breach, out to the dying flames. After a time, she followed. She smelled of the march—sweat, mud, and the delicate, iron fragrance of demon blood. She smelled far better than he, not that he cared. There'd be plenty of time for bathing at sunrise. If he had the taste for it, he might invite her to join him in the river. Maybe she'd stumble and fall. Maybe he'd save her. He almost smiled at that stupid fantasy. Those unoriginal things only happened in self-indulgent tales for hopeless romantics. Still, though, nothing wrong with some romance, when he thought about it.

"Tired now."

"I am too. We'll have a few hours' sleep soon enough." Thick, crimson blood caked his body and crackled when he moved. Better that than the warm sensation of freshly dead things clinging to him, he supposed. Better than the blood of his dead comrades. He thought of them and realised with a sinking heart that he knew only Keri's name. He thought of the girl with the nice smile and matching armour and felt her passing anew. He tried to remember the others, but he hadn't known them long enough to memorise their faces.

Is that a saving grace?

"Natteo will live," Seren declared, as though she were a healer in her healer's chambers and Derian a relative waiting for word. She used the same disinterested tone most healers reserved for these moments, and despite her ignorance of Natteo's welfare, it reassured him greatly.

And then she dragged a dead demon's corpse from below the break of the wall and dropped it at the edge of the dying flames in one gliding movement before sitting down on its back. Satisfied it was a comfortable seat, she held out her hands over the warmth.

"Sit with Seren." She patted the head and bade him sit—upon the sightless, still-grimacing head of a monster. He considered dragging over his own demonic chair, but being closer to her was worth a little discomfort. "Need to talk," she said, patting the beast's head a second time. Its tongue slithered free from its mouth.

"How do you know Natteo will recover?" he asked.

"Don't know. Only know that he not die this day," she said.

"How do you know?"

"Don't know. Just know."

"Right, that's polished. And me? Do you know if I will die?"

"You… will probably die."

"…"

"You should pray to not die," she said, smiling curiously.

Was that her first joke? Was that a joke at all? "I think I'll just go and stand over here for a while," he countered.

"Derian might die if Derian over there." She began tying her hair up absently. He stood to leave, and she did not stop him, so after a breath of confusion, he sat right back down. "Then again… you… might not die." She shrugged, and he was confused and unsettled.

"Do you have knowledge of things to come?" he asked—wary that she did, and wary that she would reply. He hated conversations like this. He was frightened of prophecies, and he didn't know why. Prophecies usually meant predestined death, and that shit terrified him. She squirmed slightly, adjusting her perfectly shaped rear upon the beast's back; a deathly gasp escaped its mouth beneath Derian's less impressive rear, and he felt thoroughly uncomfortable.

"Broken." She touched her forehead, suspiciously close to where he'd shot her in the head. "You broke Seren."

"Sorry."

"Sometimes, Seren… Urgh… I… can't put words, sentences, thoughts… order." She sighed, searching her thoughts for elusive words to explain further the destruction he'd laid upon her. "Hate it."

"I'm sorry."

"I know. Stop saying."

"But I really am sorry."

"Stop talking. It annoys Seren… Me… Derian… Urgh… You are better with shut mouth. I see arrow when Derian… you… when you talk."

He shut his mouth and felt worse. This was the longest conversation he'd had with her yet, he thought. From this close, he could see her lips in the dying firelight, and he wanted to touch them with his finger. Nothing unsavoury. Just a little touch. They looked so very touchable. Perhaps that in itself was a little unsavoury.

"With broken mind…" she went on, "because broken mind, I have seen things, moments, people, different… endings to what is now?" she offered, and it still thoroughly confused him. So, he apologised again, and she muttered a curse. "I see moment you not put arrow through head. That was good. We even friends. You even this night…" She made a crude gesture with her fingers and shrugged. "It was fine. First for Seren… me."

"Sorry, WHAT???"

"Broken mind see actions of what could, when actions taken different," she said, choosing a disapproving master's tone as her own.

"I do not understand any of this, Seren," he said, forgetting himself and taking hold of her perfectly formed shoulders. He wanted to kiss her. *She likes me, she really likes me. Why else does she say this?* He'd heard that stirrings of war stirred other things in the quiet moments after.

"Idiot, Derian," she said, removing his hands from her shoulders before taking them in her own and looking into his eyes.

Say it. Say that you love me.

"I do not love you, and you… you do not love me. You never love me." She sighed as though wary of revealing something he was wary of hearing, and then she went for it anyway. "There is someone, she… pretty. Very pretty. Not Seren pretty… but pretty… with… hair… and she does not know she will love you… because—" She sighed and searched for the words in the fragmented mind that he'd broken. "Because in world, shared souls… fated to meet." Her face darkened. "If both survive."

He didn't know what to say, and he didn't understand why she spoke as she did. He had a thousand questions, none of which he expected her to answer.

"Will I know her when I see her?"

"No."

"Why?"

"Because Derian is idiot." That was fair enough.

"Will we…" He made a rude gesture with his fingers, and she shrugged a 'possibly' shrug. Then she made another rude gesture and he felt his mind stumble over itself.

"Do you know her name?"

"No."

"Tell me something about her,"

"No."

"Please?"

"Whisht."

"PLEASE."

"I don't know. She is girl, she is pleasing… she has

good… knees?" Derian's head spun for the umpteenth time in this conversation alone. It was exhaustion on top of unsettling, unnatural words. "Do not ask more," she warned.

He asked more. "Will we meet soon?"

"Not in these lands. Not unless you live until night you meet. You probably die many times from here until then, in… my… Seren's… thoughts. Wait… was right first time," she muttered, shaking her head and tapping the area where he'd shot her.

"When might I die?" He was desperate to know. Also, not to know.

"You die plenty in broken mind, but next you die with me in fire. When you die, there is no coming back for Derian, no coming back for Seren… Urgh … for me … Aargh." She picked at a loose piece of torn skin upon her abominable chair and flicked it into the fire in annoyance. "That will be me," she whispered, watching the flesh sizzle. "I am afraid to die. I see nothing after die."

Leave now.

"Why do you speak to me like this?" he cried, and this time he stood. As if sensing the moment, the first glimmer of light emerged from behind the horizon, announcing their full night's survival. He'd never seen a more beautiful sight, and suddenly he was more tired than he had ever been in his life. His body ached, and his head was full of ashes. He didn't want to talk to this goddess a moment longer. He didn't want to die in fire with her, and he wanted to know more of this mysterious girl with the nice knees.

"Because you are important to Se … to me?"

"You don't even like me," he snarled, before turning back towards the wall. Stomping away was all he could do. He needed sleep, and he needed to hide. He needed to see Natteo, and he needed to cry. Oh, he needed to cry.

"I like me, and Derian could save me if Derian know must save me," Seren called out, but he didn't look back. He was thoroughly confused, thoroughly exhausted, and thoroughly terrified.

"To the fires with you so!" he shouted, and he left her to her watch.

28

MEMORIES TO COME

That went much better than expected, Seren thought, watching her former killer storm petulantly away. He would settle that growing rage of his soon enough, she imagined.

If he doesn't, his heart will explode.

She cracked her neck satisfyingly and left her demonic throne where it lay. Derian carried the weight of the battle heavily, she thought.

He is no seasoned warrior like Lorgan.

He is no tough little wretch like Natteo.

He is no iron-willed flying witch like Kesta.

He had darkness inside. Perhaps, honed as a weapon, it might offer value, she thought.

She wondered could they ever be friends? She wondered would she ever even crave his friendship? She wondered had she said too much to him? Or worse, not enough? She could see more future moments for Derian than for anyone else. She saw fewest for herself. Mostly, she saw the fire, and it scared the thurken spit from her. *Is that the saying?*

She shrugged and enjoyed the burning light of dawn a little more and decided she had said exactly the right number of broken words, and if his heart didn't explode, she knew he'd be at her side—if not for camaraderie, then for the seed of curiosity she'd planted in his mind. He would tiptoe up to her all stupid-like and beg for a little more information on what she knew, or didn't know. *Poor stupid Derian.* How could she explain what visions she saw in a way that his feeble mind could understand?

Some images were like vivid dreams with such clarity that it stung her mind, while other visions appeared like lost memories from childhood, barely even thoughts to gaze upon, and mostly inaccurate. *Mostly.* Perhaps this was exactly how she could explain it, she supposed.

She rubbed the phantom injury where he'd torn her mind apart and felt an unbridled anger form for him. "Let it sleep," she whispered of her hatred.

"Are you enjoying the morning, little one?" a voice called, and she spun around to see the rested figure of Lorgan leaning against the broken shards of the wall. Few creatures should have been capable of sneaking up on her, yet Lorgan was special, wasn't he?

He'd find a way to pull me from the fires.

The labourers had dared to leave the safety of the walls and had begun repairing the breach, and for a moment, it felt as though this town was recovering from a harsh gale. They had replaced the horror of the night with the banal duties of the day. Intending to walk, Lorgan was no longer dressed in his battle armour, instead favouring a casual shirt of grey and trousers of brown. His face was no longer covered in blood;

his eyes appeared heavy and older than before. If that was even possible.

"Did Keralynn give payment?"

All too swiftly, as though he hadn't enjoyed the company of a beautiful woman all night, he replied, "I'm certain Keralynn will offer payment when the deed is done, when the town is safe."

"You get payment now. Better for Lorgan... Urgh... no... better for... you." He laughed, and she liked the art of humour. It was wonderfully human.

His face darkened. "Did you bring the demons down upon this town?"

This isn't my fault.

"I am no beast, I am no murderer, and I am no demon master," she said.

"I never said you were, little one. But we all saw it. The townsfolk all saw it. The monsters stopped for you. What don't I know?"

"Fiore watches from dark. She is angry." Seren pointed to her navel, where the demon's mark had rested. "She whisper to beasts. Whisper them kill Seren. Whisper them kill protectors."

"So we must protect you?"

She shook her head. That wasn't what she meant. "Comrades. Crimson Hunter." She held five fingers out and pointed one to her heart and wondered did he understand? Would he value her ability? If he did, he said nothing, but his eyes warmed. Few warriors ever wanted to join the Crimson Hunters. Perhaps he saw the coup in the finest warrior in the world offering her sword. Offering her allegiance. Until the war. Or until she died in a day or so.

"Would the monsters chase if we left? Would we save the town?"

"No. Drawn to this place." She tapped her navel again and then held out her left hand. "Fiore whisper them chase Seren." She held out her right hand and waved it vigorously. "But peasant town, easy food."

He sighed, and she said no more. Instead, they stood watching the dawn for a little time.

Most of the fires were nothing more than embers now, and their dying glow brought memories from another life flashing before Seren's eyes. She couldn't decipher their meaning, but she desired breakfast all of a sudden. She wasn't sure what food she liked most, but the prospect of cooking some meat over the embers appealed to her above anything else at the moment. *Meat with honey and onion.*

"Tonight must be better," she said.

"I have a few ideas, little one."

"More flames?"

"More flames."

"More stakes?"

"More stakes."

"Didn't work last night," she muttered.

"It'll work tonight," he countered.

"Perhaps it will," she said.

"How was the watch?" he asked.

"Silent. No signs, no howls, no beasts." She eyed the forest, as she had done all night with Derian at her side.

"Good," he said with no surprise. "And where is Derian?" he asked.

"He stood until dawn break," she countered quickly, lest he become irked with the young man's disappearance. Who knew what Derian might say, explaining his absence to an angry leader?

"You both did well tonight, little one, and I think you've

watched long enough. Let me walk you to your lodging lest
your followers ambush you."

As they walked through the breach, a stream of eager children
flooded out carrying axes and blades. They leapt through the
fire's breach but did not mutilate the corpses like before. Instead,
they charged for the treeline, ignoring any fear of demons
hovering beneath the sun's rays. A few gestured to Lorgan as
they passed, as though he were their general, but none dared
greet Seren. Perhaps word of the demons' strange retreat had
reached the rest of the town's ears. Seren watched as the
children, for a moment, attacked the branches of the trees
energetically, and she left them to it. In years to come, as
adulthood struck, those who survived might suffer nightmarish
recurring dreams, but they would be tougher for it, and for now,
they were unsullied heroes. Simple and incredible and fearless,
despite what their eyes had shown them. Willing to accept things
they didn't understand. If only the town could think and behave
as they did. Lorgan had been wise to call upon their efforts.

"Your followers appear to have grown tired of adoring
you already," Lorgan said, and she searched for the right
words. Careful words. She had no desire to deceive those she
would call her allies; if there was no trust, there was no
acceptance, and there was no survival.

"They wait for miracles of fire." She looked to her
fingers. *No, still no enchanted fire yet.* "And resurrection
too."

He looked around as they walked, and when he spoke, she
could see the faith and love he had for humanity. "This town
has not likely known days as black as these. No matter how
many times you tell them you cannot perform miracles, they

know what they saw. They hoped for your miracles last night, and they'll hope for them again tonight, I would think."

She caught her frustrated hiss before it left her lips. "And when nothing happens, when they see I have no power, they will turn on… Seren… me."

"Did we turn on you, Seren?"

"You might!" she snapped.

"We didn't after your vector demon killed us."

"Did, and chained."

He dropped his head. "When we took you from that glade, you became our responsibility. We went to war with a rival outfit for you, which will probably end up getting us all killed. There is a grand demon hunting you, and still, we haven't run for the trees. What matters is we are with you. Until the end."

She shrugged and thought it was a good reply. "Then they will turn on us all."

He smiled and patted her on the shoulder. She didn't know why, but it was reassuring, fatherly. It felt like home. She immediately wanted another. "You think very little of these peasants, Seren. They will not turn on you or us, or anyone—even if things turn for the worst."

She wanted to believe him. She could see the belief in his eyes, redemption reaffirming his will. It was beautiful, and it blinded him to the good and bad in people. They'd been quick to place their unquestioning faith in her; they would be equally quick in condemning her. They thought her a god, and just as easily, they could think her a demon. Even this far from the stronghold of the Dark One, they desired something divine from the source. She had nothing to convince Lorgan otherwise, so she spat on the ground, and he seemed happy to take it as a concession.

"If I could save them, I would," she offered after a time, and he nodded approvingly.

"And if we can save you from Fiore, the grand demon, we will try."

"If you save me from Fiore, that be only beginning of horrors."

29

NATTEO

"Could somebody please cease that infernal spitting racket before I lose my fuken mind?" he screamed, but as he suspected, the noise did not cease. It continued its clamour, beginning somewhere outside and carried in by invisible fingers to lodge in his head. *'Thump,'* it went, and he hated it. *'Thump'* it went again, and the pain matched each beat as murderous thoughts filled his mind. He was frenzied, demented, and exhausted. "Can you please let the dying rest in peace?" His head hammered with every word shouted. So much for being a diminishing hero.

"You aren't dying, sir," a young man said. It came from a few feet away. Natteo turned in his bed. *Not alone so.*

"I'm rarely wrong about these things. Give me more syrup to ease my passing." Natteo chose his weakest-sounding voice. He knew how to play a healer.

"You've had plenty."

"More." Despite only darkness filling his vision, he still chanced a charming smile. He heard movement and the pop of a cork. He imagined the filling of the spoon, and he sighed as they placed it to his lips. "Thank you, my friend. You are kind to the dying," he offered, and stretched himself out, waiting for the poppy syrup to take effect.

"You are not dying. But, if you were, would she heal you?" The voice was young, male, and perfect. Natteo pulled the wet cloth from his eyes, and the room became less gloomy. He sat up and felt the cold chill of evening strike his naked chest. *Why are all healing parlours so spitting cold?* His head thumped, and he realised the hammering was louder from a sitting position.

"Do you mean Seren?"

"Would she have healed you, if you were at the source's door?" the young man asked, and Natteo eyed his prey. He was raven-haired and clean-shaven, with a weak, rounded chin, and dark, innocent eyes. Not entirely unattractive, but not exactly Natteo's type. Until a few months ago, he hadn't even known he had a type.

"She cannot heal with weaving enchantments. She is only a mercenary, like any of us!" he snapped, licking his lips, trying to discern exactly what flavours his mouth tasted of— something fetid, sweet, revolting, and delicious. He needed more to ease the thumping. He reached for the bottle in the healer's hand and was denied the ambrosia. The young man slipped away and returned the brown bottle of goodness to a shelf above his head.

The room was twice the size of his chosen shack and snugly furnished. A few more beds sat on either side of Natteo's. Bodies in various degrees of horror filled them all. Most slept, their chests rising and falling slowly with wet wheezing or staggered gasps. Some stared at the thatched roof above their heads, waiting to die. They'd seen enough; injuries of the body healed well enough, but injuries to the soul were eternal. They might leave this place, but they would never be the same.

"Will she help us if we pray to her?" the healer asked, and Natteo glared. How did a healer fall for her charms as others did? They flocked to her like desperate children, and in the face of horrors, when she brought nothing but misery, they still hoped her capable of marvels. She was no miracle worker, and only now—with a severe amount of blood loss, a dreadful tear in his neck, and an aching body—did Natteo realise Seren was not good for the Crimson Hunters at all.

"Are you peasants really so stupid?" Natteo muttered, and cursed his lack of control. His words were crude and unjust. The ruined and lost surrounded the healer; he was undoubtedly a better person than Natteo. What was wrong with having a little faith in greater things beyond the mundane?

"I know what I saw," the thick-skinned healer countered, taking little offence.

"And you think you see a deity?" Natteo mocked, wondering if he were being a little unfair to Seren. Just because their entire world had spun on its head since she'd appeared in their lives, just because thousands of demonic beasts had just 'happened' to break through the source since her appearance, just because they'd died twice since she'd introduced herself in a flaming fireball, and just because a grand demon was apparently seeking to break through and cut them all up into little pieces. *Just fuken because. And another hundred reasons after.*

True, she had fought for the town and come to Derian's aid without hesitation, but it was an unsettling thing how easily she had implanted herself into their group. What right did she have, going from captive to comrade so swiftly? She claimed she was important; she claimed warmth; she claimed friendship. But unlike the rest of her new comrades, he was not so easily won over. *Not yet.*

Natteo loved Lorgan like a father—as though he were his own disapproving father—but sometimes, the old fool searched for nobility in the wrong places. Natteo was all for helping the little waif with her torments, but deep in his bones, he knew it was Seren who would get them all killed. *Again.*

Death should have scared him, but it really didn't. There was something in the darkness. After death. Maybe he was just turning bitter like Kesta. Maybe he was just tired like Lorgan. Maybe he was listening to the darkness within him, just like Derian. He shook these thoughts from his head. Perhaps he had taken enough juice; or perhaps one more was all he needed.

"I believe in greater things, mercenary."

"Hold on to that faith, my friend. What harm can it do?" Natteo said, conceding the matter. He tested the tearing at his neck. Whoever had tended to him had chosen larger stitching than needed.

Perfect.

Scarring brought greater interest in business. Any mercenary with impressive scarring was worth more than pretty mercenaries with flawless skin. He'd been meaning to pick up another few scars to draw greater numbers to him, and this long tear underneath his chin, all the way down past his shoulder, would suffice.

"This is some polished healing. Thank you, sir." Natteo reached out and took the watching healer's hands and squeezed them tightly. May as well find out the young man's predilection before they moved any further, he thought. *Also.* "More?"

The young man held his hand more briefly than he would have liked. He did not squeeze in reply. He did, however, offer a smile, and sometimes a smile was all it took. Perhaps his new friend was a young man unprepared to admit that fathering brats was probably not in his future. Natteo would very much love to father a child. Or just be a father to a child. Perhaps down the road, he could steal a child for himself and his husband. Not an ugly one, though. Where did that thought come from? he wondered, shaking his head.

"Any more and you could collapse," his healing friend— who might or might not heal his other urges—replied. Natteo sighed in mock defeat. He still had pain; he intended to claim more syrup.

"Please?"

"No."

Natteo sat up, swung his feet down to the cold tiled floor and stood up, stretching magnificently, displaying all the nudity that he could. Perhaps his confused healing friend hadn't noticed when he'd stripped him during his surgery, or perhaps another healer had had the pleasure of preparing Natteo. As it was, the smooth shave Natteo performed upon his lower regions every third or fourth day served him well.

"You should not be up walking," the healer cried, and Natteo shook the bruising from his body, shook the sleep from his limbs, shook the different appendages to life. His young healer did not look away until he realised he had not looked away, and then he swiftly looked away, taking a keen interest in the brightly burning fire in the corner. Natteo took this exact moment to liberate a little bottle of corked loveliness from its place on the shelf.

"No, no, no—you can't take that," cried the healer, and Natteo spun around, offering his most charming grin.

"Would you like to wrestle me for it?"

"Erm… no?"

Natteo popped the cork and drank. He knew the risks. He'd spent a lifetime and a half in servitude in Castra, so he

knew pleasure; he knew excess; he knew how to dance
between them easily enough. He swallowed the milky potion
and involuntarily shook and growled as it hit his system. His
vision blurred from the earlier doses, the room began to spin,
and he adjusted his stance to compensate.

Not enough to be fatal yet.

He took another mouthful and duty brought the healer to
him, but Natteo kept his prize behind his back playfully. It
didn't matter that they might die in the next day or so; what
mattered was having fun between then and now.

"You shouldn't be up," the healer hissed again, reaching
from a safe distance, and Natteo suspected the young man
might not be interested at all. Not that Natteo would have
done anything; he was already in love.

What would he think of me, behaving in such a way?

All's fair on the march, Natteo thought. Besides, his love
didn't even know how much he truly cared for him. Maybe it
wasn't even love. Maybe he was just the first man to
consume Natteo's every waking thought. Every night as he
lay down to sleep, in fact. He really spent far too long
imagining his love coming to him, taking hold, kissing him,
and so much more.

Is that love or excessive desire?

Maybe that was all love could be. He shook his head
again and ran his fingers over his lips. He made a satisfying
sound, and he wondered if he hadn't taken a taste more of the
poppy juice than he'd meant to. *Oh well.* He'd probably die
tonight, but not in this room, Natteo decided.

"This is mine now," he whispered, clutching the bottle,
and he spun away from his new friend, searching for his
clothes.

He wondered was he late? They had curtained the
windows over, and the lack of light coming from beneath the

doorway worried him. The stitches were many hours old, and he suspected a full day had passed since the demons had breached the wall. He suspected there was more fighting coming. Perhaps his friends were fighting this very moment. Panic cut through his delirium, and he reached for his ruined clothes, in a heap at the foot of his bed.

"I've got to go."

"You will die if you leave," the healer cried, but Natteo pushed him away and began dressing. As he did, a rasping hiss of wet air distracted him, and he stopped for a moment to take the hand of the ruined man in the bed beside him. The demons had destroyed his face, his body more so, but he had one working eye, and he was staring at the bottle.

"Take what you want, friend," Natteo whispered, and passed the opened bottle to the doomed man. The healer tried to recover the bottle, but after a moment's pause, he thought better of it. They would need more beds tonight. Natteo nodded in appreciation. Sometimes mercy heralded a blissful departure. The man kept drinking until the bottle was empty, wherein he placed it carefully on the floor beside his bed and lay back to stare at the ceiling and remember beautiful things.

"Where are my weapons?" Natteo asked.

"They are with your comrades," his new friend said, before offering him his boots.

"Time to die." Natteo took the young man's hand and kissed it gently before stumbling out of the doorway into the night.

30

THE LAST CHARGE

There was no clamouring bell to alert the town. Its inhabitants already knew their routine. It was strange how swiftly bloodshed and horror had turned wide-eyed farmers and uneducated miners into hardened warriors. Treystone had only needed a few nights of dreadfulness. Those who had survived stood ready as darkness overcame them.

Though he'd slept a handful of hours, Derian felt weak and wretched. The people who'd laboured the entire day probably felt worse. Great tales never spoke of the exhaustion and the mundane. Always, defences were set. It was never *how* they were set.

If the first day's preparations had been inadequate, the second day's were a considerable improvement. Derian suspected those who had toiled in the treeline had either steadied their nerve or learned, brutally, the value of effective preparation. Perhaps both. Or perhaps they'd learned from the children's boundless enthusiasm. From his solitary place at the gate, Derian could see the damage imposed upon the forest. Perhaps had they accomplished this the previous night, Derian would still have soldiers to command.

Lorgan addressed the gathered crowd only twenty feet away. "Hold your shields longer than you think you can. Do not be the first to collapse." Twenty feet may as well have been a mile. Lorgan stood at the centre of the open gate with his shield drawn. On either side of him stood a dozen similarly armed warriors. At their feet lay a long, reinforced beam. Lorgan's plan would never work.

It might half-work.

In the distance, cutting through the darkness, Derian heard a howl, and his heartbeat quickened. There was no more fear, no panic, but he tasted metal on his tongue. *Like demon blood.* His armour was heavy. It would suit a giant's build, he thought. He didn't understand why Lorgan had come to him with the freshly cooked metal piece, only that he had commanded him to wear it. The shielding was thick and bulky, heavier than any other armour he'd seen. Every step he took was laboured. He imagined it would take an army of canis a full night's tearing to penetrate its thick shell, but that didn't make him feel any better.

They'd strapped Rusty into his right hand and his new blade, Honey Blood, into the other. The long sword was unusually wide. Its handle had a golden bronze finish with a blood-red wrapping at its grip. He liked the blade. Perhaps it deserved a better name.

From behind the thickly-grated faceplate, he could make out some part of the battlefield. The children had cut every thin branch from every tree and sharpened each one to some wonderful nastiness, before placing them all along the walls leading out towards the treeline. Thousands, all jagged and uninviting. Guaranteed to do little damage to a rushing horde, but enough to persuade the rest to turn towards easier footing.

But a wall of thicker, sturdy spikes stood clustered at every corner of the town. If the beasts circled like before, they would find their route obstructed.

Along the river, at the far end, a dozen more of the sharpened lines blocked the route, ensuring nothing but frustration would meet their vanquishers for the first charge. The fires were lit and spread out to twice the width of the previous night's. The flames would be wilder, but they would also burn more swiftly. It wouldn't matter, for the fighting would finish long before they burned to ash. The town appeared impregnable, uninviting on all sides but one, and at this last side stood Lorgan with the rest of his army.

Kesta stood atop the platform over the front gate. "Do not fire until they breach. They must breach," she commanded. She was in her element. "THEY MUST BREACH!" Perhaps it was a death-wish or the scent of vengeance she savoured. Whatever it was, her imposing smile suited her, and her determination heartened the defenders standing nearby. They did not know what horrors she had endured or that she had seen a town fall, and perhaps it was better this way. She was poised, waiting for the kill, and they watched in awe, desiring vengeance of their own.

"I am too far from any of this," Derian muttered, and sighed heavily in his armour. Ahead of him, in a handful of regimented lines, stood every warrior in the town.

Shame.

Lorgan no longer trusted Derian's judgement. He had fallen short in defending his side, and Lorgan had punished him for it. Now, Derian reinforced the rear, and it devastated him. He'd argued and pleaded, but it had come to nothing, so here he stood behind hundreds of lesser peasants, awaiting his turn.

As recently as a week ago, the prospect of fighting would

have crippled him with fear. He would gladly have taken his place at the back. But anger was a glorious tonic. Now he desired only to stand at the front, bleeding with strangers he treated as kin. He wanted to bring the fight to those who hunted them.

Was this bravery? Was this madness? Was he a warmonger? Oh, what did it matter in this moment?

Even Seren had earned her place in the battlements. Standing along the top wall with a bow in hand, she was statuesque. Though the wall was heavy with archers, they stood away from her. The townsfolk, too, had kept their distance, and Derian thought it typical. *Fickle peasants.* Maybe she'd scared them away with talk of prophetic nonsense; maybe she'd finally convinced them she desired privacy above worship; maybe they had finally realised she was no goddess.

She was still a goddess to him, though. She would be *his* goddess someday—regardless of what she suggested. If there were things like prophecies, he would defy them. Her eyes watched the forest, and he wanted to apologise to her for storming off, for fearing the unknown. He almost took a step forward so he could call to her, perhaps convince her to stay and talk a few moments, but the effort was too much, the distance too great.

In this spitting metal suit.

Lorgan was daring with his plan, and the defenders answered without question. If a typical tactic involved standing and waiting for an attack, this was the polar opposite of that approach. No, the first part of Lorgan's plan tonight was lighting no fire at the front gate, setting no spikes to block the demons' route, apart from a tight line of them on either side of the pathway leading up towards the gate. The second part was opening the gates, inviting the demons in, and then challenging them to a fight.

Not even the greatest storyteller could make this lunacy sound believable.

Derian felt excitement stir, and he gripped his weapons. Disappointment or not, he would do his part, and if this were the end, well, he would end it well. Somewhere in the forest, more beasts answered each other's braying wail. Their meaning was clear: fresh meat awaited them tonight.

"Come feast, you fuken curs."

"Let's play," Derian whispered, and his tongue felt less than his own. The howling grew to a crescendo, it echoed out through the valley, and somewhere beneath it, he heard something else. He tried to listen closer, but someone distracted him.

"Hi, Derian. I almost didn't recognise you in that horse armour."

He spun slowly to see his best friend. Natteo looked a ruin. His face was pale, his hands shook, and his dilated eyes looked like a sea serpent's. His smile, though, was warm and endearing. He'd buttoned his shirt incorrectly, he'd left his laces untied, and he'd somehow fastened his leather armour on upside down. He'd ignored the shoulder straps completely, and now they dangled below him like matching tails. Overall, Natteo had looked better, but right now he didn't appear to care. He raised a tankard of bubbling ale and sipped from it, missing most of his mouth.

Somewhere in the distance, Derian heard a man scream. Natteo may have heard. He raised an eyebrow but continued drinking.

"Why are you out of bed?" Farther away there was a second scream; it may have been a curse.

"I'm here to fight. Got a pint first, though."

"You are in no shape to fight. Get back to bed. Are you drunk? Are you high?" Derian reached for the tankard. His armour slowed him down, and Natteo pulled his prize into his chest like a newborn child.

Mine, his glare suggested. "Have you seen where my weapons are?" he slurred, mimicking a bolt flying from his wrist with accompanying noises. Derian could now hear a few voices carried by the wind. Screaming, begging for help.

People are being hunted in the forest.

Natteo now noticed them too, even through his bleary-eyed delirium. He stopped mimicking the weapon and looked uneasily into the night. The town had fallen to silence as all of them—men, women, children—listened to doomed voices from somewhere in the forest.

"That's my man!" Natteo suddenly exclaimed. "That's my man. Noooooo…" He stumbled away. "Thaaaaaat's my maaaaaaaaan." He broke through the defenders like a fish through water, leaving a gap in his wake for Derian to see fully how his demise would occur.

Catch him.

Before anyone could stop him, Natteo slipped right through the vanguard, pushing any in his way until he stumbled over the reinforced beam lying on the ground. He allowed himself a 'Who put that there?' scowl, before jogging gracelessly out through the spiked walls, down from the town's entrance towards the darkness of the treeline.

"Thaaaaaat's myyyyyyyyyy maaaaaaaaaan."

Derian heard the battle cries of the monsters. "Stop him, Lorgan!" he screamed, but they'd already lost sight of Natteo. The strange voice of growing anger in Derian's mouth broke now, giving way to sobbing pleas, entreaties to the gods of the source that they return his friend to him before the monsters broke through.

"The gods are dead."

As if to spite his begging prayer, the demons broke through now, in their gnashing hordes. In less than a pulse of blood there were hundreds of them rushing toward the town, and Natteo charged towards them. He saw what it took Derian a moment longer to see: the outline of seven familiar mercenaries sprinting for their lives, ahead of the thundering demon pack, towards the town.

Oh, no.

Derian realised Mowg and his men must have attempted to reach the town before nightfall. *So close.* How cruel of fate to deny them salvation a few breaths out. How cruel to see an entire army standing at the gate, unwilling to charge out and steal death from them.

All except one.

"Boooooooooooaaaaaab!" screamed Natteo, gathering momentum as desperation cut through the poppy disorientation that had been slowing his movements.

The Army of the Dead began to close the gap now; they cleared the trees and sprinted in one flat line across the battlefield. Free of armour, weapons, and supplies, they sacrificed it all for one ill-timed dash towards safety. With snapping teeth at their ankles, they tried, oh, but they tried, and Derian held his breath as though releasing it might release the wave of death a shadow behind.

Through tears, Derian watched Natteo careen towards them, flapping his arms as though to distract the racing pack of demons hard on their heels. Derian stepped forward, and the effort was almost too much. But for the armour, he could have followed his comrade.

Saved him.

And then another shape appeared upon the battlefield. A beauty with flowing black hair. She carried her arrows in the same hand she held her weapon in; each draw of the bow loaded the piece. Each reload released a shot. A technique fit for a god of war.

In a breath, Seren released five arrows, and five canis demons fell behind the sprinting mercenaries.

That's impossible.

She reached for a second clutch of arrows and did the same again, and the crowd gasped as she rained down death upon another five more.

She is a god.

All seven mercenaries might have made it through the battlefield, but for Natteo's influence. He got one strike in as he reached them: flinging his pint of ale, he struck one beast across the head and caused it to snort before resuming its charge. Then, tragically, he crashed headlong into one of the men, and both of them crumpled in a nasty heap in the middle of the battlefield. The six who remained veered around them, leaving them both behind, and Derian wondered would he have done the same?

Seren, however, did not leave the fallen behind. She roared as the monsters did, as Derian did—a guttural, wrenching cry of primal, animalistic hatred. The valley turned to day as a blast of light emerged from her body, clear and blue like a droplet of rain, shimmering and vast like a lake. It spread out in an arc around her, covering the battlefield like the light from a thousand suns. The shock wave punched some monsters from her path, and sent others cartwheeling high into the air. It passed harmlessly over the two fallen figures, but that was all Derian could see, for in their excitement, horror, or fear, the crowd converged in front and blocked his view.

He roared what curses he could, willing his body to carry its weight forward through the mass of his comrades. With weak, laboured arms, he shoved some defenders aside until he could see flashes of movement, and then suddenly, the crowd separated of its own will as the charging mercenaries reached the gates and kept running, unaware the demons were now far behind. They fell through the lines of soldiers and collapsed at the rear of the defences in front of Derian.

They gasped and wheezed, and Derian wondered how many hours they'd run for.

"On your feet. There is no time for any rest!" Lorgan roared as he made his way through the line. Through the break, Derian spotted Seren and a mercenary carrying an unconscious Natteo back up the path towards the town. Behind them, injured and unconscious beasts slowly came to their senses. Puzzled and dazed from the assault, they held their charge, waiting for whispered words from whatever commanded them.

Then the crowd split anew, making way for Seren to step through. She released Natteo to the mercenary and fell against the inside wall, panting. She held her stomach as though she had been punched, and Derian could see the effort it took her to breathe. No peasant came to her aid. Perhaps they feared the line of grey forming in her long, black hair.

Ageing. Ageing and weaving.

He cursed his ignorance once more and took another step forward, but Lorgan stopped him with an outstretched arm. His eyes were cold as stone and focussed upon the exhausted mercenaries, still struggling for breath. Derian could see the questions forming in his leader's mind. Could the Army of the Dead put aside their quest for vengeance for the sake of the town? For the sake of their own lives?

"The beasts are charging again," Kesta called from above.

31

THE END

Perhaps it was Seren's interference; perhaps it was genius planning by Lorgan—which would have been a break from tradition; perhaps it was the desperate chase of seven lost souls. Or perhaps it was just simple, dumb luck that had caused the beasts to behave exactly as they had hoped. They congregated near the treeline and surveyed the battlefield for what it was.

Unenticing.

Then, coaxed on by their anculus masters and maybe a nasty deity desiring a quick, bloody end to irritating things, they broke and charged down, avoiding the spikes and the childish needles placed near the open gate. Perhaps they just wanted a fair fight, Derian thought. With no wall to hide upon, the monsters looked to be accepting the challenge.

If they had knowledge of humanity's penchant for violence and tactics, however, they might have realised just how uninterested humans were in a fair fight. Perhaps, too, they might have recognised a temporary killing ground when it crept up and surrounded them. However, they knew neither of these things, and Derian thought it a beautiful thing as they charged through the two lines of spikes.

Lorgan left the exhausted warriors where they lay before swiftly taking his place at the front of the line. "Lift it!" he roared, and a dozen hands grabbed the long, reinforced beam lying innocently along the entrance to the open gates, hoisting it into the air at waist height. It held for a moment so fingers could grip better, so feet could steady themselves.

The monsters drew closer, their eyes sparkling in the night; perhaps it was a side effect of generations of darkness in the source, or perhaps it was in anticipation of the kill. Regardless, Derian could see them nearing, and adrenalin coursed through him. He wanted to fight. He wanted to bear a shield. He wanted to be there. He took a step, but Lorgan's warning stuck in his mind like a chant. Not yet, he reminded himself. *Not unless they fall.*

"Lock it!" Lorgan roared after a pulse, and the monsters' claws clattered loudly on the worn mud path in front of the town. *So close.* The reinforced beam spun and moved only a foot forward before sliding into place, into the recently chipped notches on both sides of the gate.

Lorgan had ordered six of the men to practice twisting the beam all that day. Now, they spun and locked it into place as they had done a thousand times already. The monsters charging forward took no notice of this diminutive blockade; it looked like nothing more than a sturdy tree branch, something they could duck their heads under or leap over.

Then, with the monsters only twenty feet from their prize, Lorgan raised his arm. "Block it!" he roared.

As one, with a deadly clatter of steel, a dozen long shields were drawn, lifted, and slung over the beam to face the oncoming charge. Like the scales of a massive metal lizard, the shields clinked into position, forming a wall capable of holding back a charging army of monsters.

Derian stirred again and took another step forward. *Not yet.* Suddenly, his armour felt less exhausting, less constricting. He heard a growl and realised it was his own. Death was coming, death was in the air, and he would miss all the fun.

Not yet.

Lorgan called for strength, and the defenders dug their feet into the ground. He called for fierceness, and they roared in reply. In the last few moments, he promised them the barricade would hold, and he was right.

They held against the first wave of battering bodies. Leaning as one massive body against the beam, they did not move, did not fall away. They did not shatter the perfect line.

To their left, a dozen men plunged long spears again and again into the mass of fur and snarling grey. In the hours before the attack, as they had toiled awkwardly to fashion and hone their weapons, Lorgan had pledged that these spears would devastate if cut and shaped perfectly, if slicked with grease and welded at the tip with iron, and he was right.

Not yet.

Derian took a step forward again as, to the right of the shield bearers, another dozen soldiers raised another dozen spears, plunging them deep into the monsters scrambling above the dead and dying. Each plunge knocked the creatures back before they could frenzy, before they could form a mound and breach again. Each man became a machine of devastation, and Derian roared in frustrated triumph.

"Kill them all."

He watched the next wave strike the wall. Once again, the shield held and the monsters began to panic, to howl, to search for a solution to this impasse.

"Did you think we'd fall for that one again?" Lorgan roared at them. "Burn it!" he commanded, and the world came alight with fire above his head, and Derian screamed in frustration again.

"Let me fight."

"Let me fight."

"LET ME FIGHT!"

Not fuken yet.

He took another step, easier than the one before, but still, his mind chanted at him to hold. He could see that the mercenaries were gathering their wits now, gathering their weapons too. He had seen one blond man pulling the unconscious Natteo clear of the crowd, but it meant little to him. All that mattered was killing.

A silver-haired woman collapsed against him, and he realised it was Seren. She looked beaten. She gasped as though something clutched at her throat, and she reached for Derian as she fell over. He could have caught her, but let her fall in ruin at his feet.

"Catch your breath," he snarled, in a voice that was not his. She might have heard him; she crawled towards a doorway to recover her breath. With a tremendous effort, she sat up against the door and eyed him coldly. He should have cared, but his anger was too fierce. Yes, she had saved Natteo, but she had also taken some demons from his grasp. He wanted them all.

What is happening to me?

"I'm becoming fiercer," he whispered aloud, disgusted that everything was falling into place so easily. He cursed the monsters' stupidity, cursed them for not fleeing. He cursed Lorgan's brilliant brutality. And he cursed the cleansing fire.

He turned at the sound of glass smashing. A few eager warriors stood above the manmade barricade, lighting long shards of cloth attached to bottles of clear alcohol. Then, with mighty yells, they flung the flaming projectiles into the attackers farthest away. With their next throws, they struck those closer, dousing them with dripping sheets of flame. They continued to throw, and this too Derian found frustratingly beautiful. It was strange seeing fine bottles of alcohol wasted, but that was the price of victory.

The real tragedy is the dry celebrations to come.

The demons, roaring and twisting as they burned, were now trapped between walls of spikes on both sides; they could only charge forward and incinerate those ahead as they tried to escape. On either side of the open gate, a hundred archers let loose a hundred arrows into the night towards the anculus demons, who screamed and urged their comrades forward. Dozens fell to burning arrows, and a few breaths after that further volleys flew into the night. Wild with the smell of fire in their nostrils, the monsters in the killing ground charged the wall once more and heaved mightily against it in one last, desperate effort to save themselves from flaming death. Those few who had not fallen to the jagged spears died under the crush.

Then, at last, with a terrible creaking like a breached wall failing, the beam buckled and snapped, and the mighty shield collapsed with it.

"NOW, DERIAN!"

He knew that voice. The same voice he'd answered these past few years. The same voice that had placed him at the rear, and placed him in chains, now released those chains with no warning.

Now.

The shield bearers fell back as dead monsters rolled through the gate like a deathly black avalanche, ushered in by demented, burning demons. Those with fight still in them scrambled forward, and it was Derian they met first.

"My turn."

He moved now with the swaying of his body, and he was unrelenting. He roared and leapt upon the mound of the dead, right into the patches of fire, meeting the wretched swarm in an unfair fight. He felt their heat, but he was not drenched in alcohol. He was not burning as they were. He swung and heads rolled, and he cursed them for dying so easily. He swung again, and he laughed at those monsters who snarled and snapped and tried to wound him and failed, as their teeth could not penetrate his armour. He charged forward with limbs belonging to a giant, and he delivered death upon all who charged upon him. Time became nothing but glorious moments of slaughter as he quenched his primal thirst. If he felt pain, he ignored it. If he suffered fatigue, he swallowed it down.

Dimly, he felt the presence and sway of more fighters with him as he led the fierce counterattack. The Army of the Dead stood closest, and they delivered what killing they could, and it both inspired and enraged him in the same breath. Soon, he sensed Lorgan hammering into the curs, knocking them back down the path, and he charged after them, eager to kill as many of them for himself as he could. He'd never known himself capable of such hate, and he loved it so.

He charged out into the battlefield knowing his life had led to this moment. As though he had emptied every ounce of fear he'd ever carried upon the monsters in one gushing flow. He felt his destiny take hold and wring out all his savagery, and it was the greatest moment of his pathetic life. And then he felt nothing but darkness.

. . .

He was asleep. It felt like sleep, and he stirred but could not wake. He felt like a spirit in death and wondered had he died? Was this it? Was this what death was? The absence of everything, with a little free-thinking still intact?

Well, that was horrible, but it could be worse, he supposed. He tried to open his eyes, but he had none, nor did he have sight. His body ached, yet still, he felt at peace. He could feel war ever so near; he could feel the wet, slithering warmth of blood from a thousand miles away, yet still upon him; he could feel himself charge forward; and if he desired, he could grasp the living world. But instead, he fell back towards this darkness. Something was waiting for him. Calling to him from the darkness. It was not pleasant.

A strange voice whispered in his mind. *Protect... her.* He imagined himself spinning around in a darkened room to meet this voice, and to his surprise, he found he had a sliver of sight now. Nothing spectacular, just a blur in the dimness. Something dark and golden just beyond, and he reached for it but had no hands to grasp.

"Who speaks?" he screamed, with a voice, a mouth, not actually there.

Silence met him.

"Protect who? Seren?" he asked, and felt the coolness of mist on his skin. His body became more than fastened thoughts. Almost corporeal. He stepped forward, heard his feet echo upon nothingness, and felt something deep inside him dwindle. As though something pulled essence from him. Then something else was there with him, something worse than the voice, and it scared him. It stirred at his thoughts, it neared, and he felt panic.

"Take... no... more... steps." The voice spoke more, but the words echoed, screamed, tore his mind, and he wailed.

The voice silenced, and he was afraid because they were not alone. And fear turned to anger.

"Fuk this." He took a step forward, towards the fires, with the strange voice and the creepy presence accompanying him. They were there. Yet they were not. If he was dead, so be it. He felt his very core fade as though clawed and chewed away, so he swiftly took a step back and heard the voice, frantic and lost. Like a dream from childhood.

"… Dellerin… In Dellerin…"

"Dellerin is spitting massive!" he shouted back. Something near began to bray like a beast.

"Protect… the… girl… with… the… stones…"

"Face me!" he roared, and without warning, his head spun as though shaken by a vengeful deity, and he lost what vision he had. With it came a terrible emptiness. He felt himself fading, dying. He tried to breathe with lungs that were not there, and distantly, the sounds of horrors returned. Screaming, snarling, tearing.

Breathing.

Pain.

Suffering.

Waking.

Derian found himself in the middle of a horde of dead demonic monsters at the edge of the treeline outside Treystone. The night was dark, and he was very much alive—though he believed himself mad or possessed by a demon. Had he just encountered Fiore? Had he walked in the source world? Was he a weaver? Was he evil? What did any of this mean?

"What did you mean?" he screamed, and received no answer. *Isn't this how madness strikes?* The world he'd stepped into was already fading, and he wondered if he hadn't imagined it all. Perhaps keeping it to himself was the best plan. Though he knew he couldn't hold his tongue. And besides, how often did things get so much worse by keeping deep secrets? Perhaps Seren would have answers?

"Spent."

Suddenly, he felt the full weight of his armour upon him, and he wilted like a flower beneath a drift. Around him, a few monsters who hadn't died were fleeing into the forest. Visions of the journey from killing ground to treeline struck him like a hazy dream, and he felt oddly satisfied as though sated by a fine meal. He looked across the battlefield, where several comrades still stood out among the spikes with vengeance on their minds. They were slaying the other few remaining monsters. Among them stood a deeply peaceful-looking Kesta. After a time, when none remained, she came to him.

"You did well, little one." She pulled the helmet from his head, before unwrapping his sword and sheathing it at his waist. Every movement almost felled him.

"We all did," he replied, and she allowed him to lean on her as she led him from the forest.

"Apart from Natteo. What an idiot!" She laughed, and tears spilled down her cheeks. He had the good grace not to ask why she cried yet smiled so openly. They walked to the gates and stood watch. He stripped the rest of the armour free, for his exhausted body could take no more. Halfway through the ordeal, Lorgan appeared and assisted as though he were a lowly apprentice assisting a master.

"How do you feel?" Lorgan asked him, and strangely enough, leant close and placed his ear to Derian's chest. "Not too quick," he muttered to himself.

"You took me from the battle?" Derian asked, and Lorgan

smiled uneasily. Derian knew that smile. Nothing good ever came from it.

"When things are quiet, I think we need to speak of your new… abilities," he said, and patted him on the shoulder. His eyes were sad, his body shook, but still, in a few words, Derian felt reassured that he was not losing his mind or soul.

Seren had left her place at the door, and Derian wasn't too disappointed to delay speaking with her. Around them, the crowd of victorious defenders were sombre in their celebrations. Perhaps they were right. The attack had wiped out most demons, but they feared that more would be returning the following night. Was Lorgan capable of springing another tactical master plan on them? Derian didn't want to ask him yet. He was happy to stand watch at the open gate until dawn.

The three mercenaries weren't alone in their vigil. The Army of the Dead stood with them. For now, they'd silently brokered an uneasy truce between the factions. Conversation was occasional, but, oddly, Derian noticed Mowg answering to Lorgan as though he were his commander. Perhaps, until they understood the situation, the mercenaries would answer to a new master—at least, until other matters raised their heads.

When dawn arrived, most of the fighters still stood ready. Children emerged from their keeping to the joy of absent tragedy; there was a levity to the air that hadn't been there before, and with sleep calling, Derian finally surrendered his watch just as a low rumbling began to emerge from somewhere deep in the forest.

"Look lively, comrades!" Blair shouted from the gate. He took up the long shield that had served him well and drew his sword. He looked less the slithering weasel Derian had first met, and more a grizzled mercenary like the rest of them.

He'd stood beside Lorgan at the end, he'd held his shield, and he'd roared resolute defiance. In his own way, Blair had led the town to safety as much as any of the Crimson had.

"Monsters won't be out in this light. It's not even raining," Derian suggested, but he still reached for his long-dagger. Beside him, Lorgan cracked his neck loudly, then his shoulders, and stood ready for violence as the rumble became the welcome vision of cavalry emerging from the northern path. Those still standing watch gave out hearty cheers, loud enough that even Natteo might have heard them from his self-induced coma.

Blair grabbed Lorgan's shoulders and shook them in excitement. "Gold Haven received the message." He turned back to the battalion of riders making their way through the ruined path of demon mulch and waved wildly at them, receiving hearty waves back.

Derian could swear that their banners, emblazoned with Gold Haven's sun crest, shimmered in the dawn's breaking light. The riders waved triumphantly in their saddles, and they were impressive.

Blair dropped to a knee. "Thank you, Lorgan of the Crimson Hunters. You have done us a great service. You have earned yourself a great debt from this town."

Through a devilish grin, Lorgan bade him stand. "Do not kneel in my presence, friend. We have shed blood together. Now then, I believe there was talk of payment… something about swimming in gold."

32

SAVED

I t was a beautiful morning. Derian decided as much because he was alive. It was always nice to start a day being alive. A trait he'd lost the knack of in recent times. He watched the riders draw near. He might have counted hundreds, but with so many shiny, polished helmets bouncing delicately in the morning sun, it was a difficult task. A shame, really, because though he suffered as a slow reader most of the time, he was a fine counter of numbers. He could count to ten real swift and all. There were definitely more than ten approaching, and he thought them a magnificent if somewhat unsettling sight. They brought salvation, which was always a welcome thing, but for any mercenary, beyond salvation lay payment. Delicious, deserved payment, and they deserved a hearty amount. Still, though, soldiers could change the generosity of the deal and all. Strange how brave a flock of peasants became once an army of soldiers appeared.

"Yes, yes, Lorgan. You will swim in all the money. You have my word," Blair blurted out, and Derian smiled. A mercenary's word was worth his weight in gold. A peasant's word, less so. Still, though, the sun was out, and everyone had survived the night. Perhaps everything would be fine. *As if it would.*

The town, which had suffered nothing but cautious silence these last few hours, came alive as the last rider emerged from the north path. Everyone was joyous except the three watching defenders, who watched them uneasily.

Behind the shimmering guardians of gold followed countless foot soldiers, and now Derian really began to worry. Had word already reached them of Seren's "abilities"? Was this the army sent to contain a weaver so the Dark One could have her all to himself?

He shook his head and felt the exhaustion of the night anew. Word would spread swiftly as a plague in the shanty towns of what had transpired here. An army of demons rising was news no matter the island. And Anguis, the Dark One, would learn of the weaver called Seren.

Just not yet.

Anguis had marched for less these last few years, Derian knew, and he would not allow the rebels any opportunity to fill their ranks, pathetic as they were. What else was an all-encompassing dictator supposed to do when ruling with an unyielding iron fist? *Eventually a solitary ant might gather enough forces to...* Derian groaned, trying to form symbolism. On a morning like this, every thought hurt in and of itself, without the need for poetic absurdity. He needed sleep, he needed food, he needed out of this spitting town with a few sacks of shimmering gold. Perhaps then they could pay off the Army of the Dead, allow them to live.

"They are magnificent," Blair muttered, and Lorgan nodded in careful agreement. Dressed in heavier armour than their rider comrades, the new arrivals stamped every step heavily, and the ground shook. With banners waving in the morning sun, they appeared as conquerors. Derian could have sworn he heard Lorgan growl under his breath.

"Ugh—fuken soldiers," muttered Mowg from behind. He'd spent the last hour leaning against the outer town wall in unsettling silence. Derian had watched his eyes blinking open and closed against the burning of the dawn as he fought exhausted sleep. His eyes were bloodshot now, though they were grave and serious.

At the word "soldiers," all the mercenaries recoiled. Even the Army of the Dead.

"Reckon we won't get much payment," Mowg hissed, spitting into his hands and wiping them together. He looked as ruined as Derian felt. Countless miles of running without rest would ruin anyone, Derian supposed.

Although Derian had spoken a few words with him throughout the night, he had the distinct impression the older mercenary had little interest in getting to know him.

So much for auditioning in a real outfit.

Derian suspected it was the monster he had been in the battle that was causing Mowg's coldness. Better that than believing he didn't want to know his victims before he killed them. He had made an impressive bush, Derian recalled. And as an unarmoured warrior, he was just as intimidating. He stood beside Lorgan and Derian now, as though facing a new wall of charging monsters, and perhaps that's exactly what the golden army was.

From this close, Derian could see the first few riders' shocked faces as they trotted forward through the battlefield. And why wouldn't they be shocked, he supposed. Around them lay a thousand shredded demonic carcasses, and ahead were the impressive remnants of spiked defences, still smoking away. Savagery was in the air this fine morning. Along with the fetid stench of demon skin sizzling in the sun.

Blissfully unaware of the anxiousness of the three mercenaries, Blair offered a smile of camaraderie to them. "Duty calls," he announced, setting his shield at his feet and walking carefully down through the remains of the smouldering spikes to greet their guests. He marched as only a town official could. It didn't matter that his armour was marred with the blood of the demons, that his face was red from the touch of flames. What mattered was welcoming their saviours.

However, it wasn't Blair who greeted the leader of the golden riders first. That honour belonged to Keralynn, who burst through the gates in an explosion of elegance. Dressed in fine armour, she scampered down through the ramparts, somehow appearing both graceful and in control. She glided past Blair, eager to meet the marching army as though they were the bringers of a divine naked god.

Her urgency must have impressed the riders, who swiftly brought their mounts to a stop in front of Keralynn, who now stood where the bloody ground met the beginning of the scorched pathway. Though Derian tried his best to hear, her stately words were muffled and lost beneath the cheering. Her tone sounded playful, though; that much he could tell. *That's good, right?* And regardless of what she said, the golden army general appeared most pleased with her attention.

"The traditional stately welcome," Lorgan growled. His eyes were cold. Perhaps he didn't like the good-looking general who dropped to his knees in a grand bow, or the way she took hold of his face and kissed him passionately. Or the way he spun her around as though he were wedded to her.

"She only kissed me once when we landed in this little shit-hole of a town," Mowg muttered, shaking his head in disgust. "Thought it could become something. Ah, well."

They were still kissing.

"She's all dressed for war," Lorgan said, eyeing Keralynn's armour. He spat into his hands and rubbed them fiercely. "Didn't see her standing at the wall, though." A fine point, thought Derian as Keralynn broke the kiss and gestured for the grinning warrior in gold to follow her towards the town.

Blair met them halfway, and from here Derian could hear the tales the warrior told as they walked.

"I hate this part," Mowg hissed, and Lorgan agreed with a simple nod. Having reinforcements was one thing, but soldiers had ideals contrary to any mercenary's actions. They didn't play together.

"Derian," whispered Lorgan, taking hold of the younger mercenary's shoulder. "Go take your armour back to the smithy and get him to work on the parts worn down by your endeavours." He gestured to the heavy armour Derian had left by the gate wall. Derian's heart dropped at the thought of carrying such a weight alone. "And find Seren while you are at it."

Oh, please order me to rest for a few hours.

Before Lorgan could dismiss him, Mowg took the older mercenary's shoulder as though he were a friend, a companion of war. "We are far from finished discussing our matters, Lorgan," he warned, and Lorgan stared back without word.

An anger grew in Derian. He wanted to remove the offending hand from his leader. *Maybe with my teeth.* He took a step towards Mowg. It didn't matter what pedigree the legend was; no brute was ever allowed to accost any Crimson comrade. The mercenary guessed his intentions and seized Derian's wrist, twisting it sharply before shoving him away from the argument. If he'd feared the darkness deep in Derian, he showed little on his face. In fact, he never even looked Derian's way. Instead, he kept his eyes locked with Lorgan's. It was polished.

"Be still, Derian," Mowg said.

He knows my name. That's something, isn't it?

"Yes, and go pick up your armour while comrades of the Guild discuss matters," Lorgan added.

Ah good. We are all friends.

Nevertheless, he wouldn't go quietly. "We just fought an army of demons together. Does that not settle some matters?" It was a fine argument; Derian had spent the night waiting to offer it.

"True, little one," agreed Mowg, releasing his hold on Lorgan. "You could have killed us at our camp. Probably should have. You could have left us to fall beneath the demon charge, too. I might have, had I been in your boots." He patted Lorgan's chest absently. It was a fine pat, though not as impressive as one of Lorgan's love pats. "But we struck a deal, Lorgan. This matter is not rested, yet."

Behind them, they heard the golden army drawing nearer. Already the soldiers had fanned out on either side of the wretched valley with supplies and tents. Derian cringed at the awfulness of pitching a tent in the middle of a field of entrails. Now that they were out of regimented march and away from the glare of the sun, he guessed at least five hundred soldiers. There may have been thrice that. Or even half. Definitely more than ten.

"Oh, we can settle this like proper aggrieved mercenaries," Lorgan said coldly. He clenched his fists a few times. He stood a foot taller than Mowg, but that meant little. Since when did such things as natural advantage matter to any mercenary?

Mowg shrugged weakly. He might even have shaken his

head. "You wish to endure a duel of blades over Seren's value and your actions?"

Lorgan laughed loudly. "No, brother. Why would I risk either of our lives over something so trivial as being cheated? No—how about a fair bout of the fist?"

At this, Mowg laughed heartily. Perhaps he had noticed their size difference too. "You think I'm foolish enough to step into a ring with you? Are you fuken mad?"

"I'm an old man, Mowg. True, I am bigger, but youth is a fairer balance. Or is the great Mowg of the Army of the Dead too afraid to face little old me?"

Mowg laughed again.

Keralynn reached them now, her face flushed with nervousness—or else excitement. Mowg barely noticed her; his eyes were still on his quarry.

"You don't get to lead an outfit like ours without knowledge of unknown things, Lorgan the Fist," he said, and Lorgan fell silent, though Derian caught the flash of embarrassed anger on his face for a pulse before turning to greet their saviours.

Lorgan the Fist?

Derian very much looked forward to asking Lorgan how he had earned such a polished title. He also had questions about his own, darker secrets. He'd spent most of the night thinking over his newly-found powers, and why he'd had a pleasant chat with a strange voice in another world. Lorgan clearly knew more than he'd let on. Still, the day was young and questions could rear their ugly heads after some rest, when they were well away from eager ears.

So, instead, Derian allowed himself be swept away in a wave of cordial greetings as Lorgan and Mowg resumed their more stately roles. Whatever anger had been shared between the two mercenaries was swiftly lost as a tall, impressive rider, dressed in gold and steel armour, stepped forward. Keralynn went and stood with him; her eyes were upon him and no one else. On her finger rested her wedding band.

So, it wasn't love then, Lorgan?

"This, my fine comrades, is Grand Protector Dorn, lead golden knight of Gold Haven," Blair declared grandly, and the knight removed his gloves and offered a customary hand. Derian felt an immediate pang of unease: he did not trust the man who met the hearty grip of both older mercenaries. However, he bowed when the soldier looked his way and received a casual nod and nothing else in reply.

"These fine mercenaries stood proud and held the town," Blair continued, and Derian felt a little ashamed at his previous disdain for the man. Despite Blair's exalted role as mayor, he had unhesitatingly dug into the mud alongside his fellow townspeople. "Mowg, of the Army of the Dead, and Lorgan, of the Crimson Hunters," Blair continued as though showing off prize vegetables at the local fair. "Without them, we would have fallen." He gripped Lorgan's shoulder at this last gift of praise. He did so as a real companion and Lorgan nodded in mild consent.

Keralynn was less impressed with Lorgan's heroics and eager to tear Dorn away from the rest of the fighters. With her hand firmly clenched around his arm, she avoided Lorgan and Mowg's eyes.

Awkward.

"Who knew mercenaries could do such a thing, eh?" said Dorn gravely, and gave a mirthless laugh. A fine trick to master, no doubt. Though his eyes suggested disdain, his tone was cordial. "Well done, gentlemen, and to your comrades, wherever they may be, please extend Gold Haven's sincerest thanks," he offered. If there was insincerity to his words, neither Blair nor Lorgan caught it; they laughed along with him, gamely playing their parts. It came down to numbers every spitting time. After all, Dorn commanded the numbers to bury them deep enough that no Guild would ever find the truth. They played their parts, and they played them well. Derian had a sinking feeling. He half expected it to rain.

As the little gathering continued to share false niceties of demonic things and casual recollections of masterful tactics, Lorgan took Derian aside. "Get clear of here before beastly questions emerge," he whispered fiercely.

Derian only half-heard the words; oh gods, how he needed to rest. Sometimes one had to read through the lines when exhausted, battered and weary. He too desired to know of Seren's and Natteo's health, but more than that, he desired sleep.

Like a child slipping away from its parents' feast, Derian snuck away with little notice. Even when his heavy armour screeched as he dragged it along the ground, the adults took no notice. He himself, however, noticed a few worrying things. First, no villager offered to help him with his burden. They all avoided him completely as he dragged it down through the streets in search of the smithy. But more worrisome were the superstitious signs of the demons the villagers made as he passed.

With an army at your gates, who needed the lesser rats to fight for you? he thought.

"Ooh—the Lesser Rats," he declared loudly, as though struck by lightning. "Now, that's a good name for a mercenary group." Suddenly his worries lessened as he realised how much he needed to share this epiphany with Natteo.

33

MARCH OF THE DEMON

What is happening to me? Seren fell away from the doorway onto the muddy ground, unable to catch her breath. She tasted metal in her mouth. *The taste of the dying.* She also tasted raw dirt mixed with bitter, unhygienic grime, along with a twist of blood from her bitten lip. She could feel her soul tearing away with every moment, and oh, she feared the cost of her actions.

Derian stood beside her. She reached for him, wordlessly begging him for help, but the monster was taking hold. She had lost him to the darkness. Her hand wavered before exhaustion took it. She knew this terrible drain. She'd felt it before, in another life, in a controlled cage, when she had had a mind worthy of coherent thoughts and a fierce and kind master.

Breathe. To most, this was as natural an act as thinking. To Seren, it still felt strange. Stranger, too, when she couldn't quite catch her breath either. *Is this drowning?* She tried another tactic as her chest recoiled in agony. Holding her breath, she imagined suffocation was a mere fleeting habit that she'd picked up since becoming human again. Within a pulse she was gasping more heavily than before.

"Stupid Seren," she hissed, then discovered to her dismay that talking was even harder—and that she'd also referred to herself in the wrong person again. *Breathe like a newborn.* Her mind reeled from the effort of weaving her soul, and she sought clarity among her spinning thoughts. She remembered the sensation of the source tearing through her as she charged out into the battlefield. She remembered the triumph of saving her comrade. The cost, though, was something she hadn't prepared herself for. How could she? *Gelded.*

Remember what you are.

"Seren should... have... remembered..."

You thurken cur, stop talking.

"I will stop."

She sat up unsteadily in the mud, her hair covering her grimy face. Where it had once been rich and dark, it was now tainted with grey like strands of straw. *I can reverse this.* "When I learn to breathe again," she whispered, and whispering was easier. Who knew words spoken aloud carried more breath away than whispering? She wasn't sure how she felt about whispering. "Thurken curs," she whispered, and didn't like the sound. "Thurken cur!" she shouted, and that was much prettier. More painful, too.

Remember what you are.

Around her, the defenders had turned to warring, and it was wonderful. She felt their anger overcome their terror, and she liked this most of all. Sitting huddled in the doorway, she enjoyed the feel of wrath. And then she realised her breathing had returned to normal. Normal enough for her to rise, at least. As she did, her body almost collapsed and she whispered a moan and discovered it unsatisfying. Spitting the mud and blood from her mouth, she tried to wipe her face clean. Thoughts of dirty muck all over her face displeased her. "A noble warrior should look the part," she remembered her master saying, and his face came to mind. She saw him almost clearly now beside her. He was torn and broken, maimed and fierce. He had fought a terrible beast, and Seren reached out as she had for Derian. Her master faded away without a word or smile or acknowledgement, but he'd been there with her.

Remember what you are.

"Find him," she demanded to her broken mind, and pictured him near, and thinking like this hurt dreadfully, because a beautiful idiot whom she hated more than anything in the world had broken her in two with an arrow. So, she did what she never did: she wailed for her master and found it rather rewarding.

What is happening to me?

She did not know how long she despaired, only that Derian's sudden howl of anguished rage tore her from her misery. As Fiore scratched upon the doorway between worlds, so too did Derian's monster. She wondered if Derian had the will to control such a thing. If he were foolish enough to attempt to control such a thing. She could see things more clearly now, even if they made no sense to her. Even if she saw nothing beyond tomorrow.

I've only just arrived. I'm not ready to leave.

A few warriors ran past her and she felt their burgeoning hatred, pure and terrible, like an arrow through the forehead. It never took long for a mob to form and set about destroying, and the tides were already turning. She'd seen this. Or at least a version of this. The coming awfulness would not be in her hands.

And I can do nothing to stop this. Who knew weaving a little destruction could reveal forgotten things? She caught his face, caught his voice. So very far away from her. Right in front of her. Where he said he'd be.

"Bereziel!"

Her heart skipped a beat, slowed, gave up on her for a moment. She held his name close to her mind, so close that she forgot the pain. The terrible pain of sudden aging and the tearing of the soul. It was something to do while scrambling away from battle. *Like a coward?* They would believe as much. *Peasants.*

At first, her feet carried her slowly from the noise. Each step taken through a muddy path was akin to marching through… through… snow? Was that sensation something she recognised? Whatever it was, she scrambled forward like a wretch, conscious that only moments before she'd been a glimmering god. Now she was dying.

You know these steps bring you to doom?

She knew, but that was her place in this world: to disrupt the natural order of things. Oh, god: she was remembering. She increased her pace. Along the way, she'd lost a shoe. She couldn't remember when. Probably among the demons. Something terrible was afoot. Well, terrible beyond the fate of this unforgiving town. Bereziel struggled. Seren struggled as much.

I should not follow this path. Should not step into the dark. Even if he needs me.

Without warning, her body suddenly shuddered, and she fell again, gasping. *Too much of my soul torn away.* This dying felt nothing like rebirth. *Birth boom.* This felt terrible, as though some enchantment worked upon her. She sensed Fiore the demon ever near. Scraping now, as the last barrier collapsed upon him. And she felt the cruelty of those she protected.

"Seren… broken. Not ready," she cried, as though anyone

would care. As though any master could hear. She needed to sleep. To close her eyes and rest herself for the horror to come. She was not ready, for if she looked beyond the fire, all she saw was herself, flying into a grand demon's domain with fire upon her fingers. The source reviled her. Both worlds conspired against her. She had no right to walk in either. Yet she danced.

I am not ready for this.

"Where are you, master?" she wailed aloud, as the roar of demon war erupted behind her. Curiosity got the better of her. She'd seen this victory in her mind before, yet still, to see it with open, human eyes was a beautiful thing. For she was still a newborn. Entertained by wondrous, gory things.

The warriors of this wretched town were incredible. She was proud of them. Even if she hated every one of them. She didn't want to: she chose to. Hate was as easy as joy. Easier when she felt like dying herself. It made their cruelty easier to understand, to accept.

Scrambling to her feet again, she wiped the mud from her tightly-fitted dress and whispered a curse. Unsatisfied, she cursed aloud and continued on her way. "I'm not ready," she muttered every few steps, and unsurprisingly, this mantra did not help. Through the streets she marched, a little demoness from the source, until the screams of terror and triumph and horror and beauty were far behind. Only then did she listen for her true prey, for her deeds were not done this night. Soon enough, she heard it and followed, each step solidifying her fate in Treystone. Each step changing the natural order of things.

This path leads to your doom. She knew this, but her quarry was touched by a darkness greater than all the seven demons put together. She did not know how; she did not know why. Only that it was better she follow the path she had been destined to take. Perhaps others marched towards her salvation.

"Hold him still," someone cried, and she fell still mid-step. *Last chance.* Her body was broken. Her will sapped dry to a husk. "Hold him still, damn you," they cried again, and Seren had the sudden desire to climb into a little ship of flying metal and sleep for days until her body returned to itself, but the voice cried out again.

"He is comrade," she whispered, trying to rouse herself. *Save him, Seren.*

Ever since she'd stormed into this world, she had been destined to die. The world had no place for such a being as her. Now, it was about doing what she could before death took her. A lifetime under Bereziel's watch had reassured her that even delicate moments could reshape the world. Weaving that pulse towards the monsters had brought forth her mind.

She followed the piercing cries and came upon the fallen ruin of Natteo. Her comrade. Her friend? His lover held his quaking hand.

"Save him," the mercenary cried as the healer knelt in front of his dying patient. "Please," he added, punching the ground, but the young healer was shaking his head as the blood spurted skyward. *Like beautiful spray from the sea.*

His body hadn't been ready for his adventures. The tear had ruptured further, causing more damage. Instead of carrying him a step further, the two men had tended to his draining wounds in the middle of a muddy lane. No place for anyone to die, except perhaps a mercenary. Natteo's companion shook as the blood continued to drain. Halting the flow was a futile battle. Even in this dim light, she could see the agony on Natteo's face, and she did not hate the sacrifice he placed upon her, as the world was illuminated by a hazy blue shimmer. She saw others, though, drawn to the cries and watching his demise. She was disgusted.

"He fades away," the healer said, releasing his hold on the neck wound. His eyes were already back on the battle at the front gates. His mind was so cold—regretful, yes, but cold, nonetheless. There were others to attend to; Natteo was lost to the night. A miserable sentiment, and Seren did not judge him. Even if his own distrust of her shone brighter than that of the rest. Beside him, the young mercenary wailed his curses as though broken-hearted, and she felt the glow of blue as though it were a physical thing.

It's not. It's the destruction of your soul.

"The boy is dead," the healer said, and his lover wailed, and it was beautiful, for such emotion could change the world. Change the turning of war. Change the destiny of the sun, the moon, the stars. She collapsed down in front of Natteo's already-cooling body and emptied her agony into the ether. She felt her heart suffer, and still she pushed deep into her essence. It was natural. *Necessary.* This was how the first weavers had found their way. They had followed instinct. Those heroic few in the beginning had often sacrificed themselves, all in the name of pushing back against the night. She knew this because Bereziel had told her. Had shown her. For the source lay in every place, in every time. Everything happened as it should. But sometimes great injustices could be undone.

Especially when un-fated girls appear to wreak havoc upon the natural turning of things.

Un-fated.

Is that a word?

It is a meaning.

That was her calling. To tear the paths the future told. Natteo's journey had ended this night. She sensed nothing for him beyond. Unless she interfered, for that was her gift to this world. She was a soul created by gods. Lost and moulded into human form. She strayed outside of the paths of time. She knew this now; knew her importance. How did she know?

I've always known.

I just wouldn't remember.

Absently, she touched her forehead and felt her body weaken, and she took the anguish. This was no frenzied release of power towards a pack of demons seeking easy kills. This was the perilous release of eternal primal power, stealing life from the source. To heal was the greatest skill of a weaver. How else could a being like the Dark One become invincible? How else could Bereziel live among the source realm for a thousand years?

How did I?

Were she whole, this would have been a simple release of healing for her. However, a gelded little waif was no match for the powers of death, and death wreaked its assault tenfold upon her. She felt the fibres of Natteo's skin recover themselves, felt the blood refill his veins, felt his rebirth boom from the intimacy of her touch. Only a little healing, yet the blue shimmer grew as though it were a fountain of fire, and she dimly heard distant, terrified voices. They howled at the heat emanating from her body, and she remembered the burning. She remembered to combine both. So close. Oh, she was so close to remembering her way.

And then she felt his heart quiver and quicken, and her own heart quivering too, as she fought for both their survivals. She fell away from him, back into the mud. A finer place for a heathen demon to die, no doubt. She was gasping again. There was no breath; she waited for the end. Her soul felt as empty as her thoughts. In her ears, she could hear their gasps, their curses, and then she heard their pleading.

"My boy—he fell on the first night. His body… his body lies cold…"

"My sister fights death even now…"

"Save us…"

"Ave Seren… Silencioooo." *Whatever that means.*

They were more plentiful than she realised. Those broken wretches unwilling to fight. Unwilling to relive the horrors they had endured. All drawn by a beautiful, cleansing light in the unforgiving night. Those few silent watchers now became aggressive acolytes. She felt their zealous belief, and it was potent and devastating, and she hated them all and wanted to die. The world spun as they pulled her to her feet, and she struck them away with her last bit of strength.

"Leave me," she howled, for she was empty. She could heal a torn vessel of blood. A body still warm. What this hateful few desired was beyond her. How could she tell them? How could she explain? She knew the truth and knew her doom. *This is how they turn.* "Thurken curs," she hissed, pushing them away fiercely. "I hate you all."

It had not happened as before, but she knew her soul was dissipating beneath her actions. Looking at Natteo, she saw the healing, and it was beautiful. He stirred and opened his eyes, and she called him a friend. More than that, she called him a companion.

"I cannot heal dead," she cried, knowing her words doomed her. Her mind was awash with maddening visions of Dellerin, and she knew she had tapped into her potential a little more.

Like the first weavers who killed themselves.

The last of the healing light faded, leaving her mob in hazy darkness, and she searched for words that would settle their grief. "Leave me, peasants." She was harsh and cold, for she knew no better. She was a spent force. A lifetime without the body taking such abuse had ruined her. Her body became weary, as it had at the gate. With what energy she had, she pushed through the gathering into the darkness.

She did not speak aloud; she did not gasp for air, for she was learning. *Always learning.* She accepted death, even were it to stroll up and knife her in the back, because the world believed she had no right to life.

An abomination to natural things.

So be it, she thought. She marched from the bitter acolytes and she knew they would not follow. Not yet. Not until they had the numbers to justifiably tear her apart. Not until they knew their town was safe. Her feet became heavy, so she challenged her own agony and ran. She endured this self-inflicted horror until she fell through her shack door. When they came for her, it would be swift. She knew this, for she saw it. She would have no strength to save herself.

No strength.

Gelded.

"Come for me, Derian," she whispered to the dark as she collapsed upon her bed, already asleep. Already dreaming.

And her master awaited her upon his throne in another realm.

34

THE FIGHTING MONGOOSE

"Don't let any of them out of your sight, Kesta," Lorgan had whispered beneath the shadow of the front gate, and Kesta had held her tongue. A fine plan; the right plan. Who knew how long this uncomfortable truce between the two parties might last? The long night could have gifted the disgruntled mercenaries plenty of time to form some tasty vengeance. From the few words she'd shared with them, standing watch covered in demon remains and well-earned sweat, she suspected they were a decent crew. Strange thing for any mercenary group to have decency. Especially one so renowned. Truth be told, they were entitled to their vengeance. She wouldn't think any less of them for it. She just wasn't enthused at the thought of getting stabbed this morning. She wasn't finished killing demons.

Kesta accepted the orders without argument and slipped away from the front gates in silent pursuit of the five mercenaries. Lorgan and Derian could handle Mowg, she supposed, and she herself could handle tracking the rest of the small, exhausted group. Follow, observe, know their threat.

She wasn't used to levity, but recent events had blessed

her with a warmth beneath the hollowness she lived with. Perhaps that was why her steps were so light as she trailed the walking mercenaries down through the darkened streets. Dawn was hours away, but the battlefield lay in reassuring silence. The monsters were licking their wounds, resting for the day to follow, and it was a wonderful thing. She could still smell the smoke in her hair, in her clothes. Who knew killing hundreds of those bastards would instil something in her? Something grander than misery, at least.

She had not smiled warmly in a decade. She could offer an insipid smile when the occasion called for the gesture, but mostly, she hid behind a frown of emptiness. Only Lorgan knew the true horror of her life. It was he who had discovered the broken waif half-dead on that last terrible night when everyone else had left her. She had carried the small town of Annise with her for a decade now. These last three nights of slaughter, killing, and punishing had quenched her loathing ever so, but she would never again know happiness. Nor would she want to.

She would not live many more days and felt strangely relaxed about the matter. She'd been waiting for death for ten years now, and had known the last few sand grains were slipping through the glass since the demons charged through their camp.

She slipped past a couple of wandering defenders who had earned their own reprieve from the watch. They didn't even notice her pass; their exhaustion had taken their wits, and their own muffled words concealed her footsteps. She recognised them from her stand. An older couple; they'd held hands before the first charge. Kesta understood that love. Slipping into an alleyway, she watched them for a moment, still hand in hand as they reached their home. They had left their door unlocked before they left; they hadn't expected to live through the night. At this realisation she smiled bitterly. Another day's grace earned.

As the door closed behind the couple, she snapped the memories from her mind and returned to task, following the shuffling mercenaries. Their steps were impossibly laboured. After so long running, followed by a war and a long watch afterwards, it was hardly surprising. They walked as a family and, despite their threat, she felt a kinship to them. Probably the one who called himself Clover, the most. She grinned. Facing her demons and tearing them to spitting shreds had earned her a desire she rarely allowed herself to endure.

Luck of the clover.

He was no leader, but something in his walk, his arrogant laugh, his tone, was familiar. Like home. She wouldn't lie: as they'd battled in the Army of the Dead's impressive camp, she had struck him fiercely across the chin and found him attractive enough. *Even with the vomit.* He had a strong Venistrian jaw, and, curses upon her, she'd always liked Venistrian blood in her man. They were the charming, devilish ones; they were the finest lovers too. She knew this from experience. Any layovers in Venistra were interesting times. For a moment she thought of Mika, and her stomach clenched and her quarries disappeared down through a dimly lit pathway, out of sight.

"Hope you enjoyed tonight," she whispered to the absent spirit of her husband, and he made no reply. "Now, leave me to my task." Steeling herself, she followed Clover and his band, wary of the precariousness of following skilled mercenaries down a dark pathway, where a simple ambush would have been a justified manoeuvre on their part.

They made no attempt on her life, yet she remained cautious. She froze, seeing their sixth member appear. To be fair, it wasn't only she who froze. Boab's companion, holding his hand, did so too.

Natteo—out for a midnight walk?

She couldn't hear the words shared, only the gentle mocking tones of both parties before they went their separate ways. Normally she cared little for such matters, but Natteo deserved a little joy in his life. The minor disaster of a man hid his horrors just as she did.

Don't all the interesting ones do that?

As the exhausted mercenaries turned to leave, Clover spun her way and stared into the shadowed corner where she hid. She froze a second time, not daring to breathe lest it give her away.

"We will not kill you, Kesta of the Crimson," he called. "You may as well come out of the shadows and come play." He sounded dangerously charming. She'd heard such charming words a thousand times in her life. She knew she wasn't unattractive. She was simply a maiden, albeit an older one. "Come, let us… share a mug of ale together," he called as she revealed herself. Her heart quickened at his smile. But charming or no, he was a threat. Any mercenary hailing from Venistra was a threat. Even when a person was in their good graces. She considered offering a polished reply before turning on her tail and returning to Lorgan, but thought better of it. She had learned little of their intentions. And fuk it, she was feeling adventurous this fine night.

"As long as you do the pouring," she countered, offering a smile unnatural to her. When the right time called for it, she could pull this smile from the ether. She rarely revealed tepid emotions like hope, joy, or interest, but when she needed to play the part, she could. Even with those she cared for. Those who tried their hardest. Like Lorgan, Derian, and especially Natteo.

"Ha—I think it would be safer that way… comrade," Clover countered, bowing magnificently. His own brothers disappeared into the night while he waited for the spy to gather her wits.

He was taller than she. A decade younger, too. He had cold, dangerous eyes, mercenary eyes, and she approved. The first lesson Lorgan had taught her was to peer into an opponent's eyes and understand them within a breath. She stared at his dark eyes glistening in the starlight, and she knew well his dangerous threat. He knew his appeal and he would play his own petty part. She understood the danger she could be in.

She bowed deeply, answering his gesture, and he smiled and took her hand, kissing it before beckoning her to follow.

"I need to rest," he told her. "I need to wash this spitting mess from my clothes… from my body. I need a thousand and one things after. Mostly, though, I need a drink," he said smoothly, and she walked with him. She wasn't truly scared, for when someone had lost everything in the world, fear was a wasted state of mind. Instead, she was wary. She worried about being stabbed before she had another crack at killing a hundred more demons. To most mercenaries, their ability was a status to pay attention to. For Kesta, it was a distraction. She was a terrible fighter. She had ability and strength but couldn't read a tactical moment coldly. She'd charge forward and be reckless. She'd have made a fine, bumbling soldier, had she desired wretched regimentation. Taking orders, as long as they involved killing demonic curs, would have been a fine life, she imagined. Not that she wasn't wily or intelligent. She just couldn't help herself, and the Crimson just weren't equipped to take advantage of the genuine gifts she offered.

She rested her hand on the pommel of her dagger as she

walked. All casual like. That was the second lesson Lorgan had taught her. *Look relaxed despite your threat and despite the threat.* If Clover decided to kill her, well, he'd succeed. But she might deliver a few devastating blows before falling. Sometimes, it was the little things.

For the first few steps, he did not kill her, even though the path was tight and dark and perfectly suited for a swift stab and drain. "My place or yours?" he jested, and she almost smiled at his brazen Venistrian charm.

"I assume a company as rich as yours can afford the finest quarters," she countered as they passed the last cluster of houses with no stabbing incidents. They continued on out into the main square of the town, where the huge warehouse housed the children and the stores of coals or barrels of black water or whatever Keralynn had been so reluctant to share with them.

Ahead, the rest of Clover's comrades were slipping in through the warehouse's main door like thieves, and Kesta held her step.

"What are you doing?" she hissed. Admittedly, Natteo had suggested breaking in to find out what was inside, but the first night's disastrous events had taken precedence.

Now, what right did the mercenaries have going in there? she wondered.

For a flicker, Clover lost his charming tone. Perhaps her question had thrown him. "We have our own beds... um... on the barge."

Barge?

There was no river deep enough to hold a barge, she thought, and her heart skipped a beat. Now, perhaps, she had a reason to smile. To really smile. "You have an airbarge in there?" she asked, struggling to keep her face neutral. Her fingers twitched when he nodded. She felt fresh beads of sweat form in her armpits, and suddenly the worry of him stabbing her was lost to the thrill of excitement. How long had it been since she'd seen one? Since she'd stepped aboard one? Flown to Venistra on one?

"You want to see how a real mercenary group travels?" he said, puffing out his chest.

Aboard an airbarge was a finer place to be murdered, she told herself. This relaxed her far more than she would ever admit.

"It must be rather small," she said, as he led her towards the open doorway.

"Oh, don't speak ill of my baby," he said, mocking her gently. He pointed to the railed wheels along the bottom of the wall. Perfect for sliding aside and revealing a wall-sized gateway. A tight squeeze, but wide enough to fit a small airbarge through.

"Where did all these spitting children come from?" he shouted suddenly. His outburst caused a stir among a group of older children, who stared up in excitement and terror from beneath their wrappings of blankets. The smaller ones remained tucked up, scattered along the floor of the massive warehouse where they'd been sleeping the horrors away. Her heart broke as she spied the young girl called Eveklyn. She stood with no blanket against the far wall, her face stern and alert. Beside her, the heavy axe rested against the wall, at the ready in case things took a tragic turn. Kesta wanted to reassure Eveklyn that everything was fine. At least for tonight. She also wanted to tell her there would be plenty of desecrated demon entrails to use for decoration come the dawn. Instead, she offered the girl a bow and forced an approving smile. Eveklyn took it with a simple shrug and returned to her grim watch. She was built of fiercer things, Kesta saw. She hoped the girl succeeded in her task swiftly when the time came, earned a few demon kills in her last few moments to ease the passing into the night.

"Spit on me. Well, at least they didn't get aboard," Clover muttered, glancing up as Blood Red went to task unlocking the front door of the monstrous flying machine.

Beautiful.

"It's a strange-looking beast, large as it is," Kesta gasped, taking in the airbarge in all its glory. Most flying beasts were wide, with long, heavy iron propellers sticking out at every corner, but this one was different to most others she'd ever seen. The body was massive—as long as a couple of comfortable houses shoved together, and just as tall. However, the propellers were folded upwards as though in prayer instead of hanging out on either side, like the wings of a Waylor peregrine in flight. Massive chains with links as thick as her fist held them upright. It allowed for easier parking, she supposed.

"Easier to store away from eager eyes," he said proudly as the third lock clunked free and Blood Red pulled open the thick iron doorway and slid in. A few children watched with as much eagerness as Kesta, though they made no move to stir.

Kesta wanted to stir. She wanted to hop aboard and know this beast's innards for herself. Still, as though in a courting dance of her own, she played it coy. "We could have used this on the first night," she said, tapping the hull, hearing the strength in its glossy green finish. Without the keys to gain entrance, it was as impenetrable as a safe. It was probably for the better that she'd been unaware of this monster. Three days in and she'd still be trying to get through that metal plating.

I'd have missed out on all that killing.

"As if we would allow anyone near our baby... *my* baby." He stroked the hull, and she realised it was he who piloted this monster. *Familiar and charming.* And oh, she liked his charm that little bit more. Especially if he wasn't intending to stab her. "Do you have any idea the dangers of flying such a beast?" he asked, and she grinned. Anyone who'd lived in a city knew well the dangers—and the exhilaration, too. Oh, he could stab her now. As long as he gave her the tour first.

"You piloted this beauty through those doorways? I'm impressed," she said, and his smile faltered as though she had challenged him. He kicked absently at the wheels by their feet and tried his best not to acknowledge the suspicious-looking toe bar at the rear.

"Course I did. No problem at all."

She was in love with this machine. Doing her best not to disturb a few young ones sleeping beneath its massive body, Kesta glided around it in a daze, checking its exterior, exploring the outer mechanisms. It was a mercenary machine, no doubt. Built both to protect and to endure assault. For a bitter moment she wondered if Seren wouldn't be better suited with this group of mercenaries, after all? They had an airbarge to call upon and enough fuel to keep them flying. A grand demon would have an arduous time tracking her down.

"The *Fighting Mongoose*," he said, wiping a little smudge of grime from the painted title on the hull. She stood close to him, as though enchanted, and ran her fingers along the name as he did. Around airbarges, she could remember what it was to be alive. *To smile.* She wanted to stand upon its bridge, to look out across the clouds of eternal nothingness. She wanted to delve into the engine room and smell the sour aroma of black water. She wanted to deafen herself as the clunking turbines spun to invisibility in front of her eyes. She wanted to fly just once more.

"I'm the only pilot, so that makes me indispensable," he boasted, and laughed at his jest.

"Oh, if this were a tale, you would be signing your own death warrant with such a stupid statement," she mocked, turning towards the closed doorway far above.

"I'd best not die, so," he said with a laugh, and she liked this, though she did not know why. Perhaps the adrenaline of the battle was affecting her. Perhaps she just had a thing for airbarge pilots. It had been so long since she'd spoken with a man like him, and strangely enough, it was a fine distraction —for the now, at least.

Who knew killing and a machine of the sky would get me in the mood?

She knew her time was short; she knew that, after dawn, the Army of the Dead would take to the skies, leaving Treystone behind. She couldn't blame them. She wasn't bitter at all. She was bold. Didn't Lorgan want her to monitor them?

"I want to see it all," she said, and he smiled like a hunter.

35

CHATS IN THE DARK

The blacksmith took one disapproving look at the heavy armour and cursed. Then he took Derian aside and shouted at him awhile. He used a fine collection of profanities unsuitable for retelling. Derian immediately committed them to memory for the next time he caught Natteo cheating at cards. And then he pledged he'd be more careful the next time he waded into a pit of demonic beasts all heroically, preventing the town from incurring even a single casualty.

"Sorry, sir," were the actual words he used. Derian suspected the blacksmith understood the hidden connotations.

"Come see me after noon. I'll have your piece as polished as before," the blacksmith muttered, before calling his apprentices from their cots. Derian watched for a few moments as they went to work repairing the damage to the connecting segments of heavy plating as though it were no matter at all. He'd never understood the finer points of metal working, yet was always fascinated watching those skilled in the craft get to work with such intricate things.

"Double stitching this time, and…" He looked at Derian absently, as though sizing him up. "Line some more chain through the strands." One apprentice wiped some sleep from his eyes and protested, but the blacksmith dismissed him. "Whisht. He can take the weight, slight as he is."

Derian turned to leave and heard a whispered, "Thank you." He looked back, but the man was already ordering the apprentices to duties like any stern master. For a moment more, Derian watched the bellows blow fiercely at the pit flames. A few sparks took flight into the morning air, followed by a thin stream of fading black smoke, and he found a strange comfort in this mundane activity. Battles came and went. All anyone could do was treat them like any other day. The Crimson Hunters had gifted this unlikely day to the blacksmith. And perhaps many more after that.

He wondered if genuine heroes felt this satisfied every waking morning. Uplifted. Content. Proud... Tired. He thought on this and his relaxed smile faded a little. They probably felt tenfold the pain he felt in his body, and that was from only two days of fighting in the season. Three, including the whole 'getting blown up by a vector demon' thing. Was a life lived in awful pain a worthy one?

They probably have a giant's will, a cantus's heart, and a god's resilience.

"Heroes," he whispered to the silent morning, and plodded down through the deserted streets, searching for Seren. His mind was awash with worries. Not only about his brutal actions and the fact that he had possibly stepped into the source, but also about Seren's prophetic words, which terrified him. And the matter of a strange voice in the darkness talking to him.

It wasn't the largest town, but he somehow lost his way twice on route until, eventually, and with bleary eyes and a terrible headache for company, he finally came upon her shack. Wondering how to approach, he followed his gut and snuck a glance in through one of her grubby windows.

She lay there among rumpled bedding and half-discarded battle garments, looking tossed and unkempt, and a surge of relief struck him. He knew the ravages of the source upon the body, and now he clearly saw the streaks of grey prevalent in her beautiful, long hair. Her face was a grimace and, oh, despite the faded wrinkles, the mud, and a spattering of crimson brown, he still thought her beautiful. And he? Well, he was similarly ruined. He felt as grey and dishevelled as her hair. His insides felt as though a beast had attempted to claw free of his mortal body but had been denied.

"For now."

Every breath he took offered no relief from the terrible exhaustion dragging at his aching limbs.

He gazed at her and wanted nothing more than to curl up and sleep in her arms—for now. Desired the fantasy of her opening her eyes and beckoning him in. For that is what demented young men did when in lust. Or love. Or in the throes of demonic possession.

He wondered how long he could gaze at her before it became unsettling. At least a few moments more, he told himself, ever hopeful she would stir and smile and remove her garments. Or that no one would happen along and recognise his deplorable behaviour for what it was.

Am I a freak if I marry this girl?

"Yes, you are."

He didn't like his mind answering so sternly. He didn't like that it had a point.

"Freak."

With a shameful acknowledging nod, he turned away from the sleeping goddess and left her to her privacy. Plodding over the muddy ground, he dimly noticed that

Natteo's shack was unoccupied, but thought little of it. He'd be spending another day in the healer's domain, no doubt.

They might keep him away from the dream syrup, though.

With memories of Seren strolling wonderfully through a glade of green and life, he slipped through his doorway and stripped naked before dropping into a mostly clean bed. A while later, having tended to his desires as any young man would who was in lust, in love... or possessed by a demon, he lay back in the bedding and fell asleep and met her master in the dark.

————

Seren stumbled and fell through the foggy world, knowing terrible things were afoot. It felt different to the realm where she'd spent most of her life. Though she'd escaped a few days ago, mere moments might have passed within it. Or decades; she had no way of knowing. Time meant nothing there.

Things within here were clearer than in the world of the living. She knew which steps to take, even if she stumbled as she marched forward. She was one of the few capable of walking between both worlds. Not even Bereziel matched her abilities, and he'd spent an eternity within already. As he was destined to do. She had no destiny. She belonged in neither realm. That was the sin of being conceived by gods, yet never born.

A thousand miles away, in a different moment, her body took a deep, terrified breath as it stirred uneasily in its slumber, for it knew as she did the horror to come.

Home.

This was the only home she understood. Understood and feared.

"Master," she cried aloud into the darkness with a mouth that was not there, and she sensed him. Watching, calling. Fighting?

From the moment I left.

How could she forget his sacrifice? Still, she sought him out through the hazy darkness as though walking through a foggy moor on a starless night.

She knew the longer she stayed the more she would recognise; nothing in this realm behaved naturally, at least to a fragile human mind. There were advantages to blindness, for it went both ways. The less she saw, the less she was seen. Only Bereziel saw everything. As did Anguis, the Dark One. She counted her steps for a time until the buzzing in her ear became alive with the sounds of torment. Around her, she heard the maddening bray of unspeakable, brutal things crying out their agonies. Their ecstasies too. She stepped further into the source, and her broken mind cleared more and her soul glowed a little more brightly.

How do I know this?

She knew because she had returned to her hunting grounds. Her arena. To the kingdom of Bereziel the ancient. Bereziel the timeless. She'd studied under his guidance for many years. But it had been only a moment since she'd been freed from Fiore. Flickers of his teachings returned to her and she grasped for them. Some she held; most dissipated, like most of her thoughts. *Gelded like a waif.* She knew the precariousness of her step the way a spider knows without seeing the threat upon its web. Had she a breath, she would have sighed. Instead, she sought her master out. As she had done a thousand times before, from her place of chains.

"Master, come for me," she wailed aloud into the misty darkness. All the while fearing what might approach from somewhere deeper within. Something that moved between existence, between time, between entire universes. She did not know how she knew this, only that she did. She howled again and felt the disturbance of a terrible presence.

"Is it you, Fiore?" she asked, though her voice was a whisper. She knew Bereziel would be most displeased if the demoness took her at this very moment, so she called for him again and sensed his reply like a whisper in her ear.

He wages war, and you cower like a waif.

Beneath the cries of beasts, she heard the delicate song of a city of light and recognised its beauty. That was the wrong path to take, she reminded herself, and stepped away from its tune.

She stepped further into the night, feeling her heart quicken as her body become more. *Birth boom?* Soon, she passed where most other weavers had been lost. Had been left to die. Only two foolish weavers had ever stepped into that path beyond and lived. One ruled the world in anguish; the other was her wonderful master, lost from his time, gathering what strength he could.

"Oh, Serenity," he whispered now, and she smiled and opened her mind to him. And as her mind's eye focussed, he stood before her with open arms, a kind smile, and a grimace of such silent torture she suspected he had been stabbed through the heart. "Why have you returned to me?"

"Bereziel of the Seven," she cried aloud, for that was his favourite title. That would always be his title. Even if the Seven were lost. *Dead and entrapped forever.* Her words, not his. Perhaps that was why he had shunned the inevitability of death in favour of undoing a terrible act. *No, nothing can be undone. But certain injustices can be rectified. Certain terrible acts can be twisted to goodness.* His words, not hers.

Her part to play was immense. She was a great cog in his eternal machine, which strove to influence the fate of the world more favourably. She was honoured, and she was willing, but oh, the omens were wretched.

"Master, I am sorry to have returned to you in this gelded form," she whispered.

"Ruined by a dog." His voice was as old as the mountains. Older. It reverberated through her, and she remembered his terrible strength, his unforgiving lessons, his heartlessness in driving her onwards. But mostly, she remembered his kindness when she broke beneath his teachings. "A thurken dog with a bow."

He held her, though she knew well his seething anger. And why wouldn't he be furious? How much had it cost him to free her from the shackles of a cruel demon? How could she explain her mistake?

I'd forgotten how the world worked, and this pretty boy with a bow came along, and I tried to say hello, but he had a bow...

"Help undo this horror, master," she whispered, and her voice was strong. Stronger than in her native realm. She felt her body become more as her master wept for her fate.

———

"Oh, spit on this, not again," Derian muttered from his place in the mist. This visit felt different. He felt more at ease; stronger, too. As though this world were familiar. However, he'd only been there once. He felt his heart hammer, felt sweat drip down his armpits. Felt an overwhelming spasm of panic take hold of his chest. He couldn't breathe.

It's just a dream, or else I've lost my mind.

"*No dream, Derian. Try again,*" the voice in his head whispered.

"Definitely a dream. Shut up," he countered and thought

it a fine comeback. The voice in his head must have thought
so too. It shut up immediately.

What is this terrible place? he wondered, all the while
trying to ignore the eerie comfort this dark place brought him.
The same comfort of home.

"*Home is where you tear apart demons,*" the voice
whispered.

"This is a dream. Also, I told you to shut up."

"*Ripping and tearing.*"

"Shut up, shut up, shut up."

"*Eating and swallowing…*"

"I'm losing my spitting mind."

"*No, you are not. Walk a few more steps.*"

He hadn't noticed the panic drift away, but he felt its
absence now. He looked and saw nothing but blurred
darkness, as though he were wandering home from a drunken
night in a tavern. *Home.* He tried to focus his vision. Tried
really hard. Slowly, things sharpened against the blindness.
Like staring at a burning candle before quickly looking away.
He couldn't comprehend exactly what he saw, though. A few
shadowy forests of strange trees. A distant horizon stretching
out across a vast, empty plain. Something that might have
been a mountain peak, poking out through the clouds. He was
no master of mountain peaks, but he imagined it to be a very
impressive mountain peak. And then it shifted a little and
ambled away, and he suddenly didn't want to imagine a
creature that large.

"*Run into the darkness.*"

It felt like the most natural thing to do. He was no Natteo
at running, but he tried his best. Time felt different as he
charged forward into blurred nothingness, and it was
wonderful. To either side he saw glimpses of this terrible
place, and he ignored them. Following his instincts. And he

felt stronger, fiercer, more aggressive. All fear had diminished now, and he chose to enjoy this dream. Or this madness.

"Not either."

He was more than Derian of the Crimson now. He was primal. Ancient. And this was his hunting ground. He did not fear the mountain peak anymore. Instead, he wanted to leap upon it and kill it from the top downwards. Whatever that meant. Suddenly he sensed the creatures beyond the fog. He saw them in his mind, and he sought them out. Against his own will.

"What are you doing?" he demanded of his limbs.

"It's fine—I have this."

"What are you?"

"I am you. I am your kin, I am your legacy, and I am wrath upon them all."

"Is that all?"

"I am your darkest desires, I am your brazen defiance, I am you at your best. I am your hidden little monster, Seeva."

"Oh."

He sensed them ahead. Then he heard their voices, heard the tantalising call of a caged grand demon as it wailed its venomous roar, seeking out a fight from somewhere among them. Derian roared aloud in anger, in reply, and in challenge.

"Derian?" she cried, and her voice cut through his charge. Slowing to a jog and then a slow walk, he followed Seren's voice. His desire to protect her was as potent as his desire to destroy.

"Helping her will cause plenty of bloodshed. I approve," his mind whispered, and he grinned. This burgeoning personality from within was giving him a taste for warfare, if nothing else.

———

"Oh, Master, return to me my mind so I might walk the path," Seren begged, and Bereziel shook his head sadly.

"If I could, little one. If only I could."

"It is unfair to leave me in this way." She gripped him and knew how pathetically she behaved. Desperation had drawn her into this world.

"It was not my intention for you to step within. I called another to help. Your own desperation made you slip towards comforts unworthy of you."

She knew this, and her heart sank. Had Bereziel been capable, he would have saved her mind. He saw the fires as she did. Perhaps he saw more now. It was a terrible thing to lose the one advantage she'd had. The more her mind returned, the less she foresaw. All she knew was the fear to come. The terrible burning, too. With nothing after.

And then she sensed something.

"Derian? You brought Derian through the darkness?" She spun away from him in panic. At the end, when the fires took her, she'd seen Derian come for her. "You cannot bring Derian into this fight, into this war. He is wild, careless… stupid. And he is to help me."

"He has value in this world, in this moment," Bereziel countered. She almost smiled at the familiar, fatherly tone. He did not like to be challenged, but he expected it regardless.

"He could be more," she hissed.

"A Seeva serves no master. Not anymore."

"He is still human," she begged, and took Bereziel's hand. She hated Derian, really hated him. Even with a dormant demon hunting beast inside him, she hated him, but there was something to the boy. Some unlikely destiny just trying to fulfil itself, and it began with him saving her that very day.

"I know what you fear, little one," Bereziel whimpered, and now she could see the anguish in his features. Could see the love. "But if she rises untouched, no army can stop them all," he said.

"At my expense?"

He reached for her, and she wanted his embrace. Oh, she wanted to forget this nightmare, but she shoved him away. "Oh, Serenity. We knew the world would not take kindly to your emergence. I couldn't protect you from the horror." He touched her forehead and tears streamed down his cheeks. He made a terrible point. *That fuken arrow.*

"I'm so scared."

"Have faith, little one. The hour is late, but the tide can still turn."

As he spoke, he gasped, and something stirred in her mind. A flicker of memory, from before an enchantment had been cast to grant her access into another world. It was one thing for a soul to pass between worlds, but to move an entire body from the clutches of a demonic prison was something else entirely. *He fights Fiore now, this very moment.* She remembered the chains. She remembered Bereziel freeing her. *Naked, chained, ruined.*

The book had been opened. The ending had begun.

She loved him as only a granddaughter could, and she could see, beneath his stern features, the agony of battle. Fused by a deadly enchantment that had cursed the world, he was a bitter old wretch, out of place. In the same breath, he was now at his fiercest and heroic. She knew his soul's essence was split across a thousand years of time. *Or more.* She knew that, as he spoke with her, he watched events from a thousand years before, easing actions where he could. He saw things in the days beyond and moved them to better the world, to undo what evils he could. *No, not undo.* Nothing could ever be undone, but terrible events could be twisted favourably.

Oh, what he would give to be able to influence the world as I do.

Oh, what he would give to carry my burden.

Oh, what he would give to face down a vengeful realm, intent on rectifying a stolen fate.

"When the fires come this day, you *can* save yourself," Bereziel said, and his voice broke, as though he were caught by his own lie. *A beautiful lie.*

"I am so tired, so scared, so unprepared." She reached for him again. This time gently. "Come away from this realm, Master. Heal my ruin, so we might bring about the end of these times."

He stared into her eyes. His face was strained with anger and helplessness, and she knew her selfishness. For he was kind and caring and loved her with all his heart, but such a task was beyond him. Even now, as he fought for his life, delaying the marching beast, she craved more. That was not how she had been trained. "My tasks within the night are not yet done, granddaughter."

The time has come.

Before she could beg him, she felt the great tearing away and knew terrible things were afoot. Distantly, she saw Derian charge towards her. "I'm scared. I'm…"

"Be strong and live," Bereziel whispered, and she was pulled from the realm of the source into the burning haze of the day, where countless cruel hands clawed and pulled at her, and she, well, she was a gelded waif unable to weave the source to save herself from the burning to come as they placed the manacles upon her.

———

"It's you," Derian hissed in a voice not his own. He saw Seren standing before the impressive beast, saw her dissolve to nothing, and he felt her absence immediately. His rage became too much, and he charged towards the wraith of the source, for that was where he was. *Unless it's a dream.*

"Ah, Derian," the strange figure of the dark said, bowing to him. He was taller than Derian, smaller than Lorgan, but there was a strength to him that was terrifying. More terrifying yet when he reached out and took hold of the charging Derian by the scruff of the neck and held him as though he were a rampaging child. "I wasn't aware we'd actually met yet," the figure added, examining him curiously. Though he appeared human, there was something unmistakably ethereal about him. His sharp features were cut too fine, his eyes dazzled too much in this dimness, his movements too graceful and somehow unnatural to the human eye. He was old as time and as young as a child, in the same moment.

Despite himself, Derian was awestruck and struggled unsuccessfully in his grasp. "You came to me out on the battlefield," Derian whispered, and as he spoke his voice became richer, more vibrant. Alive. *Within the darkness?* Again, he felt a realness to this world that was comforting and exciting.

"In here, I can kill easily enough."

"Did I now?" The figure shook his head as though dismissing Derian's suggestion.

"Yes. You told me about the stones—"

"Whisht, hound," he interrupted, and Derian felt his hand form into a clawed fist.

Clawed?

The figure saw this and smiled. His eyes glimmered a little more. "Oh, I like that contemptuous anger. Forgive my candour—I was not sure what part of you would greet me," he said. For an entire breath he held his hand out as though he were going to pat Derian on the head. It wouldn't be like a Lorgan love pat at all. "You say we spoke before? I will take your word as a mercenary that we did." He looked straight through Derian as though he were invisible—and perhaps he was. Perhaps he saw something beyond. A wash of energy flashed across his features. The figure smiled and waved his withered hand in a strange motion before gliding past Derian. The world around them shook without noise, without essence; glimmered from dimness to something else. "Allow your eyes to see this world a little more clearly. Allow your soul to reveal itself. Be swift about it, too—I'm losing this battle," he added, grinning.

Distantly, Derian sensed something fierce and deadly, and he felt his body tense like a hunter's, sniffing the prey. Or better, sensing a threat walking across his domain, spoiling for a fight. Derian remembered swinging above a hundred gnashing teeth; he remembered tearing apart the monsters of the night upon a battlefield and beneath a shattered wall. Finally, he remembered being entrapped within impossibly heavy armour and freeing himself from fear, sorrow, and all terrors.

"Kill them all."

"Who are you? Where is Seren?" Derian demanded as the figure glided effortlessly away from his grasp. He wore a cloak. Strange that Derian hadn't noticed it before. Or the golden throne he passed as he walked. *What's a throne doing in the middle of the source?*

The figure froze as though time had fallen still. He watched something beyond what Derian saw. It was an unsettling thing.

What is going on? Derian wondered.

"You've come home to kill, Derian," his mind replied.

This is my home?

"It was my home in the beginning. Now it is ours."

He heard a deep sigh and realised it was the figure. He remained watching the dark, and when he spoke, his voice was distant. "She's returned to die at the hands of peasants. Or rise above death."

Wait, what?

Suddenly Derian wanted to free himself from this strangely familiar place and aid his Seren. "Where is she?" he demanded, feeling his heart quicken as he slept in his bed, so far away, and he remembered this was simply a dream and nothing more. "I wish to wake," he cried, and struck his face.

"Shush. Save the fight for the actual fight. In no time at all…" the figure said, and chuckled to himself at some wittiness Derian hadn't caught.

None of this made any sense, and Derian wanted to roar aloud. To take hold of this strange brute; to get answers. Instead, he listened, hoping to glean what he could, hoping even more to wake from this dream. And hoping to stay here a few moments longer. He felt as though he'd spent his entire life using a fraction of his mind, while the rest of him lay resting, concealed in an unforgiving cage of darkness. Something stirred within. Something that didn't like cages.

Am I possessed? he asked his mind.

"We are, by each other," it replied, and that made little sense, yet he knew it to be true.

"How did you know my name, strange cloak-wearing man?" Derian hissed, trying not to listen to his mind, which spouted reassuring nonsense. Nonsense that tasted like agreeable things.

"My apologies, little hound. I am Bereziel of the Seven. I speak to you from the darkness. The pages have been opened by Erin; the demons are gathering. The world is going to war. You will play your part." He took a breath and offered Derian a look that said "Was that enough of a grand reply?"

"Wait, who's Erin?"

"It's irrelevant, little hound."

"And what pages? What war?" Derian imagined himself spitting in disgust. "There's always a fuken war."

"The less you know, the less Anguis will learn," Bereziel said, and his face darkened at the name he had used as though saying it aloud was a precarious thing.

"I am sick of ignorance. Who is this Erin?" Derian demanded. He thought hard on his next question. "Does she have nice knees? Is she the girl with the stones? Is she the girl you told me to protect?"

At this, Bereziel of the Seven, who was bringing war and spit to the world, or something like that, leapt upon Derian, gripping him tightly, whispering fiercely. "Say little more in this realm."

Spit on this.

"Tell me what is going on! Tell me, or I will roar aloud everything I know, and damn those who listen." It was a fine threat. He wasn't certain how much he had to share, but that didn't matter. Bereziel had no memory of his own words; who knew what damage Derian could do?

"If it brings the demons quicker, say plenty."

Bereziel sighed again. "I see things, and I use moments where I can. But only because I've already done the action, or will do the action, or, in the moment, am doing the action." At this, he waved his hands at the world around them. "You see moments as a line with a beginning and an end. This world, though, ignores the rules of night and day as we understand them. Time, life, and death are different here. Actions taken are eternal in this realm. But that's only because they've always occurred. In the now, in the then, in the to come." He eyed Derian as though what he said made perfect sense. Neither part of Derian's mind had a spitting clue what he meant.

"I understand completely," Derian lied.

Bereziel saw through the lie. "When thinking as a human, it might take madness to fully comprehend this darkness." His face darkened. "I've spent millennia within, and even I can't fathom it completely. However, that does not stop me from manipulating what I can to my wishes." He frowned in thought. "All of us have chosen paths. For that is the will of things that came before us all. Terrible things. No matter what we do, we were always destined to do it. I was always destined to be here, as were you. Everyone in the living realm has a path, apart from Seren. Such a soul can taint these paths to different moments. She can change the world. She is chaos to the natural order of things. For when things are torn from their rightful path, great evils can be undone."

Derian nodded as though his newest gathering of words made a semblance of sense. He knew well the trick to negotiation: sometimes when you had no hand at all and your opponent had locked you into a dead end, and all your bets were open and your stack was precarious… and you'd just rolled a three… and it wasn't even your bet… and you had no idea how the spitting game worked… Well, then, sometimes you revealed all your cards… and lied.

"You say I've spoken to you from a different time, and so it will come to be. It is your past but my future," Bereziel went on, and wiped his forehead as though tending to a wound. "Unless it was simply an echo you heard. Tell me, did we speak? Did we converse?"

Derian nodded, though his mind shook. Had they spoken?

· *Of course we did.*

Didn't we?

"Don't ask me. I was busy tearing the beasts apart."

"Wait, tell me—did I speak of the Seven?" Suddenly Bereziel gasped and fell to his knees, as though speared by a claw. Derian sensed a terrible evil nearby, and his darker part became enraged like never before. Around him he saw fire, shimmering metals—and an arachnid leg striking out at him. Within a pulse it was gone, but Bereziel remained on his knees, gasping. "You shook my will," he croaked. "I cannot hold her very much longer."

All thoughts of Seren were lost. All thoughts of girls with knees and insane talk of things he couldn't understand. All that remained was a terrible desire to rip the legs from whatever beast he had just glimpsed.

"In the world of Dellerin, you are reckless and wild, unable to control your ancient form," Bereziel said. "I have witnessed your discipline, watched you, for longer than you can know."

"What is it that takes control of me?"

"Your lineage, your wonderful ancient blood that was awoken after your death," he replied, and his eyes were wild with fire. His gasping had ceased. "Out there, you are a shadow of your true self, but in here, little Derian of the Crimson, you might give Fiore a little trouble."

Fiore. The name burned deep in Derian's mind. He really wanted to give this Fiore some trouble. He felt his body become whole, and it was not human. It was divine and wild and real. He'd seen pictures of these beasts in his studies. He knew their name, for he'd always feared meeting one in battle. The true, fierce creatures of Venistra.

Venandi night hunters.

Bereziel was beside him now. He had attached a terrifying long blade of serrated bone to his right forearm. He waved his left hand again, and magenta fire surrounded them, burning away the world to reveal the battle beyond. The battle that was being waged now, and then… and maybe in the future.

Derian really hadn't a clue how it worked.

Because of the source.

"Want to tear at a grand demon?" Bereziel cried.

"That would be spitting polished," roared Derian, and the world shook one last time.

36

STABBED

"Oh, spit on me," Clover muttered, climbing up the little iron ladder ahead of Kesta. "Stupid thurken peasant idiots."

She looked up at his hindquarters as they bobbed ahead of her and thought it a fine view, and then she saw the reason behind his outburst. *Spitting peasants.* He ran his fingers along the clinks in the heavy, plated hatch door, muttering curses under his breath.

"It would appear the fine residents of Treystone felt it excusable to be graceless hosts."

"It looks like the peasants were at it a while," Kesta offered, watching him run his fingers along the damage. It was minimal. A few shallow chunks had been dug out, and there were some careless scrapes on the surface. She thought it a good sign of a sturdy ship. That plating *was* thick. They'd built this airbarge to withstand some nasty things. Looking down to the settled children below, she understood the peasants' behaviour. A vessel as impressive as this might cart dozens away to safety, on voyage after voyage, if there were a skilled pilot to handle the machine. She ran her fingers along the little dings in the finish. Were the peasants able to get aboard, they could have stored the children in safety.

Clover stepped into the massive barge and she followed. He swiftly slammed the hatch behind her, and she felt that stirring of worry again. *He could stab me right here. Nobody would know.* Truthfully, the threat of assassination paled compared to the excitement of being aboard an airbarge again. Oh, she wanted this wonderful machine. She wanted to know it intimately.

"Mowg will cause quite a stir once he learns of the damage done to the *Mongoose*," Clover muttered, inviting her to follow him down a narrow corridor towards the far end of the barge. It was wide enough for two people to slip by. Every few steps were wooden doorways on both sides, suggesting sleeping quarters.

"He doesn't seem much of a forgiving man," Kesta countered, running her fingers along the corridor walls as she followed. She couldn't help herself. She wasn't used to nice things. Or enjoying herself. She'd never been aboard this model of airbarge; the vessels were relatively rare, and this wonderful machine was like nothing she'd seen before. This was turning into a great day, she thought, even if she walked into death.

Clover turned back and stood over her with arms spread wide as though to embrace her. "Still worried about coming aboard, eh? Don't worry; there isn't much any Crimson mercenary could do to earn the ire of our fearless leader," he said, winking as though he knew something she didn't. Which he did.

"What does that mean?"

"A life debt is a life debt," he said, as though that would reassure her. "But enough of this crap. Come—you are my beautiful guest. Let me show you the finer parts of my baby."

He played the charming Venistrian lover impressively, and she enjoyed his bravado as he swept away. He didn't put her at ease with familiarity, but still, it was a subtle taste of home. A taste of a different life. *Worth getting stabbed over.*

"You have carpet?" she exclaimed in delight as they stepped into another corridor. She fought the compulsion to remove her boots. *Carpet on an airbarge?* She dropped to her knees in the corridor and felt the softness. Carpet was a thing mercenaries rarely engaged with. It was a needlessly luxurious veneer, reserved for the richest of all traders or for wealthy brigands pretending to be royalty in their oversized mansions. It hardly belonged on an airbarge, and she ignored his sniggering before getting to her feet again and following him to a door at the end of the corridor.

"We like to relax here. After a hard day saving the world," Clover said, ushering her in with the sweep of a hand. "It has nice carpet for you to inspect too, if you'd like."

It was a wonderful, regal, red carpet, and it covered the floor of the finest room she'd ever seen. It resembled an exclusive tavern suite in Dellerin City, down to the painted walls of deathly, seductive black. Thick silken curtains of ludicrous unnatural purples and pinks adorned all four walls, which not only ensured privacy but also kept the cold from the room during flights. She shivered for a moment, thinking of some of her early flights in unstable death-traps and the biting wind stealing the warmth from her body. Expensive curtains would have helped.

"What do you think?"

Grinning, she imagined at least a dozen mercenaries whiling away the hours in this room. There were three thick couches and a few down-filled chairs scattered artfully about; Kesta felt the need to drop herself into the fluffiest-looking couch that she could find. So she did, and spit on her. She giggled as though she were a child, spreading her feet wide on the impossibly soft cushion.

A profitable career could be had in this unit.

From behind a small marble and oak counter, part of the pretence of being a small tavern in the sky, Clover pulled two crystal goblets from their place of holding. He took a moment and then plucked a bottle of brown sine from a shelf and filled both glasses before holding them in the light of a candle for inspection. He was enjoying the game. She was his prey, and she was happy to play along. She could think of no better place to be—apart from at the helm, of course, controlling all their lives with a delicate swipe of a few levers. Now that would be impressive.

"We like to treat our guests as royalty," he whispered smoothly, and she saw the desire in his eyes. Whether it was desire to tear the clothes from her or desire to plunge his blade deep into her gut, she couldn't tell. She took the glass of sine and sipped the burning ambrosia. Even the spitting sine was the finest she'd ever tasted.

"I feel honoured," she countered, and clinked his glass. "But I want to see it all. Show it to me before you do whatever needs doing."

He chuckled coldly. "You speak like a peasant who's never been aboard. Tell me, dear Kesta, what extravagance could best this room?" The grin returned, and she wanted to kiss him or strike him. Whichever, really. She thought his question fair, but she wouldn't be dissuaded. Draining her drink, she left it on the couch's armrest, got to her feet and walked through the room, searching for interesting things to add to her giddiness. He caught on swiftly. Snatching up her glass and securing it behind the tavern counter, he said, "Fine, fine. I'll take you around the *Mongoose*. All of it. Before I do… whatever needs doing."

To this, she offered a smile. It was nearly genuine.

"This way," he said, marching through a doorway that had been concealed behind a curtain. The luxuriousness disappeared again beneath the more usual grey metals, and this felt more familiar. A ladder led down to a room below. He slid down, and she followed and found herself in darkness.

Here is where it happens.

She raised her fists in futile defiance as Clover brought light to the room with a few caught flint ignitions over some candles wicks.

"Whoa," she gasped. They were standing in the engine room, among the innards of the *Mongoose*.

"Yes, she is impressive."

Kesta ran her fingers along the vessel's machinations, studying its workings, taking in all she could and loving every divine valve, piston, cylinder, and rotor. She'd been in love several times in her life. This engine caused similar stirrings. It was the shiny things.

"Whoever keeps this beast running keeps her smooth and oiled, shined and tight," Kesta whispered. Her eyes darted from part to part, her fingers touching, inspecting and adoring. He had the excellent sense not to disturb her. Perhaps he'd realised by now how deep her appreciation of this barge was. Appreciated her knowledge and ability too. "No carpet down here," she offered. Her knees ached as she crawled beneath the engine, but she ignored the discomfort. "Does she hum? Does she screech?"

"She purrs like a dream, Kesta. Maybe, if you hitch a ride, you might hear it too," he offered, leaning up against the wall. He wore an inane smile. Warmer now. Appreciative of her respect.

"It must require a fortune running this," she said, eying

the many cylinders of black water stacked neatly on top of each other at the far end of the room. She walked over to them as if in a dream. Almost unconsciously, she pulled at their straps and found them adequately secured. A few of those volatile containers coming loose could turn this beast into a firefly a few miles up. Black water burned quicker than oil. Burned quick enough to keep a monster like this flying as well.

"That's probably why Mowg dislikes my baby so much," Clover said, shrugging. "Still, though, who needs riches when you can fly?"

She wanted to hop on him right there and then. Just a quick act of decadent furrowing. Just to finish the most memorable day of her life... since becoming a mercenary.

As he showed her around, he began to behave less like the charming lover and more like a respectful peer. It probably wasn't every day a lady matched his passion.

They made their way down to the stables, deep in the lower section of the vessel. Away from natural light and terrifying sights, the mounts would be safe with grass, feed, and sturdy straps to keep them secure as they flew across the sky. There were no mounts in the hold now, however, as they had recently been stolen by a rival band of mercenaries. There was only a moment of awkward pause before he suggested they visit the galley next.

This large room was as far from the engines as they could get. The bitter stench of engine oil was replaced with the rich aroma of exotic spices, and her mouth watered. A long stove covered half of one wall, and a long table with a dozen seats filled the room out. The table was already set with ornately decorated tableware. *No expense spared.*

"We can stay in flight quite a while without touching down," he boasted, opening a cupboard to display tenfold the supplies the Crimson had pilfered from their camp. Kesta's guilt was allayed somewhat. They had secured sacks of vegetables in a larder, along with countless jars of fermented foods and dozens of thin strips of hanging meat, both salted and dry. The Army of the Dead took no chances where food was concerned. Were she a fine chef, she could have cooked a week's feast for an entire battalion and still have room for desserts. With all the black water below, the ship could stay afloat for months, she thought, with a few less mouths to feed.

"Convenient if the world ends," she muttered.

"Try this," he whispered conspiratorially, opening a jar of pickled carrots. "Assassin of… um… Death, or whatever he's going by these days, has an unnatural love for these bitter things. Every port, he ships a few new jars. Always carrots. Gets mighty attached to them too." He fished carefully in the jar, and the bitter, tasty aroma struck her nose. "I would be remiss in my duties as a blaggard if I did not pilfer these delicacies in honour of a beautiful woman." He tossed a carrot over to her. "Or I could find some honey bread?"

Ah, honey bread, the ever constant.

"I want to go out there," she said, forcing the fermented carrot down her throat more easily than she expected. She looked past the simple riches of food and cooking hobs and pans and plates and everything a decent airbarge galley should have, and gazed longingly at the little hatchway leading to the outer deck beyond.

"Of course you do, my dear," he said. Setting the carrots aside, he unlocked the door, and she soon stood high out on a deck, with the small reinforced glass sphere of the flight deck beyond. It was a stunning deck. Cut of the finest oak no doubt, and kept nicely polished against the unforgiving sky. On either side of the outer deck, only a waist-high wooden guardrail protected them from a steep drop to the ground below. She imagined the exhilaration of marching across this deck mid-flight and chuckled. It was in making the trek while caught in a gale that her nerve would be tested.

Again.

Below them, the children were already settled again, and she wondered just how many people might this monster have lifted to safety the first or second night? How cruel for them to know salvation was but a sheet of plate metal away.

The cockpit was large enough, with two seats displaying similar controls, and she slid into one leather chair without permission and ran her fingers across the levers as though they were her oldest friends. If he was irked at her boldness, he held his tongue. In fact, he ran his fingers through her hair, and she allowed him.

He leaned in closer now, and she could smell the aroma of battle on him. She cared little for the perfumed oils most men might wear, but his muskiness was enthralling.

"I love this machine," she whispered, and he caught her fingers as they neared the four ignitors. One for each propeller.

"You can't fly her… just yet," he whispered, and she imagined how easily he could stab her through the back and she would sit at the controls and take it.

"'Just yet'? Oh, Clover, you say the most interesting things," she said, leaving the controls unloved. Absently, he mimicked the actions of launch, and she suspected they hadn't changed too much over the years.

He stroked the pulley and the lock that held the controls in place. "It's a wonderful thing to release these monsters from their chains, but it's a thurken nightmare reeling them in." Oh, he was doing a fine job seducing her, with little effort.

That type of girl.

Behind the seats was a hatch, with a ladder leading back to the more luxurious segments of the airbarge below. She followed him down the steps as though drunk. She felt lighter than she had felt in a lifetime and willingly allowed him to lead her to one last room.

"As pilot, I took the finest room," he said, leading her into his chambers, and it *was* fine. The bed of a thousand different silks was glorious. As were the many books on aviation, monsters, poets, and artists that lined the wall. The carpet here was soft too, and this time she removed her boots without a moment's hesitation. He slipped behind another curtain on the far side of the room to tend to natural duties, and she continued to inspect his choice in literature.

"You like my collection of books?" he called out from behind the curtain.

"Of all the things, your book collection has impressed me most," she said, and smiled. Had she just cracked a joke? She thought she heard the crack of flint and the burning of fire, followed by the loud gushing of water, and she suddenly became very suspicious as to his endeavours. Suspicious yet oddly untroubled. He'd had ample opportunity to stab her many times already. She was settling.

He said nothing for a few breaths, so she climbed upon the bed and stretched out and felt at home. Not with him, of course—he was fine. He was a potential transient lover, and such things had been wonderful when she was younger. No, this was a pilot's room; this was *home*. She closed her eyes and thought of the sky and of lifting this bitch deep into it. She imagined the roar of those chains releasing the massive propellers. They could cut through this entire spitting warehouse if needed.

"Well, it would be a terrible shame to waste a perfect

night with something as mundane as a little sleep," he whispered, drawing her from her near dream. She sat up and saw that he had drawn aside the curtain, revealing a bathtub, just large enough for two. She smiled, enjoying his naked manhood, his naked muscles, his naked grin, and his manhood again. She looked back at the tub. Well, two people if stacked appropriately.

"It appears I am to be stabbed tonight after all," she said, slipping free of her garments and climbing into the bath after him.

37

LORGAN

L organ stared at the doorway and sighed gently. He looked to the picture behind her and sighed again. He looked at the wall surrounding him and thought about punching it a few times and resisted the urge to show his unease, so he sighed again. Really spitting loud. Keralynn continued to talk, and Lorgan felt the room closing in; felt the turning of the tide; felt the traditions of peasantry spilling out all over him. There was danger brewing. Not just for him, but for the town itself. And she had no idea what trouble she stirred.

Shouldn't have furrowed her, either.

Mowg could see the danger too. He leant back in his chair behind the gathering, playing his part, pretending he had no hand in this turning of events. There was talk of payments among the arguing, but Lorgan had been here before. The last time he'd walked into this room, he'd had all the power. Until an hour before, he had continued to hold the power—and then the Gold Haven army had arrived. Now the power had shifted.

Blair, a previous enemy, now sat behind his desk as his

only ally. "They stood with us when they could have fled. Now you feel the need to challenge our debt to them, Keralynn?" he hissed, shaking his head in disgust.

This isn't about money, friend.

Seren was on to something.

"You were the one who had issue with them first. They are no heroes," Keralynn snapped. She had little issue revealing her unease. Or her temper. She stormed around the room, her anger increasing. He'd known there was a worrying zealousness to her, but something had caused her to lose her sense. She'd chosen Dorn as her ally. He was the biggest hound in the room, in her eyes. In her pretty, fanatical eyes.

How unpredictable is a terrified fanatic?

"I was wrong. And I am glad to have been," Blair muttered, eyeing the Gold Haven general, who sat listening without word. Dorn probably thought himself the biggest hound in the room too. Easy thinking that, with an army waiting outside.

Blair was the lone voice of reason, and listening to him defend the Crimson's price was unexpected. He wasn't used to changing people's minds through heroism and honourable deeds. He was, however, quite used to broken deals where payment was concerned. Lorgan could see Blair's genuineness now. He should have seen it before, but stubbornness had blinded him. Keralynn thought of her welfare and beliefs over the benefit of the masses. She had no place in this position. Blair, however, was a fine leader of Treystone.

"The town of Treystone is grateful," he said, eyeing Dorn. "Gold Haven is in their debt too," he added.

Dorn won't take your side on this one, comrade.

Lorgan looked to the painting above Keralynn's head again and sighed. He might have stayed and defended the town regardless of its most famous son. Knowing this was Heygar's home had confirmed his decision. He hadn't even come close to redeeming his sins, but standing firm was a few drops removed from a brook of regret.

Dorn, for his part, cared little for the town's obligations. He was here to protect the town's value. Treystone grew as a fine mining town under its larger brother's eye. (Though probably not as much as it could have, were it allowed to take advantage of its own bounty.) "Yes, we are grateful, and along with my soldiers here, they are relieved of their duty," he said, and for a moment Lorgan almost laughed. He always found humour when everything was about to fall apart.

This is not about payment.

Lorgan had sensed a threat on the walk up from the gate. Sensed it in every zealot that passed them humming religious nothings. The unease in the air was more than the heavy stench of smoke. Some called it a gut feeling. Lorgan considered it inevitability, for he was a man cursed. And a man deserving of his curse.

A silent prayer to the painting was all he could offer now. It was a prayer he'd spoken these thirty years now. He'd received no reply from the source beyond, and he desired no reply. Silence was all he deserved. When a childish fool's actions doomed the entire world to ruin beneath the Dark Bastard's grip, there weren't any words that could heal a broken old man.

The only thing he desired from the source was the call into death. A deserving death. A fitting death. Truthfully, he'd sensed death for thirty years now. Waited for it eagerly. He sensed it much closer these days. Ever since Seren had appeared.

The room fell silent as those aggrieved took a moment to

gather a breath, form new arguments, slip further from a positive outcome.

He offered a few words in the vain hope of reaching a suitable agreement. "I'll take what payment you deem fitting, and we'll be on our way."

He stood up from his chair and offered Keralynn a charming smile. He remembered her writhing in his arms, and it had been pleasurable. Welcomed. Unexpected, too. It had been fine times, silencing her fanatical ramblings, even if only for those few hours. Knowing his death likely followed the next night had been worth the few sermons.

Truthfully, he'd worried as the golden army had approached that Seren's activities might draw unwanted attention. The promise of gold had placed him in this room. He should have known better.

Should have grabbed my clan and bolted.

"Yes," agreed Blair, believing in the power of a fair deal. "Pay them their weight in gold and send them off upon their mounts." It sounded reasonable, and for an entire moment Keralynn appeared to think on this.

Mowg glanced his way, clearing his throat, and Lorgan almost smiled in reply. As if it wasn't bad enough that the Watcher of Treystone had issue with him. The matter of ownership of said mounts was a matter he might care to discuss. Though probably not with fists. "Any mercenary who stood in defence of this town deserves payment," he said, stretching easily. He knew a mugging when it happened. He knew her threats, too.

"I have no issue with the Army of the Dead, nor with their payment. They may fly away with rich pockets and clean souls," Keralynn countered. Her tone was dangerous, for she played a very dangerous game in this moment. Her face was flushed with rage. Or was it from embarrassment for lying with an old man?

This isn't about payment at all. This is far more serious.

"Oh, Keralynn, be wary of your words," Lorgan said carefully, stepping slowly towards the door. Each step creaked loudly on the varnished wooden floor. Two or three more steps and his hand would reach the door handle. Everything after that was a golden river of possibilities. However, waiting for those thurken steps felt like swimming in a deep river with heavy armour. He stopped to look at the picture one last time. *I'm so sorry, Heygar.*

"You are criminals," she hissed.

Mowg stood up from his seat casually, but his eyes were as wide as Lorgan's. Her words signified that things had taken a terrible turn. Not just for the Crimson, but for all involved. This was no matter of withholding payment. It was bad for business not to pay any mercenary outfit once the contract was agreed and completed. A town like Treystone would suffer dearly at the hands of the Guild, once word of their actions reached them. Gold Haven would suffer too, just for having an authority present. They could not simply pay one and punish the other.

Easier to remove both outfits from the equation.

"Oh, yes," they would say reassuringly to eager ears, asking about their accomplishments. "Both heroic outfits rode off as gallant champions and we never saw them again, honest to the gods. By the way, don't go searching around the dozen mounds of dirt over there."

Dorn was wise enough to see the precariousness of her words. "Oh, Keralynn, you do not want to pay one outfit and not the other. That is simply not done, my love," he declared.

'My love'? Aw, spit on this.

"I choose my words just fine, husband," she hissed.

Aw, really, spit on this.

Keralynn wasn't finished; those steps to the door seemed distant now. "My issue is with the one they call Seren." She spat her name, and Lorgan remembered her fanatical queries as to Seren's powers. Her pleading to know of her healing abilities. *Of how she could return the dead.* He had been removing her dress at the time. It had stubborn knots and too many buttons. Fumbling thumbs were a perilous affliction in the moment of passion. *Oh, Lorgan.* He dared not look her husband in the eyes. Any guilt he'd lost clung on to him anew. Worse, Keralynn was risking Lorgan speaking of her unfaithfulness now, all in the name of condemning Seren.

Zealots.

"Seren is no matter. We do not answer Anguis's laws in Luistra," snapped Blair, but Dorn was intrigued.

"Among them walks a weaver," Keralynn said.

And this is where a polished mission gets rightly scuffed.

Dorn leapt to his feet, slamming his fist upon the desk. "You waited until now to tell me?"

Lorgan formed a fist of his own and thought about making a break for it. Beside him, Mowg did the same.

"A weaver in this place will never remain a secret," Dorn snarled. "Oh, my love, what possessed you to allow such a beast to roam free?"

My manly manhood?

"Terrific. A fuken Acolyte of Anguis," whispered Mowg under his breath, and Lorgan nodded, sharing his disgust. Only things worse than zealots were fools believing in the dream of Dellerin. Most settlements feared the Dark One and his reach, but there were some vile bastards who would serve him in an effort to keep his eyes from their activities. Or worse, to be rewarded for them. Lorgan could see it in his eyes before he spoke another

word. Who knew what advantages such a gift would bring
Gold Haven? Who knew the riches a captain might earn
delivering such a gift?

Preferably dead, as the law goes.

Keralynn smiled. "We believed her a sympathetic soul,
believed her capable of saving us at our time of need. We
were wrong. Her actions proved as much," she said, facing
Lorgan. He had nothing to say. Mowg spoke up again. It
sounded like he was protecting his investment.

"She saved us, brought fight to the monsters attacking,
and you wish to deliver her to the authorities willingly?" His
words were slow and deliberate, for he was a legendary
mercenary used to hazardous negotiations.

Blair agreed. "She did all that and you intend to condemn
her to death?"

Keralynn would not be swayed from her beliefs by such
well-constructed arguments. She looked ready to let loose a
tirade of superstitious nonsense about the end of days and the
rise of demons. "She returned a dead mercenary to life, yet
would not grant such a gift to those suffering."

"Which mercenary? What are you talking about?" Lorgan
growled.

"It matters little now," hissed his former bedmate, and he
wondered what he had ever seen in her. Apart from her
staggering beauty and sublime shapely body. "We are dealing
with her now."

What?

"What did you do?" demanded Blair, but Lorgan was
already leaping away from the door towards her. She stepped
from his grasp; she was swift. Dorn was almost as swift. He
raised his sword and stood between his wife and her attacker.
Without thinking, Lorgan struck him fiercely across the chin,
knocking him from his feet.

"Your wife has some stamina," Lorgan hissed, and ignored the pang of guilt that struck him anew.

Keralynn ignored them, her fanaticism returning now in full force. "She will burn," she screamed, and Lorgan almost struck out at her a second time. Just once, across the chin. Leave her asleep in the arms of her zealous bastard of a husband.

"What have you done, you stupid cow?" demanded Blair. His face was pale, for he knew full well the depth of her actions. He looked to Lorgan, who stared back at him in panic, for he knew the consequences. Treystone would not survive the season if word reached the Guild.

Lorgan held his strike, and Mowg grabbed his shoulder. "You slept with her? Nice! Anyway, doesn't matter. We have to go," he cried, dragging Lorgan away. An explosion of light nearly blinded him as Mowg pulled him from the office, down the steps, and out through the early morning streets. It should have been an escape. Should have been the beginning of another adventure, but both mercenaries stopped in their tracks. Standing in a circle outside the building was Keralynn's little army of sycophant zealots.

"We can talk about this," Mowg announced, as the mob drew in around them.

38

WAR IN THE SOURCE

D erian wondered if there were any tavern bard skilled enough to describe the source to a watching crowd and call themselves no liar. Oh, those silver-tongued peasants might describe the primal cries of a thousand different beasts and still never do justice to how beautiful their terrifying anthem was to the ear. These masters of poetic licence might have described this realm as a place of sunless skies with eternal dark that could steal a hero's will. They might sing of the cold mist, as thick as a blossoming bonfire's smoke, that hung in the air and still never describe the eeriness of this shadowed land. They might accurately describe one solitary moment in this place as a thousand years and still be ten thousand years from ever explaining what the source truly was.

To Derian, stepping down into the throng felt like wading through a bowl of curried soup. Or any soup. (Apart from Fayenar wheat soup. That was closer to lightly salted warm water.) His movements were reduced as though a legion of grasping fingers placed themselves upon him. Dragging, slowing. Repulsing. He hated this place so very much. He never wanted to leave. Even when he sensed his foe.

Click, click, click.

Each cracking noise sent shivers down his spine as his instincts took over. Oh, he wanted to fight. He felt the growing hatred. Like the calling of sleep, he succumbed and was left unfulfilled. The world slowed and he could only stand and crave, his body taut and ready.

"Be still, Derian. Allow the moments to return to themselves," Bereziel whispered, and Derian snarled. Ahead of him stood the beast named Fiore, and she was dreadful to gaze upon.

Click, click, click. Her ashen, grey face resembled no human he'd ever seen, but there was a femininity to her that he could not quite explain. He was no bard.

Her piercing eyes shone blood red in the night, like a demon's catalight, and their glow left a thin blush across her impossibly sharp features.

Click, click, click.

She was underdressed for marching into war with him. Her long hair almost concealed her naked chest, but it did not conceal the many shards of horn protruding from her head like a crown. *Perhaps she is a queen?*

Click, click, click. That spitting noise cut through him like her claws might, were she to deliver a telling blow upon him. Claws instead of hands were a demon thing, he supposed. Massive, jagged claws as sharp as diamond shards were probably more valuable in a realm such as this.

Click, click, click. If she was a beauty of this demonic dominion, his own demonic part felt little attraction. For, below her navel, her body resembled nothing human at all, for she moved like a grotesque spider, clicking with every step. Her many long, spindly legs jutted out from an obese globular abdomen, which bobbled hideously as she moved. She scampered across the darkness and oh, he wanted to bite into that body and spill her vileness all over him. But it was covered in armour. *No, in shell.* A vile shell, like a crustacuus's. Impenetrable and thick—and he without a sword. He watched her as she did battle, and she was impressive.

As though held in place by heavy armour, he felt movement slowly return to his body as the battle whispered of his arrival. She struck out at a blurred figure; only then did Derian understand the source better.

Bereziel whispered from beside him, "In this moment I am with you in mind and word, but I am a faint echo of my true self." The figure came alive in sharpness. It was Bereziel. He struck fiercely at Fiore with a weapon of blinding blue light, and Derian realised it was the long, sharpened bone Bereziel had attached to his forearm. The strike was laboured. "She caught me there," Bereziel whispered, touching his forehead as she tore at him again with her claws and struck a terrible blow. With his other hand, he pointed to the figure as he fell away from her strike and crumpled to the ground. "That is me this very moment. No echo, just a breath from here." He gasped heavily. "Time and actions are irrelevant in this place. Seren has her gifts; controlling moments is mine." Beside him, Bereziel wiped absently at the fresh wound. Derian hadn't noticed it before, but it had been there. Had always been there.

"This is you, as we speak?" Derian asked. He was a terrible student when ordered to read and learn annoying words, but in action, in seeing happenings, he was astute.

"I am holding this moment for as long as I can. I have fought her so very long and I am tired, I am weak, I am beaten." He dropped to his knee again and bled a little into the ground. "The bitch is tougher than I'd expected. I cannot hold her off for much longer. I cannot weaken her alone. I must allow both these moments to become one," he wheezed, and Derian saw him fading away as though he were a wisp of smoke, and the world resumed its turning once more.

Within a pulse of time, Derian stood watching the battle between both combatants. He saw the wretch who'd collapsed beside him become the wretch felled by Fiore, and he charged towards her. Even with the sound of his panting and snarling, even with his strange four-limbed charge, she did not hear him approach. No matter. Within a breath of time, she realised his presence.

"My turn."

His body was not his, yet completely his, and he felt the rush of wind beneath him for a second breath before colliding with her. In his mind, he'd imagined tactics. Fine tactics from the little experience he'd earned as a useless mercenary. He imagined himself attacking her appendages first. Delivering unto her savagery that would save the world. Take a limb, weaken her, tear her spitting throat out.

That didn't happen at all. He lost control, and it was beautiful. With clawed paws, he ripped at her shell, at her skin, at whatever he could, really. His movements were a blur. He gored into her like a hound upon a fresh, delicious kill. And she *was* delicious. The first bite he took from that unprotected, grey flesh was ambrosia. It might have been from her shoulder, or a spindly ankle; he couldn't say for certain. He never stopped. His howls matched her shrieks of surprise, and it was the greatest moment of his life, and he decided this was ecstasy. Time stood still, and she wavered and fell away from the assault and he grasped her bulbous abdomen and this was most succulent of all. He heard her body rip, heard her hate-filled wails shake the world around them, and it was art.

"Where is the blood?" he howled as he tore thick, leathery slabs free. Blood would have been better, he told himself. He wanted to eat his prize, to claim her meat as his victory, but she was far from succumbing to his assault.

Click, click, click. Her legs bobbed in his sightline as she stumbled through the darkness with him clutched tightly next to her, all the while delivering strike after strike. Still, she staggered away, howling in horror and agony but not falling.

She spun and jerked violently, and he dug in deeper for as long as he could until, eventually, she shook him away before delivering the first counter-blow of her own, and it was excruciating. He flew backwards and landed in a ruined heap, and pleasure was replaced with anger again.

"Seeeeeva!" she cried, and he did not like her voice. Not one little bit. It shook him more than the blow itself. It was an old voice. As old as the newborn beats of thunder rolling over the world's first mountains. He did not know how he knew this, only that he did.

"Because I was there."

He roared in reply, a terrible whirlwind of snarls, equally as primal as she. He cursed her to the fires. Cursed her to the dark. Cursed her to her prison for ten thousand more years. The beast within him had come alive, and he saw flashes of its origin. Created by the old ones to destroy the old ones. Oh, in pure form his kind had been divine. Now, though, lanced through the soul by a human vessel, he was gelded. Such a shame. Such a waste.

But gelded or no, he knew her too, and she was no more impressive. He was an instrument of righteous war. She was merely a grand demon, as powerful as the world and twice as old. What fear could she bestow upon him?

"To the fires with you," Bereziel roared in the old language, and a wild magenta fire lit up the dark. He cast enchantments of fire upon her and she squealed in horror and the battle turned. The aroma of charred meat struck Derian. For a moment he imagined a fresh steak sizzling on the spit after a hard day's fighting. *Rare steak.* The smell was tantalising. As was the aroma of burning hair. Her screams were worse than before, and he enjoyed those most. He allowed himself a moment to savour them before leaping back into the fight. The human part of his mind feared the fire, yet he charged into the flames, regardless. A little burning was a small price to pay for enjoyment. She spun away, attempting to bat the fire from her hair and skin, but it was a futile task and Derian saw her falter.

"We might kill her, after all," Bereziel roared in unexpected triumph. Though weak and battered from a timeless battle, he appeared to grow stronger with every passing moment. Derian, on the other hand, weakened. Exhausted or not, he went after her with savage claws and found sudden, devastating success. Perhaps her belly was a weakness. Perhaps he'd just given into his more savage self a little more, because suddenly he broke through skin and muscle before finding an appealing gathering of bones deep within. He wasn't sure which cluster of bones he'd discovered, only that he gripped the largest tightly and pulled. Oh, he adored the ripping, the cracking, the squealing that followed.

"Yes, Derian, tear her apart," Bereziel howled, and Derian agreed it was a fine idea. Bereziel appeared beside her, sacrificing his magenta flame for a moment in the name of a little slicing and stabbing on his part. Derian had never been a fan of spiders. Not one little bit. It was the way they walked. Who needed that many legs? He'd have asked that of anybody who mocked him for his fears. Destroying this arachnid bitch was going some way to overcoming that terror.

He pulled another bone free and Fiore fell to her side as though broken in half. Her lower legs remained moving, clicking horribly in Derian's ears, and he savoured the near ending of the battle. Who knew he would be the first mercenary with a grand demon's pelt to his name? *Without scars, as well.*

Dying, she opened her mouth, and the sight of countless vicious incisors lining that vile cavern was a thing he would remember in dreams for years to come. He would also remember the pain they inflicted when she bit down onto his shoulder, drawing a flood of warm crimson; the pain was maddening as he fell to the ground, writhing in frustrated anguish.

I should not be felled as easily as this.

"Another takes our burgeoning strength."

"Seeva," she hissed weakly. She had no strength to deliver another strike, and Bereziel took advantage by driving his blade deep into her heart. Before she could pull it free, he fired a fresh volley of magenta fire upon her. At such a short distance, it should have scorched the life from her. Should have burned right through her ruined form and finished the fight. Instead, the flames dissipated away into darkness and Derian collapsed weakly. *Poisoned spider bite?* His body convulsed, and he felt a dark, invisible fist take hold. What was this? He gasped and felt a terrible darkness. The monster within him roared in anguish as it suffered the taking of strength tenfold.

"Seeva," Fiore whispered again. She was weak. So weak, and he had no strength to tear her throat out and be done with it. He tried to rise, but his body would not obey him. He did not belong in this realm; did not belong among such evils.

Bereziel howled in anger and cast more fire upon her. "What is this vileness?" he roared, sending a second and third volley back towards the demon—all for nothing as a blue glow formed around her. Blue and clear, and Bereziel held his blow. He looked around in fear.

"It cannot be," he cried.

Derian clamped a hand over his shoulder wound and felt his heart hammer from a thousand miles away. He was terrified and called for Bereziel's help and in the same breath for Bereziel to finish her.

"Save Seren," Derian gasped, but his voice became lost beneath Bereziel's growing panic.

"I concealed this. How can it be?" he cried, backing away from the broken grand demon. "No, no, not yet."

"What is happening?" Derian hissed as Bereziel stood over him. His hands glowed with the same blue shimmer as that which protected Fiore.

"Waken from this nightmare, Derian," Bereziel whispered. He spun around on nimble toes, looking into the darkness. Searching deeper. "You must wake or your soul will burn in this very breath," Bereziel whispered. "He has found us. He has found *her*."

There was silence.

And then there was a voice. It carried the sound of a dozen hissing Fiores. Trapped and enraged, furious and lamenting. When it spoke, no anger stirred in Derian, for who could carry anger when such terror had engulfed him?

"Old man," the voice said. "The Seven have waited an age for you."

"Anguis, the Dark One, has found us," Bereziel whispered, gripping his sword.

39

ANGUIS, THE DARK ONE

No matter one's station in life, there were rules to surviving the unforgiving Dellerin world. For the Crimson Hunters, it was no different. To start, to be any reputable group of any substance, you paid your dues to the Mercenary Guild, and you paid them before the collectors came calling. It wasn't debts the collectors bought. Apart from the obvious need to stay mostly within the blurred lines of the Guild's code, there was one rule that all members were charged with obeying. The Guild played no part in the treacherous game of politics, no matter how noble the man or woman might be. No matter the fortune offered. The Guild was an army in itself, spread out across all islands of Dellerin, and this was bad for business where uprisings were concerned. It hadn't always been like this, but as any politician would insist that "all constitutions were written to be amended." Not everyone agreed, but when a dictator of pure evil took to power, The Guild had little issue with writing themselves away from the inevitable headaches that entailed. If those in power and those with great power ever fell out, the world might never recover.

So, when Anguis, the Dark One, appeared before them, Derian had every right to be wary of doing or saying something to bring ruin upon his comrades. He'd never expected to see the famed overlord in the flesh, in the spirit… in the source. Yet here he stood before them. He thought about bowing, thought about introducing himself, but Bereziel's mutterings made him think better of it. Attacking a source demon was one thing; pissing off the demonic leader of the world was something else entirely.

"You should not be here, Anguished One," Bereziel snarled, and for a strange moment Derian felt like the sober comrade of a drunken lout facing down a massive bouncer who'd removed them from some exclusive establishment. *Sorry, friend. Don't listen to him. We'll be on our way.*

Bereziel's hands became a fire of blue as bright as dawn, and within a flash, a shimmering blue shield of energy formed around them both. Derian knew of these weavings. He's studied a little of them and knew not to touch them. Lorgan would have approved.

If truth be told, Derian had expected a giant of eight feet. He'd expected leathery, discoloured skin with horns and claws protruding from every orifice; he'd expected a vision of such impressive mightiness that all would cower beneath its disapproving glare. He'd expected the same fiend that stepped through fires, through darkness, and returned with Silencio at his beck and call; the legendary brute from Venistra who hunted down most of the grand demons of this realm and wrapped his will around them. Well, that's what the bards sang about, at least.

"You must flee," Bereziel whispered, and Derian heard the fear in his voice. Derian saw little threat. He should have known better. While Bereziel cowered, Derian gazed upon a normal, unimpressive man. His heavy, dark robes looked expensive. They were probably silk. Probably really comfortable, too. His perfectly ordinary clean-shaven face was a little pale; his body was built no more impressively than Derian's traditional, less monster-y form. His hair was cut tightly beneath the hood he wore. He did not march towards them like a demonic warmonger of history. Instead, he strolled as though he were out in a forest during harvest season.

Are we sure this is the dark weaver responsible for a hundred thousand deaths, the destruction of the monoliths, the breaker of worlds?

Only then did Derian notice the silence. The constant cacophony of the ever-present braying beasts had fallen silent, and a shiver ran up his spine. *The monsters of the night fear his presence, and I'm interested in the comfort of his clothing.* For a pulse, nothing happened, and Derian wondered if Bereziel had affected time as before.

Because I've no idea how time works here.

Casually, the Dark One waved his hand in the air, and a massive, deathly black fire formed up around them as though they'd stepped into a dome of nightmares. The shielding veneer of blue remained, but the fire was far more impressive.

Trapped within a haven.

He waved his hands again, and the black fire looped and rolled like a tempest at sea. With every breath it thickened, and anything Derian had seen beyond its borders disappeared to nothing, leaving them all alone, nice and cosy, in a spitting cage of death fire.

Anguis reached out and cautiously touched the shield between them. When he spoke again, the horrid tone was gone, replaced by a younger voice. *Human.* "You might have been wiser to shield your quarry before saving yourself, old man." He knelt down to the ruined arachnid demon and stroked her scorched skin. She groaned but kept her eyes upon Derian, staring with unrivalled hatred.

"She knows what lies within," the distant voice whispered in his mind as it crept further away to lick its wounds, and Derian felt his body in the real world settle as it slept. He wanted to wake, wanted to flee, wanted to enjoy normality. Oh, to be allowed a few hours with his book or with Lorgan at his side, happy to answer a thousand and one burning questions. He looked at the flames around them and thought his words badly chosen.

Bereziel held up both hands, and they glowed fiercely in reply. Around them, the shield hummed as he drew energy from his soul.

"You should not be here," hissed Bereziel again, and Anguis ignored him.

"Oh Fiore, I have searched many years for you," Anguis whispered as though tending to a lover. Maybe they were lovers. Maybe the Dark One was into crazy things. Anguis looked at Bereziel and grinned. "Longer than we've hunted you, Bereziel." He touched his chest and a glow from deep within him erupted beautifully for a moment.

At this, Bereziel whimpered. The shield flickered, but he recovered.

"You can sense her, can't you?"

Who?

"You vile bastard," Bereziel roared, and the fear, the sorrow, disappeared. The world seemed to shake, and Derian felt a wave of heat emanating off him. He stepped towards Anguis and the surrounding fires roared wildly.

Anguis laughed, and it was terrifying. No, it was worse than that. It was the sound of countless deep voices, the things of nightmares. They echoed around them, and Derian felt his beast recover ever so. He imagined a different cage. Imagined a four-legged beast pacing back and forth, seeking a weakness.

"Who is the man-beast? I sense something in him," Anguis hissed, peering through the shield. Below him, Fiore squealed in fury and Anguis appeared to find this very interesting.

"My name is Deri—"

"Whisht, idiot," Bereziel shouted, standing in front of Derian. A fair interruption. Maybe telling the Dark One his name wasn't the best idea.

"He's one of the little pawns you are gathering? I thought after Karkur you might choose a different path." His casualness was probably the most unsettling thing, Derian thought. That, and the demonic undertones in his accent. Anguis went deathly still before turning back to Bereziel. "Want to know what they have to say to you, Bereziel?"

Who?

"I want nothing from you, Anguis." The shield flickered again.

Anguis nodded his head as though conversing with someone else entirely. After a moment, he laughed. "She misses you."

"Now is not the moment, Anguis," Bereziel roared, and Anguis laughed again. A vile, cruel laugh like a demented murderer mocking their victim as they drowned in their grip.

"You still believe in the source, believe that events can be unchanged." His eyes grew colder now. "You think Silencio hasn't granted me the vision to see beyond this veil?"

"To the fires with you."

Anguis shook his head. "Tell me this, do you see victory? Do you see my head upon a block?"

"Do you see a life lived eternally?" Bereziel countered.

"Do you see no end to your reign? I might see horrors. But I see hope in something beyond you. Beyond us all. I see their release," he cried, and the world shook and Anguis looked around in mild amusement before nodding in approval.

"A reminder of your strength, I'll admit. We were not meant to meet in battle today. I was not meant to take Fiore, yet here we are. Something has changed, hasn't it? Something new to this world. What is it, old man? Come out from under your shield and tell me. Come play with me and we can settle this matter. Let us tear our paths from destiny's grasp together."

Like Seren?

"Do not tempt me, cur."

Anguis shrugged and stroked the grand demon's cheek a few more times before muttering a few words in a language Derian couldn't understand, yet in the same moment it felt natural to him. Around her, the blue veil glowed brighter now, and Fiore recovered from her wounds.

"Be ready," whispered Bereziel, and strangely, Derian could see he was older now. Greying in parts, with wrinkles deeper than before, as though time had slipped behind him and added three unforgiving decades in as many breaths.

"Will you answer to my will?" Anguis asked, and she finally looked from Derian to her healer. With an injured claw, she struck out at him. A fine strike that might have taken his head off, but a shadow from around him held her strike, and she shrieked in agony.

In terror.

"Oh, Fiore, my beauty, why fight us all?" he cooed, like a smooth charmer seducing a young virgin.

Fiore roared again, and around them a thousand monsters roared in unison. At this, Anguis recoiled, watching the dark as Bereziel had before. *What hides in the dark that even*

Anguis fears? A stir of hatred ignited in Derian, but he controlled it. The healing around the demon slowed and petered away to nothing, and Anguis gripped her by her throat, lifting her skyward as though she weighed nothing at all.

"You dare go against your own kin? Your lovers?" he roared, and his voice was truly terrifying. His countless tongues echoed like a choir in a Venistrian cathedral. Derian had never visited Venistra, believing that sound made little sense. What also made little sense was knowing that when the stones called and an incredible girl walked willingly into death, he would be there in Venistra. In a cathedral. That was an entirely different adventure to come, he knew.

Wait, what?

"Calm your mind, Derian," Bereziel whispered. "Don't stray from the now."

Fine advice.

"Be with your kind," Anguis howled, and the world shuddered, and suddenly Derian sensed them. The grand demons enslaved, charmed, adored, threatened. But more, he sensed something beyond them. The seven gods of the realm, still alive but broken. Torn, lost, entrapped.

He fell to his knees, not as a lowly mercenary but as their servant, and he saw a charge and it was beautiful. He howled like before; suddenly that shield looked like the easiest, most breakable barrier in the world.

"I deliver unto you a gift, Fiore," Anguis said, and his chest glowed and Derian hated him. Hated his sins, for they were unforgiveable. He sensed the madness, and his hands became claws, his voice a snarling roar of vengeance. "I give you freedom. Do you yield to me?" Around him, Derian saw the beasts that lived in his shadow, and they paled compared to the first gods, dead and lost. He tried to form words and met only primal cries in a language not spoken for ten thousand years.

Fiore howled her acquiescence, and within a breath she was released. A breath after that, she faded into nothing and Bereziel cried out in fury.

The effort caused Anguis to drop to a knee. He remained there for a moment before the shield of fire fell around them.

Distantly, Derian heard Bereziel command him to wake, but he remained. He felt the desire to climb from this darkness towards the world of the living, and somehow, he knew how to shun this urge.

"I cannot allow this beast to live."

Any other day, he might have cowered, but his inner, monstrous voice offered an interesting argument.

"Let me rip him apart as I did with Fiore."

Why not?

Such worries, like facing Lorgan with word of foolish, dooming actions, were lost as he charged forward through the barrier and shattered it as though it were a sheet of the thinnest glass.

"No!" roared Bereziel, and suddenly Anguis was on his feet, charging towards him. His demonic eyes were alive with furious triumph, his hands illuminated in terrible fire. "Not yet!"

Suddenly, the world shifted from darkness to brightest dawn, and Derian hit the wall of his shack and fell back onto his bedding.

40

GIRL ON FIRE

They fell upon Seren brutally, and she allowed them, for she had no choice. She was empty. A fragile vessel ready to crack and break and be gone forever. The vision of Bereziel still stung her mind, and she clung to him as the vision faded and left her cold and weak and scared. So very scared.

Scared.

A powerful word.

Just like love.

She loved Bereziel as much as he loved her. She saw the knowing sadness upon his face as they dragged her from the source. He knew the horror to come. *No, the horror that is happening.* The gift of sight faded with every breath that her mind returned to her, but she could still remember the horror to come.

Unless you come from the darkness and save me, idiot.

"Take her!" It was a cruel, feminine voice, and she knew who spoke, for though some moments seen could be tainted, even twisted, this moment had not transformed. She had seen

343

it before Derian had appeared and after, everything had gone
dark.

Because you die.

He cannot pull you from the torment.

"Stupid wench," a voice hissed in her ear.

Seren tried to open her eyes, but the daylight burned. She
was so very tired; so very ruined; so very human.

"Beware her fire," another voice cried. It was just as
frantic, just as zealous. She was alone among a dangerous
pack of animals, and she could not bite back at those few
who snapped. They dragged and pulled her roughly from
her bedding, dropping her painfully on the floor before
reaching for her again. Many hands, all eager and vile. She
hissed, but her voice failed her as much as her own
soul did.

All spent saving for things to come.

It was violence that drew her from her blindness. The first
few strikes took her courage and her breath. She recoiled as
they dove down upon her stomach. They tore at her dress, and
only the revolting shriek of Keralynn held their hands,
allowing her a mugging with a measure of dignity.

Another fist struck her belly, taking her wind, causing an
involuntary retch.

Scared.

She fought in their grasp and opened her eyes to her
assailants. They'd broken in through her door, gathered
around for entertainment. A few blocked the door. They all
appeared the same: their eyes excited, their raucous cries
growing in frenzy as they became drunk in their assault.

Thurken curs.

No delicate spoken word brought a respite from the fear.
Her shattered mind had not feared anything like this.

"Thurken, curs," she whispered. Those nearer were

warier, their actions both violent and controlled. She felt their single-mindedness, and they were assured of their actions.

Burn the witch from the source and feel just fine about it.

"Please, I mean you no harm," she gasped, and oh, words were as difficult as her grasp on imaginings. It was as difficult for her to speak, to imagine, as it was for them to see the dreadfulness of their own actions. Conviction was a thing of pride; however, conviction brought about more sins than anything else ever could. She wondered had Bereziel once taught her this lesson, or was it knowledge she'd lived long enough to learn? Already, what she'd gleaned from the source was fading, but it was no matter. When her weak human body recovered, she knew she would be fiercer than before. She only needed to survive the day. Afterwards, she would face things that could really fuken kill her.

But at least I'll have myself alone to count on. Mostly.

"You had your chance, demon."

She felt Fiore near now. Felt her own death even nearer. Felt her failures nearest of all. Her exertions upon the battlefield had taken their toll. Aye, she had drawn from the well of her soul and tapped a little more understanding, but there was only so much a frail body like hers could sustain when dealing with impossibly potent energies. Tending to Natteo had exhausted her reserves. She caught sight of her fingers as her killers wrenched her hands away from protecting her head. They were older now, like a barge captain's.

Can I un-age this ravaging?

Un-age?

Is that a word?

"We saved you," she screamed as hands pulled her to her feet. The forcefulness was the worst. They cursed her loudly, with the vilest gathering of words they could muster, but they meant little. She'd gladly take some wounding words over a fist. They called her a "smelly bitch," and struck her fiercely across the chin, knocking out a tooth, and caught her before she could fall to the floor and curl up in a ball.

She definitely preferred being called silly names.

"You came as saviours," Keralynn hissed, taking hold of her hair and standing over her. As she spoke, the rest of the crowd fell silent. Theirs was not to talk when their queen spoke, after all. "You came as an angel of the source, with miraculous promises of healing." Seren tried and failed to spit in her face. It appeared more as a wet gurgle than anything else. If she survived this, she would master the art of spitting in bitches' faces.

"I promised nothing," whispered Seren, and her voice was frail and humbled. Even supported by foreign hands, standing was nearly beyond her. Her knees gave in. Her head fell to the side. Her body gave up completely. Gripping her tightly, Keralynn pulled her from her keepers' hold as though she meant to display her to the remaining zealots waiting outside with torches. Despite herself, Seren screamed out as strands of hair were pulled free, and, without support, she fell once more. Her knees took most of the shock, and she fell back against the bed. She knew the act of crying and knew the advantage. Tears fell from her shaking body now, for she was not ready for any of this. She was still new to this world. She didn't want to leave it. She'd spent a lifetime within the source's hold, suffering helplessness like this. Tears were nice. She appreciated that lesson.

"That's it, little one," Keralynn hissed, and Seren heard the clink of chains. She knew this moment to come, knew the horror, and she dropped her head as they wrapped the chains around her. She'd seen many moments from different times. Moments where Natteo died and the next age burned.

Moments where Keralynn chose kindness over cruelty. The steps bringing her to this moment could not be changed. The paths she'd followed were of her own making. She could have taken no other. She only prayed to the lost gods that Derian would follow the same path.

That the Crimson Hunters would follow his afterwards.

She sought Derian's will and found him absent. Lost to the source. She willed him to hear her anguish. To understand how fuken late he was. She felt nothing. So, she tried to be brave. Tried to look into Keralynn's eyes and threaten her.

Keralynn knelt beside her. "Yes, cry it all away. Your sins are pure. Your soul, tainted. Whisper your evil aloud. Redeem yourself in our eyes." Releasing her grip, she stroked Seren's head gently.

"What would you have me do?" Seren whimpered. She had delayed the inevitable. Why? Because even heroes feared horror, tried to avoid unmentionable things a little longer. And who knew, perhaps those extra few moments might deliver godly power upon her.

You are so very late, Derian!

"You can avoid this fate. Return to us our dead," Keralynn whispered, and the crowd agreed now. They called out the names of those who'd fallen, and Seren shook her head.

"It is beyond my power, woman." *Is that the right term? Mostly.*

"You brought them back in front of our eyes the first night. You claimed the miracle was beyond your ability, yet many saw you breathe life into the little one." Her voice changed from smooth and suggestive to fervent and wild. "Time is precious, Seren of the Light. I will ask you once more."

Before Seren could answer, there was a commotion

outside. Her heart fluttered with excitement. And then she felt a crushing disappointment. There were excited shouts, triumphant laughter, victorious cheering, and she knew the fate of the Gold Haven army and the town to come. She'd seen this, in barely grasped moments.

Next come chains and fire.

Derian should have been here by now.

Seren cursed Keralynn as they tightened the chains. Weakly, she tried to fend them off but nothing happened. She willed her fire, but she was useless, weak-willed, a shadow. And he was fuken late. They bound her hands behind her back before pitching the chains around the support beam above her head and dropping them down the other side. With a sickening clatter, they began the terrible act of hoisting her up. Keralynn began threatening her as she rose into the air, but Seren heard nothing. The pain took her senses. The terror took her defiance. The chains jerked under her weight as they dragged her skyward, and she kicked out a few times half-heartedly. Her feet had only left the ground for a pulse before both her arms popped out of place, and her squealing filled the room. She fell silent only when a fierce crack across the cheek from the vindictive blonde stunned her.

"Return our dead to us," Keralynn cried, and this time Seren formed the right amount of spittle. It took flight and struck her tormentor's cheek. The bitch didn't flinch. She snarled and struck Seren one more time before retreating from the little shack with her mob behind her. Secured tightly, Seren remained held up, swinging a few inches from the ground, all the while howling at the pain. She heard the door close behind her and nodded in acceptance as she listened for the placing of tinder around the shack. Probably as shrewd a move as any, she supposed. Keep her contained within and control the furnace from outside.

Cook the little weaver witch.

She wept again for her failures. She tried to understand how else she might have stepped, and cursed Derian one more time. A spitting arrow had undone her. The flames were slow to ignite. She wondered why this was so. She thought on it as a distraction from the agony and realised the wood was likely damp. More smoke with dampness, too. Or else that was just with leaves.

It was something to ponder while waiting to die for the third time in as many days.

———

Late. Spitting late. Thurken late. Fuken late. There were enough debilitating feelings in the world; few were as panic-inducing as chronic lateness. At least for Derian. He understood the panic of being late better than most. Would his mother's terrible fate not have differed had he woken up at dawn? If he had accompanied her as he'd pledged he would?

Maybe her path was always to get trampled.

He believed these wonderful, helpful thoughts while suffering another bout of lateness. Struggling from the grip of his sweat-covered bedclothes, he sought coherence. He knew Seren was in peril. Knew it as though she'd whispered it in his mind. His mind still spun with visions of the darkened world. His understanding of time and moments was as skewed as a rodenerack. Something about a spider lady, a dark hooded brute, and Bereziel watching on. Thinking on these matters hurt his mind as though his thoughts attempted to conceal the nightmares they'd experienced. Bereziel had suggested the source was too potent for the human mind to accept; he was probably right. As Derian's memories flickered away, he welcomed ignorance. Unexplained things? It was the spitting source.

Fine thoughts to have while she burns.

"Or else it was just a dream," he told himself, donning his pants and his boots after that. *Just a dream, but real fuken late.* His heart hammered. It had hammered since he'd wakened. Since before. Distantly, he heard the chanting, and he quickened himself. The sound had been a constant these past few days, but there was a different clamour to it now. He tried to calm himself but only felt worse. How did he know what demented chanting sounded like?

Suddenly he froze mid-knot. His fingers quaked as though taken by another entity.

"Are you there, monster?" he asked the empty room.

Are you there, monster?

He received nothing but silence in reply. Not even a festering, hissed reply claiming to be a deity from before the age of humankind.

An insane dream brought about by dark deeds.

Buttoning his shirt, he opened the doorway and stepped out into the fresh morning air, and immediately began coughing from the heavy smoke drifting on the breeze. Further down the path he saw the gathered crowd, clustered and agitated. Chanting her name, though more in fear and revulsion now than in devotion and respect. Also, they had placed great stacks of burnable things in a great, deep circle around her shack. The smarter manoeuvre would have been just to fill the shack with wood and run away, but if nothing else, the zealous peasants demanded a protracted sacrificing. As he watched, they cast planks of timber upon the blaze and rolled empty barrels into the blazing furnace, and it was an impressive, burgeoning inferno.

Seren.

"We could have used that for the defences," he muttered in dismay.

Fear dragged at his every step, and there was no monster to push him. What dreadfulness would they inflict upon him, he wondered? He remembered his wildness upon the battlefield. They would too. Still, he went towards them, hoping courage would catch up. It didn't. He looked through them; he looked around them, searching for his comrades, and he felt terribly alone.

They moved like a herd of livestock, and they were just as mindless. His fists tightened, but there were too many to strike. He dropped to his knees and looked to the flames growing above their heads. She'd told him of the fires, told him he'd had a hand in saving her, but he was a coward without a plan. Once more he called upon his monster, hoping it was no dream. Nothing happened. No monstrous form took over. No heroism gathered his limbs and commanded greatness. He wandered forward, knowing that at any moment they'd turn on him, shackle him. Pitch him into the fire beyond. Maybe he'd make it through one of the unbroken windows and survive a little longer within. Maybe he'd save her from the flames. More likely, she'd save him.

Help me, monster.

"Help me," he begged his mind, and craved the adrenalin of the hunt, the strength to tear through that fire and pull her free. If she lived.

Or else it might rain?

Something sparked a little inside. It took his fear and his rationality. Truthfully, he was just as scared, but through the shrieking, the bodies, the smoke, and the horror, he sensed Seren alive within, and it was enough to drive him forward.

Whoa, there.

He peered at the fire with a colder mind than before. Saw

the fury in the growing flames and found a godly scheme, worthy of winning the day. They had made a perfect, unforgiving circle of fire, unconquerable by one so insignificant. To race into the thick blaze would be death. Even for one as un-killable as he. So he looked to the heavens.

"I'm coming," he hissed. His muscles screamed as he hoisted himself up to the unsteady roof above. It shuddered under his weight, and he was certain his usual luck would follow him. "I can't make that jump," he argued, and nothing replied, so he threw caution to the winds and leapt for the next roof and, miraculously enough, as though gifted by unnatural ability, made the distance with a foot to spare.

"I am a godly thing," he whispered, because godly as he was, he feared the acolytes would discover his plan. *I am a sneaky, godly thing.* Leaping to the next roof and the one after that, he believed in himself. The roof after that had an enormous wall of burning amber in front of it, but he never stopped. Spurred on by the sudden outcry of the zealots catching sight of him, he leapt one last time. He shouldn't have looked at the crowd as he jumped. He might have landed properly.

———

They came at Lorgan and Mowg recklessly. They carried no blades, so neither mercenary drew theirs. And why would they? A massacre in the town square would not help their cause when the Guild came calling. After the disaster of these contracts, the Guild would most certainly be investigating.

The gang of zealots came with fists and fury and the worst of intentions. They were a couple of dozen, and it was a mugging worse than what Lorgan usually walked into.

Mowg, the younger of the two and relying on aggression to break through the crowd, leapt at them first. He met the first cur's strike and countered with a swift kick between the legs, taking the man from the fight. Three more came after, and Mowg offered what resistance he could, swinging indiscriminately for an impressive few manoeuvres. Were the rest of his team at his side, they would have waded through the assailants. As it was, he was knocked to the ground with a busted nose, leaving Lorgan to fight them off alone.

Lorgan had learned the art of prolonging a bout of fists for the benefit of an audience. A handy skill to learn in the golden streets of Castra, where pleasurable companionship was worth a few bruises. He'd mastered the art without too many shots to the face. Bobbing, weaving, swatting away strike after strike until the crowd began to enjoy the spectacle and the opponent winded himself was the most natural thing in the world to him. That's where a champion earned titles and enjoyed exotic exile a little while longer. *A few years.* He didn't miss the fights. *Not really.* Didn't miss the art, either. *Not really, either.* He liked to think it had been a means to an end. A distraction from his chosen life as a wretched drunkard. *The Fist.* They'd called him a master of the ring. Whispered amongst themselves that he danced as gracefully as a royal Luistrian player with the stinging snap of a punishing Venistrian cantus. They also said that, when meeting a better fighter, he was truly brutal. When he was in command of all his strength, all his menace, all his spitting regret, he was devastating.

The zealots met this beast. He offered no grace or entertainment. He offered only violence, and, for a sweeping moment, it was glorious. He charged into them, throwing devastating blows at all who moved with hands untouched by the ravages of the march and a thousand bouts. Men, women

—all took his strikes and were lesser for it. They charged, screaming and mocking, all of them unproven in violence like he was, and all of them fell. He moved like a Seeva beast caged within devastating armour as a pack of demons snapped at his heels. Their numbers fell to his ire.

"Where is Seren?" he roared as he met a young farmer's fist with his own fist. He heard a crack and fell away from the young lad with stinging fingers and nothing more. The farmer fell to his knees, his fingers splayed at an unusual angle. The crowd edged away from him in terror as he single-handedly brought the fight to them. They'd likely never seen a man as broken as he was come alive and fight in this way.

For a moment he believed he might win this day out, until a devastating strike took him from the fight. It came from behind. His body still swung for a few breaths, even as he stumbled, and then a second blow brought him to his knees and defeat. For him, for her, for the entire town as well. His vision blurred, his senses jangled, and the golden glove of Dorn wrapped itself around his neck.

"What did you do to my wife?" Dorn hissed, holding him so tightly that Lorgan couldn't breathe. Dorn was no peasant. His arms were thick with hardened muscle; he had a fighter's build, bulwarked by strength from a sturdy frame.

Of the deaths I've endured, this will be the least impressive.

He stopped struggling, saving the last of his breath to answer the man.

What did I do to her?

"Everything," he replied, and forced out a snigger as though recalling one particular memory out of everything imaginable. A crude and dishonourable thing, admittedly, but the man was married to her; he was aware of the sordid things Lorgan hinted at. The ruse worked, and Dorn released him to strike him more intimately. This Lorgan took. It was only fair. After a few blows, the zealots gathered around him and finally the champion of Castra was defeated. He expected bindings, and he was not surprised. They wrapped a thick, leathery cord around his hands before leading them both down towards Seren's shack.

Lorgan's throat was raw by the time the fires were lit. He screamed out for Seren, but his voice was lost to the demented chanting of the zealots and he hated them. Oh, he hated them so very much. They relinquished their hold upon him as the flames overcame the outer walls of the shack in a terrible, crackling wave. He begged for her release, knowing the impossibility. He screamed for her to weave some miracle and tear herself from this terrible end, but she hung lifelessly from the chains and he cursed himself for not seeing to her sooner. He knew the ravages of weaving. But he was old and careless. Neither affliction absolved him.

The heat stung his eyes, but he wouldn't look away. She'd never know he was with her at the end, but it was all he could do. He'd lived a wretched existence; this was no fitting way to step into the dark but he was lost. Oh, to conjure one fine, godly, plan to pull them all from the fire, so to speak. All he received was a gentle breeze, which helped the flames catch quicker.

The air thickened with hot ash and dancing sparks, and hope left him. Beside him, Mowg appeared. His hands were unbound. "Let us slip away before they seek a second… sacrifice," he whispered, slipping a tiny blade between Lorgan's bonds and cutting them with a flick of the wrist. Lorgan made no move to flee. "Come on, old man. Gather the rest of your clan and leave this spitting ruin of a town."

Around them the zealots, drunk on death, howled and revelled and ignored both mercenaries as though under an enchantment. Still, Lorgan would not sneak away like a noble coward. He knew he was giving his life up for no reason, yet still his feet would not move. Through the deathly black plumes, the flames attacked the walls of the shack, and the fire took on a deathly life of its own. Looking past the zealous fools, he peered through the glass and saw her choke and thought it a finer fate than burning like a beast upon a spit.

"Please, do not do this, you monsters," he cried out, and met nothing but excited cries of sacrifice. Oh, how swiftly the zealous had turned on their godly protector. He spun to scream at the Gold Haven army, still stationed down near the front gates. A dozen had entered, but none had dared get involved with this disgraceful act. Were they unaware the Guild would hold them responsible? Were they that assured of their captain's approval of such an event?

"Are you mad, Lorgan?" Mowg cried, shoving him fiercely before slipping away from the lunatics. Within a breath he was gone, and Lorgan offered no condemnation of the younger man. His responsibilities were to his comrades. Were it one of Mowg's mercenaries, Lorgan would flee this place just as swiftly.

Liar.

"I will stay with you until you fall, little one," Lorgan whispered, knowing her fate was sealed. The fire overtook the outer wall now, and they cheered at this. A loud roar of screeching metal filled the air and suddenly, Derian appeared above Lorgan's head, leaping from shack to shack as though skipping over rocks in a calm brook. "Do it!" Lorgan roared, filled with a surge of unlikely hope as Derian cleared the last roof before her shack. "Do it, you thurken cur!" It wasn't much of a plan, but it was an act of wonderful lunacy and

Lorgan approved, until his young apprentice landed awkwardly and crashed right through the roof. It was a spectacular Derian-flavoured event, yet Lorgan barely noticed because the great warehouse in the centre of the town exploded with a sound like a thousand stars collapsing and the world went to hell.

————

"It should have held," Derian squealed as he fell through the roof and kept going. From smoky daylight to horrific burning darkness, he crashed through layers of wood, breaking every bone in his body as he did. Well, it felt as much; he was no healer. He understood pain, and he was in dreadful pain. The landing was worst. He didn't know what he hit first, but he knew he broke through and took it with him. As he landed in a ruined mush, half a support beam fell on top of him, crushing his knee agonizingly.

"Help me," he cried, forgetting in that moment that he was supposed to be the saviour. It was this sobering thought that shook away his bleariness and, with a groan, he rolled from beneath his burden with more strength than he realised.

Where is the pain?

Incredibly, his body healed as though infused with a miracle tonic. His knee hurt less than it had, and his torn and broken body was knitted as though reborn in a birth boom, as Seren had called it. The only problem was the lack of air to breathe.

And any spitting way out of the furnace?

He had that terrible late feeling again, and he fought his panic. "Seren, wake up," he roared, taking hold of her. She swung lifelessly at his attempts. Behind him, out in the streets, where the bastard zealots prayed in fire and honoured in murder, he heard fresh screams as they separated from the mob they'd been. "Open those pretty eyes," he demanded, but her pale, bleeding face remained locked in a sleeping grimace.

Tugging at her chains, he began easing them to the far end of the broken section where an idiot had fallen through. Somehow freeing her from the beam was the only plan he had. It seemed better that she be in his arms, in the middle of a pyre, than hanging like meat on a spit. He looked to the broken beam she hung from and the daylight above, and the obvious solution struck him. *Escape.*

"Sorry, my... friend," he whispered, leaping up to grab onto her holding chains before climbing up towards salvation. Even with smoke taking his vision and most of his breath, and the fire's searing heat scorching his skin, he carefully avoided touching most of her more delicate parts as he left her behind. Despite the awfulness, it was mostly a painful and uneventful climb. (Apart from when the beam shifted under their weight, and their bodies swung wildly and she inadvertently head-butted his groin, making him squeal in a higher pitch than normal.) If asked about it later, he might have mentioned that he'd meant to go through the roof, and that breaking the beam on the way down had been a shrewd calculation on his part.

Eventually he reached the top of the beam and climbed back out through the hole he had cleverly created. It wasn't the most heroic escape, but it was one that best suited his makeup.

Allowing himself a few breaths and a moment to gaze in puzzlement at the crowd running away from what looked like an attack from some flying death spheres, he wrapped the chains around his arms and began pulling her free of the support beam.

"Help me," he roared, attempting and failing to summon his inner demon monster thing to share the burden. Wedging his feet against the edge of the hole, he shunted and pulled until the chain slid free. Her body swung, almost taking him with her, and he cried out again for his demon to wake, for her to wake up and weave them all to safety, or for Lorgan to come save him, or for something else to come save them all.

And then something else did, from above.

And by the time he'd pulled her free, he'd discovered what it was.

41

GTA TREYSTONE

Natteo hated waking up to the sounds of shouting. Especially while naked and nestled up in silken sheets. He hated that he was no stranger to waking up in this exact way, too. Stretching out, he dared a yawn and set about ignoring the commotion for as long as he could. Hiding beneath the blankets, he could still hear it, though. *Is there anything worse?* It came from somewhere out in the hallway. Better that than in his room. Had he the energy to rouse himself, he might have. There was panic in the shouting. That too was a familiar memory. He ignored the commotion and felt grand about it.

"Shush," he called out weakly, manoeuvring himself across the lavish double bed into a better position; somewhere in the middle, there were plenty of pillows and warmth for all. Why was it when duty called that bedding offered its most alluring embrace? he wondered happily. It didn't matter what drama occurred: an army waited by the gates; the town was safe; the Crimson were polished. He was taking the day for himself; he'd earned it.

"Nat, get up, you lazy bitch," Boab hissed from somewhere beyond the warmth of his silken sheets. *Spit on this.*

"Um… no," Natteo countered wittily.

"We must go… my…." Boab searched for words and found nothing. Natteo smiled from his cover. Easier saying emotional things in the dead of night.

"Come back to bed." Finally, he looked up from his sheets and grinned. Shouting could come and go. They had locked the door, and neither wanted to leave this lavish bed chamber. He just needed to put his foot down, was all.

"Fine mercenary you are. I'll see to the commotion. Stay there all you want. Do you want to give me your breakfast order now? Or when I return?" Boab mocked as he dressed swiftly. Had Natteo had the drive or the energy to enjoy the spectacle he would have; but he was as spent and useless as his docile manhood after the long night. It *had* been a long night. It wasn't every day (though it felt as much) that he died and then was drawn back from the clutches of death by a weaver girl. *Again.* It also wasn't every night, when the dizziness of the resurrection had dissipated away, that he lay nestled in the arms of his lover, who wept at what he'd seen.

I've seen worse, my dear.

He knew he'd died. Knew he'd ventured into the night. He also knew he'd sensed something truly terrible lay in that darkness beyond. Something older than the mountains, with power that could split the world apart. He'd whispered this to Boab as they both sobbed, and his lover had smiled and called him an idiot. It had been the perfect response.

"You'll make breakfast too? I'd like eggs. Do you have eggs?"

"This is why my outfit are the top of the rung and your

group languish in wretchedness. You are an idiot, Natteo. Get up, get dressed, and get out of here."

Outside, there was the clatter of footsteps running down the hallway and as alertness reared its unwanted head, he felt the itch of apprehension. Still, though, he tried to ignore that perpetual mercenary feeling that everything was about to take a nasty turn; to remember this moment for however long he could. Who knew when he'd feel as sated and satisfied with his choices in life as he did this fine breakfast-less morning?

"If you loved me, you'd come back to bed and sleep a while longer."

"Then you have your answer, Hunter," Boab countered with a wry grin, and grudgingly, Natteo climbed from the warmth and stretched wide on the carpet, scrunching his toes as he did. He loved a good stretch. Especially when naked. He always looked his best, stretching out with no shame. And he had no shame. Shame was for people like Derian, too unsure of their own footsteps and too certain of their own embarrassments. "Own them," he'd happily tell his best friend when his face turned red over a humorous matter, and Derian would invariably do the opposite.

"What is happening?" Boab cried, opening the door to the sound of raised voices. One of them was familiar.

Natteo leapt up, pushed through after Boab and caught the vision of Kesta emerging from another room opposite. She was as bare as he. She, however, had had the decency to at least drape some silk sheets over her shame.

Wait a moment.

Why is Kesta emerging from that bedroom without clothes?

He laughed hysterically. And why wouldn't he? To discover the reserved Kesta in a state of undress was fantastic, but to discover her emerging from the salacious chamber of a rival mercenary was truly wonderful. So, unsure of what else to do, he laughed like a demented idiot. Up and down the narrow corridor, the rest of the Army of the Dead emerged from their chambers and the galley beyond, already clad in armour, already prepared for war. They'd heard the shouting and prepared for the worst. As they hurried down the corridor, they buckled their straps and checked their weapons almost languidly, conversing in low, relaxed tones as though a call to arms was just another task in their day. And perhaps it was—gathering as one, going to war, their voices light and easy and drenched in a camaraderie Natteo had rarely enjoyed in his own pitiful outfit.

"She said Mowg's getting a right mugging," said one.

"Ah, not again?" another replied.

"Who was supposed to have his back?"

"Lorgan was with him. The peasants are up to their peasantly shit."

"Just like in Focquer?"

"Ugh—that was a nightmare."

"No weapons. Just fists."

"Keeping it nice and clean?"

"And legal too. Last thing we need is the Guild's questioning."

"What about my daggers?"

"No daggers for you, Clover."

"But they're really small."

"That's what Kesta thought too."

Laughter.

"Gather up. Usual crowd control."

"Just once, I want to go to one of these backwater towns and get paid my due."

"A mercenary's life…"

"Is a charmed life."

"Is a charmed life."

"Is a charmed life… Hey, who took my shield?"

"Probably the naked Crimson boy."

More laughter.

So many mercenaries all scrunched together, falling in love, shouting at each other, suffering the hangover after a battle's revelries. There was a dreamlike sense to the moment. Probably because of Natteo's laughter. *Fuk them if they can't take a joke.*

"Put your manhood away, you idiot," Kesta hissed, wrapping the sheets around her, and he started sniggering again. Then he thought about the loud moans he'd heard through the walls and he slapped his thigh loudly, chortling as though possessed by an ancient relative from even more ancient times. This earned him a few disapproving glares from the mercenaries squeezing past.

"What is happening? Where's Lorgan? Who is foolish enough to mug Mowg?" she demanded as the one named Clover slipped out of the doorway in his polished armour. His underclothes beneath looked hastily buttoned. A good mercenary equipped the armour correctly, though. Everyone knew that. Especially Natteo.

"The peasants have started some trouble," the Assassin of Death shouted from the hatchway beyond. Boab had told Natteo the brute's name was actually Brin. According to Boab, only a brave fool would call him by his given name. "With Mowg and Lorgan, and the girl too," he added, and leapt from the hatch to the bottom of the ladder.

Kesta was already back in her room, donning her clothes, and Natteo's manic laughter finally died away to a few deep breaths. The realisation of threat finally sank in. He was a terrible mercenary, he'd be the first to admit it, but he'd do anything for his comrades.

Even Seren.

He'd been in no mood to face his comrades after dying, though, and had convinced himself easily enough that he'd earned a few hours' reprieve. Learning of their spectacular successes in the field had eased any guilt he'd had about not standing watch with them, but guilt never disappeared, he knew. It only slept in, and usually roused itself to the sound of shouting voices. Just once, he'd love the shouting voices to be good times. His mood swung like a pendulum.

Grabbing his clothes, lacing his boots, buttoning his buttonables, he heard the last Army of the Dead mercenary drop from the flying fortress and he felt terribly late. "Go on without me, Beo. I'll catch up," he called to the waiting Boab. With both groups of mercenaries united, they could stop any mugging. Forced reassurances offered little comfort, though. His hands shook, and he felt the darkness from his death stir.

I died, and something drew itself to me.

"We can go together, Nat," Boab countered. Natteo loved being called Nat. He'd never been called Nat by anyone before.

"Whisht with that. Nothing has changed since last night, Beo. Nothing at all," he said, knowing Boab liked being called Beo. Neither was the cleverest term of endearment, but it was a good start. He pressed his lips to his lover's hand. It was six months to the day since they'd met during the Feast of Wrath in the Guild's stronghold. In the basement to be more precise. They'd met only a few times since that night, but every meeting was more wonderful than the last. Not just the pleasure, although that was divine, but also the words shared, the emotions gifted, the happiness earned. They'd even survived their third argument. Not to mention the poisoning incident, a case of robbery, some disastrous heroism, and a little death between them. Who knew how

strong a couple they could become? Natteo was even ready
to reveal to his comrades his current attachment. He had
dearly wanted Derian to know of his endeavours, but
somehow, he struggled to open up to his friend in these
matters. Natteo had never believed in love and happiness. He
believed only in unfaithfulness and inevitability. Still,
though, what was the soul, if not something that could heal
itself?

"As you wish," Boab muttered, strapping on his sword,
despite the warning, before charging out through the door.
The shouting continued in the little hallway as Natteo
continued to dress. Only when he loaded his wristbows did he
feel in any way polished. Donning his cloak, he stepped out
into the hallway and into the calming grip of Kesta. He eyed
her and then looked down at her hand on his shoulder. She,
too, was dressed in her finest; her eyes were alive with
excitement. It was a good look to her. What had Clover done
to her?

"Delay, little one," she hissed. At the hatch stood her
conqueror. He looked as tired as Natteo felt. Always the sign
of a memorable night.

Clover was listening to a youthful voice below and Natteo
recognised it. Swiping and spinning away from Kesta's grip,
he walked down towards the waiting Clover and gazed below
to the shaking figure of Eveklyn. At her side rested a massive
battle axe. Upon her chest hung an ill-fitting breast plate. A
perfect attempt at a child's vision of battle preparedness.

"What happened? I wish to hear for myself," Kesta said,
appearing beside the two men. Natteo couldn't help but
notice the affection she had for Clover, even in such a
perilous moment. She ran her fingers down his uncovered
arm as the child, in a frantic, breathless voice, related the
story for a second time, emphasising the important parts.

"Massive army at the gates in control! Lorgan and Mowg fighting! Pretty Seren tied in chains in shack! Lots of fire!"

Her tale was quick and concise, despite her panic, and Natteo admired her for this. She'd seen horrors, had taken on responsibility, and now attempted to undo an evil her neighbours were attempting with strangers who did nothing more than treat her with a modicum of respect. As she spoke, Natteo fought the urge to leap down and follow his comrades.

Surely, it is madness for Kesta to delay.

He suddenly regretted laughing happily while the rest prepared to save their comrades. He tried to push past Clover, but Kesta held him again. He stared at her coldly, but her eyes were upon the diminutive figure below.

"Little one," she called, and Eveklyn snapped to attention. "Send away any children wandering around this building." Eveklyn nodded but appeared thoroughly confused. "When we retreat with our comrades, this area will become a precarious place to be. Go now."

At hearing a direct order from a mercenary, Eveklyn took to the task. "Very well," she squeaked, and Kesta turned to her bed mate.

"We need everyone if we are going to save them," she said, and Clover nodded in agreement. "Is everyone off ship? Is there anyone else we can call upon to assist our numbers?"

Clover shrugged, raising his hands. "We're the last to disembark."

Without warning, Kesta shoved Clover out the door. He cursed loudly as he dropped awkwardly to the floor below. Natteo turned to follow him, but Kesta pulled him back from the doorway.

As though the world had suddenly slowed to a crawl, Kesta moved silkily. Slamming the outer hatch shut, she twisted the key before kicking the lock violently. What followed was the delicate clink of half a snapped key falling uselessly to the carpet below, and Natteo stood watching in bewilderment. A moment after that, Clover climbed up the ladder to the outer porthole and began shouting every curse he could think of. There were quite an impressive few. Natteo had been called most of them at least twice in his life. He offered a confused wave as the lock spun and failed to open.

Kesta kissed her two fingers, placed them to her heart and spun away from her lover as he roared, threatened, and pleaded for entry. "We only have moments to take advantage," Kesta said in an eerily calm voice. Whatever they needed to do sounded in no way advantageous. Still though, as she glided away from the vitriol, he couldn't help but follow her.

"What are we doing?"

"Taking advantage of a spitting awful turn of events."

It seemed like a fine answer, full of dreadfully violent repercussions, but he'd cast his lot in with her. "What of Lorgan, and Seren? What about Derian?" His stomach sank as he thought of how shitty everything had become since he'd gotten out of bed. He passed the doorway and considered slipping in and climbing back under the covers to hide. Instead, he followed her up a ladder to where two pilot seats and a gathering of confusing-looking mechanisms were tucked up beneath the cover of a dome of thick glass. He had more questions. "I am a skilled thinker," he lied, "but I've never flown on an airbarge... well, not technically... My point is, Kesta, I can't fly this and I sincerely doubt you can either... You aren't listening. Why aren't you listening? Why are you strapping into that chair?"

"Shut up, Natteo."

"What are you doing with that lever?"

"..."

"What is that thing there with the button?"

"…"

"Why is it clicking?"

"…"

"What's that humming?"

"Shut the fuk up, Natteo, and strap yourself in."

42

INSANITY

"Have you lost your mind?" Natteo cried. It was one more question. It was rhetorical too, so he imagined Kesta wouldn't have an issue. Since the world had turned on its head, all Natteo could do was talk. "They'll kill us for this. You know that, right?" Talk, and ask loads of questions.

"Of course I do!" Kesta snapped, pulling a thick metal lever all the way down with a grunt. On either side of the airbarge, the massive cylindrical propellers screeched loudly as the chains keeping them upward were released and they began dropping slowly. Natteo eyed them for a moment like a fat man might view a tantalising little tunnel where they stored the honey cakes. It would be a tight squeeze getting this ship out of the warehouse—and that was an optimistic view. A practical person might have said the propellers simply wouldn't fit.

Natteo *was* that person. "The propellers won't fit, Kesta. They won't fit at all."

She whisht him, instead focussing on the countless other dials and knobs and levers and buttons littering the front of the cockpit. Her hands moved in a blur, dancing from one instrument to the next. She relaxed back in her seat, humming under her breath. Truthfully, this humming worried him as much as her attempted thievery.

Dying has taken her mind, and I'm along for the ride.

"A small matter," she countered. Her face scrunched up for a moment as though the realisation of their imminent demise had struck her. He expected a pause, a moment of clarity and a panicked outburst. But no. "When we take off, can you hop out and fix the mirror? I'm not as tall as Clover." She tapped the glass and indicated the long mirror attached on the other side, giving a view of the beast's rear. Behind them, he could see Clover climbing slowly up towards the pilot's hatch. Things were about to get interesting. "Come on, you bitch," Kesta hissed, dragging the lever up and back down fiercely. The dropping propellers whirred to life and Natteo's seat vibrated.

This is happening.

He took hold of her hands and held them fast. "Kesta, we have to save Lorgan. We have to stop this shit."

She stopped, shrugged, and sighed. "I am taking advantage of the situation. Lorgan will get out of whatever he's gotten himself into. It is Lorgan, after all." It was a fine point.

"So, what are we doing with their airbarge?"

She stared at him with burning, excited eyes. "This is my airbarge now." Releasing herself from his grip, she giggled. He missed the humming. She pulled the lever one last time, and the four elevated propellers dropped smoothly into position. The walls of the warehouse might have disagreed with that assertion; the propeller blades tore through the thin sheets of metal with a piercing screech, and Kesta grimaced. "Time to go," she muttered, peering out through the daylight created by the heavy rotors. He couldn't see the blades now.

All that remained was a thin haze from their spinning and the feeling of heavy vibration coursing through his body like some vile anti-elixir.

"Ah, there we go," she exclaimed, taking hold of two controls. The airbarge danced in answer, giving a violent shudder over the sound of screeching metal. She began humming again. Natteo was terrified. He'd been here before. At the mercy of a lunatic. Last time, it had been a predictable brute with a heavy pocket of coins and salacious tastes, followed by the appearance of a savage dagger. This time, it was the closest thing he had to a mother, shattering her sanity and dragging him towards imminent death.

Lorgan won't save you this time, either.

"I've made a huge mistake," he cried, and she reached out and took his shoulder.

"There, there, little one. We have a home now. Let's go save some people, start some shit, and escape this ungrateful town." He didn't hate her words.

With one more shudder, the *Fighting Mongoose* rose a few feet and Natteo caught sight of Clover's hand flailing out over the balcony as he reached the summit. Kesta spotted it too. She moved her hands rapidly, and the airbarge answered her demands. It veered violently back and forth, and Clover's hand closed on empty air.

"Bye, beautiful," Kesta muttered, watching him crash against the far wall. She held her breath, and the *Mongoose* hovered over him, all the while ripping shards of warehouse metal with its deadly blades. He stirred and climbed to his feet, and Kesta exhaled. "Ah, brilliant. He's not dead. I like him." She suddenly looked at Natteo. "I look forward to hearing about your boy, as well. Don't think your little Natteo dance threw me off the scent."

While Derian believed in the source as reason for

strangeness and incredible tales, Natteo believed in inevitability. Unlikely events were an inevitability. It kept him on his toes. Kept him ready. This, this right fuken here, was just another unlikely inevitability in his life, because, since he'd picked up a nasty habit of dying, the world had spun on its head. Why bother questioning the small matter of stealing an airbarge? It was inevitable.

Kesta was in her element, which was a pleasant thing. Since the day they'd met, he'd feared waking up to the tragic discovery that Kesta had had enough. Insanity was a good look to her.

She looked skyward, and the airbarge followed suit. It lifted higher, and the metal walls on either side tore like paper as the propellers spun. "Don't fret, Natteo." She pointed out at the shards of metal whirling in the air as they lifted. "This beauty is Castra made. Much better than the shit these peasants believed would keep monsters out." She certainly knew her metals, Natteo thought. With a last groan, the warehouse shuddered and collapsed around them. The airbarge juddered under its efforts, but continued rising. She held the controls, easing them as though becoming acquainted with an old dance partner, and for a moment her certainty reassured him. Not much, but enough to keep his bladder full. She leaned forward in her seat and began looking left and right. "No one left below." She looked back at Natteo, grinning again. As she did, the *Mongoose* shot upwards at a terrifying speed. The deafening roar of screeching devastation took all his senses. It sounded like death, and Natteo screamed. They broke through to daylight, only for the starboard side rotors to snag on some debris from the collapsing warehouse.

"Shit."

"What happened?"

"Whisht."

The *Fighting Mongoose* reared sideways like an ocean barge dashed by a squall in a storm, and Natteo caught the bile that reached his mouth and swallowed in panic as the building crumbled around them.

Fuk, fuk, fuk.

"Meant that," she muttered, pulling on the controls as the airbarge teetered close to turning right over. As all manner of loose objects—a pair of pilot's gloves, a few silver coins, a wonderfully-crafted pocket knife, and an empty glass jar of some uneaten delicacies—took flight and clattered against the side glass, now below him, he suspected she had not meant that manoeuvre at all. He lifted off his seat as the airbarge clunked heavily. The sound of tearing metal pierced his ears again and somewhere below he heard the roaring of engines, like a thousand beasts of the night, as Kesta forced them upwards.

"No problem, at all," she added. This too was a lie. He knew this because the propellers shuddered and slowed. And then they fell back down.

"To the fires with this," he screamed, as gravity sucked them from the brightness of blue to the darkness of death waiting below.

"Be polished," she hissed, and flicked two switches, pulled another lever, pumped a pedal below the controls a few times, and suddenly the beast levelled. "I should have adjusted the mirror," she muttered, and the airbarge froze in mid-air before shooting back up through the hole in the roof.

Natteo gripped his belt straps as death came for him… again. However, within a few breaths, he realised just how skilled she was at flying. She pulled at the controls and the ship answered her every demand. He watched the propellers twist and move in near silence, and marvelled at how easily the *Mongoose* glided through the air now.

Below, the town of Treystone was alight. To be more exact, one part of the town was alight, and it had quite the audience. He could see the congregating crowds and the result of their vile actions. He growled under his breath and cursed the peasants for what they were. At the gates, some soldiers in golden uniforms stood staring skyward, their mouths open, watching the airbarge rise. Perhaps, just like they had refused to intervene in a barbaric burning of innocent mercenaries, they were also unwilling to attend to the matter of an airbarge breaking apart the biggest building in the town. Then again, this was Crimson Hunter business; who knew what they'd decide to do? And how much it would fuk everything up?

"It's time to save our clan," Kesta hissed, bringing them back around. Natteo knew they looked rather impressive to the fiends below.

"Yes!" he cried in excitement. Seeing the smoke billowing out from the flames was stirring the fight in him. "What shall I do?"

"Go out, fix the mirror, and—I don't know. Save whoever needs saving," Kesta said. Natteo shook his head.

"I'm not stepping out there. Not a fuken chance."

She released the controls and grabbed Natteo fiercely. He shrieked in reply. A fine reply. He expected the ship to plummet, but it remained upright, stable, unmoving. He didn't understand flight at all. "Get your rear out on the deck and get ready to help," Kesta growled, "or I'll fling you over the side."

"No, you won't, and there's nothing else you can say or do that'll make me walk out there."

· · ·

The deck was finished in seeping oak planks, and polished with a dark varnish. It was a fine deck, and he wished he had an extra pair of boots with better grip more than anything in the world. Around him was the endless blue, littered with a few patchy puffs of white. Overall, it would be a nice enough day, he thought. He liked to look at the sky. It was a fine distraction from the ground below. He'd argued his best, but the crazy glint in her eye had convinced him to step out into death's windy grasp. It was inevitable, and likely less dangerous than staying in the cockpit with her.

The *Mongoose* lowered down through the smoke and he could hear the chanting, the shrieks, the growing riot in the streets below. Leaning over the side, he tried in vain to spot his comrades. Closer to the gates, he saw some soldiers marching towards the centre of town with weapons cautiously raised; he saw the gathering of zealots praying to the flaming wreck of Seren's shack. Midway between that and the shattered warehouse, he saw the charging Army of the Dead sprinting through the side streets towards the melee in search of their leader. And then he caught sight of Lorgan, climbing up one of the shack roofs. *Now, why is he doing that?*

Seeing the airbarge above him, Lorgan waved wildly up at Natteo who, unsure of what to do, waved in reply.

"Hold on," shouted Kesta, and the *Mongoose* angled sideways like before and circled the inferno. Only then did Natteo spot the two figures within the burning building, and it all made sense. Well, some of it made sense.

First, he saw Derian reaching for the swinging body of Seren, and a fury overtook him. This was no simple anger, but a hot, bottomless fury from another realm. Perhaps this was loyalty incarnate. He hadn't been sure about Seren at the beginning. Truthfully, he still wasn't sure, but she'd saved him three times now. The least he could do was call her a friend. And seeing his actual best friend struggle with the unconscious girl, surrounded by flames and with no hope of escape, goaded him into action like never before.

"How dare you burn my friends, you spitting peasants!" he roared, charging down towards the galley door. Suddenly he no longer feared falling overboard. He didn't know what he was doing, only that he needed to do something. The door gave way under his charge. It might have been unlocked, but he'd taken no time to check. His heroic friends were burning below.

I have to do something.

It wasn't his finest moment. Were skilled bards to tell the tale, they might have said he attacked the town with a weaver's gift of fire and might. That he emptied every last one of his wristbow bolts into the zealous bastards and sent them scurrying. That his ferocious demeanour, along with the terrifying sight of the airbarge, had chased them away, screaming like children.

Tragically, this tale wasn't told expertly at all.

In the end, it was tableware he called upon.

Mostly dinner plates, at that. He did not want to kill indiscriminately. They were idiots, but they were also humans, led astray by idiocy. He'd seen such things up close. If the plates didn't work, he told himself, he'd take greater measures involving wristbows. He dashed back into the galley, grabbed an armful of plates from a shelf, and sprinted back out onto the deck, hurling plates like a child at play. Truthfully, a lunatic standing out on the outer deck of a massive, hovering airbarge hurling heavy plates at a mob of open-mouthed peasants would have been an interesting spectacle to a casual observer. But to the unfortunate peasants who were pelted by crockery flung from above, it was a recipe for a stampede, and stampede they did.

The army of Gold Haven seemed entirely unsure of what to do, and Natteo was unsurprised. They were not used to thinking on their feet, he knew. He'd never met a soldier quick enough to hold his attention for long, and in his opinion, any fool who answered all orders without question was a bore. *Even in the bedroom.* Sometimes a little breaking of the rules was called for. *Especially in the bedroom.* He thought of Boab and grimaced. All was fair in love and thievery.

"I'll ruin you all," he roared, and continued tossing plates into the mob. He didn't hit a villager with every strike, but every few moments he was rewarded with the sound of a satisfying crack and a shriek of pain, followed by the sight of a wounded villager stumbling away clutching a bruised head or a bleeding arm. There were worse ways to save the day, he supposed.

With expensive tableware shattering all around them and the sudden appearance of five heavily-armoured mercenaries bent on a scuffle, the zealots finally lost their taste for savagery. Seeing the crowd thinning out at last, Kesta brought the airbarge close over the inferno, and Natteo took to throwing little jars of fermented delicacies, which burst fragrantly on impact. Perhaps believing the concoctions were bombs filled with poison, tossed by a demonic acolyte, the last stragglers scattered, howling with fear.

Hovering over Derian and his prize, Natteo climbed out over the deck's ledge and threw down a rope ladder which had been suspiciously and just a little too conveniently positioned for such an unlikely event.

"Up here," Natteo cried to a thoroughly confused Derian, who, having pulled a girl from a burning pyre suddenly found himself unsure of what his next step should be. That step was upwards.

He just needed helpful instruction, Natteo realised. "Hey idiot, you take the rope and use it to climb up," Natteo shouted, and the possibility of survival finally struck Derian. Hoisting Seren upon his back, he climbed onto the ladder, and Kesta brought the airbarge away from the shack as the outer fire finally caught along its walls.

We had loads of time.

A better tale would have involved the shack collapsing as both young heroes leapt to safety. Natteo vowed to include that when he retold the tale to willing ears.

The *Mongoose* drifted over the fire now towards the battered, waving figure of Lorgan. Natteo climbed down the side to help Derian with his burden. Somehow, through panic and adrenaline, both mercenaries dragged Seren back over the edge onto the attractively finished deck.

"Is she still breathing?" Derian asked, collapsing beside her, and Natteo shrugged. He was no healer, nor had he memorised the chapters about healing tricks to use on a march. Derian probably didn't have a clue either. For now, he attempted another tactic. He began kissing Seren passionately on her eerily dead-looking lips.

"Not the time, Derian."

He continued kissing. Badly, too. A proper kiss involved tongues and passion and frequently two or three willing parties. Derian looked like he was blowing warm air into her mouth. When this was all over and their severed heads weren't rotting in a ditch somewhere, Natteo was going to have a very uncomfortable conversation with Derian, instructing him how to kiss better. Start with her eyes being open, he'd say. Or at least with her being alive. Slipping your beloved the tongue while she was asleep was a definite no.

And maybe steer clear altogether of someone you've already killed.

"That's not what comrades do when one of them is unaware," Natteo hissed, just as Seren gasped and spluttered out a few hacking breaths. "Oh," Natteo said. Perhaps he had this all wrong. "Well, she's alive. Why not leave her be?"

"I was just trying to save…"

"Just leave her to wake up."

"But it's from chapter forty-two of the book…"

Whatever Derian was trying to explain was lost in the sound of Kesta's incessant tapping at the window. She gestured to the mirror beyond, and Natteo shrugged. Here he was saving the gang single-handedly, and she couldn't get up off her rear and fix her view. He had half a mind to go tell her that, and to add a few delicate profanities to emphasise his point, but an arrow landed on the deck at his feet.

The Gold Haven army had taken to action after all, and more deadly barbed arrows soon followed the first, all of them searching for mercenary blood. Suddenly, the treacherous outer deck became an even more dangerous place to kiss a sleeping, defenceless girl, as the soldiers found their range. Some of their arrows clinked uselessly against the heavy metal hull or met death beneath the spinning propellers, while others arced down and struck the deck they stood upon. It was a shame. With every clunk, the varnished surface was marred that little bit more. The airbarge's beautiful finish had survived tearing a building apart, but a few sharp little barbs and it was all for spit.

"We're not the problem," Natteo cried out to the attackers, ducking away from the edge. He'd learned enough in warfare to know no army was inclined to stop attacking a stationary target just because of a convincing argument. Nevertheless, he tried again. "The lunatics with lit torches and crazy eyes are the actual problem." It was a fine point, and the army below might very well have thought on the matter as they unleased salvo after salvo at them.

"Get her inside," Derian cried, grabbing the semi-conscious Seren by the arm and pulling her towards the galley, away from the hail of projectiles. Though her eyes were closed, she let out a terrible moan as he took hold and Natteo couldn't help notice how misshapen her arms were. They appeared... longer. He reached for her legs and helped Derian drag her from harm's way. Below, he could see the soldiers reloading and he cursed them passionately. Typical warmongers, he thought.

In reply to the attack, Kesta reared the flying monstrosity and allowed it to drop again as though an engine had failed. Natteo felt his feet leave the deck for a breath before she kicked the *Mongoose* back into the air and his boots connected with the surface again. The screams of terror below suggested her success; he nearly screamed with them.

Suddenly, the airbarge rolled sideways and drifted over the rooftops towards Lorgan. It was an impressive feat of skill, and the archers below were denied any further shots. Despite his legs betraying him as though he were sliding down a greased decline, Natteo played the hero once more. Edging out towards the suspiciously convenient rope ladder, he somehow flung it back overboard.

Natteo considered himself a master storyteller. Unlike Derian, he enjoyed the words spun by a loose-tongued bard, or a crotchety old verse from a bitter old storyteller. Whenever he himself was telling a tale, he always kept the truth floating among the current of entertaining nonsense—and always made himself or his Crimson comrades, or both, look polished as fuk. However, there was no way to retell the next few moments without making the Crimson Hunters look like vile criminals.

A Guild's bounty was soon to be posted condemning their name, and everything was about to change. Truthfully, it was all Lorgan's fault.

It didn't matter that it was the right thing to do.

The *Mongoose* whirred and hummed on its merry way, and as though touched by a deity itself, Lorgan leapt from the shack roof and reached for the swinging rope ladder as it arced his way. So far, so spitting polished. But then things went sideways. Had Kesta been able to confirm his escape in her mirror, things might have turned out differently. However, unable to do this, she spun the airbarge around to check whether she'd caught her prize fish, and that was all it took.

The world slowed to nothing. Natteo could have sworn he saw each individual propeller blade as it spun. The wind ebbed away to silence, and even the smoke stepped aside without argument so the Crimson could commit their unforgivable act for everyone in the town to see.

If asked, Lorgan would have sworn he had been alone on the roof of the shack. After all, who would have noticed an old mercenary climbing atop a shack roof, with all the mayhem erupting around the town? *Eveklyn did.* For she had seen a strength in Lorgan that only a heartbroken child, bent on vengeance as rich as Kesta's, could ever see. With her outsized battle axe strapped awkwardly to her back, she spotted Lorgan and scrambled eagerly up to join him.

The *Mongoose*, with a wild-eyed Kesta at the controls, swung around, its massive bulk casting little Eveklyn in shadow. Her eyes widened in terror as the wind from the propellers whipped at her hair. Natteo, leaning over the railing to reach for Lorgan, locked eyes with her and screamed at Kesta to pull up.

Lorgan swung by one arm from the bottom of the rope ladder, his armour glinting in the early morning sun. His face was red from anger, relief, and a fine amount of rage too. He looked up as Natteo screamed, then followed his gaze and saw the child below, her hair a halo of gold, reaching for him. As the *Mongoose* turned skywards, away from the devastation below, the momentum swung him back again towards the brave little one, that fierce child without a family, without anyone at all. Her mouth opened in a wail as she reached for him, for the hero of the town, for her hero, as he left her behind. For a moment, time stood still.

"Don't!" Natteo screamed, waving his hands.

But he did.

Lorgan reached out his one free arm, and stole a fuken child from Treystone.

With a final burst of strength, he reached out and snatched her from the roof, and she shrieked in excitement, in relief, in terror, in all the emotions a child could ever have, as he locked her into a sturdy embrace—safe, fatherly, eternal. And then the ship rose into the sky, leaving Treystone far behind.

Natteo covered his face with his hands and sank to his knees. "Well, at least we'll have a good mode of transportation for when the Guild hunters come searching," he whimpered miserably as Lorgan began climbing up the rope ladder with his little burden. Natteo wasn't yet done giving out about things. "He stole a child. I need out of this spitting outfit." He looked over at Derian, expecting him to agree, to say something useful and make him feel better, but Derian was staring in the other direction. On the floor of the galley, Seren, her hands blazing with magenta fire, had begun convulsing violently.

43
———

THE GANG GET HIGH

"What are you doing, idiot?" Derian cried, wiping the water from his face. As shocking as the needless drenching was, it eased the smoke's stinging in his eyes. But still.

"I was putting out the fire," Natteo countered, shaking the last few drops from the bucket as though they'd finish the task.

Derian knew little of weaving, but he suspected a weaver's magenta fire was unlikely to be quenched by a bucket of water. He was right. The flames did little more than flicker and whoosh before resuming their menacing wave. He could see Seren's fingers alight beneath the fire, and they did not burn. Instead, each finger fidgeted eagerly, as though restlessness had the better of her.

"I'll get some more," Natteo said.

Lorgan dropped beside the convulsing girl and tried to steady her with powerful hands, but swiftly learned, as Derian had, the futility of this task. Blessed with impossible strength, her body contorted and twisted like an Addakkas eel. She moved as though an enormous invisible hand had taken to shaking her. "Natteo, help us drag her back onto the deck. If she sends off a flare, she could set this barge alight," he roared, fighting her flailing limbs as they dragged and rocked him.

Give me the strength to hold her.

As usual, no monster deep in his mind assisted Derian's needs. Between the trio, they dragged her from the cover of the galley back out onto the deck. As they fought her unconscious violence, Derian couldn't help notice how nice the airbarge's deck was. Was that seeping oak? he wondered mid-shake, and almost smiled at his foolishness. *The things idiots notice during a crisis.*

Cursing, roaring and fighting, they pinned her flat without setting the vessel alight. As they struggled, the barge swayed gently against the cutting wind and rose higher into the sky, away from the outraged town below. At last, she yielded to their efforts.

"That's it, hold her still. Let her muscles relax," Lorgan hissed, pinning her shoulders down and taking most of her struggles. To them he roared. To her, he was gentle. "There, there, little one," he crooned. "Come wake from this stupor."

Lorgan turned now to Eveklyn, who had been standing off to one side, watching and clearly wanting to be of use. He motioned her to hold one of Seren's legs, and the child trotted forward, crouched, and grabbed on. She struggled, but her grim determination was impressive. Derian nodded his approval, but inwardly he winced. Why, oh why, had Lorgan invited yet another nightmare upon them? he wondered, although he, too, had seen the desperation in the child's face. That was how younglings disappeared into mercenary life, he knew. They chose to be taken. *Not like me.*

A veneer of blue flowed from Seren's burning fingers and surrounded her body. She gasped loudly, and the flames flickered, then diminished and dissipated completely. Shuddering one last time, she fell deathly still, and suddenly Derian felt the exhaustion of the day strike him. He fell away from her against the edge of the deck, gasping himself. He felt as though he'd never learned the art of sleeping and had simply grown more and more exhausted as the years passed. Lorgan must have felt it too, for he relinquished his hold on Seren and sat down beside Natteo. Each of his movements was laboured, accompanied by the sound of breathlessness. A moment later, Natteo collapsed and lay flat out beside Seren. His eyes were open, although his voice was weak.

"I don't think they built me for a life so high."

Derian looked to the world below. Having never been in an airbarge, he'd expected to be terrified. But as he watched the little aggrieved people disappear beneath the plumes of smoke and cloud, he thought it an oddly peaceful thing. "Bye, Treystone! Go fuk yourself, you peasantly assholes," he said dreamily, and somehow gathered enough strength to wave mockingly at them.

"Language in front of the little one," Lorgan muttered, and patted Derian weakly. Was that a scoring blow, he wondered, but found himself too tired to care. He saw Seren's fingers glow blue for a few breaths and wondered if she had cast an enchantment on them.

Only Eveklyn seemed untouched by this exhaustion. She remained beside Seren's newly subdued foot, observing it. She was probably as terrified as the rest of them, but she'd set herself a task and stuck to it.

With a metallic clink of controls being locked into place, Kesta emerged from her domain. Stopping momentarily to readjust one of her mirrors, she marched out onto the deck. Derian had never seen her face illuminated in such joy, and he smiled in reply. As she neared, however, her smile faded and she stumbled mid-step before falling awkwardly to the deck.

Seren shuddered again. Her fingers glowed brightly and, with a yelp, she sat up slowly. Eveklyn grabbed her leg, but there was no further struggle. Seren gasped as though emerging from a deep swim, and suddenly Derian felt relief surge through him. More than that, he felt giddy.

"I feel polished," Natteo declared, and leapt to his feet, only to have the gentle sway of the deck flatten him again. "Sort of polished."

"I'm sorry, oh, I'm so sorry," Seren cried, shaking her hands as though they were still alight. "I took from you with no asking." She pointed to her chest. Tears were streaming down her grubby, beautiful face, and Derian rushing over to wipe them away. That was what overly enamoured little cubs did. She bowed to each of her comrades in turn, offering delicate apologies for whatever she had done, and then she turned to Derian and smiled and he really, really wanted to wipe the tears from her face. He also really, really wanted to bathe with her until they were both clean. He wanted to… No, he wanted to respect her for the fierce warrior and comrade that she was. So, he bowed as a comrade did and prepared to ask her how she was feeling. Prepared to ask her how, only moments before, her arms had been so misshapen and ruined but now worked perfectly well. And then she wrapped them tightly around him and planted her lips on his.

This isn't happening.

"It happens to heroes."

So, we are a hero, then?

"Why aren't you trying to enjoy this, idiot?"

As swiftly as she had gathered him in, she tried to pull away again, and he realised there was only a taste of passion from her. The kiss was a gift and little else. A gift not from a lover, but from a companion. The hug would have been sufficient, then, he thought, but couldn't wipe the smile from his face. He'd just kissed the most beautiful girl in the world.

"After the girl with the nice knees."

"What the fuk was that?" Kesta said, climbing to her feet and leaning against the deck's guardrail. With her hair catching majestically in the wind and a straightness to her pose, she looked a different person altogether. She appeared to belong in the sky, among the bobbing clouds and the cool air.

"Release me," Seren said. Her tone was less cutting than normal, and this was a win for Derian. Begrudgingly, he released her from his tight hold and ignored the intrigued look from his best friend. He'd saved her from the burning flames. A brief kiss was a fine payment.

"I took from all of you," Seren continued. "As I slept. Had no right."

"What did you take?" Natteo asked, and Derian knew that careful tone. It was a deeply suspicious tone he saved for brutes in taverns, right before he did something stupid involving fists. It was a tone of both warning and disarming.

She shuffled her feet. She actually shuffled her feet. "I took from your souls."

"Ah, that's fine, so. To the fires with my soul," Natteo declared in his warmer tone. A tone impossible not to feel happy hearing. He'd mastered that tone long before he and Derian had met. Derian had once asked him how he was so clever with his use of language and manner, and Natteo had looked ready to break down and cry before breaking into a fit of demented laughter instead. Then he'd taken to mocking Derian as an "uneducated peasant" for the rest of the day, and Derian hadn't asked again.

Natteo continued in that jovial, kind tone. "A soul

suggests deities watching over me. Watching me. If my soul is a beacon for them to glance at, I'd rather not have them see everything I do."

Seren frowned. "I do not understand."

"He's talking shit again, Seren. Pay no heed," Kesta said, placing a hand on her shoulder—a gesture of forgiveness if ever Derian saw one. "It's his way."

"I am, and it is," Natteo said, using his most 'stirring shit' tone. "Anyway, we've stolen the Army of the Dead's airbarge. We've incited a town to riot. We've earned the ire of the Gold Haven army, and that lunatic Anguis the Dark One will soon know of Seren and come searching. He must get in line, of course. Isn't there a grand demon called Fiore coming after her first?" The others nodded glumly. "Polished. Was there anything else? Oh, yes. We also stole a child, so the Guild is going to be pissed with us. There's no coming back from that."

"We can return the airbarge," Lorgan mumbled.

Kesta turned to him and unleashed the past few days of anger and frustration on him.

It was like watching parents arguing, Derian thought dazedly. It was not a long argument, but it was heated. He'd seen Kesta argue with Lorgan before, but this was something else entirely. Their words went back and forth without break. He'd never seen her stand her ground, attack so openly and truthfully, from the first bout. Lorgan, on the other hand, looked exhausted, already set to lose.

"You aren't thinking, Kesta," he protested weakly. "We are better than this."

"Right—we only steal children and naked girls. Anyway, it's my airbarge now, and I'm taking the biggest room."

"Now, that's not fair. That's a completely different matter altogether. And we never stole Seren. We just needed to keep her chained a while. And no choosing rooms."

"The Army of the Dead started this. They mugged us first, and we saved them at the gates." She crossed her arms, looking around her at the vessel. "We've earned this. It's my airbarge."

"The Guild will murder us for this crime. It's one thing stealing a cart and a few horses. It is another taking out the Guild's number one unit. Taking the airbarge has denied them escape from Treystone. I forbid this as leader of the Crimson."

"We can't exactly fly back down and give it back to them. They are big brutes with a bigger name. All they have to say is we are enemies and the zealots will consider them allies. No, no, I've followed you for years, dear friend, but I will not lead us back to Treystone to return the *Mongoose*, for it is my airbarge."

"See sense, woman."

"It's my airbarge. I'll throw you over the side before I relinquish control, and I'll throw you over the side if you call me 'woman' in that way again."

"In what way?"

"'Woman.'"

"Oh, well, I didn't mean it like that."

"Oh, well, I'm still not giving them back my airbarge. Let them come for it."

Natteo joined in. "They'll need a big ladder to reach us."

"Shut up, Natteo."

Kesta stepped forward and took Lorgan's hands. "I have gifted us something incredible." She pointed to Seren. "The girl is hunted by a grand demon. Would you condemn her to death over the vague notion of honour?"

Lorgan shook his head weakly. "I've done terrible things, my comrades. I've doomed noble warriors to die. I cannot willingly do so again to the greatest mercenaries in the land."

"How about we rescue them from Treystone?" Natteo said thoughtfully, as though he cared deeply about the mercenaries. Perhaps he did. "We have an inside guy," he said, pointing to Eveklyn.

"I want to travel with you, Crimson Hunters," the little one said. A fine, heartbreaking argument.

Moments passed, and Derian had seen this before. The slow whirring of mechanisms as Kesta's words won out. It was insane but, spit on him, Derian wanted this beast too.

At last, Lorgan exhaled deeply. A good sign. "And you will travel with us, Eveklyn, upon this airbarge," he muttered. "But you must earn your right of entry."

"Whatever it takes," she said staunchly.

The *Fighting Mongoose* was a thing of beauty, and Derian fell in love with the machine as Kesta had. Derian and Natteo suffered only one minor falling out over choice of room, but Natteo's argument that his more lavish choice still smelled of him and his previous night's conquest was the last word on the matter. That, and the fact that Seren's chosen bedroom was located right across from Derian's. Some quiet night, she could open her door and slip into Derian's unlocked bedroom for some play…

"Stop it, Derian."

———

Before enjoying the fruits of their labours, however, they had a set of elite mercenaries (tenfold the ability of the Crimson) that needed rescuing. All they had was a plan. It wasn't the greatest plan, but it was a start. If the townsfolk hadn't burned the mercenaries to ash by now, then phase one of said plan was sending a young girl strolling innocently through the gates and gathering information about the Army of the Dead as she skipped along. Once her new comrades aboard the *Mongoose* knew of their plight, they could put phase two of the plan into effect. So far, Lorgan had no firm strategies to address any of the hundred eventualities Eveklyn might discover, but recently his plans had been unusually successful.

They decided to wait until near daybreak so the *Mongoose* could approach without being seen. Derian, Natteo, and Lorgan would disembark with the child and walk the last few hundred feet with her to avoid inadvertently feeding her to any demons still wandering around. After that, well, they were semi-skilled at thinking on their feet.

Knowing he should sleep and eat and recharge for the following day to come, Derian remained alert. His mind still reeled after the recent events, so he distracted himself by watching Kesta keeping the *Mongoose* airborne. It was a wonderful experience, and he took in what instruction she gave. Her ease with the controls as she brought the ship to land a few dozen miles east of the town, where it would stay until nightfall, made him realise how little he knew of her. Whatever life she'd known before, it had clearly been far more impressive than the nothingness he'd experienced.

No matter how hard he tried, he couldn't understand how the airbarge remained in the sky. Watching the four spinning blades was an unnerving thing, yet he couldn't keep his eyes from their silent threat. Kesta, seeing his confused interest, assured him that no human, beast or object would survive even a glancing blow from any of of these blades. She also reassured him that the airbarge could stay airborne with three, possibly even two propellers, but most certainly not with one solitary propeller, no matter the skill of the pilot. He wondered if he would ever need to be aware of such a fact in the future and swiftly decided that no, he would absolutely never need to know this.

Not at all. Definitely not.

He asked her whether the blades were unnatural mechanisms from another world, but Kesta had gently insisted that the source was not required to keep this beast airborne. When she began using words like "aerodynamics" and "propulsion" and "thrust" and "gravity," though, he just nodded and listened to the rush of wind. It was a fine distraction to confusing things. *Less confusing than speaking of the source.*

When she returned to the galley to ensure that her peace with Lorgan was solid, Derian took to walking the outer deck, inspecting the four sets of blades as the sun set on an incredible day.

Lost in his own thoughts, he never heard Seren approach. Her face was as marred as before. Her hair was tangled and her smudged clothing smelled of three-day-old sweat. She hadn't learned the art of presenting herself as the goddess she was just yet. The old Derian would have suggested he show her what to do, starting with how best to scrub when naked. Might have even suggested he do her back if needed. He'd have been happy to do it, too. The new Derian, however, was about ready to fill a bath, offer soap, and run away. He almost said something, but she spoke first.

"You are ordinary kisser, but good comrade," she said very slowly. "Bereziel chose you for… for… the reason… No… For *a* reason. So, I should forgive." She tipped her forehead. "Someday. Maybe tomorrow?" She sighed as though the words she chose were not the ones she wanted. He thought them fine words, though. "You saved me from… from the fire. You came for me when no one… no one else could." She spat over the side and groaned in frustration. "My words come slowly."

"You are improving," he offered, and she smiled.

"Can you tell Ser… me? Thurk. Can you tell me of source… aagh, of theee source."

I'll do anything you want. I'll scrub your back.

He did not say that, but he spoke of the source. He spoke quietly of his dream and the events that had taken place as best he could, and she did not interrupt. Only at the end, when he spoke of waking to the smell of burning girl, did she act. It was another kiss. This one was on his cheek, and Derian's heart hammered.

"Thank you, stupid Derian. For saving me."

He had a fine, honourable reply ready. About duty and doing the right thing. But then Natteo appeared from the galley, a half-eaten sandwich in his hands. He'd wasted no time at all cleaning himself. His clothes were of silk and rich leather, and brightly coloured. His hair was straight and combed, his eyes touched up with attractive paint. He appeared as alluring as a male escort in the pleasure nests of Castra. Though he looked polished, his face was grave.

"I think something happened to me when I died," he whispered, offering Derian the rest of the sandwich. It was made of strangely cured pickle and carrot and an unusual cheese. It needed mustard. "Maybe all of us. You ever see Kesta behave like that? You ever see Lorgan's battle plans meet such successes? I heard what you did on the battlefield, Derian. And hearing about this Bereziel, I think something big has happened."

Derian offered Seren a piece of the sandwich. She licked

it a few times to taste, before swallowing in one bite. It looked like she could have used some mustard with it.

"What do you mean, something big?" Derian asked. An icy shiver ran down his spine.

"Maybe not big. How about colossal? Or titanic? Vast and terrifying? Or momentous? I sensed something in that … death. Stronger than the last time I died."

"You sensed Bereziel? Or Fiore? The Dark One?"

He shook his head and Derian could see the unease. "Somehow, I know it was something older. Greater. It scared the living piss out of me." He shrugged. "I figured you'd fuk up with Seren, so I eavesdropped on you. I'm sorry. I couldn't stop listening. I can't shake the thought that something beyond everything we know is moving in the dark."

"That thinking will serve you no good, Natteo."

"What trapped the demons? What killed the gods? What broke Dellerin in half?"

There was a near mania to his words, and Seren shushed him gently as though trying to quiet his dark thoughts.

"Well, perhaps it'll stay hidden. For now, I think we have enough to worry about," Derian muttered, and Natteo smiled hopefully. *Ignorance is a cursed gift.* Something in Natteo's few words terrified Derian. That was a matter for another time.

"Another tale after the end of the world."

Shut up, monster mind. Where were you when I needed you?

"Resting."

Well, that's just spitting wonderful.

Natteo waved his hands in front of Derian's eyes. "Are you okay, Derian? You've been staring at me for the last few moments like an idiot. Is it the silk shirt? Does it dazzle you? Are you ready for a Natteo spin? Seren can come play too."

Seren gently stilled Natteo's frantically waving hands. "He's talking to beast. His beast. Um… himself… who is also beast."

"She's a smart one," his beast, which was himself, said.

Oh, rest for another while, will you?

"I can't. The time has arrived."

For what?

Nothing happened for a few breaths. Derian felt the eyes of his comrades on him, and he felt the stirrings of terrible anger surge through him. This was different to before. He had more control and more ability to focus it. He was a monster, but he was also human.

"For this."

Suddenly, Seren collapsed, screaming. Not a human scream but a terrible, violent outburst that tore at Derian's mind. From her fingers came the magenta fire once more. This time, though, the flames flew out into the darkness in two deathly fireballs. Derian took hold of her and held her and the flames disappeared again, but the screaming remained as though the demon spider bitch from the source was tearing her apart. At last, with a piercing cry, a desperate sob, she fell silent.

"It is done," she whimpered, and Derian embraced her. Behind him, he heard Lorgan and Kesta rushing over to investigate the commotion. Somehow Natteo had gotten hold of another bucket of water, but this time he held off an assault.

"Are you okay?" Derian whispered.

"No, no. Seren is not." She gasped, shaking in terror. "Fiore has emerged. She walks this world once more."

44

FIORE THE SEVENTH

The evening was still and cool. Barely a breeze in the air and certainly none blowing ill things. For one seeking omens, this might have seemed a perfect night for nothing extraordinary to happen. For those tired few warriors standing along the walls of Treystone, it was an improvement on the menacing feelings they'd felt the nights before.

As they donned their armour, sharpened their blades, lit the fires, there was optimism stealing through the ramparts and it was most welcomed. Torches lit their wary faces, yet gone were the battered grimaces of the doomed. No longer were they staring into the night, restless and grim, waiting for four-legged death to emerge from the surrounding forest seeking their flesh. No, tonight they watched on through unblinking eyes, for survival had toughened them—though it had broken their souls too. Though still traders, farmers, and miners, they were all hardened now by bloodshed and horror.

They lined up as they had before, in groups, their arrows focussed on the farthest spikes. One lone master stood on each wall to give orders; the five hundred warriors of golden grandness had left them to their own devices. They were but peasants, after all.

But although they watched, they did not see the speck of crystal nothingness appear in the darkness down from the gate, in an area where a patch of green grass remained alive and vibrant.

————

Seren's escape had robbed Keralynn of most of her zealots' frenzy. As though a veneer of unnatural hate had been pulled away from their zealous eyes, peace had suddenly fallen upon them as the airbarge had disappeared into the sky above.

While Keralynn had struggled to keep her flock under control, to justify her aggression towards those who'd come to their aid, and to save her fractured marriage after one too many discovered dalliances, Blair had been the voice of reason. And that voice had taken to beginning fresh negotiations with the remaining mercenaries. It was a shrewd move that would save the lives of the stranded outfit and the townsfolk alike. Keeping the Mercenary Guild happy, after all, was a smart tactic.

Blair was a generous man, so Mowg, sporting a black eye, had kept listening. Talk of "swimming in gold" had been a fine opening gambit on Blair's part, and by the time negotiations were concluded the sun was already setting and every soldier had been needed at the wall.

Meanwhile, the Army of the Dead had gone to task, lining their pockets and striking deals as though they had little choice in the matter. They stood now like any fine mercenary outfit, with threat glittering in their eyes: getting paid, getting back what was theirs, getting a little vengeance too. They'd been in the mud before, been lowly grunts earning a crust.

But they still had their name now, and nothing else mattered. And besides, the Crimson had taken care of most of the demons anyway. The golden army could take care of the rest. It was an agreeable contract.

At the front gate stood Dorn, the leader of this great defence. To anyone but a hardened mercenary, he appeared almost impressive. At home among the ramparts in a battle that would never be waged, with polished armour and his sword raised as a sign of grandeur, he looked inspiring. His masters in Gold Haven would have approved of this.

Unfortunately, he knew of the silence to come. He craved a little demon slaughter, all in the name of Gold Haven's honour, but the Crimson had denied his march a glorious epilogue. Sometimes the epilogue is more important than the actual lost tale. For what greater legend was there than the tale of the heroic local leading the finest army against the beasts of the night? At least this way, the saga of the lost weaver might be more easily forgotten.

On either side and stretching along the outer wall stood the rest of the soldiers. They drew no sword, nor loaded any crossbow. Most still carried the stains of mud from the deep trenches they'd helped build around the town; others still smelled of tree sap and bore splinters in their flesh from the hundreds of sharp spikes embedded within those same trenches. They had heard the terrible stories all day, from willing peasants with loose tongues. Most had never seen a demon, but with an army dug in and secure, they were confident in their abilities.

As the sun sank below the horizon and no shadowed beasts appeared from the dark, relief spread like wildfire through the ragged ranks, and ever so slowly, the defenders of the town embraced the near-silence. For the first time in days, there came sounds of nature. Of foxes shrieking, night hawks roaring, hissects buzzing. And soon enough, the wind played its part, carrying gentle mocking jests among the defenders as camaraderie raised its reassuring head.

An hour passed, and a few more after that, and nobody noticed the slow changing of the darkness as the night creatures fell silent one by one, stilled by an unseen, terrible threat. What could they sense that their human conquerors couldn't? Had the soldiers taken note as the last hissect buzzed and suddenly fell quiet, they might have noticed the threat. Had even one solitary soldier spoken aloud of the sudden chill running down their spine in those last few moments, they might all have taken heed of the menacing things at play. More likely, though, nothing could have prepared them for what was to come.

———

With the vile human's words still reverberating through her thoughts, Fiore cursed him with everything she had. *How weak to be saved by a mortal, bent to his will, broken to a knee.* She knew his name. Knew his shameless deeps, incredible and impressive as they were. However, as he was anguished, she was regal and divine. Aye, the Anguished One had collected the finest of her brethren and sought out her soul for his own, but breaching into the living world was worth a lifetime in his servitude. *His lifetime.* She'd waited long enough to break free, and his cleansing touch was a tainted gift. As he gifted her passage with his human words of weaving, she eyed the diluted Seeva and hated him most. Sniffing his scent, she committed it to memory. No beast dared lay such a claw upon her beauty and live to their fitting end. *I smell you, Seeva.* And then, wonderfully, she faded into nothingness. Nothingness and then very much everything.

She stretched her gorgeous legs out and felt the touch of air upon them and gave thanks to her keeper. *No, her master.* She spat this thought away, enjoying her birth. *No. More than birth.* It was a demented, sacrilegious act against the old god's will, and it was beautiful. *Was it worth the sacrifice?* She stepped farther through and began her hunt, for who knew how long she would enjoy this wonderful freedom before the Anguished One came for her?

"Serenity," she whispered to the world; it was a scream to the living who heard. "Bring her to me," she hissed, seeking out mindless, feeble humankind as she had before. Oh, whispering into their easily influenced minds had been a rare treat this close to the world. But with failure came absolution in the form of her own limbs tearing at Serenity.

The Soul without body.

She could have whispered to her master about the girl, but that might have delayed his pledge to release her. She would suffer horrific torment when he learned of her intentions; her actions, too. She would grasp his torments, for pain was majestic, but being denied her hunt was her anguish. Oh, no; her pledge to serve him was unbreakable, but it had nothing to do with saving his bloodline from a terrible, wonderful end. And after Serenity died, Fiore herself would gorge upon her stolen soul.

Licking her lips, Fiore, the seventh demon after the fall, stepped through into the world of the living after thousands of years, and it was perfect, for she was not alone. Far below, hundreds of illuminated souls scurried. Smeared with bone and blood and the muck of wretched humanity, she'd forgotten how diminutive and unimpressive they were. She clicked loudly in excitement, for none of her kind ever forgot the taste of raw flesh.

———

It appeared as a crystal-clear speck of black light afloat in the air. Not even a sharp eye could have spotted it, for it was silent, even as it grew in size. Were an adventurer brave enough to peer through this speck of nothing, they might have looked through a keyhole into a twisted, horrible realm of madness. Were that same adventurer to go against their primal instincts and remain peering through for a dozen breaths, such a concentration of warped horror and timelessness would have taken their sanity. Were that same unfortunate adventurer unlucky enough to fall upon their back as the madness overcame them, they might well have been split in two by the silent emergence of a massive arachnid talon as it stepped through. For as twisted and confusing as the source's notion of time was, so too were the manifestations of mass within its realm of demons.

The grand demon's leg stepped through and the rest of her followed slowly after. The doorway grew in scale as she passed through it, from a speck of irrelevancy to a vast seventy or eighty feet in diameter. She dipped her head as she dragged her bulbous form through, and the hundreds watching below screamed in terror as the gigantic spider appeared in the middle of the battlegrounds.

A few hundred demons clinging to her will like swimmers riding a wave, were dragged through from the dark to freedom. The spider moved slowly now, out in the open air of Treystone, for her body was not built for such a realm, but the demon parasites dropped away like fleas and charged into the night towards the scent of human flesh.

The chorus of barks and howls and the thunder of charging beasts stirred the incredulous defenders to action. A group of mercenaries led the defence. They wasted no time regretting their contract or their bad luck; instead, with the promise of payment driving them onward, they went boldly to war. Surely a demon-covered arachnid was worth a bonus hidden within the fine print. Stepping away from the gate, they aimed their crossbows into the darkness, enjoying the familiar feel of weapons in their hands. They fired bolt after bolt towards the charging horde, and this stirred the rest of the army to action. Orders erupted, and the whooshing of arrows filled the night, answered by the piercing, terrifying cries of the grand demon as she tasted defiance in the air.

At first, no fool attacked Fiore, for they all knew the stories. Instead, they sought to eradicate the lesser problem before dealing with the insurmountable one. A sound tactic, if truth be told. Many of the lesser canis demons fell to the barrage swiftly enough. Those not felled by bolts were struck with flaming arrows, and soon the night was alive with the flicker of flames and the truly terrifying shadows of the unholy invaders.

Though they were terrified, facing death was nothing new to the townsfolk. They did not cower at the vision of a towering spider; rather, they met the attack as though led by Lorgan of the Crimson Hunters.

At last, the barrages of arrows tapered off, and the surviving demons fell silent as they sought protection behind their master.

"Serenity," she screamed, for the blinding souls had put up a fight and this disgusted her. No human ear understood her words or her plea, but they read her intentions, heard the horrific clicking of spider legs as Fiore turned her massive body toward the town and began marching forward.

If Lorgan had been among them on the battlefield, he might have been blessed with a moment in time to pat every one of the defenders' backs. "Well done," he would have said, as the first group of townsfolk fired upon Fiore's ghastly form, striking her with countless projectiles. "Again," he would have insisted with iron assuredness, and they would have been certain of his plan, even as every last arrow bounced ineffectively off her shell.

They could have turned to him as this horrible event unfolded and looked to him for guidance. But Lorgan wasn't with them on the field of battle.

He was above it.

45

LAST STAND

"She's taller than I remember," muttered Derian from his place at the edge of the *Mongoose*'s main deck. High up, away from terrifying things, the world was peaceful. A fine thing before violence erupted. No one saw them approach, and it was no surprise. The soldiers had more pressing matters to attend to, and Fiore had little need to look up when prey was plentiful.

"Prey."

His mind was a gathering of imprecise memories, but he distinctly remembered goring into her with his horrible teeth; it had seemed so much easier back then. Another of the spitting traits of the source, he thought, cursing himself for having bragged about his victory to his comrades. He was no skilled storyteller; few were. He'd claimed to have ruined her. Pledged to them that his inner monster was truly magnificent. Now, well, she was impressive and carried few scars from their meeting. A doubting comrade might claim mischief on Derian's part. A classy comrade might say nothing of it.

Natteo was *not* that comrade. His new armour clinked

loudly as he stood beside Derian, gripping the wooden edge of the deck and looking over. "Really, Derian? You tore that giant apart? Are you sure you weren't dreaming?" Derian could hear the terror in his best friend's voice. His own voice would likely quiver as much when he dared to speak. There was no shame in fear now, though, for the beast had begun its march on Treystone. She strode across the battleground as though she waded through a swamp. He felt his dinner of carrot soup churning in his stomach. Would leaning over and throwing up all over her be a shrewd first attack, he wondered.

Below, Fiore suddenly roared, and the world shook. Soldiers standing to meet her charge at the ramparts were knocked from their feet as an invisible wall of energy pulsed across the battlefield and thundered skywards. Even as Natteo and Derian were pushed back from where they stood, the airbarge held her position with little more than a slight tremble. As big as Fiore was, the *Fighting Mongoose*, of handcrafted wood and finest Venistrian steel, was just as large, just as dominant.

Regardless, her roar was impressive, and Natteo said it best. "Her spitting roar is more powerful than most gales of wind. Think we've bitten off more than we can chew." He peered down at the mounting confusion. "I've changed my mind. I've no issue leaving here with my life." He jested, but there was an enticing grain of truth within.

"No fleeing this fight," Derian's monster hissed, as though the suggestion of fleeing disgusted it. Perhaps it did. He remembered hating her. Being compelled to rip her throat out. That had been nice.

"Well, they weren't burned alive," Lorgan said, pointing down at the Army of the Dead. Even as a thundering spider monster marched towards them with grotesque legs and snapping claws, they moved as though this were nothing more than a common skirmish. Perhaps they believed themselves capable of being the first outfit to take out a grand demon. Perhaps had there been a thousand more of them fighting, it would have been a fairer fight.

"Look at them," Natteo said wistfully. Casually, he pulled an unfamiliar silver chain from beneath his chest plate, kissed the decorative green stone it held, and returned it to its resting place. Natteo had never been the superstitious type, nor was he sentimental. Derian could have asked him about it, but a second roar erupted and thoughts of the beast surpassed curiosity.

"They are magnificent," Natteo said softly.

They were.

They were not intimidated by unstable ground, thundering bolts of energy, or jagged spindly legs. They kept clear of Fiore's marching, choosing swiftness of foot over stubborn, ineffectual defending. Moving into position for a breath before moving again, they fired volley after volley of arrows, all the while searching for a break in her armour. A clue to her manoeuvres. Any chance of victory. It was all a skilled outfit could do, short of throwing themselves foolishly into harm's way in the chance of scoring a telling blow for the warriors who followed.

But where the Army of the Dead were impressive and sly, the defenders in gold were woefully inexperienced. No doubt under orders, they stuck to traditional tactics, digging in and waiting to hold off the assault—as if holding territory in this battle meant a spitting thing. Fiore moved along the side of the trench, swiping out at the defenders, and it was devastating. Each swing reached thirty feet either way. She resembled a swimmer striking out against a wild tide. Tragically, the defenders offered no nasty current to catch her in. They died brutally, one after the other, before earning a taste or a flair for battle.

In the first few moments, Derian watched as dozens of soldiers dressed in gold were slain by the flurry of her claws, and it was terrible. Those who met their end after one blow were the lucky ones. He saw limbs torn free, bodies crushed all in one swipe, and he was petrified. Though he could hear the screams from this high up, they were faint, and it made the horror easier to witness. One sound was undiluted by the distance, though, and it pierced through his head.

Click, click, click.

Her many horrific legs shuffled unnaturally around the battleground, stabbing as they went, seeking victims. And he tasted metal in his mouth. He gripped the edge of the balcony and desired to kill her. To end this horror. And the horror worsened, for she began to feast. Reaching down and grabbing what pulpy remains she could, she gorged herself greedily on the dead, the dying. Lesser soldiers might have fled. Perhaps they should have.

"Poor peasant soldiers," growled Lorgan, joining Derian on the deck. "Retreat is the only move." For once, he'd forgone his light leather armour in favour of a heavier steel suit. He looked impressive and threatening. As he'd dressed, he'd jested quietly that it was unlikely the river would be the death of him this night, and he was probably right. He wouldn't last long in that melee.

"What are we waiting for? We should fight," whispered Seren. Her voice was stronger than before; she'd eaten some of his soul, after all. He'd imagined there might have been a heavier conversation to have on the matter, but knowing she'd healed herself at the expense of a little bit of his

mystique or aura or whatever the fuk they thought it was…
well, it was no matter to him. Besides, he hadn't been using it
at the time, nor did he feel any less of a man for it. Neither
did his monster.

"I feel just fine."

That's nice. Any chance of that strength from before?

"Not yet."

"We are waiting for the moment," Lorgan mumbled, still
watching the battle intently. His eyes darted from one group
of archers to the next, from beast to mini-beasts, as he
formulated a plan. A plan involving the first-ever beating of a
grand demon. Derian felt less hopeful. He could have
watched all night and still spotted no crack in the beast's
armour. By dawn she would have slain the town, eaten what
she desired, then turned her attention to seeking Seren. He
prayed she did not look up.

"The soldiers will fall, but the Army of the Dead might
give fight. They truly are a skilled outfit," Lorgan said. He
sounded sadder than Derian had ever heard him. "They are
the best I've ever seen… After the Seven," Lorgan added,
and he was not wrong. The Army of the Dead did their Guild
proud now. They never stopped moving, calling out orders,
suggestions, and warnings as they manoeuvred around the
demon, and taking out the straggler canis demons as they
attempted to earn a kill beneath the tempest of their master.

The mercenaries kept wide of the terrifying arachnid and
focussed on the one weakness they had discerned in her dense
shell and her thick, impenetrable skin. As she fed, they fired
upon her mouth and the fleshy innards within. Their arrows
lit the night and disappeared into her churning maw. Soon
enough, the demon's feasting was halted by a terrible dose of
indigestion. Twisting with pain, she ceased eating and began
to howl. Suddenly the night came alive with fireflies.

Far above her, Lorgan, Derian, and Natteo looked on in astonishment.

"It won't be enough—she is colossal," Lorgan hissed. His fists were clenched, his foot tapped as though listening to a tune, and Derian realised that the torment of staying afloat watching people die was almost too much for him. Lorgan would find it easier to drop from here and sacrifice himself, saving those fated to die this night, than to stand idly by as a battle raged below him. Derian, however, was happy to stay put. Stepping foot on the ground was inevitable death, even with Seeva blood coursing through his veins.

His Seeva blood thought differently.

"He'll never send you down, but he knows the distraction we can make."

No chance. We are fine here with bow and arrow.

"Let's jump."

Shut up.

"It'll be fine, trust me."

Shut up, shut up, shut up.

All too swiftly, Fiore discovered their tactic. Protecting her face, she took to lifting any fool too slow to avoid her gaze and throwing them at whatever group of archers was nearest. It was a terrible thing to see soldiers feasted upon; it was a worse thing to hear their wails suddenly fall silent as they were dashed messily against walls, ramparts, comrades.

Derian opened himself to his monster's anger. Its hatred. Its impressiveness. Its lack of desire to urinate all over his new set of armour.

"I can smell her. I can smell her."

Breathe her in.

Down below, there was a roar and a clash of swords as the cavalry appeared. The sight should have been far more impressive than it was, but it was a failed charge, the order given by a general unprepared for such a battle. They emerged from the town in a line, two abreast, with swords raised. The remaining soldiers cleared the way, and the riders charged valiantly down through the battlefield towards the demon.

"Brave and foolish," Lorgan whispered, shaking his head.

The cavalry split apart now and thundered to either side of Fiore, seeking out limbs to sever. She had many to offer, and for a bemused moment she stopped flinging her human prey and watched the strange mounted creatures surround her.

It was a fine tactic, and terribly executed. From both sides the riders raised their blades and struck fiercely at her vile, spindly legs as they charged past. Were there a thousand more soldiers with earless mounts, this approach might have earned victory. But Fiore's shrieks of agony were an ungodly, deafening thing, and the brave mounts, trained though they were for savage battlefields, struggled against their primal instincts. The noise was ear-splitting, and hearing pure evil so close was simply too much for the poor beasts.

They reared, they broke, and almost as one, they turned tail and fled the monster. Many of the Gold Haven riders were tossed off and left behind, and Fiore pounced, greedily exacting swift vengeance for their sins. She raged and hissed and stabbed and killed, and the riders fell to her in less time than it took a bard to order a drink before beginning a performance.

"Let us be free of this airbarge."

It's a lovely airbarge. Are you insane?

"Are we insane? Yes, we are."

Lorgan shook his head. "I can see no way to beat her, short of dropping this heavy beast on the bitch's head and shattering her senses. How would she do against the propellers?" He shrugged at his own ineptitude. It wasn't much of a plan.

"She's not *that* heavy, Lorgan," Kesta countered, stung. "But you know what we must do. We've delayed for long enough. We can't beat Fiore—we can all see that. But we can still play our part if I can just set this ship down on the far end of town…" She frowned.

"What's at the far end of town?" Derian asked nervously.

"Not our destiny."

Quiet, you.

"Kesta can load as many innocents as she can," Lorgan said. "This town is doomed. Better some survive to tell our tale." Beside him, Natteo grabbed his head as though it were about to fall loose.

Derian didn't like this plan at all. Not one little bit. "You mean *we* load, right? *We* survive to tell our tale, right? *We* aren't joining this horror show, right? Right?"

"Yes, we are. Come on—let's go. Now!"

Whisht, monster.

"We do what we must," Lorgan said, tipping his forehead before bowing to Kesta. "The rest of the Crimson can add to this fight, delay her for however long we can." She touched her fingers to her lips, touched her heart, bowed, and sprinted back to the cockpit to take her seat beside Eveklyn, who was already strapped in. Whatever unspoken words they'd shared would be their last.

Derian shook his head. "But they tried to kill Seren. They beat you up, Lorgan… They didn't even pay us." His heart was hammering. It felt less his own and more his beast's. A finer way to meet death, he supposed.

The *Mongoose* descended, and beside him Seren hissed a curse under her breath. She still wore her blue dress. It was torn and ruined, and she was beautiful.

"Seren, for all that I did, I am sorry."

She shrugged, and at the tips of her fingers the magenta fires came alive once more. "Don't kill me again. We fine," she muttered, but her eyes were wild.

Dorn was the last rider to emerge from the gates. As the soldiers with legs still able to carry them fled past him, he brought his beast in line with the huge, multi-legged monster and charged forward.

"He's got a lance. A fuken lance. What is that spitting fool thinking?" Lorgan hissed as the airbarge dropped all too slowly to stop the insanity.

Fiore was close to the gates. Dorn didn't have far to charge. With all his strength, he raised the long lance at the last possible moment as though he were a grand jousting champion and struck up at the beast as he charged beneath her. She took the strike well and did not fall, even as the long metal shaft bent beneath the force of her shell. *Bent, but did not break.* And then, with a wet pop, it lanced her bulbous body, and she shrieked in agony. She swatted at him as he charged past and struck him a glancing blow. The horse, blessed with terrible hearing, continued its charging as though still following a master. Dorn sat in the saddle, still gripping the reins. His head, however, lay spinning fifty feet behind.

Derian's eyes widened in horror—and the Seeva burst forth. Suddenly, leaping from such a suicidal height was nothing at all. His legs were built for such drops, he told himself. Not to mention the river of blood he'd need to drain before he died. He looked down with two sets of eyes and liked his chances.

He heard a roar of outrage and saw Keralynn charge out towards the beast, brandishing her sword and shield. If she had called for her zealots to follow her into death, none followed.

Beside him, Lorgan shouted for her to hold her charge. Even Seren gasped and held her breath. Ignoring them, Keralynn had almost reached Fiore, and as the airbarge dropped, Derian heard her cursing even as one of Fiore's legs stretched out to kick at her.

"Oh, no," Natteo wailed as the screaming Keralynn was flung skywards like a child's toy. The world slowed and Derian lost control of his limbs. The beast was nearer now; he could smell her, and found the scent familiar. And awful, too. He dashed towards the edge of the deck, as did Lorgan, though their reasons were different.

Lorgan leaned out into the air, one arm outstretched, and perhaps had Kesta seen it, she might have angled the beast better. But this was no outstretched hand of a child upon a swinging ladder. Keralynn flew towards the airbarge, her broken arms and legs flailing. She was alive, and she screamed as she ascended and then fell silent at the sight of the massive barge on its collision course with her. Derian wondered what might have been going through her mind, whether she saw Lorgan reach for her as she passed. It all happened in a pulse, and no godly reflexes could have allowed him to reach her in time.

At least it was painless.

The *Mongoose* was unaffected as Keralynn met her doom in the right front propeller. One moment she was in front of them, sailing through the air. And then there was a terrible haze of red and ruined mist splashing over the deck, a few metallic clunking noises, and then Natteo began to scream.

"Ugh! Some of her hair is on my face. Get it off. Get it off. Get it off. It's still warm."

He roared in horror, wiping a chunk of tangled, ruined

crimson and blonde hair from his face. As he did, he had
more to say. Perhaps it was his way of enduring traumas as
they occurred. After the screams of disgusted horror, came
the disgusted cursing, after that it was a witty remark. On this
occasion it was something about his "gut feeling that Lorgan
and Keralynn's dalliance had little to no future."

Derian barely heard him. He had lost control of himself
completely and now did something truly stupid. Only Seren
saw him, and she screamed in triumph. As he killed himself,
he thought her scream was ever so adorable. "This bitch
needs to die!" he roared, leaping over the edge.

It was wonderful. The entire world fell to nothing but the
rushing of death as the land drew closer, and Derian howled
with delight. He allowed himself a moment to enjoy the
lunacy as he careened through the night sky, fuelled by a
crazed, monstrous version of himself. The closer he drew to
Fiore, the more powerful his hatred grew. He feared no death.
He feared only failing to kill her. His hands were his own,
and that was fine because he pledged to tear her throat apart.
Even with human hands. He'd just need to tear more
viciously.

He smelled her.

She smelled him.

She looked to the sky.

He landed on her face.

He felt every bone in his body shatter from the fall, but hatred
infused him and pain was no matter at all. What mattered was
the pain he delivered upon her.

"Fiore the Seventh, know my wrath," he snarled with
Seeva breath.

She wailed aloud at the attack and bit at him

instinctively. He remembered her teeth from the source. Up close, they were that little bit more impressive. They were as large and sharp as long swords, and she forgot everything in favour of tearing him apart with them. With arms barely able to support a fist, he punched her teeth and shattered three with one blow. Whatever agony he suffered dissipated in this shared moment of mortal combat. He tore at her face, kicking, screaming, biting and hurting, and she reached up to crush him, but he reached into her fetid, foul mouth through the newly-formed gap and took hold of her tongue. It didn't matter that it was half the size of him or that its slime was sticky and burned to the touch. What mattered was pulling that horror loose. With a terrible burst of strength, he tugged violently. He heard the tearing of demonic muscle and were he granted another breath, he might well have pulled it out. But Fiore's panic caused her to bite down hard, and the fresh agony caused her head to rear back suddenly. Derian flew upwards like the Watcher of Treystone and then fell back like a treat to be caught and consumed.

"Not like this."

It was the magenta fire that saved him. He never knew how Seren erupted with such violence, or why it took his near consumption to force her hand; only that the fire consumed them both swiftly enough that Fiore snapped her mouth shut and he bounced off her ugly, horrible lips and fell away from her. As he did, he knew his task was done. In this world, his monster could ravage only for moments and little beyond that. He felt it weaken as he fell, no doubt exhausted by the few breaths of mindless violence it had dealt upon a vile undefeatable monster. He bounced once more against her bulbous abdomen. It was a terrible thing, really, and he thought of little demonlings all scurrying inside, waiting to bring further ruin to the world. He wished he hadn't thought of that at all.

With a terrible crunch heralding further injury, he fell to the ground and waited for death. Above him, he heard the terrifying clicking of spider legs. And all around him, he heard soldiers and mercenaries resume their defence. Buoyed by the emergence of the *Mongoose* and the heroic Crimson Hunters, those who hadn't fled behind the gates or from the walls took to firing further bolts and arrows, and Derian's resting place became an even worse place to be.

"This is how I die."

"Worth it."

Perhaps so, monster.

"I'm you. Never forget that."

He lay in the ruined grass and watched the sight of Kesta bringing the *Mongoose* tantalizingly low. From the deck he watched Seren fire volley after volley down upon the beast, and it was glorious. He could smell the burning of skin and it was delicious.

"We need to rise."

He felt the terrible pain lessen as death came to him, and he smiled at Seren's divinity. His story was done, but his actions had brought something to the world. A foolish soul might lose their sanity upon realising their impact upon the world and eternity beyond. Most people never saw the influence they had, but with his dying steps, Derian saw it wonderfully.

Wait, steps?

He did not remember climbing to his feet, only that he stumbled away from the wretched spider's legs, the defenders' projectiles, and the stunning weaver's fire. Each step felt stronger than the next, but his desire to tear the demon apart was gone now.

"Live, and we fight another day."

His inner voice was weaker than before. So distant it was easy to imagine it was just a voice in his head. Stirring himself, he scampered away with his life, determined to study everything about his kind, about the source, about Anguis, the Dark One. About Bereziel, too.

A bard will say no hero is ever happy when denied their destiny, but Derian would argue differently any month of a season. Scrambling away towards the treeline, he found cover and watched the ending of it all.

Fiore did not take the assault silently. Rearing up on her terrible legs, she chased after the airbarge as though she were a cat chasing a butterfly. To Kesta's unexpected credit, and with her mirrors assisting her at every twist, she led the beast away from the town, accompanied by the blazing symphony of Seren's onslaught. Any who saw the event would swear the night burned magenta, and they would be right. Fiore was alight as she charged, yet no matter how many fireballs Seren struck, it could never be enough. No weaver had ever killed a grand demon, nor had an entire battalion.

He saw it in her fire at first, as Fiore did. The break between strikes grew longer as Seren emptied her soul and weakened herself.

At the end, in the moments before Fiore tore them from the sky, he watched Seren collapse against the edge of the deck. He saw Natteo take hold of her and scream into her ears to take his soul. Perhaps had Kesta been aware of this, she might have brought the *Mongoose* higher, allowed them to regroup and then return to torment the walking mountain and coerce it away from the town.

Kesta also didn't know that grand demons could jump

when needed. With wounded but supple legs, Fiore leapt high and caught hold of the monstrous airborne beast, as big as she was, and pulled her back to the ground.

Running on shaking legs towards the distant airbarge without a weapon to his name, Derian tried once more to summon his hatred, but the moment was lost. Behind him, the Army of the Dead realised the battle had shifted and followed him. Few followed them in turn, but one of those brave few was Blair, with shield in tow. It was the last charge they would offer, for the moment would pass, the demon would kill them all, and their lives would be lost in time forever.

The beast held the *Mongoose* in its vile claws as it shunted violently left and right, fighting like a doomed Delfina trout to clear itself of a fisher's line, all to the sound of screeching metal. Derian knew not even a master sprinter could reach them in time. Not that he could do much, but it seemed very important to be beside his comrades when they died.

He watched the attempted clipping of the airbarge's wings helplessly. Watched as, like a Seeva learning its limits the hardest way, Lorgan leapt gracefully over the edge with shield in hand. He did not attack Fiore as Derian had; instead, landing on her nose, he drove his shield directly into her left eye. He was no thin, concentrated point of an arrow or the sharpened tip of a lance, but he was fierce. The shield, sharp enough along the edge, sliced into gelatinous vileness and held. Fiore howled again, and deep within himself, Derian roared with approval.

With a roar, she released her hold on the airbarge which shot up like an arrow let loose at the moon. Unsure of what to do next, Lorgan leapt from the beast's terrible face as her talons scrabbled for the embedded shield. He rolled once off her belly as he fell and landed almost gracefully on the ground. Spinning around and aggrieved at her wounds, Fiore howled once more, louder than ever, before turning towards Derian.

"She smells us."

What do you mean, 'us,' monster?

"At least the others made it out alive," Derian muttered to his monster as Fiore forgot Lorgan and charged towards him. He summoned the strength for one more desperate sprint away from the spider demon, towards the treeline. He imagined for a wonderful moment he might clear the line and immediately discover a deep cave—too small for demons, with a nice mossy patch deep within where he could rest. Perhaps he'd even discover a stash of honey cakes while he was at it.

"Ah, spit on me," he gasped as she covered the ground between forest and Derian in a few steps, cutting off his attempted escape. "I'm a spent soul," he muttered to the wind as he gave up. He didn't even have Rusty to call upon, he thought miserably. He'd have loved a honey cake before the end, he thought with equal misery. He felt the dampness in his pants again and muttered a curse. *Nobody will ever know.*

The ground shook as she neared, and he fell to his knees. Seeing his defeat, she slowed, and a booming noise erupted from her, and he felt the shame of her mocking laughter. He was no true Seeva beast at all; he was a weak imitation of what heroes should be.

"To the fires with you," he hissed as she raised her claw to decapitate him. And the *Fighting Mongoose* fell out of the sky and landed on her head, tearing a deep gash in her leathery hide. He watched in silence as she reared forward, unable to hold herself up. The propellers, which were still slowly turning, now accelerated again, and as the monster shoved the airbarge away from her it took flight just a foot from the ground and shot up over her head once more.

"Flee from here," he screamed in panic. Knowing his comrades lived would have been enough for him. Anything else was too cruel, too savage, too unfair for a warrior's final moment.

But that final moment turned out to be an incredible moment. And not his final one at all.

The *Mongoose* dropped once more. This time, however, it appeared to make an emergency landing. He knew the term because Kesta had told him the dangers of such an event. She'd also mentioned the dismal survival rates of most everyone involved with emergency landings, especially anyone unlucky enough to be near one of the propellers.

In this case, the "anyone" was Fiore, who met the front left propeller, which was the only propeller head on, as it were. They collided, and the *Mongoose* kept going.

Even his monster may well have lost the taste for such savagery, yet Derian couldn't look away as one of humanity's finer weapons met a grand demon as old as the world, and cut her spitting head off. No, that wasn't accurate at all. Mulched the demon's head to nothing was a fairer description. The stunning blades cut and severed inch by inch, foot by foot, and it was like thrashing wheat in the harvest season. Fiore could not scream, for her mouth was taken. As her body convulsed, Derian cursed her loudly. The airbarge's engines roared as the remaining spinning spheres of death came back to life, and the *Mongoose* held and swayed, glided left, glided right, all the time removing more and more of the grand demon.

Anguis is going to be pissed.

And then it was done. Within a few breaths, they had conquered the beast. Her quivering body fell still as they tore her ancient mind to nothing, banished her demonic essence to venture into the night and never return. The last of her viscera and brain and whatever other spidery bits too disgusting to mention ceased spraying, and with a heavy clunk and no lesser skill, Kesta pulled away from the dead beast and sped towards Derian.

Distantly, he saw the Army of the Dead cheer and celebrate, and somewhere beyond them he imagined those who'd viewed the spectacle in the town behaving in similar fashion. Though exhausted, he rose and waved to the barge as a dripping wet crimson rope ladder was thrown over the edge by the diminutive figure of Eveklyn.

"Kesta says we have to leave… because it's her airbarge," the girl called down to him, and fuk it, Derian felt they'd earned themselves a little thievery, all guilt-free, like. They were heroes, were they not?

Far behind, the cheers of the Army of the Dead waned and fell silent as the realisation struck them. As one, they thundered across the battlefield trying desperately to catch the Crimson before they took off again.

As he took the rope ladder and began climbing, Derian felt the presence of an ally watching from his place beyond the dark. He tried to hold the thought for a moment, but it was lost in the momentum as the *Fighting Mongoose* rose from the fallen demon and drifted along the battlefield towards the shuffling form of their battered leader. If Lorgan held any residual guilt for stealing the airbarge, he relinquished it the moment he took hold of the ladder and soared upwards, offering a wave to the approaching mercenaries and gesturing crudely to the town of Treystone as he and his comrades left them behind.

.   .   .

Any skilled storyteller or bard would finish such an epic legend with tales of grand, euphoric celebrations. Of bitter rivalries giving way to solidarity between comrades of the road. Of payments made and pockets filled with coins well earned. But this was only the beginning of unfortunate things to come. On the far side of the world, someone had opened the book. The lost Seven were stirring. And the last war in this Dellerin age had only just begun.

EPILOGUE

"For one so old, you are swift," Anguis spat, waving his fingers where Derian had been but a moment before. The effort it had taken to banish him from this realm by way of this barrier was more than Bereziel had expected. He almost stumbled from the effort but held himself.

"I am, as I always was."

"Old man, there is no need for this," Anguis said gently. If attempting cordiality was a tactic he still called upon, he had learned little these thirty years gone. They were not friends; they never had been. Their paths had crossed fewer times than most, yet still, and perhaps rightfully so, he blamed Bereziel for the terrible deeds that had taken place.

It's no excuse for his savagery.

The hooded figure placed his hand upon the shimmering blue barrier to test its strength, and Bereziel felt the strain. With Derian gone there came a changing of events. Something unusual had arisen from the boy's interference, and despite the struggle, he grinned. *Serenity to the world.*

Anguis did not grin. He shuddered as though struck and drew his hand to his chest. If nothing else, seeing fear living within the twisted beast was encouraging. Where there was fear, there was advantage.

He was not ready to face the ferocity of the Anguished One. He might never be. But there was safety in numbers, and safety for others to continue the fight after his passing.

"Can you feel the change?" Bereziel mocked, playing the part of the wretched old master that Anguis would recognise, all the while searching for a swift escape from this realm. *From this moment.* It was one thing returning a young boy he'd summoned; it was another thing escaping this plane himself. He could withstand quite a beating if need be. It was revealing his strategy that he feared the most. All those years of steering insignificant moments would be for nothing if Anguis took hold and wrenched the truth from him.

Wrenched his soul from him while he was at it.

"I feel nothing, old man. Come out of your shell and face me so we might finish what you started."

It was an appealing challenge; Bereziel's hatred for Anguis was evenly matched. Anger would not serve him this day. Better he not show his full strength, either. At least for now. Something had changed again. Something in the living realm had been lured from its natural path. He recognised that moment as he had thirty years before: Anguis struck fiercely at his shield and shattered it. Within a pulse, Bereziel formed another one around him and held off the next powerful strike from the dark weaver.

"I could do this for eternity, Bereziel," he hissed, and Bereziel felt the souls of gods and of demons present. It was only natural that Anguis believed himself invincible.

"I will hold you for as long as I can. I will never yield to your will," Bereziel cried in frustration. He felt the world changing once more. Anguis charged forward and struck fiercely, and again shattered through the barrier. Desperately,

Bereziel erected another faded shield of blue, though it was weaker than before, and Anguis charged through it with a defiant, ungodly roar. Once more Bereziel held him off. It was Anguis who breathed more heavily, though. Backing away to the edge of the terrible black fire, Bereziel sought escape eagerly now. He could sense his own panic and he forbade it to weaken his will.

"Is this how you survived so long? Hiding in terror, as gods walked? Tell me, old man, how much better might your *imagined* world have been, had you met me after Venistra? I called upon but one demon at the beginning, and you were a master. It could have been war most divine. It could have been worthy of me. Of us both."

It was a fine question, but it had never been about the Dark One. It had only been about undoing the terrible sin of the lure.

Once more, the world changed and Bereziel laughed. He had not seen this at all. Even in thousands of years searching. "Fiore," he cried in delight, and Anguis hesitated. For a moment his body trembled as though taken by the very demonic souls he mastered. Perhaps that was exactly what happened.

"This cannot be," he roared, and struck weakly at the shield. As he did, Bereziel released his hold upon it and leapt upon the monster. With his ancient essence, he weaved his horror upon Anguis. Grabbing at his chest, where terrible, beautiful things were enslaved, he delivered his soul. The Dark One, unprepared for the counterattack, fell away in shock, but Bereziel, seizing the moment, never relinquished his hold.

"She has the stones," Bereziel roared, for Anguis feared the breaking of the lure. Feared other things too. "She has my protection, too."

"You have grown stronger," Anguis gasped, but the moment was already turning. Bereziel could sense the terrible power he called upon. The oceans of reserves.

The world shook, and they separated. Around them the wall of black fire, trapping Bereziel in Anguis's hold, shattered. Within a pulse of time in the real world, or perhaps a year and a day, Bereziel vanished from the moment, but his form still remained, standing in front of the fierce, dark master.

From the safety of his domain, where no weaving could come between them, Bereziel panted in relief and cried out for the pain and suffering he had endured. *It is nothing to theirs.* He also cried out in joy for Seren, and for the unknown paths to come.

"The future is unseen and precarious, little one," he whispered. He'd never felt as spent as he did now, and knowing now the power he warred against brought upon him his own fears.

"It must be done. They must rise once more," he whispered to the source, hoping distantly that they could hear his pledge.

Anguis, the Dark One, reached for the old man, and his hand faded through him as through mist at midnight. Cursing, he searched out in the source for the ancient, broken soul who had defied him and felt nothing. The old man faded away, and only then did he feel the weaving upon him. Clasping his chest, he sought the world of the living.

"What have you done, Bereziel?" he cried as fear etched itself into his soul. "What have you done?"

FIND OUT HOW IT ALL STARTED

They were sent to stop the Dark One. They Failed.

Set thirty years before the events of The Crimson Hunters, The Seven; The Lost Tale of Dellerin is a set in a grimdark fantasy world where evil reigns, demons roam, and enchantments cost your very soul.

"A truly dark work that is not for the faint of heart" - Readers Favourite

"Characters that feel alive with soul, the author captures true human emotion" - Amazon Reviewer

THANK YOU FOR READING THE CRIMSON HUNTERS

Word-of-mouth is crucial for any author to succeed and honest reviews of my books help to bring them to the attention of other readers.

If you enjoyed the book, and have 2 minutes to spare, please leave an honest review on Amazon or Goodreads. Even if it's just a sentence or two it would make all the difference and would be very much appreciated.

Thank you.

EXCLUSIVE OFFER FOR NEW READERS

When you join the Robert J Power Readers' Club you'll get the latest news on the Spark City and Dellerin series, free books, exclusive content and new release updates.

You'll also get a short tale exclusive to members- you can't get this anywhere else!

Conor and The Banshee
Fear the Banshee's Cry

Join at www.RobertJPower.com

ALSO BY ROBERT J POWER

The Spark City Cycle:

Spark City, Book 1

The March of Magnus, Book 2

The Outcasts, Book 3

———

The Dellerin Tales:

The Crimson Collection:

The Crimson Hunters, Vol I

The Lost Tales of Dellerin:

The Seven

ACKNOWLEDGMENTS

For Poll, Jen and Jill. Thank you ladies so much for taking my shit coming up to launch. And for the shit after launch. And when I'm just around in general.

For Jean and Paul. Here's to raising a toast in my honour because you were the first guys to suggest such a brilliant idea. And, yeah, the incredible support is appreciated as well.

Massive thanks to the amazing Cathbar who has been an incredible champion since I began this endeavour and for returning to me the beauty of our native language. An bh-fuil cead agam dul go dti an leithreas, a cara? I think we know the answer.

For Eoin, whose kind words and unwavering support with early drafts throughout my career has been so greatly appreciated. Honestly man, I don't know how you get through some of the rubbish I've sent you. Like really. I've been sending you a ridiculous story about a kleptomaniac squirrel the last few weeks and you still come back to me with well constructed suggestions.

For Bren and Shane. I had to use your real names for obvious reasons. I'll see you at practice one of these days. It's Bren's turn to choose, and I'm winning the Podge and Rodge competition this year. Fuk ya's. Army of the Dead for life!

For the DNF THIS crew- much respect and love across all four corners of the world. You haven't quite gotten rid of me yet. Stay the course guys. Any day now.

For John, who sends me a text message every fuken morning telling me to write quicker or else I'll lose my fan base. You are fighting the fight for the silent readers and I hate you for it. Annoyingly, you only listen to my audiobooks so this victory is tainted. I'll still take it.

For Ant, the legend. I'm sorry for pointing out the continuous low hum in your house. It's definitely not me under the stairs with an anti white-noise machine. I hope this acknowledgment eases the pain. I hope you remove that old hoover from under the stairs. It's a terrible seat.

Special mention to my editores=Jen for taking a dumpster fire and filling it with marshmallows. And for Steven for suggesting I add some sprinkles of chocolate on top to make it pretty. Also thank you for somehow finding a couple flaws in an otherwise perfect manuscript.

Special shout out to my nemesis Lcass. Or Lisa Cassidy for those of you in need of a cracking fantasy read. I just put a plug into my acknowledgements. Top that!!!

Finally, to the fans who own this story now. Thank you a thousand times over for the support you guys have shown me. (I expect as much because I'm a genius but it's nice to be reminded.) Your kind words and wonderful interactions are what make this writing lark so rewarding. Without you all I'd have never made it this far. Let's go a little further.

ABOUT THE AUTHOR

Robert J Power is the fantasy author of the Amazon bestselling series, The Spark City Cycle and The Dellerin Tales. When not locked in a dark room with only the daunting laptop screen as a source of light, he fronts Irish rock band, Army of Ed, despite their many attempts to fire him.

Robert lives in Wicklow, Ireland with his wife Jan, two rescue dogs and a cat that detests his very existence. Before he found a career in writing, he enjoyed various occupations such as a terrible pizza chef, a video store manager (ask your grandparents), and an irresponsible camp counsellor. Thankfully, none of them stuck.

If you wish to learn of Robert's latest releases, his feelings on The Elder Scrolls, or just how many coffees he consumes a day before the palpitations kick in, visit his website at www. RobertJPower.com where you can join his reader's club. You might even receive some free goodies, hopefully some writing updates, and probably a few nonsensical ramblings.

www.RobertJPower.com

facebook.com/AuthorRobertJPower

twitter.com/robertjpower

instagram.com/robertjpower

#SaveTheSeven